Praise for Ellery Adams's previous novels

"Love *Chopped* and mysteries? This delightful character-driven cozy is just the treat for you."
—*Kirkus Reviews* on *Murder in the Cookbook Nook*

"Creating a group of suspects that will keep readers intrigued until the last page, Ellery Adams has proven one thing with this book: This is one series that should and will go on for a long time to come. In fact, the author has done such a brilliant job, readers will find themselves wanting to live in Storyton, no matter how many people end up dead there."
—*Suspense Magazine* on *Murder in the Locked Library*

"Ellery does a wonderful job in capturing the essence of this whodunit with visually descriptive narrative that not only lends itself to engaging dialogue, but also seeing the action through the eyes of Jane and her fellow characters."
—*Dru's Book Musings* on *Murder in the Locked Library*

"A love letter to reading, with sharp characterizations and a smart central mystery."
—*Entertainment Weekly* on *The Whispered Word*

"Adams launches an intriguing new mystery series headed by four spirited amateur sleuths and touch̶e̶s̶ ̶̶̶̶̶̶ of magical realism, which celebrat̶e̶̶̶̶̶̶̶̶̶̶̶̶̶̶̶̶ and women's friendships. A̶̶̶̶̶̶̶̶̶̶̶̶̶̶̶̶̶̶rah Addison Allen, and ̶̶̶̶̶̶̶̶̶̶̶̶̶̶̶̶̶ve around books will sa̶̶̶̶̶̶̶̶̶̶̶
—*Library Journal* (sta̶̶̶̶̶̶̶̶̶̶̶̶̶̶̶̶̶̶̶̶̶) on
The Secret, Book & Sco̶̶̶̶̶̶̶̶

"This affecting series la̶̶̶̶ from Adams provides all the best elements of a traditional mystery. . . . Well-drawn characters complement a plot with an intriguing twist or two."
—*Publishers Weekly* on *The Secret, Book & Scone Society*

Also by Ellery Adams:

Book Retreat Mysteries:

Murder in the Mystery Suite

Murder in the Paperback Parlor

Murder in the Secret Garden

Murder in the Locked Library

Murder in the Reading Room

Murder in the Storybook Cottage

Murder in the Cookbook Nook

Murder on the Poet's Walk

The Secret, Book and Scone Society Mysteries:

The Secret, Book & Scone Society

The Whispered Word

The Book of Candlelight

Ink and Shadows

The Vanishing Type

New York Times and *USA Today* Bestselling Author

ELLERY ADAMS

MURDER ON THE POET'S WALK

Kensington Publishing Corp.
www.kensingtonbooks.com

KENSINGTON BOOKS are published by

Kensington Publishing Corp.
119 West 40th Street
New York, NY 10018

All Kensington titles, imprints, and distributed lines are available at special quantity discounts for bulk purchases for sales promotion, premiums, fund-raising, educational, or institutional use.

Special book excerpts or customized printings can also be created to fit specific needs. For details, write or phone the office of the Kensington Sales Manager: Attn.: Sales Department. Kensington Publishing Corp., 119 West 40th Street, New York, NY 10018. Phone: 1-800-221-2647.

The K and Teapot logo is a trademark of Kensington Publishing Corp.

First Printing: October 2022
ISBN: 978-1-4967-2948-4

ISBN: 978-1-4967-2949-1 (ebook)

10 9 8 7 6 5 4 3 2 1

Printed in the United States of America

This novel is for all the folks on Bookstagram, BookTube, and BookTok. Your videos, photos, shout-outs, reviews, and enthusiasm for all things bookish amaze me. Whether you have a million followers or just one, what you're doing matters.

Keep reading.

Keep sharing.

Keep shining.

A poem begins as a lump in the throat, a sense of wrong, a homesickness, a lovesickness.
—Robert Frost

If I feel physically as if the top of my head were taken off, I know that is poetry.
—Emily Dickinson

Welcome to Storyton Hall!

OUR STAFF IS HERE TO SERVE YOU.
Resort Manager—Jane Steward
Butler—Mr. Butterworth
Head Librarian—Mr. Sinclair
Head Chauffeur—Mr. Sterling
Head of Recreation—Mr. Lachlan
Head of Housekeeping—Mrs. Templeton
Head Cook—Mrs. Hubbard
Spa Manager—Tammie Kota

SELECT MERCHANTS OF STORYTON VILLAGE
Run for Cover Bookshop—Eloise Alcott
Daily Bread Cafe—Edwin Alcott
Cheshire Cat Pub—Bob and Betty Carmichael
Canvas Creamery—Phoebe Doyle
La Grande Dame Clothing Boutique—Mabel
Wimberly
Tresses Hair Salon—Violet Osborne
Pickled Pig Market—the Hogg brothers
Geppetto's Toy Shop—Barnaby Nicholas
Hilltop Stables—Sam Nolan
Storyton Outfitters—Phil and Sandi Hughes
The Old Curiosity Shop—Roger Bachman

CURRENT MOOD CARD COMPANY PERSONNEL
Jeremiah Okoro
Gilbert "Gil" Callahan
Stephanie Harbaugh

NOTABLE POETS
Professor Dodge Ashley
Gretchen West
Connor Jensen
Farah Khan

Village of Storyton

BROKEN ARM BEND

STORYTON HALL

STORYTON CEMETERY

LA GRANDE DAME

THE OLD DUSTY CURIOSITIES

CHESHIRE CAT PUB

SPOKES BIKE REPAIR

CHILDREN'S COTTAGE

PHARMACY

HAIR SALON

DAILY BREAD

RUN FOR COVER

DECEPTION TOY FACTORY

DOC'S OFFICE

CANVAS CREAMERY

POTTER'S SHED

STORYTON SCHOOL

CHURCH

PICKLED PIG MARKET

MAIN STREET

Chapter 1

Jane Steward always looked forward to afternoon tea, but never more so than today. She couldn't wait to share her exciting news with Uncle Aloysius and Aunt Octavia.

I hope I beat Mrs. Hubbard to the punch, she thought, hurrying out to the terrace. Mrs. Hubbard's culinary skills were exemplary, but the head cook of Storyton Hall also possessed a taste for gossip that was as insatiable as Aunt Octavia's sweet tooth.

Catching sight of the tea spread, Jane hoped her great-aunt wouldn't overindulge on sugary treats. The plucky octogenarian was the uncrowned regent of all she surveyed and tended to do exactly as she pleased, but she was also diabetic, which meant eating foods that were good for her health over those that *felt* good to eat.

"Hello, dear!" Aunt Octavia cried as Jane took a seat at the table reserved for the Steward family. "Don't these apple-cinnamon scones look glorious? Mrs. Hubbard is so clever. She put a rolled-up copy of Robert Frost's 'After Apple-Picking' inside our napkins. Should we each read a few lines in between bites?"

This suggestion was met by a pair of groans.

On the other side of the table, Jane's twin sons, Fitzgerald and Hemingway Steward, wore matching expressions of disapproval.

"That's a lovely idea," Jane said, plucking a turkey, Brie, and apple finger sandwich from the tray.

Uncle Aloysius beamed at his wife. "You should start, my dear. Your voice is pure poetry."

The twins rolled their eyes and sighed. Though Jane knew they wanted to eat and run, she wanted to savor such moments. During the workweek, this was their only chance to gather as a family. Jane's responsibilities as resort manager kept her busy from sunup to sundown—if not later—which is why afternoon tea was sacred to her. She'd miss it only if faced with a crisis.

Unfortunately, the luxury resort catering to bibliophiles from all corners of the globe had been plagued by one catastrophe after another. During her tenure as manager, she'd dealt with challenges that were part and parcel of running a country estate–turned–hotel. The upkeep of its aging structures and extensive grounds demanded a great deal of time and money, and as if that wasn't enough to worry about, Storyton Hall seemed to be a most favorable setting for murder and mayhem.

However, on this sultry afternoon in mid-August, Jane wasn't thinking about the numerous acts of violence that had occurred in her ancestral home. Her thoughts were of the future. Her sons would soon be heading back to school as middle schoolers, and her best friend, Eloise Alcott, was getting married in two weeks.

These weren't the only changes on the horizon either. The ruined folly was being rebuilt, and the orchard, which Jane was tentatively calling Chekov's Orchard, had finally been restored. The cherry and apple trees wouldn't bear fruit this year, but guests still loved to wander among the trees. The boughs provided welcome shade, and the soft grass muffled all sounds but the songs of insects and birds. Bees and butterflies drifted through the field of wildflowers dividing the orchard from the untamed forest. It was the perfect place to escape the oppressive heat and humidity.

"Mom?"

Jane started. She'd been gazing over Milton's Gardens and the great lawn toward the blue hills surrounding the village of Storyton and had been too lost in thought to realize that the table had gone quiet.

"You're meant to be picking apples, not gathering wool." Her eyes twinkling in amusement, Aunt Octavia tapped the Frost poem with a flamingo-pink nail that matched the flowers on her pink and green dress.

"Your turn, Mom," Fitz added impatiently.

"Did I ever tell you how sweet and cute you were as a toddler? *Before* you learned to talk?" Jane teased. Then, she read a few lines of Frost's poem aloud. " 'There were ten thousand thousand fruit to touch, cherish in hand, lift down, and not let fall.' "

She passed the poem to Hem, who raced through five lines before holding out the paper so that Fitz could recite the remaining six.

When Fitz was done, he popped an apple-sausage ball in his mouth. After chasing it down with a swallow of cider, he said, "It doesn't sound like a poem about apples. It sounds like a poem about being tired."

Looking pleased, Uncle Aloysius said, "Very percep-
tive."

"What gave you that idea?" asked Aunt Octavia.

Fitz dropped a spoonful of maple cream onto his
scone. "He says he's overtired. And he mentions sleep a
bunch of times."

"He has aches and pains too," Hem said, chiming in.
"He sounds like you first thing in the morning, Mom."

Jane was tempted to throw a sausage ball at her son
but restrained herself.

"If your mother wakes up with stiff joints, it's because
she works so hard," Aunt Octavia said loyally. "And
since we're on the topic of hard work, Mrs. Hubbard
tells me that you two have taken excellent care of her
kitchen and vegetable gardens. We're all very proud of
how dedicated you've been to that job while also working on your jam business."

Fitz flashed his most winsome smile. "Thanks. Would
you please pass the mini candy apples?"

"Only one treat at teatime," Jane reminded him.

"But we're growing boys," Hem parroted Mrs. Hubbard so perfectly that everyone laughed.

Uncle Aloysius doffed his fishing hat and used it to
hide his face from Aunt Octavia as he leaned closer to
Fitz and Hem. "If you boys were older, you might be
more interested in poetry. Men have been wooing
ladies with romantic poems for centuries."

The corners of Hem's mouth dipped down as he
turned to Jane. "Do all the guests write love poetry?"

"No. They write all kinds of poems. A few are working on novels written entirely in verse, some are song-
writers, and others write free-verse poems about
everything and anything. Most of them are interested
in writing short poems for greeting cards." She smiled

at her sons. "You might not know it, but you've created poetry. Think of how many verses you've come up with about Broken Arm Bend. And that jingle you're working on for your jam business? That rhymes too. Songwriting is a close cousin to poetry."

"Maybe that's why I like hip-hop. Remember that song I played for you the last time we slept over?" Fitz directed his question at Aunt Octavia.

To Jane's utter astonishment, Aunt Octavia replied, "The one from A Tribe Called Quest? I most certainly do. Such clever wordplay."

"Was I there?" asked Uncle Aloysius. "I don't remember."

Seeing his confused expression, Aunt Octavia patted his hand and told him that he'd probably been in his study.

"I ran into two of the poets in the garden. We had a nice chat about nature and Whitman. I showed them one of his poems and told them we'd named our spa after him. We spoke all the way—" After a pause, he said, "I don't remember where I was headed, but it doesn't matter."

Jane and Aunt Octavia exchanged worried glances. Uncle Aloysius had been more forgetful as of late. He'd even gone fishing without his beloved hat. Her uncle was never without his fishing hat, much to Aunt Octavia's consternation, and when Jane drove down to the lake to return it to him, he touched the top of his head, clearly confounded to find that he wasn't already wearing it.

After the poets are gone, I should talk to Aunt Octavia about this. Doc Lydgate could pop over—just to be sure Uncle Aloysius is okay.

Hem gulped down the rest of his cider and swiped

his napkin across his mouth. "Can we go back to the kitchens? Mrs. Hubbard needs more cucumbers for the dinner service."

As soon as Jane excused the twins, they leapt from the terrace with the nimbleness of two jungle cats and trotted down the path leading to the kitchens. Once they were out of sight, she turned back to Aunt Octavia and said, "I have news."

"Oh?"

"Tobias was working the deli counter at the Pickled Pig this morning," Jane said, referring to the village grocery store. "I've never seen a man slice salami with such gusto, but he has every reason to be happy."

Aunt Octavia leaned forward in her chair. "Does this have anything to do with his children's book?"

"In a way. His book launch is scheduled for the second Friday in September, but it doesn't look like he'll be able to have it at Run for Cover."

"Why ever not? What better place for a book launch than a bookstore?"

Jane grinned. "Because people have been calling Eloise for days, asking to buy tickets for the event."

"I didn't realize we needed to a ticket to attend Mr. Hogg's book launch. Such things should be free to the public. We wouldn't want to discourage future readers," Aunt Octavia grumbled.

"Neither does Eloise. She'd never dream of selling tickets, but apparently, Tobias has become a legitimate celebrity. No, not Tobias. *Pig Newton* is the celebrity. Hundreds of thousands of people follow him on social media. And now, thanks to the publicity, *The Near-Sighted Pig* has had so many preorders that it's already hit several bestseller lists. Tobias has offers from toy and clothing companies interested in producing merchandise featuring the pig from his book. A sweet little pig with glasses. I can just see backpacks and bedsheets. Poseable figures. The works!"

Aunt Octavia put her hand on her heart. "Are we about to witness the birth of a storybook icon? A pig as adored and revered as Wilbur?"

"I hope so. Tobias is a sweetheart, and his book is as heartwarming as they come. And even though his big brothers have teased him mercilessly, Barbara supported his writing dreams from the get-go. Imagine having two authors under one roof. Barbara's already writing two romance novels a year, and Tobias has tons of ideas for *The Near-Sighted Pig* series. Storyton has its own famous author couple."

"I wonder if he'll retire from the grocery business," Aunt Octavia mused.

"You can ask him at his book launch, seeing as it'll be taking place in Shakespeare's Theater. The Storyton Players are going to perform a puppet show, Mrs. Hubbard will whip up a few hundred pig cookies, and Eloise will handle the book sales."

Aunt Octavia glanced around. "I love it when we host creative types. At the moment, Storyton Hall is full of poets. I see them scribbling away in the reading rooms and the Henry James Library. I see them in the Anne of Green Gables Gazebo, the dining rooms, and the lobby. I don't think we've ever had such an industrious group of guests before. I can practically feel their energy. It's electric! Wouldn't you agree, Aloysius?"

"I would. In fact, when I was out on the lake, I saw a young man walking and writing in a little notebook at the same time. He was inches away from going in the drink but looked up just in time. After avoiding that mishap, he ended up wandering into a dense patch of poison ivy." He chuckled. "If you see a young man scratching his ankles this evening, that's the Poison Ivy Poet."

Jane laughed. "I can't really blame him for being zealous. He has to beat out fifty poets to win the greeting card contract."

While selecting a green apple macaron from the tiered cake stand, Aunt Octavia said, "I always wondered how a person made a living penning greeting card messages. Is the pay any good?"

"Not for freelancers. For every submission, they're lucky if they make enough to cover the cost of dinner and a movie. Sometimes, they're asked to submit original artwork in addition to a poem. But this new company, Current Mood Cards, wants to shake up the greeting card industry. Their slogan is 'cards for every situation,' and they're looking for a very versatile writer. Whoever wins will leave Storyton Hall with a signed contract containing more zeroes than most poets see in a lifetime."

Uncle Aloysius grunted. "I guess Robert Frost was wrong. He said, 'There's no money in poetry.' He also said, 'There's no poetry in money, either.' "

"Stuff and nonsense." Aunt Octavia gave a dismissive wave. "You never know what feeds a person's muse. Money, or the lack of it, can be an inspiration. Greed, envy, pain. Love and longing. Loss. Intense human emotions are what inspire poets."

Having finished her tea, Jane put down her cup and rested her hand on Aunt Octavia's hand. "Let's hope that intense emotion stays on the page. We've seen what happens when it can't be controlled."

"Yes, we most certainly have."

When Jane got to her feet, Uncle Aloysius followed

suit. His eyes twinkled with mischief as he gave her arm
a pat and said, "Don't worry, my girl. No one's hunched
in a dark corner, scribbling, 'Roses are red, violets are
blue. I'm a poet and a murderer too.' "

Don't tempt the fates, Jane wanted to say but didn't.

Instead, she gave her uncle a quick hug and turned
away before he could see that his joke had failed to
make her smile.

That evening, Jane met her book group, the Cover
Girls, in the lobby.

Mabel, owner of La Grande Dame Clothing Boutique, stopped fanning herself with a copy of Amanda
Gorman's "The Hill We Climb" long enough to greet
Jane. "I am *so* glad this event is inside. Even Satan must
be sweating. I honestly don't know how people survived
without air-conditioning."

Mrs. Pratt, retired schoolteacher and romance novel
aficionada, bobbed her head in agreement. "Women of
a certain age and body type should be applauded every
time we venture out from June to September. April is
not the cruelest month. That's a tie between July and
August."

"Humidity really messes with people's hair too. I get
them red-carpet ready, and the second they leave the
salon—*bam!*" Violet mimed an explosion around her
head.

Phoebe shrugged. "I love summertime. Even if my
business didn't depend on selling lots of gelato, I'd still
love it because the days are so long. It's the only season
I have enough time to work on my art and get a ton of
reading in before bed."

"I like the summer too," said Betty, proprietress of

the Cheshire Cat pub. "And *this* summer is even more magical because of Eloise's wedding."

Mrs. Pratt craned her head. "Where is our bride?"

Jane checked her watch. "Running late. I'd better explain how this wine party is supposed to work. I can fill her in later."

Violet raised her hand. "Do we get to taste-test everything? You know, so we can be knowledgeable hostesses?"

Jane laughed. "Of course. It's billed as a wine-and-cheese event, but Mrs. Hubbard had the kitchen staff make enough food to feed the whole village."

"Better than a roomful of drunk poets," said Mrs. Pratt.

Jane couldn't argue with that. She led the Cover Girls to a round table with a sign reading SHELLEY'S SYRAH and pointed at one of the wine bottles on the table.

"Each table features a wine named after a famous poet. Each poet wrote about wine or the act of drinking. For example, Percy Shelley wrote a poem called 'Fragment: The Vine-Shroud.' His table has a Syrah and foods to complement the wine, like smoked Gouda, black olives, and dark chocolate bacon."

"I need a piece of that," Mabel said, hungrily eyeing the platter.

"We'll eat as soon as we finish the tour." Jane walked to the next station. "Okay, so here's Pablo Neruda's pinot noir. This wine is being served with pear slices topped with goat cheese, mushrooms stuffed with salami and garlic, and barbecue pork skewers. The table near the grandfather clock is Emily Dickinson's zinfandel. The strawberry ricotta bruschetta is amazing, and the spicy shrimp wontons aren't too shabby either."

Phoebe held up a book of poems by Mary Oliver. "What about my girl? Does she have a table?"

"Yep. Mary Oliver's merlot. Her wine is paired with Parmesan potato skins, lamb kebobs, and teriyaki chicken wings."

At that moment, the door to the staff corridor flew open, and Eloise stepped into the lobby. "I'm so sorry! For being late, for using the staff hall, for looking like a hot mess."

Eloise's maxi dress was a sunflower print on a field of cobalt. The blue brought out her eyes. Her face was gently sun-kissed, and her honey-colored hair was gathered in a loose bun. She was a vision of casual elegance.

"Ha! Hot mess is me at five in the morning after staying up to read one more chapter that turned into ten," murmured Mrs. Pratt.

Mabel put an arm around Mrs. Pratt's waist and said, "We can't let lack of sleep get us down, Eugenia. At our age, we might not get back up!"

"Didn't you hear? Fifty is the new thirty," Betty told Mabel.

"You're here!" Jane beckoned for Eloise to join them. "I was just showing everyone the poets' tables. I'm asking each of you to keep an eye on the food and wine at your assigned station. We want to make sure all the guests have plenty to eat or drink, but not *too* much to drink. Butterworth and Sterling will be here as well, so if any of the poets go from tiddled to tap-shackled, let one of them know."

"Are those synonyms for *tipsy* and *totally drunk?*" asked Phoebe.

"Yes, and if you don't want to hear more of where those came from, don't ask Sinclair about the poetry trivia contest. I put him in charge of coming up with the questions," Jane said, referring to Storyton Hall's head librarian.

Having finished her instructions, Jane asked her friends to follow her to the Walt Whitman Spa.

The spa had closed an hour early, allowing Storyton Hall staff members to set up an intimate cocktail party just for Jane's book club.

"How lovely!" Betty exclaimed as she entered the spa's tranquil lobby.

Candles flickered on a crowded buffet table, soft music floated through speakers concealed by potted palms, and a floor-to-ceiling waterfall cascaded over teal tiles on the back wall.

Eloise looked at Jane. "You know how to spoil us."

"I know how to thank my friends for helping me out. How many times have you showed up for book club only to end up as co-hostesses at one of the hotel's random parties?"

Violet examined the wine bottles in the center of their table. "You say that like it's a bad thing. My social life only has a life because of you and your parties."

"And we get to have so much fun with our clothes," added Phoebe. "In just one season, we might go from being *Great Gatsby* flappers to fairy-tale characters to famous detectives with a ton of cocktail and tea parties in between."

Jane volunteered to pour wine while her friends helped themselves to food. She then filled a plate for herself and took the empty chair between Mrs. Pratt and Eloise.

"You're not still dieting, are you?" she asked, gesturing at the meager amount of food on Eloise's plate.

She sighed. "Not intentionally. I don't know if it's nerves or what, but I'm just not hungry."

"That's a problem I never have," said Mrs. Pratt. "But one of the delights of being a mature woman in a mature relationship is accepting who you are and how you look. Luckily, Roger loves food just as much as I do. I may have to put some of that dark chocolate bacon in my purse for him."

Jane grinned at her. "I think we can find you a better doggie bag than that. Okay, ladies. Tonight, we'll be sipping a cabernet sauvignon from Cliff Lede, aptly named Poetry. While I was searching for the perfect wine for us, I learned there's a sign on Highway Twenty-Nine in Napa Valley that says, 'And the wine is bottled poetry.' Shall we see if Robert Louis Stevenson was right?"

She raised her glass, and her friends followed suit.

"I can definitely taste berries," Mabel said after her first sip.

Phoebe nodded. "Blackberries, maybe? And vanilla."

"We're just so posh," Anna said in an exaggerated British accent.

The Cover Girls sipped wine and tasted one delicious dish after another. Finally, Jane tapped her wineglass with a clean spoon. Hearing the gentle chime, her friends fell silent.

"Should we go around the table and read our favorite lines?"

The other women murmured their assent and bent to collect the books of poetry they'd stored under their chairs. The group often selected books based on activities and events occurring at Storyton Hall, and this time was no exception. Instead of reading the work of one poet, however, they'd agreed to read the works of different poets. They'd each picked out one poem to share with their friends.

The first poems they heard were Amanda Gorman's "The Miracle of Morning," Mary Oliver's "Song for Autumn," and Maya Angelou's "Life Doesn't Frighten Me."

As the women read aloud, the words grew wings. They flitted like moths, soared like birds of prey, and darted like bats. Sentences hummed like dragonflies or sighed like a moth alighting on a moonflower.

After pausing to discuss the first round of poems, the Cover Girls heard Emily Dickinson's "'Hope' is the thing with feathers" and Joy Harjo's "An American Sunrise."

Jane completed the circle by reading "Belly Dancer." Penned by her favorite poet, Diane Wakoski, the words danced around the center of the table, conjuring images of a woman in silk pantaloons, swaying and clinking her finger cymbals.

When the poem came to an end, the Cover Girls exchanged looks of contentment.

Mabel said, "Before this week, I wasn't sure if I liked poetry. I guess I do, because this has been a wonderful experience."

"I can't imagine how hard it must be to pack a whole story into a few dozen lines," added Violet. "I have new respect for the writers we're about to meet."

The other women echoed this sentiment. Except for Mrs. Pratt, that is.

Holding up a warning finger, she said, "Don't forget that we've met sketchy writers before. And by sketchy, I mean dangerous."

It was true. From the moment Jane had become the resort manager, her ancestral home had been plagued by violence. From petty theft to premeditated murder, she'd seen it all. She had yet to fully recover from the traumatic events that occurred when a famous cooking show had decided to film at Storyton Hall. She'd been so excited by the idea of hosting a group of celebrity chefs—and receiving a large check for her trouble—that she hadn't stopped to consider the possible ramifications.

And the ramifications had been significant.

Jane hoped she'd learned from her mistakes. Following the cooking show disaster, she refused several lucrative offers, including one from a group of medieval lifestyle enthusiasts interested in hosting a jousting tournament, a canine protection coalition that wanted to train dogs on the premises, the Society of Political Impersonators, the League of Extraterrestrial Communicators, and the National Association of Mimes, Clowns, and Ventriloquists.

Poets are dreamers, she reminded herself. *If the worst thing they do is drink too much wine, I'll count myself lucky.*

"For tonight, we just need to be our friendly selves and provide a steady flow of wine—and by 'flow,' I mean a gentle stream," Jane said.

Anna gleefully rubbed her hands together. "This is going to be fun."

As it turned out, she was right. All the poets, the Current Mood Card Company VIPs, and the Cover Girls had a ball.

But as dark fell and the flow of wine became a trickle, the guests wandered off to order cocktails from the Ian Fleming Lounge or to seek the comfort of their beds.

Jane was ready to kick off her shoes, put on her pajamas, and spend the rest of the night on the sofa, snuggling with her man. Edwin had his own apartment

above his restaurant, Daily Bread, but he rarely slept
there anymore. He and Jane had been a couple for so
long now that strangers assumed they were married.

But Edwin wasn't Jane's husband. Nor was he the
twins' father. Not on paper, anyway. Legalese aside, he
was Jane's devoted life partner and unofficial father to
her sons. Over the years, the four of them had become
a family.

"Is Edwin working late tonight?" Eloise asked on her
way out. The other Cover Girls had already left.

"It's a Friday night, so I'll probably be asleep when
he gets home," Jane said.

Eloise smiled. "If you want, I could call the fire department and claim I smelled gas coming from the
restaurant. My brother would eventually forgive me."

"I don't want him glowering when you and Landon
are standing at the altar. Besides, I want the TV to myself so I can finish watching *Persuasion*."

Eloise sighed. "Landon will never appreciate Jane
Austen, but I guess I'll keep him anyway."

After wishing her friend a good night, Jane helped
her staff clear away the dirty plates and wineglasses. She
was heading to the Pablo Neruda table to collect an
empty platter when she spied a piece of paper on the
floor near the grandfather clock. It was no bigger than
an index card and contained a black-and-white clip art
image of what appeared to be a Victorian funeral
hearse. Below the image were a few lines of poetry.

There is a silence where no sound may be,
In the cold grave—under the deep deep sea.

Jane frowned. The words sounded familiar, but she
couldn't place them. She examined the font, which was
meant to resemble old-fashioned handwriting, and

stared at the horse-drawn carriage and its driver, who was clothed entirely in black.

Turning the paper over, Jane's curiosity quickly morphed into dread. The words were knives, sharp and menacing.

Tell no one, or I'll silence you forever.

Pressing the paper against her chest as if she could smother the threat, Jane whispered, "Not again."

Chapter 2

Jane sensed rather than heard someone approach from behind.

"Miss Jane? Is something troubling you?" Butterworth inquired in a voice as deep as a mountain cave.

Jane turned to meet the concerned gaze of Storyton Hall's butler. Butterworth was one of three men who'd served as a surrogate father to Jane after her parents died in a tragic accident when she was very young. Butterworth, formerly of Her Majesty's Secret Service, was a formidable man in every way. He was six-foot-four and had a chest like a redwood trunk. At fifty-five, he was quicker and stronger than men half his age. His facial expressions alternated between inscrutable and censorious. He reminded most people of a grizzly bear, but to Jane, he was just a big teddy bear.

"I found this on the floor," she said, handing him the paper.

He read the verse on the front, flipped the paper over to read the message on the back, and then held it up to the light. "Standard copy paper. The Victorian funeral hearse is a bit odd, but seeing as we have a hotel full of poets, I wouldn't read much into the poem or the image. The threatening language on the back is another matter."

"I don't like it one bit." She pointed at the lines of poetry. "Do you recognize this?"

"I'd be ashamed to call myself an Englishman if I didn't. They were written by a Victorian poet named Thomas Hood. He wrote about contemporary issues, like the plight of the working poor, London smog, grave robbing, and selling corpses to anatomists."

Jane muttered, "Lovely."

"These lines are taken from a sonnet called 'Silence.' I don't remember every line, but the theme is the absolute power of silence."

"The lines on the card include a reference to the grave. Between those and the note on the back, it's clearly a threat."

One of Butterworth's giant hands came to rest on Jane's arm. "Whoever wrote this would probably be surprised to learn it had been left it in the lobby for us to find. The message is troublesome, yes, but we now know to watch our guests with increased vigilance. Just in case."

"Will you show this to the other Fins?" she asked.

Butterworth's gaze flicked to the clock. "By the time the next chime sounds, they'll have been informed. Go home now, Miss Jane. In the words of William Wordsworth, 'rest and be thankful.' "

Jane obeyed. As she walked through Milton's Gardens, her path lit by star shine and fireflies, she did feel thankful.

The Fins would do anything in their power to keep

Jane, her family, and her guests safe. They'd all taken an oath to protect the Guardian of Storyton Hall. Butterworth, Sinclair, and Sterling had been hired by Uncle Aloysius back when he was the Guardian. Landon had come aboard shortly after Uncle Aloysius passed the title to Jane.

For centuries, the Steward family had devoted their lives to the protection and preservation of a secret library. For over two centuries, the library had been filled to bursting with priceless literary treasures. Most of the scrolls, folios, manuscripts, and books had been given to the Stewards to hold on to for posterity, and some of the materials were considered subversive— even dangerous—at the time they were locked away in the fireproof, temperature-controlled room in an attic turret by the Guardian of Storyton Hall.

Over three hundred years ago, the manor house had been an English country estate. It had been dismantled by Jane's ancestor, Walter Edgerton Steward, and rebuilt in a remote valley in western Virginia. Walter believed the relocation would dissuade rogues and thieves, but he was wrong.

Rumors of undiscovered Shakespeare plays, the sequel to *Jane Eyre*, or a completed version of *The Mystery of Edwin Drood* never stopped circulating. So the thieves kept coming. As did the violence.

Because Jane didn't want her life, or the lives of her sons, to be permanently marked by violence, she'd made the momentous decision to sell or donate the treasures stored in the secret library. This process had to be done slowly and carefully, but within the next decade, there would be no need for a Guardian because the library would be empty.

It hadn't been easy for Jane to break with tradition.

Before her, the Guardians had all been men. She'd been the first woman to take up the mantle, and it wasn't long before she realized that keeping her sons safe was more important than keeping secrets, no matter how valuable those secrets were.

As she approached the former hunting lodge that was now her home, Jane heard excited yips mingled with high-pitched laughter. She opened the gate leading to her front garden and saw her sons stretched out on the grass. A pair of black standard poodle puppies with white bibs and socks danced around and over the boys.

"We're teaching Merry and Pippin to hunt," Hem told his mother.

Fitz glanced up at her, his face shining with pride. "We're using our slingshots to shoot treats all over the yard. The puppies have to find them."

"I thought I told you *not* to use those slingshots within a mile of a building or any living creatures?" Scowling, she gestured between the dogs and their house.

"It's only treats," Fitz protested.

"We only use rocks when we're in the woods," Hem added.

Jane examined the puppy treats. They were small and soft, and since she didn't want to cast a cloud over such a happy scene, she gave the puppies a pet and wished her sons luck.

Inside the house, she was pleasantly surprised to see that the twins had cleaned up their dinner things and washed the dog dishes. The kitchen and downstairs living areas were tidy, and though Jane could imagine what she'd see if she were to peek into the twins' bedroom, she remembered Wordsworth's advice.

Rest and be thankful.

Leaving the door to their room firmly shut, she went to her room to change into pajamas. After that, she filled a glass with sparkling water and stretched out on the sofa to watch *Persuasion*.

Jane didn't remember falling asleep, but she came to when someone gently shook her shoulder and whispered her name.

"Edwin?"

"Yes, love. It's late. Let's get you to bed."

She remembered him turning off the TV before pulling her to her feet. Holding her hand, he led her up the stairs and into the bedroom.

"Work okay?" she murmured, slipping under the covers.

"It was pretty calm for a Friday. I thought we'd have more poets, but I guess they had a better offer."

Jane knew she was being teased, but she was too drowsy to come up with a reply other than, "Sorry."

"Go back to sleep. I'm going to take a shower."

Edwin always showered after coming home from the restaurant. He'd get in bed smelling of the lemon verbena soap made for the hotel's spa. Jane loved to run her fingers through his damp hair while they talked about their day.

Jane wanted to tell Edwin about the note. He'd listen attentively to every detail and would carefully weigh his words before responding. Not only was Edwin tall, dark, and handsome, but he also had a sharp mind, a quick wit, and a killer sense of humor. Jane admired his ability to remain calm and think clearly in any situation, and she wanted his take on the funeral poem.

But her drowsy brain couldn't stay focused. The softness of the bed and the rhythmic sound of the shower water lulled her to sleep. It seemed like she'd barely closed her eyes before she was woken by a sudden weight on the bed. The weight shifted, and she heard rapid sniffs and energetic grunts. When one of the puppies began covering her cheek in kisses, she rolled away and tried to hide under the comforter.

The excited snuffles and whimpers intensified until suddenly two puppy noses managed to burrow under the sheets. As they licked her face and neck, Jane hugged each of their soft, little bodies until they squirmed out of her grasp.

"Hey! You're supposed to be outside!" Hem scolded from Jane's doorway.

Shooing the puppies off the bed, Jane squinted at the clock. "Must be piddle time." Looking back at Hem, she said, "Isn't this Fitz's week to do mornings?"

"We traded."

Jane's maternal radar pinged. Her sons hated getting up early, and she couldn't imagine what could have inspired Hem to take Fitz's place. Before she could ask, Hem turned and ran down the hall. The puppies yipped with joy and sprinted after him.

Hem had left the room quickly, but not fast enough to hide his flushed cheeks.

Jane smiled. *He was blushing. Could this be a first crush?*

She'd have to wait until Fitz roused himself to find out because Hem responded to her subtle probing over breakfast by stuffing a piece of toast in his mouth and darting outside. A minute later, she heard him reprimanding the puppies and winced. The little terrors were probably digging more holes in her bee and butterfly garden.

Instead of investigating, she drank the coffee Edwin had made an hour ago. He'd left her a note saying he went for a ride with Sam and would be gone for most of the morning. Sam owned Hilltop Stables. He and Edwin were longtime friends, and both liked to get a ride in before the sun had fully risen. Edwin claimed that these predawn excursions were the only way to avoid the heat, but Jane suspected he and Sam wanted the trails all to themselves so they could ride like they were being chased by the devil.

Jane didn't know how Edwin could work until eleven o'clock at night and still be up and out of the house before the coffee finished brewing. She couldn't function without at least six hours of deep sleep followed by two or three cups of coffee.

Her mug—and a very large one at that—was empty by the time she called Fitz down for breakfast.

Ten minutes later, a preteen zombie lurched into the kitchen and dropped into a chair. Fitz's sandy-brown hair stood up in hedgehog spikes, and the creases on the left side of his face meant that he'd fallen asleep on his book again.

"Someone was really into his book," Jane said.

Fitz's reply was an unintelligible, "Huunnnhh."

After a glass of orange juice and a piece of toast slathered with the jam he and Hem had made earlier that summer, Fitz started showing signs of life.

"Hem says he traded with you for morning puppy duty. What brought that on?"

Fitz rolled his eyes and said, "A girl," before sinking his teeth into another piece of toast.

The only way Jane could play it cool was to avoid making eye contact, so she began wiping the counter with a damp cloth. With her back to Fitz, she asked, "What girl?"

"Someone from school. She was hiking on one of our trails. Is there any bacon left?"

Jane put the three remaining strips on his plate. "Were you there too?"

Fitz shrugged. "Yeah. She was taking pics with her phone, and Hem started talking to her about photography. I was hot and my water bottle was empty, so I kept walking, but he stayed to hang out with her."

"Huh. So he traded with you because he wants to see this girl again?"

Having polished off the bacon, Fitz carried his plate and juice glass to the sink. "I guess," he said while loading his breakfast things into the dishwasher. After a perfunctory, "Thanks, Mom," he headed back to his room.

Jane considered refilling her mug and carrying it out to the patio along with her book, but when she saw the huge red heart on the wall calendar, she thought of the matron of honor dress she'd be wearing in two weeks.

"I'll listen to an audiobook instead," she said, addressing the comment to her empty mug. "It's not too hot for a hike. Maybe I'll get to see the girl Hem has his eye on."

Twenty minutes later, she took the path leading to the staff cottages until it merged with the gravel driveway. She walked past Storyton Mews and its resident raptors until she reached the archery field. At this point, she had to choose between Alfred Tennyson's Trail or Phillis Wheatley's Way. Tennyson's Trail had less shade, but Wheatley's Way had more hills.

In the end, Lachlan made the decision for her.

Exiting the archery hut, he caught sight of Jane and waved both arms at her. He then grabbed something from inside the hut and jogged over to where she stood.

"Are you headed for the lake?"

"I can be. Do you want me to deliver that water bottle

to—oh." Recognizing the bottle, she said, "Uncle Aloysius forgot again?"

Lachlan, a taciturn man by nature, gave her a short nod.

"I'll take it. Thanks for looking out for him."

Two Gators filled with guests crunched down the driveway en route to the archery fields.

"Good luck with your lesson," Jane said, hurrying away before she was detained exchanging pleasantries.

Entering the stretch of woods that divided the estate grounds from the road leading to the village, Jane decided to leave her earbuds in her pocket and listen to the sounds of nature instead. She heard red-bellied woodpeckers chipping away at segments of tree bark, the coos of mourning doves, and a tufted titmouse whistling *peter-peter-peter*.

The trail was postcard perfect. The branches were thick enough to provide blissful shade while still permitting ribbons of sunlight to stripe the pine-needle carpet. Because the undergrowth was sparse, deer and wild turkey were easy to spot, and Jane was unsurprised to see a doe and her fawn investigating a cluster of grassy weeds just off the path ahead. The white speckles on the fawn's coat were fading. By October, they'd be completely gone.

Suddenly the doe jerked her head up. Her ears twitched in alarm, and she took off running, her fawn following behind.

"Am I that scary?" Jane called after the deer. She couldn't see them anymore, but the crunch of their hooves over dead leaves told her they were moving deeper into the woods.

She'd taken four steps at most when she heard

voices. A minute later, Jane saw what had really startled the deer. A group of three hikers was approaching.

When they were a stone's throw away, Jane smiled and said, "Good morning."

A bearded man with acorn-brown skin raised his hand in greeting. Jane instantly recognized Jeremiah Okoro, co-owner of Current Mood Cards. "We're taking in your beautiful trails."

The company's co-owner, Gil Callahan, wiped sweat from his ruddy brow. He then removed his baseball cap, releasing a cloud of russet-colored curls, and used the hat to fan his face. He and Jeremiah were both in their forties, but Gil's wild hair and flushed cheeks made him seem a trifle younger.

Clasping his hands, he moaned, "I need rescuing. Please tell me there's a shortcut to the hotel."

"What? Come on, man. We don't do shortcuts." Jeremiah gave his colleague a friendly shove.

Gil shook his head. "You're wrong. I need a soft chair and a big cup of coffee. And possibly a defibrillator. If a shortcut gets me those things, then I'm taking it."

Jeremiah smiled at Jane. "Your coffee *is* amazing, but this guy needs some sun. When people see him in the hall, they think he's a ghost. Every writer's going to think the hotel is haunted."

Replacing his cap, Gil scowled. "Very funny. You know I have a toxic relationship with the sun. Every time we go out, I get burned."

The leggy brunette standing next to Jeremiah stuck out her bottom lip in sympathy. She was in her mid-thirties and looked like a fitness model. Not only was she toned and tanned with shiny hair and a lovely face, but she was also an incredibly upbeat and organized person. Jane had enjoyed planning the four-day poetry conference and competition with her.

"You seem totally unaffected by the heat, Ms. Harbaugh. Did you have fun last night?"

"Oh, call me Stephanie. And yes, I had a blast. The wine was perfect, the vibe was positive, and the *food!* Just, wow. This whole place is a PR person's dream. If these guys ever fire me, I want to come work for you."

Jane shot a glance at Jeremiah and Gil. "If they're smart, they'll never let you go."

"Current Mood couldn't get off the ground without Stephanie." Jeremiah stepped aside and gestured at the trail. "I'm sure you don't get much time to yourself, so don't let us keep you."

"Unless you want to show me that shortcut." Gil waggled his brows.

Stephanie looped her arm through his and began pulling him forward. She waved at Jane with her free hand and said, "See you later."

As Jane continued walking, she went over her mental list of the day's activities. The writers would spend the day working with Professor Dodge Ashley, lecturer and published poet. At the end of the session, Jeremiah and Gil would review the first round of entries and begin ordering the writing samples from best to worst. Jane knew that the winner of the Current Mood contract had to exhibit a talent for capturing a wide range of emotions to complement an even wider range of circumstances.

The village of Storyton could use cards like the ones Current Mood would be producing, as the current options were limited. Eloise carried cards with literary themes at Run for Cover, Phoebe sold cards made by local artists at the Canvas Creamery, and the Pickled Pig

had cards for life's big events like birthdays or weddings, but not much else.

Do you carry cards in your hotel gift shop? Stephanie had
asked Jane by email.

Jane had replied, *Just postcards and notecards with photos
of the resort.*

*Have you ever thought about using literary quotes or lines
of poetry on your cards? Watercolors of the reading rooms, the
garden, or the rockers on the terrace might be more appealing to
your guests than photo cards. Current Mood could design some
samples for you if you're interested in changing things up.*

I'd love that, Jane had replied.

At last night's wine tasting, Stephanie had told Jane
that she was incredibly excited to show Jane the cards
Current Mood had created for Storyton Hall.

"I didn't bring them tonight because I'd probably
spill wine on them. I'm seriously clumsy. But I promise
to show them to you tomorrow," she'd said.

Jane couldn't wait to see them. She knew many of the
products sold in the gift shop needed to be updated—as
did the website—but other, bigger projects kept her
from addressing these things.

She had a corkboard in her office covered with multicolored index cards. Jane's Hopes and Dreams board
was full of ideas on how to improve Storyton Hall. She'd
already made some of the wishes come true by building
a top-notch spa and a storybook village for children,
but not all the hopes and dreams were as fun. Repairing
the roof, replacing the furnace, restoring the orchard,
and rebuilding the folly accounted for four of thirty-
something index cards. And somewhere on that board
was a card that read, UPDATE GIFT SHOP PRODUCTS.

Jane pictured the current layout in the boutique and

realized they'd been selling the same products for years. Other than the tea towels, most of the items featuring the name or image of the resort were lackluster. Story-ton Hall needed a branding overhaul.

"We need color. Book spines and teacups. Wildflowers and literary quotes. And homemade products like the boys' jam, honey from local hives, and artistic cards."

Energized by ideas, she soon reached the lake.

Though the trail followed the curve of the lake and disappeared from view behind a stand of dense cattails, Jane veered to her right, where a small dock jutted out into the lake. The large dock on the opposite bank was the launching spot for the canoes or fishing boats maintained by the Recreation Department. No one used the small dock other than her great-uncle, which is why Jane always referred to it as Uncle Aloysius's Wharf.

She walked out to the end of the dock, shielding her eyes against the sun's glare as she searched for a jon boat with a royal-blue sunshade. Luckily, he was on her side of the lake. His line was in the water, and his feet were propped up on a bucket.

Jane smiled. She knew that most of her uncle's time "fishing" was actually spent snoozing.

He didn't startle at the sound of his name, but slowly raised his head and waved. A few minutes later, he motored over to the little dock, cutting the engine when he got close.

"You forgot your water bottle," Jane said, grabbing the bow and pulling the jon boat against the dock. She handed the water bottle to her uncle and then stood, straddling the boat with one foot while keeping the other foot on the dock.

"Thank you, my dear. I'm mighty thirsty."

Jane gestured at his bucket. "Still empty?"

"'Fraid so. They were biting earlier but have gone quiet. I'll give it another hour before calling it quits."

Jane glanced around. The glassy lake was undisturbed by boats. A few ducks paddled around near the middle, but other than that, there was no activity. "The trails are seeing some action this morning. Maybe the fish heard voices and decided to hang out near the bottom."

"Yes, some folks have passed by. I don't know how many because I can't see over the cattails. They might still be over there. Every now and then, I catch a flash of white from that spot."

Jane pointed to the clump of vegetation. "Behind there?"

Uncle Aloysius readjusted his hat. "That's the place. They startled my blue heron friend, which is probably why I can't catch anything. He's my good-luck charm."

Jane smiled tenderly at her uncle and then blew him a kiss. "That's for luck."

He mimed catching the kiss and pressing it to his cheek. "Just what the doctor ordered. Thank you, my dear."

Jane put both feet back on the dock and watched her uncle deftly maneuver the flat-bottom boat toward the center of the lake. She waited until he'd turned off the motor and cast his line before returning to Tennyson's Trail.

She'd barely rounded the curve when she saw the bow of a Storyton Hall canoe poking through a cluster of reeds. Jane loved the bright colors of their little fleet of canoes. There was mango, canary yellow, lime green, and purple. The one caught in the cattails was a vibrant turquoise.

As Jane moved closer to the water's edge, she noticed more colors. A white dress. Long, brown hair. Scarlet ribbons wrapped around milk-white hands.

It took a moment for Jane's brain to play catch-up with her eyes, but she soon realized that she was looking at woman in a white sundress. The woman's head had slumped forward, and her face was hidden by a curtain of long, dark hair. The red ribbons around her wrist had been looped around either side of the bench seat and seemed to be holding the woman upright.

"Ma'am?" Jane called. "Ma'am! Can you hear me?"

There was no reply.

Jane wanted to keep calling. She wanted to delay the truth, to preserve the idyllic stillness of the morning.

But she couldn't.

Her hotel was booked to capacity. At any moment, a guest might walk by and see what Jane saw.

A dead woman in a turquoise canoe.

Chapter 3

Jane's first call was to Butterworth.

"We have a Rip van Winkle in the lake. We need to rope off Tennyson's Trail immediately, but Lachlan's in the middle of an archery lesson."

"I'll see to it at once."

Jane tried to catch sight of her uncle, but the reeds were too thick. "I'd also like someone to take my uncle back to his apartments before the cavalry arrives, so could you send a driver to collect him? And ask Sinclair to come with you, please."

"Certainly."

There was a note of triumph in Butterworth's voice, and Jane wondered just how dusty Sinclair's clothes would be by the time he and Butterworth reached her.

Storyton Hall's head butler and librarian were extremely fond of each other, but they had a strange way of expressing their affection. For example, Butterworth ruthlessly teased Sinclair about his fashion sense, while

Sinclair would poke fun at Butterworth's bearlike appearance.

Usually, Jane found their friendly banter amusing, but this was no time for levity. After ending her call with Butterworth, she placed a second call to the Storyton Sheriff's Department.

When she reported the death to Sheriff Evans, she wouldn't use the term 'Rip van Winkle.' This code name, which was specific to Storyton Hall, referred to the unexpected passing of a guest. The code made it possible to alert the staff about the death while protecting the privacy of the expired guest.

Most hotels had code names for such occasions. Once, at a hotel conference, Jane's colleagues had shared the names used by their staff. The most memorable were Elvis, Marilyn Monroe, Casper, Raven, and Mr. or Ms. Halo. With guests coming and going every day, death was part of the business. People had heart attacks, accidents, or slipped away in their sleep, and any hotel manager worth their salt had a plan in place for dealing with a guest who was alive when they checked in but no longer breathing when they checked out.

The officer who answered Jane's call connected her to Sheriff Evans without delay. She didn't even have a chance to state the reason for the call.

"Good morning, Ms. Steward," the sheriff's voice boomed in Jane's ear. "I expected to hear from your sons, or have they roped you into handling the customer service division of their business?"

Jane was nonplussed. "Sorry, but I don't know what you mean. Is this about their jam?"

"It sure is. They're making a special batch of Happy Huckleberry for my family reunion." When Jane didn't reply right away, the sheriff's tone shifted. "Ms. Steward. Has something happened?"

"There's a dead woman in our lake. Not in the water. She's sitting in one of our canoes. Someone tied her hands to keep her in an upright position."

The sheriff drew in a long, slow breath. He then asked Jane a series of questions, which she answered as succinctly as possible. He finished by asking if she'd already contacted Doc Lydgate.

"Not yet," she said.

"I'll call him on the way over. Be there as quick as I can."

Sheriff Evans didn't bother telling Jane to keep her guests as far away from the scene as possible. They both knew that she and her staff would secure a perimeter and do everything in their power to make his job easier.

"I was hoping this kind of thing would stop happening," Jane said in a small voice.

"I make the same wish every day. Hang in there, Ms. Steward. We're on our way."

Jane turned back to the woman in the boat.

Her body was absolutely still. The canoe wasn't bobbing in the water, which meant the hull was likely stuck in the muddy bottom. No wavelets lapped at the canoe's sides. No breeze moved through the woman's hair or ruffled her cotton dress. The insects had yet to find her. She looked like a photograph of a woman, unmoving and expressionless.

The world has gone silent, Jane thought.

It wouldn't last long, she knew. Soon, this corner of the lake would be corrupted by sound. Voices, engine noises, ringing phones. Sound and movement would replace the preternatural quiet.

For now, there was only the wide sky, the tall reeds, the water, and two women facing each other. One stood by the lake edge. The other was propped up in a canoe.

Jane wondered whether the woman had died in the canoe, surrounded by the cough of frogs and the beat of dragonfly wings. She wondered if the blue heron had seen someone wrap red ribbons around the woman's wrists.

The sun beat down on Jane's shoulders. Sweat trickled down her neck and soaked into her shirt collar. The strands of strawberry-blond hair escaping her baseball cap were damp. Unlike the rest of her body, her mouth was dry.

And yet she was alive. The fact that she was hot, sweaty, and thirsty was evidence of her good fortune. She could look forward to a drink of cool water and a refreshing shower. In her future, she'd share countless meals with Edwin and the boys. There would be get-togethers with her friends. Weddings and Christmases. Fall bonfires and snowflakes on her mittens.

The woman in the canoe would have none of these. She'd never hug another person again or sit down to a glass of wine at the end of a very long day. Her hand would never again pet a puppy, her teeth would never again bite into an apple cider donut, her eyes would never again watch flames dance in a fireplace, and her ears would never again hear the whisper of book pages.

"I'm sorry," Jane whispered.

The subtle whine of an electric engine made her turn around.

Sterling, the head chauffeur, drove the first of two utility vehicles. Sinclair and Butterworth were in the second.

Pulling to a stop along the side of the trail, Sterling said, "Are you okay?"

"Yes. Thanks for getting my uncle."

"I'm going to hear it from your aunt when she finds out there's a Rip van Winkle and I didn't race to her with a full report."

Jane smirked. "She'll know as much as we do by the end of the day. That woman has a network of spies."

"After she dresses me down, I'll keep an eye on our guests from the surveillance room."

"Good idea," Jane said.

For a moment, she was disconcerted by how calmly they were responding to such an unusual death. But then she quickly pushed the feeling aside. Bursting into tears or having a fit of hysterics wasn't going to bring the woman back to life. The best Jane could do for her now was to protect her dignity and aid the sheriff's department in its quest to find out what happened to her.

Butterworth parked his vehicle in the intersection between Tennyson's Trail and Whitman's Walk. While he tied a length of yellow caution tape to the sign, Sinclair walked over to Jane.

He searched her face. Seeing no sign of distress—only concern—his gaze shifted to the canoe.

His expression revealed nothing, but Jane caught the slight tightening of his jaw muscle. Like Butterworth, Sinclair had been trained to hide his emotions, but Jane had known him her entire life. He was worried.

"What are you thinking?" she asked.

"When I look at her, I see a poem."

Jane didn't understand the allusion and told him as much.

Sinclair brushed road dust from the lapel of his seer-sucker suit coat and began to speak in a clear, melodi-ous voice.

> *"'And down the river's dim expanse—*
> *Like some bold seer in a trance,*
> *Seeing all his own mischance—*
> *With a glassy countenance*
> *Did she look to Camelot.'"*

Butterworth approached the lake edge, his hands clasped behind his back. He added his voice to Sinclair's and their words mingled until they were more prayer than poetry.

> *"'And at the closing of the day*
> *She loosed the chain, and down she lay;*
> *The broad stream bore her far away,*
> *The Lady of Shalott.'"*

Jane was instantly transported to the Tate Gallery. It had been less than two months since she'd stood in front of John William Waterhouse's haunting painting of the beautiful, damned maiden, *The Lady of Shalott.*

How she'd stared and stared at the figure in that painting. Her white gown, her red-golden hair, the gloomy trees and dark water. Jane remembered the hollow look in the lovely young woman's eyes, as if she'd just been at the Tate instead of standing by a lake in western Virginia.

"A poem," she murmured. "When we have a hotel full of poets."

"Indeed," grumbled Butterworth.

While they waited for the sheriff and Doc Lydgate, Jane headed back to the small dock, scanning the ground as she walked. Sinclair searched the lake's edge, and Butterworth stood guard.

Jane didn't see anything in the grass or in the cloudy patches of water between cattails. When she heard the rumble of Sheriff Evans's SUV, she returned to the spot where she'd first noticed the canoe and waited for him to approach.

After greeting Butterworth, he turned back to his car and waved at the fair-haired man who'd alighted from the passenger seat. "Join us, Doc."

"I thought Doc Lydgate wasn't retiring until September," Jane whispered to Sinclair.

"He must be tied up at his office. It would've been better if the new doctor's first Storyton Hall patient had a pulse, but this is the hand we've been dealt."

Having introduced the doctor to Butterworth, the sheriff led him over to Sinclair and Jane. Touching the brim of his hat in deference to Jane, Sheriff Evans said, "Deputies Phelps and Emory are right behind me. Doc Lydgate is in the middle of setting a broken arm, but we're in luck because the younger Doc Lydgate is at our service. Ms. Steward. Mr. Sinclair. This is Doctor Charles Lydgate."

Doc Lydgate's son didn't look a day over forty. He had a pleasant face, a warm smile, and dimpled cheeks. He was of medium height with wide shoulders and Wedgwood-blue eyes. Jane thought Charles was the perfect name for a man who looked like *Pride and Prejudice*'s Charles Bingley. If she were to dress the new doctor in Regency clothes, he and Edwin could masquerade as Bingley and Darcy.

"Thank you for coming, er, should I call you Doc or Doctor Lydgate?"

"I go by Doc Charles." He smiled as he shook hands with Jane and Sinclair. Then he shot a questioning look at the sheriff. "I've never had a case like this, so you might have to give me some direction."

Sheriff Evans pointed at the car pulling in behind his SUV. "We'll wait for Phelps and Emory. Phelps has the evidence kit, and Emory has the camera. They'll document the scene and search for evidence. After that, you can do a preliminary examination."

Impatient for the process to begin, Jane started talking to Deputy Emory the moment she got out of the car.

"She's in the reeds. I'll show you," Jane said. The young, female deputy would have been at home in a John William Waterhouse painting. She had the same creamy complexion and red-gold hair as Waterhouse's *Lady of Shalott.*

Prior to becoming a member of law enforcement, Deputy Emory had studied art. She was also a talented amateur landscape painter. Jane overheard her tell Phelps that the woman in the canoe reminded her of Jane Morris, the wife of William Morris. Phelps responded with a blank stare before focusing his gaze on the ground. He examined the area in an orderly manner, moving from right to left. He then searched the area again moving backward from the lake's edge.

The rest of the assembly remained at a distance until Phelps and Emory informed the sheriff that they'd taken all the images they needed and had found no evidence to collect.

It was time to shore the canoe.

"May I be of assistance?" Butterworth asked, brandishing a pair of wading boots.

Sheriff Evans's relief was apparent. He and Butterworth were close in age, but the sheriff wasn't nearly as fit. Butterworth trained every day and kept to a strict diet while the sheriff had a penchant for ham biscuits, cold beer, and anything made by Mrs. Hubbard. Evans might have a slight paunch, but Jane had seen him chase after criminals. He could really move when the occasion called for it, but he preferred not to.

Butterworth slipped on the boots and waded into the water. Sinclair handed him a telescopic boat hook, and in less than two minutes, Butterworth had the canoe within reach of the sheriff and his deputies.

Emory took another round of photos while Phelps and Sheriff Evans gloved up.

"I smell bug spray," said Phelps.

Jane did as well. She wondered if the scent explained the lack of insect activity on the body or inside the boat.

"Let's get her on dry land," said Evans. "Slowly, please. I don't want her to fall."

Butterworth stayed in the water and pushed from behind until the canoe slid smoothly onto the grassy bank. The woman's body bobbed back and forth, but her sightless eyes and slack face offered no reaction to her new surroundings.

Unsettled, Jane focused on the woman's hands. She wore no jewelry. Her nails were short and unpainted.

"She looks posed," Deputy Emory said.

Jane said, "Mr. Sinclair believes she may be the heroine of a tragic poem, 'The Lady of Shalott'."

The sheriff looked a question at Sinclair.

"The poem is about a woman imprisoned on an island. She spends all her time weaving and watching the world go by in her mirror. She understands that if she ever sets eyes on Camelot, she will be cursed. One day, she sees Lancelot in her mirror. She gets up from her loom to look at him through her window and, in doing so, breaks her mirror. Despite the dangers, the lady leaves her tower and boards a small boat. The river takes her to Camelot."

The sheriff and his deputies were captivated by the story, as was Doc Charles. Though Jane couldn't recall the poem as clearly as Sinclair—the head librarian had a photographic memory for all works of fiction—she remembered feeling so sorry for the Lady of Shalott.

"Then what? Did she meet Merlin?" asked Phelps.

Sinclair continued as if Phelps hadn't spoken. "Dressed in a snowy-white robe, the lady sings as the water brings her closer and closer to Camelot. She sings and sings until her blood freezes, and ultimately, she dies. When the boat arrives in Camelot, the lady is dead. The lords and ladies cross themselves at the sight of her. Only Lancelot looks at her face, deems her lovely, and speaks a short prayer over her."

Indignantly, Phelps said, "That's it? She didn't even get to see Camelot."

Butterworth moved into the sheriff's line of sight. "Ms. Jane noticed the canoe while walking on Tennyson's Trail. The poem in question is by Alfred, Lord Tennyson. The lady in his poem wears a long, white dress."

"And our hotel is full of poets," Jane added.

"Of course, it is," the sheriff muttered. "Do you know this woman's name, Ms. Steward?"

Jane felt compelled to look at the dead woman's face as Lancelot had. "I probably met her at the wine tasting event last night. I don't mean to diminish her in any way, but I met several lovely young women with long, straight hair. Luckily, the event was held in the lobby, which means she must have been captured by our security cameras."

"Good. Doc? Would you take a look at her now? I don't want to untie her until you've had a chance to examine her."

Doc Charles was gloved up and ready to perform his duties. He approached the dead woman and softly said, "With your permission."

At this show of respect, Jane's vision blurred with tears. She blinked them away and watched the doctor examine the woman's eyes, nose, and ears. She saw him gently part her dark hair, searching for evidence of a head injury. He looked at the skin of her neck and upper back. He carefully pivoted her hands, studying her fingernails and her bruised wrists. Finally, he forced her mouth open and pointed his penlight inside.

"What're your initial thoughts, Doc?" asked the sheriff. When Doc Charles hesitated, Evans gestured at Jane, Butterworth, and Sinclair. "You can speak freely in front of them. Not only can I count on their discretion and cooperation, but Jane and her staff have helped me with more investigations than I care to mention."

Doc Charles nodded. "I'd estimate that our patient died between midnight and six o'clock this morning. The heat has sped up some of the postmortem processes, making it hard to be more precise. From what I can see, she had no injuries other than bruising around her wrists caused by the tightness of the ribbon and the weight of her torso. She has what I assume are pen marks on the side of her right hand. I also smell bug spray, but her face and neck also smell strongly of soap or some kind of cleaning agent. I don't think she died in the canoe. I think she died elsewhere and was posed in the canoe soon after."

"Any idea of the cause of death?"

"Her tongue and throat are inflamed. She may have ingested a toxin of some sort, but I couldn't say without additional tests."

Sheriff Evans said, "It seemed important to the person who did this that she appeared, I don't know, dignified? Elegant? A poetic figure?"

"This might sound strange, but when I first saw her, I thought she was beautiful," said Jane. "A lovely woman stuck in the reeds."

The sheriff looked inside the canoe and frowned. "There's nothing here. Nothing obvious, anyway. I'll have to take the canoe back with me. Ms. Steward, would you loan us a pickup truck? Ah, here's the ambulance."

The sound of the vehicle's back-up beeper nearly drowned out Jane's voice as she called Sterling to request a truck.

"I'll bring it myself," he said. "I don't think I'll be able to find this woman on our footage without taking a closer look at her. There must have been six women with long, dark hair at last night's party."

"You'd better hurry. They're about to load her into the ambulance."

Sterling took her warning to heart. Only a few minutes had passed when he pulled up alongside the ambulance and, after asking the sheriff's permission, studied the woman's face.

When he was done, he pulled the sheet over her and murmured, "Such a waste. She had so much life ahead of her. Who knows what she might have done with it?"

Jane, Butterworth, and Sinclair lined up like party hosts watching their guests leave. One by one, the vehicles drove away.

Sinclair took Jane's arm and wordlessly led her to a Gator. Butterworth wanted to take a last look around before returning to the manor house.

"The sheriff is heading to the main dock, so I'll join him there. Afterward, I plan to launch a canoe and paddle into the cattails." Butterworth glanced around the lake. "I want to follow the lady's path."

Jane said, "Maybe you'll find something in the reeds. And since Mr. Lachlan's archery lesson should be over by now, I'll ask him to walk the length of Tennyson's Trail. Sinclair and I will be in his office. I'd like to identify the woman as soon as possible."

Sinclair drove Jane to the main garage. After parking the Gator, he said, "Why don't you go ahead to my office so you can cool down? I'll get a pitcher of water from the kitchens."

"Thanks, but I want to rinse my arms off in a big sink. Hopefully, Mrs. Hubbard won't ask too many questions when she sees me in yoga pants and a sweaty T-shirt, using her dish-washing sink to give myself a sponge bath."

Fortunately, Mrs. Hubbard was busy painting rubber stamps with black food coloring and then pressing the stamps to sheets of edible wafer paper to notice Jane.

Too intrigued not to look, Jane saw that the edible paper had been cut into butterfly shapes and that Mrs. Hubbard was stamping words into the wings. The task clearly required intense concentration, so Jane put her fingers to her lips before the kitchen staff could say hello.

At the dish-washing station, Jane washed her hands

and forearms. Next, she splashed water on her face and
dried herself with paper towels. Now that she felt slightly
more human, she stepped into the blissful cold of the
walk-in fridge and helped herself to one of several water
pitchers destined for the spa. The water was infused
with orange slices and mint leaves and was incredibly
refreshing.

Carrying the pitcher in one hand and two glasses in
the other, Jane left the bright and bustling kitchen and
entered the dimly lit staff hallway.

Footfalls echoed from all directions as members of
the kitchen, housekeeping, and maintenance staff
toted foodstuffs, laundry, cleaning supplies, and fresh
flowers through the warren of corridors once used by
servants of the Steward family. The stairs had been
warped by the weight of hundreds of feet stepping in
the same spots for over a century.

This was where the history of Storyton Hall came
alive. This was where Jane heard the house breathe and
felt its bones settle. All its creaks, groans, and reverbera-
tions were uttered to the people behind the scenes. The
people who loved the house almost as much as Jane
did.

There were a few guests in the Henry James Library,
but none of them looked up from their books as Jane
crossed the room. The door to Sinclair's office was so
cleverly concealed in the wall's wood paneling that it
became apparent only when opened.

Jane used her master key to unlock the door and
slipped inside. The long and narrow office was domi-
nated by corkboards. The paper pinned to the boards
contained biographical sketches of the current guests.
In addition to the details provided by each guest when

making their reservation, Sinclair included information on their jobs, social media handles, and hobbies. At the top of each printout was an enlarged driver's license photo or alternative form of identification requiring a photo.

Sinclair stood at the far end of the counter, scanning the printouts pinned to the topmost bulletin board.

Jane stared at him. "You look like you never left the library. I don't know how you do it. Would you like some water?"

"Please. And I only look refreshed because I keep a spare shirt in my office. It came in handy today."

He'd wiped the dust off his loafers too, Jane noticed. She filled two glasses with water and handed one to Sinclair. "I'll start at the other end, and we can meet in the middle."

Sinclair removed his silver spectacles. As he rubbed at a spot on the left lens, he said, "I'm eager to learn her name because I've started thinking of her as the Lady of Shalott, which isn't right."

"Especially since that's what her killer wanted," Jane said.

The word "killer" polluted the air and left a bad taste in Jane's mouth. After drinking some water, she focused on the printouts. She studied each image, regardless of the person's gender, before ruling them out.

Jane had paused to examine the photo of a woman named Delilah when Sinclair said, "She's here."

He removed a printout and handed it to Jane.

"Gretchen West of Knoxville, Tennessee. Age thirty-six. Unmarried. A medical librarian at the University of Tennessee Medical Center. Belongs to a social media group for medical librarians as well as an online anxiety support group." She glanced up. "That's it? One paragraph?"

Sinclair gestured at his computer. "It was all I deemed necessary for a basic profile. I'll begin a more thorough search as soon as—"

"I get out of your hair." Jane finished for him. "I'll be with Sterling if you need me. If he hasn't found any footage of Ms. West yet, I should review it for myself."

"She may have skipped the party altogether."

Jane glanced down at the printout. "Because of anxiety? Based on the support group she's in, it's a possibility."

Nodding, Sinclair sat in the chair facing his computer and said, "There's that, yes, but there's something else. After making her reservation, she sent an email asking for a quiet room away from public areas, elevators, or ice machines."

"Never a bad idea."

"True. The email included her signature in a cursive font and, on the next line, the words, 'I am, I am, I am.'"

Jane frowned. "Why is that familiar? Ah, I remember. It's from *The Bell Jar* by Sylvia Plath."

"'I took a deep breath and listened to the old bray of my heart. I am. I am. I am.'"

Sinclair's soft, rhythmic cadence reminded Jane of a beating heart. And of the heart that had stopped beating.

"We need to find the person who took away Gretchen West's 'I am'." Jane's voice was tight with anger. "We have to make sure they face the consequences for ending another person's story. No one has the right to do that."

Her hand closed around the master key in her

pocket. The fob was engraved with the motto of Storyton Hall. Every room key had the same phrase. It was also carved into the arch of the massive wrought-iron entry gates.

Squaring her shoulders, Jane spoke the Latin phrase aloud as if she was taking an oath. Sinclair rose to his feet, lifted his chin in a show of solidarity and determination, and said, "Their story is our story."

Chapter 4

In the surveillance room, Sterling stood in front of a wall of screens.

Live feed from the security cameras showed guests relaxing in the reading rooms, drinking coffee on the terrace, receiving towels and glasses of iced tea at the Jules Verne Pool, playing croquet on the Lewis Carroll Court, strolling through Milton's Gardens, meditating in the Anne of Green Gables Gazebo, catching an early lunch at the Rudyard Kipling Café, or lounging in the lobby.

The monitor at Sterling's eye level was replaying the footage from last night's cocktail party.

"Anything?" Jane asked as she closed the door behind her.

"Not yet. As soon as I got Mr. Sinclair's text, I restarted this at the beginning to look for a woman wearing glasses. Since I was mostly focusing on dark hair the first time through, there's a chance I missed Ms. West."

Jane sat down in front of the monitor. "What about this morning? Did anyone leave the manor before six?"

Sterling paused the party footage and switched the live feed from the camera over the terrace doors to the recorded footage from that morning.

"This person leaves the manor house at 5:17. As you can see, their face and hands are hidden. Their clothes and shoes are nondescript."

He pressed the PLAY button, and Jane watched a figure in a gray hoodie, black or dark blue sweatpants—the dim light made it hard to tell which—and white sneakers push the door open with an elbow. Keeping their head down and their hands tucked into the hoodie's kangaroo pocket, the early riser walked toward the gardens.

"They make an effort to look unhurried," she said. "Like they're still half asleep. But you can't see a strand of hair or a single facial feature. That has to be deliberate. What other cameras pick them up before this?"

"I can track them to the lobby, from the camera near the elevators, but I don't know where they were before that. If they came down from a guest hall, they took the stairs. The elevators didn't open."

Jane frowned. "I assume you can't see their face in that footage either."

"Nope. I've watched the footage half a dozen times."

"I'll ask Butterworth to analyze their body language. He might see something I don't, even though it's pretty obvious that this person doesn't want to be identified." She pointed at the monitor with the paused footage. "Let's start this from the beginning. We need to know who Gretchen interacted with at the party."

After viewing the footage twice, it was clear that Gretchen never made an appearance.

"Maybe wine wasn't her thing," said Jane.

Sterling held up his phone. "Maybe people aren't her thing. Mr. Sinclair said she may have suffered from anxiety. Maybe she asked for a quiet room because she wanted to be by herself."

Jane's hand went to her pocket. As her fingers curled around her keys, she said, "Let's take a look at that room."

After switching off the cocktail party footage, Sterling reached for a messenger bag containing gloves, booties, luminol spray, a magnifying glass, tweezers, and a few vials for evidence collection. His tools weren't nearly as comprehensive as those in Deputy Phelps's kit, but they'd come in handy more times than Jane cared to remember.

If Jane followed protocol, she'd restrict entry to Gretchen West's room until Sheriff Evans and his team conducted a thorough search. And though she was a rule follower by nature, some circumstances caused her to ignore—or blatantly break—the rules.

Someone had posed Gretchen West's body in a canoe. They'd used her to create a macabre tableau. This person might view their actions as poetic. They might see themselves as an artist, but Jane saw them as something else entirely. She saw them as a threat to her family, friends, and guests. A killer.

After learning the name of the dead woman from Sinclair, the sheriff's department would be tied up for a while. They'd contact Gretchen West's next of kin, run background checks, create a profile based on her on-line presence, and research "The Lady of Shallot."

As for Sheriff Evans, he'd spend the rest of the morning with the medical examiner. He wouldn't be surprised when Jane informed him that she'd entered Gretchen's room. In fact, he'd be surprised if she didn't.

Having investigated dozens of violent crimes involving Storyton Hall guests, the sheriff had come to trust Jane and her staff. After so many years, he now considered her an ally and a friend. He was also aware of the special skills Butterworth, Sinclair, Sterling, and Lachlan possessed and saw no reason why he shouldn't use their talents to his advantage.

As a former CIA operative, Sterling knew how to search a space. He and Jane paused at the end of the second-floor guest hallway to slip booties over their shoes, wriggle their hands into gloves, and slip into Gretchen's room.

For a few seconds, Jane was dumbstruck by what she saw.

"When did she check in?" Sterling asked.

"Thursday afternoon. That's two days ago. Not even two! But it looks like a bomb went off in here." Jane's astonished gaze swept the room.

Sterling unslung his messenger bag and leaned it against the wall. "Maybe someone got here before us and tossed it. Her killer could have been looking for something."

Jane wondered why this thought hadn't occurred to her, but then it hit her. This kind of mess was familiar to her.

"I can't tell you how many times I've walked into the twins' room and found a very similar scene. I don't think anyone's been in here, including the housekeeping staff. See the dirty plates and glasses? And the food wrappers? I bet they're exactly where Ms. West left them."

Jane made her way around the bed, pointing as she moved. "Chocolate bar wrappers on top of a pair of pajamas. Dirty bathroom towels under this room service coffee tray. Here's an empty pretzel stick bag on this pair of jeans. And look at the club soda can wedged between these ballet flats. If I didn't nag Fitz and Hem every day, this could be their room."

The open closet door revealed a pair of black pants, a wrinkled blouse, and a chiffon cocktail dress with a tea-length skirt. The rest of Gretchen West's wardrobe was strewn around the room. A pair of tights hung from the reading lamp, a crumpled sweatshirt and balled-up swimsuit occupied the chair by the window, and an assortment of socks, bras, underwear, T-shirts, and tank tops had been dropped on the desk, the floor, the bed, and the window ledge.

"This explains the do not disturb sign," Jane muttered.

Sterling pulled out his phone and began typing. "I'm asking Mrs. Templeton if anyone from housekeeping has been allowed in."

Jane made her way to the bathroom, stepping from one clear area of carpet to the next. "I feel like I'm playing The Floor Is Lava with the boys. Aunt Octavia got them started on the game by transforming her entire apartment into an obstacle course. For weeks afterward, the cushions from the living room sofa were never *on* the sofa because they were the only way the twins could reach the stairs without burning alive."

Sterling grinned. "Better squashed cushions than a pile of ash."

The reference to ash made Jane think of cremation. Is that what would happen to Gretchen West's body? Right now, she was lying on a metal exam table in the

ME's office. After that, she'd be buried or cremated. An entire life reduced to a box of ashes.

The bathroom was just as disheveled as the bedroom suite. Makeup palettes, moisturizers, and bottles of sunscreen covered most of the counter. Hair products were grouped on the back of the toilet, and Gretchen's hairbrush sat on the edge of the tub. A tube of toothpaste with a missing cap was partially flattened by the blowdryer. Green toothpaste streaked the hand towel and the sink basin.

Moving closer to the counter, Jane peered into a pink cosmetic bag. Nestled among tweezers, nail clippers, Q-tips, and dental floss was an orange pill bottle. Picking it up, Jane gave it a shake. Nothing rattled. The bottle was empty.

She read the label and returned to the main room to show Sterling.

"Alprazolam. Also known as Xanax. Anti-anxiety meds." He squinted at the label. "I'm getting old. I can't read the tiny print anymore unless I have direct light."

Jane hit the flashlight button on her phone and held it over the label.

"That's better." Sterling read the label. "Ms. West was prescribed one milligram three times a day. That probably means these are short-acting pills versus long-acting. I'm also guessing she's been on these meds for some time. The starting dose is usually much lower than this. A half milligram or less versus her three."

Jane said, "She brought a month's supply of clothes and toiletries. There's no way she'd travel without an equal supply of medication. This empty bottle is a huge red flag. Did you find anything?"

"Just poems. Whole notebooks full of them. She was really prolific." Sinclair led Jane over to the writing desk.

"She could draw too. Even though half of her stuff has coffee stains or ink blotches, you can see that she was talented."

Jane selected a blue notebook and turned to a random page. A short poem called "Walk with Me" was flanked by a charcoal sketch of birch trees. Falling leaves decorated the margins, and the bottom of the page featured a drawing of a couple holding hands. They both wore sweaters and knit hats.

It felt intrusive to read the dead woman's poem, but Jane couldn't stop herself.

> *Come outside with me.*
> *We don't have to talk,*
> *We can hold hands,*
> *And quietly walk.*
> *Things that don't matter—*
> *We can let them go.*
> *Like falling leaves,*
> *Or drifting snow.*

After a few more lines about traveling a rough road together, the poem concluded with the couple returning to a warm, peaceful home.

Is this for a greeting card? Jane wondered. She supposed it could be used for a couple trying to reconcile after an argument.

Behind her, Sterling said, "Sounds like an apology. Like the person who wrote this wants to make up."

"The people from Current Mood want to produce cards for real-life situations. A fight between a couple definitely qualifies. And sometimes, 'I'm sorry' isn't enough."

Jane put the notebook aside and sifted through the rest of the books and papers on the desk. Under a pile of papers was a cell phone in a floral case. There was a pocket on the back of the case, and a sliver of paper stuck out from the pocket.

When Jane pulled it free and unfolded it, she saw that it was another poem. It said:

> You are the magic
> Of moonlight on snow.
> The mystery
> Of a white hart in dark woods.
> My fingers reach for you
> like roots aching for rain.
> You're the fixed star
> of my future.

She handed it to Sterling. "This was in her phone case. It reads like a love poem."

He took a photo of the poem and passed it back to her. "I wonder if someone gave it to her or if she wanted to give it to someone."

Since Jane didn't have the answer, she wandered over to the closet. "Gretchen brought one dress for two occasions requiring nice attire. Either she planned to wear it for both the cocktail party and Sunday's awards banquet, or she had no intention of attending last night's event."

Sterling snapped his fingers. "Which was a wine tasting. Mixing alprazolam and alcohol is a big no-no. Ms. West might have skipped the event because she didn't drink. The whole thing could have made her feel uncomfortable and awkward. If she felt anxious about the party, she'd probably choose to hang out in her room instead."

"I hope she didn't avoid the event because of the

wine. We always say cocktails *and* mocktails on our invitations because there are plenty of people who don't drink alcohol. We served several kinds of flavored seltzer and sparkling juice last night." Jane imagined Gretchen in the vermillion cocktail dress, her hair falling in soft waves and her eyes shining with nervous excitement. "Maybe if she'd come to the party, she'd still be alive."

Sterling tried to shift Jane's focus by saying, "Most of the drawers are empty. She has a pair of slipper socks and what looks like a swimsuit cover-up in the dresser. The rest of her wardrobe is out in the open. I think we're done here for now."

Jane was about to agree when she paused to consider the white sundress Gretchen had on when Jane saw her in the canoe. Was the dress hers, or had someone put it on her to make her look more like the Lady of Shalott? Jane checked the label of the vermillion cocktail dress as well as the blouse on the neighboring hanger. Both were size 10.

"I'm going to call Sheriff Evans from here," she told Sterling.

He passed her the empty pill bottle. "I took photos of the label, so you can put this back where you found it."

Jane returned the bottle as she listened to the sheriff's cell phone ring and ring. She was about to hang up when he finally answered with a gruff, "Ms. Steward?"

"Sheriff, I'm standing in Ms. West's room. There's an empty bottle of Xanax in the bathroom, and she's a size ten. I thought you might want to see if the dress she was wearing is the same size." When the sheriff didn't respond, she quickly added, "In case it wasn't her dress. As far as the room goes, the things of interest are the pill bottle and a stack of notebooks on the desk. I read a poem in one of the notebooks, but I didn't look through the rest."

"Thank you. Two of my officers will be there to search the room within the hour. If they don't find any obvious clues in those notebooks, would you and Mr. Sinclair take a closer look at them? Poetry isn't my forte, and with one officer on vacation and Sergeant Cortez out on maternity leave, we're short staffed."

Jane said, "We'll do whatever we can to help. How would you like to handle telling the guests?"

"Will they be together as a group today?"

"Not until tonight. We're having a buffet followed by a literary scavenger hunt. The guests will be divided into teams, so it would be better to address them at the dinner. There'll be a lull while the servers clear the tables and set up the dessert buffet."

Sheriff Evans let out a wistful sigh. "I hate the idea of ruining a dessert buffet, but I have no choice. Avoid discussing Ms. West until tonight. If someone comes looking for her, let me know who they are and what they want with her."

"Got it. And what of her family? Should I expect to hear from them?"

"I'm afraid not. She was raised by her maternal grandparents, and her grandfather passed away last year. Her grandmother is alive, but she's in the memory care unit of an assisted living facility in Georgia."

Jane placed a gloved hand on Gretchen's notebooks and whispered, "No one's coming for her."

"Which is why we need to do right by her," the sheriff said.

After ending the call, Jane took the stairs to her

great-aunt and -uncle's apartments, where she found
Mrs. Templeton standing in the doorway, chatting with
Aunt Octavia.

Jane was glad to run into the head housekeeper as it
saved her the trouble of tracking her down. "Do you
have a minute?"

Mrs. Templeton smiled fondly at Jane. "Never, but
you can have one anyway."

"We'd better talk inside." Meeting her aunt's curious
gaze, Jane said, "Is Uncle Aloysius here?"

Sensing Jane had something important to impart,
Aunt Octavia beckoned her inside. She then called her
husband's name and made herself comfortable on the
sofa. The moment she sat down, Muffet Cat, Storyton
Hall's resident mouser, jumped onto her lap and meowed.

"You're so bossy," Aunt Octavia chided.

The tuxedo, who liked Aunt Octavia and Aunt Octavia only, slitted his eyes at Jane and Mrs. Templeton.
Having expressed his disapproval, he began sniffing
one of Aunt Octavia's pockets.

"Patience, my sweet," cooed Aunt Octavia as she dug
a treat out of the pocket and put it in the center of her
palm.

Muffet Cat inhaled the treat and meowed for more,
but Uncle Aloysius had entered the room, and Aunt
Octavia's attention zeroed in on Jane.

"We had a Rip van Winkle this morning," Jane said.
She looked at her uncle. "I found her after I saw you at
the lake. Her name is Gretchen West."

"Oh dear," murmured Mrs. Templeton.

Uncle Aloysius seemed confused. Moving closer to
his wife, he said, "I don't remember seeing anyone."

Aunt Octavia took his hand and wordlessly cajoled him into sitting down.

"That's exactly what I was about to ask you," Jane said. "When you say that you didn't see anyone, do you mean that you were alone out on the water? Or that you didn't see another person from the time you left the manor house to the time I waved you over?"

Uncle Aloysius shook his head. "I'm sorry, my girl. My mind wanders off when I'm fishing. I start thinking about things that happened yesterday or fifty years ago, and before I know it, an hour's gone by. Sometimes it takes a tug on my line to bring me down to earth."

Jane gave him a reassuring smile. "It's okay. I'm only asking because you said something startled your heron friend. And you thought you saw something white in the reeds."

"I remember the heron."

"Do you know what time it was when he flew off?"

Uncle Aloysius seemed to drift away for a moment. He came back to himself when Aunt Octavia squeezed his hand, but he was unable to give Jane an answer.

"You probably don't want to keep track of time while you're fishing," said Mrs. Templeton. She then frowned at Jane. "Was our unfortunate guest *in* the lake?"

"She was in a canoe that became stuck in the reeds. We don't know how she got there or how she died, but the sheriff doesn't want news of her passing to get out before he has a chance to speak to the guests. In the meantime, no one may enter Ms. West's room."

Mrs. Templeton put her hands on her hips. "My staff hasn't been able to step foot in that room since Ms. West checked in. My radar starts pinging whenever a guest insists on no housekeeping service. It isn't natural! Who wouldn't want someone else to make their bed and clean their bathroom for a change?"

Aunt Octavia grunted in agreement.

"Her room is a terrific mess, but it'll have to stay that way until the sheriff gives us the green light to clean it."

"I'll inform my staff right away. Can I do anything else to help?"

Jane hesitated. Though she valued the safety of her guests above all else, their privacy was a close second. Deliberately violating someone's privacy went against one of the most sacred codes of hospitality, but if a minor intrusion led to the arrest of Gretchen's killer, then it was worth doing.

"Ask only your most trustworthy personnel to keep an eye out for red satin ribbon—the kind you'd see on a little girl's party dress. Two or three inches wide. If they see that type of ribbon in a guest room, they should contact me immediately."

Aunt Octavia handed Mrs. Templeton a pencil and notepad. "What shade of red?"

"Crimson," said Jane. "I'd also like to know if any of our guests have poems by Tennyson in their rooms— particularly a poem called 'The Lady of Shalott.' If they notice a printout or a drawing of a woman in a boat or a long-haired woman in a white dress, they should tell me. Any papers or fabric found in the trash cans should be examined before being discarded."

After underlining a word on her notepad, Mrs. Templeton said, "If that's all, I'll go speak with my staff."

Struck by a thought, Jane said, "One last thing. I'd like to hear if any of the guests have a supply of pills that aren't being kept in a pill bottle. They might be in a plastic bag or another container. Mr. Sterling will text a photo of their approximate shape and color."

"Is someone dealing drugs?" asked a horrified Aunt Octavia.

"We believe the anxiety medication belonging to our deceased guest is missing."

Uncle Aloysius had been quietly listening to the women's exchange, but now his brow crinkled with worry. "Is there a chance she overdosed?"

"If that's the case, the medical examiner will let us know. But even *if* Ms. West died from an overdose, someone else had a hand in her death."

Aunt Octavia gasped. Uncle Aloysius reached over to capture her hand in his. "I'm here, my sweet."

"What I'm about to say can't leave this room," Jane continued in a softer tone. "Ms. West's death could have been accidental, but the way her body was posed in a canoe was not."

Wide-eyed, Aunt Octavia asked, "Like the tragic heroine of Tennyson's poem? Is that why you want to know if the other guests have copies of 'The Lady of Shalott'?"

Hearing stress in his mistress's voice, Muffet Cat glanced up at her and mewed.

"It's okay, my darling boy."

While Aunt Octavia plied Muffet Cat with treats, Mrs. Templeton left to round up her most trustworthy staff members. Jane also took her leave, but not without promising to keep her aunt and uncle in the loop.

Opening the door to the staff stairwell, she was surprised to come face to face with Edwin.

"I was hoping to catch you before you went all the way down. There's something I need to show you."

Before Jane could say a word, Edwin grabbed her hand and led her down a flight to the landing.

Once there, he kept holding onto her hand. In a

near whisper, he said, "Sterling told me about Ms. West. I'm so sorry, Jane. I'm sorry that she was killed and that you have to deal with the aftermath. I saw the footage of the person in the hoodie, and I *think* I know how they were able to move about without being caught on camera."

"How?"

Edwin pulled her deeper into the shadow of the stairwell. A small flashlight appeared in his free hand and he directed the beam on one of the large stones at the base of the wall, closest to the staircase ascending above them. "Do you see this big crack?"

"Yes."

"You can actually get your fingers into it. And if, for some strange reason, you stuck your fingers inside, you'd feel a lever. And if you pushed that lever to the right . . ."

Jane heard a squeak followed by a rumble. And then, to her astonishment, the stone rolled away, revealing a gap of darkness. The wall looked like a mouth with a missing tooth.

"A secret passage?" Jane grabbed Edwin's shirt. "Do you know where it goes?"

"I do, but you should see for yourself. Ready?"

Jane stared at the black square and said, "No, but I'm going anyway."

Chapter 5

Jane wriggled through the hole in the wall.

It was a tight squeeze, and she had to put her hands on the dusty ground and pull herself forward. There was nothing graceful about the movement, but she managed to clear the hole. She then crawled forward until there was enough room for Edwin to join her.

His body obscured most of the light from the stairwell, so she turned on her phone and hit the flashlight icon. She directed its small beam on Edwin and held it there until she heard the groan of the stone block sliding back in place.

They were now closed in.

"It's okay," Edwin whispered, sensing her discomfort. "Fitz and Hem discovered this a few days ago. When they overheard me talking to Sterling, they confessed they'd not only found a new secret passage but had also explored it more than once. Apparently, Uncle Aloysius has been telling them stories of the passageways he used as a boy. He can't remember where they are, but as you know, the boys are determined to find them."

Edwin raised his flashlight, and together, he and Jane swept their beams over the walls and floor. Jane saw decades of dirt and grime. Every inch of the walls and floor was coated with thick layers of dust. The space was narrow and dark. Jane felt cool air on her arms, and when she pointed her flashlight directly in front of her, she saw scuff marks in dust.

Peering into the yawning blackness ahead of her, Jane froze. She didn't want to see where it led. She wanted to get out—to return to the safety of the stairwell. She didn't want to move forward. She wanted light and fresh air.

It's your house. There's nothing scary back here, she told herself.

She tried to normalize her situation by picturing Fitz and Hem creeping zealously through the passage. If they could channel their inner Captain Nemo or Indiana Jones, then Jane could shake off her fear.

Behind her, Edwin whispered, "Keep crawling for another six feet. You'll be able to stand after that."

Jane did as he said.

It's a good thing I didn't change my clothes, she thought.

Clouds of dust billowed with her every move, so she breathed in through her nose and tried not to think about where the dust was resettling. In no time at all, her hands, her arms, and the back of her neck were coated with grit.

She assumed she'd crawled the necessary six feet when she saw footprints on the floor. Though smeared, they were an indication that it was safe to stand. She placed a hand on the wall to steady herself and raised her phone, directing the little flashlight beam at the ceiling. The last thing she wanted to do was bump her head.

Several feet above her, she saw massive crossbeams and the wink of metal pipes. Limp electrical wire and gossamer cobwebs drooped down from above, but that was all.

"Is this a secret passageway or a maintenance tunnel?" she asked.

Edwin pointed his flashlight over Jane's shoulder. "At one time, there were probably lots of access doors like these. But as the years passed and the electrical, plumbing, and heating systems were replaced, most of the entries were walled over. You've told me how the staff corridors have remained unchanged for decades, which explains why that block of stone makes so much noise when it closes. The track hasn't been oiled in ages. It only moved because the boys used it recently."

"Where does the passageway lead? Am I going to exit from behind a reader's nook in one of the guest hallways and scare some poor person to death?"

Edwin chuckled. "They might think you're a ghost. A very dirty ghost. But only for a second. The neon-orange sneakers kind of ruin the whole phantom vibe."

Jane glanced down at her shoes. "What about my Pig-Pen vibe?"

"You nailed it."

"So, are you going to tell me where we'll end up?"

Edwin pointed into the darkness. "Here's a better question: How would anyone know about this? Where it leads? How to enter it? You've lived here your whole life and had no idea it was here. How did the killer know?"

Jane had no answer.

"*If* the killer used this passageway, they might have left a clue behind. Maybe their clothes got snagged or there's a clear footprint in the dust. Maybe they dropped something. If you won't tell me where we're going, then help me look for clues."

Edwin frowned. "The twins traveled this hidden highway at least three times, and I've already been through once, which means the chance of seeing a unique footprint is slim to none. I'll take the lead, and we'll look while we walk."

Jane grabbed his shirt as he slipped by. "Is it safe? I don't want to fall through a hole and end up in the basement."

"Other than a rotten board near the end, it's structurally sound."

With Edwin leading the way, Jane continued to examine her surroundings. Other than stone, wood, and the occasional copper pipe, there wasn't much to see. But there was a host of different sounds.

Jane was used to the noises made by the old house. She just wasn't used to hearing them so clearly. Water rushed through pipes, electricity hummed, and creaks and groans came from every direction.

She's like an old woman talking to herself, Jane thought fondly. No longer troubled by the dirt, she brushed her fingers against the wall as gently as she'd once caressed the velvety skin of her baby boys.

"I wonder if Uncle Aloysius ever played in here. He's told me several times that there are more hidey holes and secret passageways than we realize, though he can't remember where they are now. Too many years have passed, and too many changes have been made." She sighed. "I know the twins want to find all of them before they go back to school. I just wish they hadn't kept their discovery to themselves."

Edwin said, "Don't be too hard on them. I think they

were hoping to give Uncle Aloysius a piece of his child-hood but were waiting to see if they could find more se-crets before telling him about this one."

They continued moving behind the walls like human-sized mice, pausing every few feet to sweep the area with their flashlights.

Eventually, Jane got fed up. "This is pointless. The sheriff will have to come back here to do an official search anyway. How much longer until we get out?"

"You're like a kid on a road trip. We'll get there when we get there," Edwin teased. When Jane responded by smacking his rump, he laughed and said, "Okay, okay! We're about to descend to the ground floor. This is the tricky part."

Jane groaned. "Now I'm really nervous. You think rappelling down a cliff face is *a little tricky*."

Edwin stopped, turned, and clamped his hand around Jane's arm. "Don't take another step. Just follow the beam of my light with your eyes."

Jane watched as the circle of light moved from Edwin's shoes to the floor ahead. About five feet from where they stood, the floor disappeared. All Jane saw was a patch of midnight black.

"That looks like the entrance to the Seven Dwarfs' mine," she said. "Or hell."

"It's not quite that deep, but there's only one way to safely descend. There's a set of floating steps against the far wall. Old, wooden ones. Most have rotted or broken in places, and the walls are smooth, so there's nothing to grab if you lose your footing."

Jane jabbed him in the side. "A 'little tricky,' huh?"

"I'll go first and tell you exactly where to put your feet. You won't fall. And if you do, you get to land on me."

"You're enjoying this."

Jane couldn't see Edwin's face, but she knew that he was smiling. "How could I not? Life's an adventure, and *I* get to share it with you."

"You silver-tongued devil, let's get this over with."

Guided by his flashlight, Edwin lowered his legs into the hole.

Jane moved to the edge so that she could shine her light into the darkness. "The boys probably climb this like squirrels, but these pieces of rotted wood won't support the sheriff and his team. Can we get a ladder in here?"

"Sure, but it will have to be lowered down from here. You'll understand once we're on the ground floor. Okay, drop your right foot first."

Edwin steered Jane's foot to a step that felt too insubstantial to hold her weight. There was no room for her left foot, so she had to lower it without any sense of where it would land. She trusted Edwin with her life, but she didn't know what to do with her hands. As her weight shifted, her hands refused to let go of the edge between the second floor and the empty space below it.

To ward off her fear, she opted for levity. "This could be a new activity for our guests. We could call it Behind the Walls yoga. With no distractions, they could reach that meditative state Phoebe always talks about."

"If you want to use yoga terms, you're about to move into *banarasana*. Your left leg is going to come straight back while your right leg stays bent at the knee. You have to grab the step with your hands and steady yourself before lowering your right foot."

Suddenly, the narrow space felt even narrower. Perspiration broke out on Jane's forehead, and her palms went clammy. She drew in a deep breath. Then another.

"Talk to me," Edwin said in a firm, but gentle voice.

"I'm feeling a little claustrophobic all of a sudden. I can't hold on to this little piece of wood while doing a split. I'm not a gymnast."

Edwin said, "You're too tall to be a gymnast, and your legs are long enough to reach the next step, so put your phone in your pocket and grab the step. I've got you."

Just like that, Jane's fear evaporated. She followed Edwin's instructions, and within minutes, she was on solid ground again.

"Ready for the big reveal?" he asked.

"Yes!"

Edwin pointed his flashlight at a mechanism attached to the wall. Jane saw chains, pulleys, and a metal crank.

Gesturing at the mechanism, Edwin smiled and said, "Would you like to do the honors?"

Jane bent down and began turning the hand crank. It didn't move easily and produced an unpleasant grating noise, but in a matter of seconds, a ray of light crept across the grungy floor.

She kept cranking, and the ray turned into a column. Jane was able to widen the opening another six inches before the crank refused to budge.

"It's another tight squeeze," said Edwin as he tried to dust himself off.

Oh no, this must be a public area, Jane thought.

Seeing no point in wiping her dirty hands over her dirty clothes, she scuttled through the opening like an oversized crab. Before she had to the chance to fully emerge, a chime began to sound.

The grandfather clock! But that means . . . oh Lord, we're in the lobby.

She quickly got to her feet, and Edwin exited the opening behind her. After tugging on her forearm to get her attention, he bunched up three of his fingers and made a pushing motion. He then reached back into the opening—aiming to the right and about half a foot off the floor. Whatever he did caused the wood panel to slide back into place with a soft *thud*.

For the moment, Jane and Edwin were partially hidden by the grandfather clock. The massive timepiece, which was over ten feet tall, was also wide enough to conceal a man. Made in the Black Forest in the early 1800s, the entire clock was covered with ornate carvings of woodland animals. An owl stared at Jane from its perch on a gnarled branch. Light reflected in its glass eyes, creating an impression of sentience.

Moving closer to Edwin, Jane whispered, "We're going to round the corner, go past the main staircase, and duck into the staff corridor near the elevators. Hopefully, no one will notice us."

"You could never go unnoticed."

"If there were more strawberry-blond guests, I might be able to blend in."

Edwin laughed. "Hundreds of people with your hair color could be milling about the lobby, and you'd still stand out. You're the queen of Storyton."

A queen in a haunted castle, Jane thought. Aloud, she said, "I won't feel human again—let alone regal—until I've had a shower and a hit of caffeine."

Keeping her head down, Jane stepped out from behind the grandfather clock and hurried past the grand staircase. Just as she and Edwin reached the elevator banks, the doors to the closest elevator opened, and Jeremiah Okoro exited the car.

Seeing Jane, he waved and was about to speak when he faltered.

Jane flashed him a grin and kept walking.

"Who's the lumberjack?" Edwin asked once they were in the staff corridor.

"Jeremiah? Are you calling him that because he has a beard?"

Edwin shrugged. "That, and the flannel shirt tied around his waist. It's supposed to hit ninety today. I don't think he'll need flannel. Or the knit beanie."

"As the twins would say, 'It's his vibe.' Current Mood Cards is Jeremiah's brainchild. If the company takes off, you can say you knew him before he hit it big."

"Nice guy?"

"Very. He's also smart and ambitious. I thought he and Phoebe would hit it off at the opening event, but Jeremiah's co-founder, Gil Callahan, was glued to her side from the time the wine tasting started until the bottles ran dry. I saw them talking and—oh no."

When Jane came to an abrupt stop, Edwin stared at her in concern.

"I told the sheriff about running into Jeremiah, Gil, and Stephanie—the top execs of Current Mood Cards—on my walk this morning. Which means I just ran away from a VIP guest who might have spent his lunchtime being interviewed by a member of the Storyton Sheriff's Department."

Edwin propelled Jane forward. "Don't worry. I'm not sure he recognized you."

But Jane already had her phone out. By the time they reached the loading dock, she had Sheriff Evans on the line.

"A secret passage? Exactly how many does Storyton Hall have?" the sheriff asked when Jane finished telling him how the figure in the hoodie from the morning's security footage could have traveled from one of the guest room hallways to the lobby without being seen.

"The twins found this one a few days ago, but there are probably more that have yet to be discovered."

The sheriff let out a wistful sigh. "What I'd give to be a twelve-year-old boy again. I'd spend every waking moment searching for secrets in that house of yours. In a way, I guess I already am. Conducting interviews isn't nearly as exciting, but I'm on my way over to tell you what we've learned so far. If I can get inside that passageway, I will. Otherwise, I'll leave the tight squeezes to Phelps and Emory."

Jane promised to have coffee and snacks waiting in the William Faulkner Conference Room by the time the sheriff arrived. She then hurried home as fast as she could.

When Butterworth opened the door to the conference room, Jane was in the middle of applying mascara. Her hair was still damp, and she wore no makeup other than the lipstick she'd applied while crossing the Great Lawn.

Jane dropped the mascara wand and reached for the coffeepot. After serving the sheriff, she gave Phelps and Emory glasses of ice water.

Waving at the food on the sideboard, she said, "Mrs. Hubbard sent cheddar and pancetta biscuits, cream cheese and cucumber pinwheels, pecan-date tartlets, two-bite blackberry scones, and chocolate eclairs."

Sheriff Evans waited until his deputies had added a few items to their plates before taking three biscuits and returning to his seat.

"Before I dig in, I wanted to tell you that the ME put a rush on Ms. West's lab work. He believes her death was the result of a fatal overdose but suspects there might be another drug involved. Something stronger than alcohol, most likely. I was able to reach one of her coworkers on the phone, and while he wasn't able to add much to our picture of Ms. West, the gentleman was certain that Ms. West stuck to water or soda during the rare times she showed up at a work-related function."

Jane threw him a quizzical look. "What kind of drugs are we talking about? The illegal kind?"

"Not necessarily. There are a number of pain medicines that would fit the bill."

"There's no way for us to know what medications our guests are taking, and I can't violate their privacy to find out. So where does that leave us?"

Because Sheriff Evans had a mouthful of biscuit, Phelps answered for him. "We need to retrace Ms. West's movements from the time she checked in. If the security footage doesn't show us whom she interacted with, then we'll have to get that info another way."

"It sounds like you have a plan."

"We do," said Emory. "I'd like to participate in tonight's scavenger hunt. Not as an officer of the law, but as a poet."

This sounded like an excellent idea to Jane. "The other guests are more likely to open up to you than to any of us. I like it. What name will you use?"

"Amelia Emerson."

"Is your false persona related to Ralph Waldo?"

The young deputy blushed. "No, but there are poets on both sides of my family. I write too, but I don't like it as much as I like painting. Writing is work. Painting is an escape. At the end of the day, I want to escape."

Jane understood completely. She pictured the book she was currently reading. It was patiently waiting for her on the coffee table. It would be there, ready to offer her its all, whenever she had the time for it. She often thought that if books were cats, they'd purr when held in gentle hands. And if books were dogs, the ribbons or bits of paper sticking out from between their pages would wag like happy tails.

The sheriff reached for his coffee. "As Churchill said, we need at least two or three hobbies if we want to be happy."

"I agree," Jane muttered. "Unless one of those hobbies is murder."

For the rest of the afternoon, while Sheriff Evans and Deputy Phelps searched the secret passage, Jane and Sterling reviewed hours of security camera footage.

It was jarring to see Gretchen West walk into Storyton Hall for the first time on Thursday afternoon. She smiled as she passed her rolling suitcase to a bellhop before politely waving off Butterworth's offer of champagne.

She moved through the lobby in a state of awe, gazing to the left, toward the conference room, before taking in the enormous floral arrangement on the round table in the center. Next, her gaze traveled up the gentle curve of the grand staircase. Her eyes roved over the giant grandfather clock, the crystal chandeliers, and the collection of elegant, but comfortable chairs and settees.

Though Jane had seen hundreds of guests with similar reactions, she never tired of witnessing the effect her family home had on people.

"It's like watching someone fall in love," she'd once told Edwin. "As soon as they come inside, they light up. Those are the guests I tend to like best."

Recalling the state of Gretchen's room, Jane assumed the young woman's appearance would be just as slovenly. But Gretchen wasn't at all disheveled. Her clothes were casual and comfortable, and she wore her dark hair in a braid down her back—a style Jane also favored.

Gretchen spent her first day at Storyton Hall in the reading rooms. Other than a brief walk in the gardens, she didn't seem too interested in the grounds. Nor did she seem interested in befriending the other poets. She didn't wear the name badge designed by Current Mood Cards or fraternize with the guests in the Agatha Christie Tea Room.

For meals, she preferred to order from the Rudyard Kipling Café. She'd either write while eating or take her food up to her room.

"Definitely shy," said Sterling as they watched Gretchen step into the elevator.

"Yes, but she's interested in everything and everyone around her. The only time she isn't casting inquisitive glances from behind her glasses is when she's writing. People were obviously curious about her too."

Sterling nodded. "That's what I saw too. Curiosity without any hostility. No ominous stares from the competition. Other than the Current Mood Card people, most of the guests were doing their own thing on Thursday. On Friday, there were two writing sessions, which kept the poets busy until the wine-tasting event. It was the first time all day that I saw them relax."

"Probably because of how much money is at stake."

On-screen, Gretchen was settling into a chair facing the fireplace in the Isak Dinesen Safari Room.

Sterling paused the footage and looked a question at Jane. "What does Mr. Sinclair think of her poetry?"

"He hasn't reported back yet. He wanted to read

through all the notebooks from her room, and he was also taking a deeper look at her online presence." Jane cocked her head. "Do you have a theory?"

"What if the other poets knew something about her talent that we don't? Maybe she won a major writing award or has had a bunch of poems published in literary journals. I'm just spitballing here, but like you said, one person is going to leave Storyton Hall with the kind of financial security most writers only dream about."

Jane reflected on how Gretchen's body had been posed. Had her killer turned her into the subject of a famous poem out of respect or mockery? Was it possible that her death had been an accident and whoever had been with her at the time had tried to undo its sting by memorializing Gretchen?

"What are you thinking?" asked Sterling.

"I was wondering if the person who put Ms. West in that boat loved her or hated her. Did she know her killer?"

After considering these questions for a moment, Sterling said, "There's something you should see."

He fiddled with the controls. People zipped across the screen like colorful insects. The numbers on the time stamp moved too quickly for Jane to follow, but she knew they were watching the hall outside the Agatha Christie Tea Room.

Sterling let the tea service begin and end before reducing the speed.

"I didn't think this exchange was worth a second look, but seeing as Ms. West barely spoke to anyone who wasn't a Storyton Hall employee, maybe it is."

Jane watched Gretchen leave the tearoom, carrying a notebook in her hand. She walked until she reached a mahogany-inlaid console table polished to a high shine.

Paintings hung above all but one of the tables, but Gretchen paused at the third table. Instead of a painting, a mirror in a gilt frame was affixed to the wall above the table.

Sterling hit the REWIND button and pushed PLAY again. This time, Gretchen moved at a much slower pace. After glancing in the mirror, her hand grazed the side of the table, and her notebook fell to the floor. A pen rolled several feet away and was promptly scooped up by a man Jane instantly recognized.

"That's Jeremiah Okoro, co-owner of Current Mood Cards. Stephanie Harbaugh, the woman on his left, is the PR director."

Jeremiah knelt to retrieve the pen at the same time Gretchen knelt to pick up her notebook. Their eyes met, and they smiled at each other.

"Those are mega-warm smiles," said Jane. "This is either recognition or the effects of Cupid's arrow. Gretchen's whole face is glowing."

"If she's glowing, then the marketing director is glowering."

Jane noted Stephanie's pinched expression and how her disapproving gaze was directed at Gretchen.

"I'm going to invite the Current Mood folks for drinks in the Ian Fleming Lounge before dinner. And I'll see to it that the bartender pours with a generous hand."

"The three of them left the manor house for their hike forty minutes before you headed out for your walk. According to the ME, Ms. West died hours earlier. The person in the hoodie and sweatpants is most likely the killer. Either that, or the killer was already outside and the person in the hoodie was Ms. West."

Jane sighed. "The questions keep piling up. I might

have to rely on something other than facts to get to the truth."

"Like what?"

"Loose lips sink ships, right? Which means we need more undercover agents to gossip with our guests." She stared at Gretchen's frozen face and added, "For her sake, I'm going to have to ask my friends to spy on my guests."

Chapter 6

The Ian Fleming Lounge was already doing a brisk business when Jane took a seat in one of the leather club chairs the staff had reserved for her party.

A server holding an empty tray materialized in front of her. "Mateo came up with a custom cocktail for your guests. It's called Poetry in Motion. He asked all of us to taste it in case he needed to tweak any of the ingredients, but it's perfect."

"Thank you, Lisa. This is my chance to get to know my special guests, so please tell Mateo that I appreciate his creativity."

While she waited, Jane wondered what kind of cocktail she'd make in Mateo's position. Poetry came in so many forms and could evoke such a wide range of emotions that it was difficult to know where to begin. Would a poetic cocktail be sweet or sour? Should it go down smooth or burn a little?

Her musings were cut short when she saw Jeremiah, Gil, and Stephanie enter the lounge. Jane stood up and gave them a friendly wave. They smiled and headed over to the group of chairs.

Jeremiah waited until the women were seated before sitting down next to Jane.

"I love this room," he said. "I've seen all the James Bond movies at least twice, but I've never read any of the books. What about you?"

"I've read a few," Jane said. "My favorites are *Moonraker* and *Goldfinger*. We have lots of Fleming titles in our library if you want to give one a try."

Jeremiah glanced at his colleagues. "This is more of a working vacation, which means I'll be reading poetry the whole time I'm here."

Addressing the group at large, Jane said, "What's that like?"

Stephanie was the first to reply. "I'm not an official judge, but Jeremiah and Gil have showed me some of their favorites so far. The poems can get pretty heavy, especially when they're about sickness or grief. But greeting card companies tackle heavy subjects. The only difference is that Current Mood is going to do that in a fresh way."

Intrigued, Jane asked, "Could you give me an example?"

"Get-well cards can be way too sappy," answered Gil. "They're thoughtful, sure, but do they make people feel better? A bit. What helps the most is laughter. Laughter makes sick people feel more upbeat. The more upbeat they are, the better they feel. I got a card from Jeremiah once that said, '*I hope you feel better soon, so you can come back to work and feel like crap again.*'"

They all laughed.

The server appeared and introduced herself to Jane's guests.

"I don't have menus to show you this evening." She gestured toward the bar. "Mateo created a custom cocktail for your group. If you have any allergies or dietary restrictions, I'd be glad to recite the ingredients. If not, are you willing to be surprised?"

Gil and Stephanie opted for surprise, but Jeremiah said, "I'd prefer a mocktail."

After assuring him that she would see to it, the server left.

Jane's guests gazed at her expectantly.

"I didn't ask you here for any particular reason," she lied. "I just wanted to chat. So many organizations and businesses have stayed at Storyton Hall, but your company is more exciting than most. The greeting card industry is in desperate need of modernization."

"And representation," added Gil.

Stephanie nodded. "Creating a diverse line of greeting cards isn't hard. The right words are universal, and we can use art to make our cards inclusive. The tricky part will be convincing stores to carry some of these cards. Cards with four-letter words, polarizing topics, bathroom humor, gender and sexual diversity—we'll probably sell the majority of those online."

"That's too bad, because a card is often an impulse buy," said Jane.

Gil snapped his fingers and pointed at Jane. "Thank you! That's one of the many, many reasons we're so glad to have Stephanie aboard. She came up with a brilliant marketing campaign to encourage people to buy an assortment of cards to keep at home. She calls them 'just in case' cards. We're going to package them in a red box with a fire extinguisher graphic and the words—"

His colleagues shouted, "Emotional Emergencies!"

Jane thought this was a brilliant idea.

"I'd definitely buy that," she said.

Gil and Stephanie exchanged high fives and went still in amazement.

"Oh, wow," breathed Jeremiah.

Very, very carefully, their server lowered her trayful of drinks to the table.

"These cocktails are called Poetry in Motion. They were made for the three of you, compliments of Storyton Hall." She smiled at Jeremiah. "The glass with the lemon twist around the handle is yours."

Jane gaped at the drinks along with her guests. She'd never seen anything like them before. Five martini glasses were topped with perfectly formed bubbles of smoke.

"How do we drink these?" Stephanie asked in an excited whisper.

Jeremiah reached for his glass. "I think we're supposed to pop the bubble right before we take a sip. I only know this because one of our interns was watching a YouTube video on cocktail trends. The bubbles in the video were made of different flavors, and they're very fragile, so someone had better make a toast fast."

"May we be the people our dogs think we are!" declared Gil.

With great care, they all picked up their glasses, raised them to their noses, and popped the smoke bubbles.

Jane caught a whiff of lemon in the smoke before it dissipated.

"Oh, that's yummy," Stephanie said.

Jeremiah held his glass to the light. "Looks like there's another surprise at the bottom. Steph, are these the things floating around in your boba tea?"

She peered down at her cocktail. "Tapioca pearls? No, these are bursting bubbles."

"Yeah, you used to put spoonfuls of pink ones on your froyo."

Jeremiah chuckled. "Man, I miss that froyo place."

"How long have you known each other?" asked Jane.

Gil jerked a thumb at Jeremiah. "We worked for the same newspaper. We bonded over some seriously nasty cups of coffee in the break room. Both of us were stressed out about deadlines and tired of being treated like army recruits by our editor. Ever read *The Great Santini*?"

At Jane's nod, Gil continued, "That was our editor. The whole vibe at the paper was negative. When you publish sensationalistic crap instead of the truth, you start losing your soul. The more our words were bent and twisted, the more we hated our job."

Jeremiah said, "We chugged along for a solid ten years until I just—"

"Lost it." Gil grinned at his friend. "I was sitting at my desk, polishing my next piece, when I saw Jeremiah unplug his computer, carry it over to the window, and toss it out. Luckily, that window was over an empty alley. Without breaking stride, my man saluted our editor and walked out. I quit a week later. The two of us met at a coffee shop near Jeremiah's place to talk about starting our own business. And here we are."

Stephanie poked her brother. "They found an office space and recruited me. Once we choose our star writer, Current Mood Cards will be off to the races."

"Have you read any of their work before?"

After draining the rest of his cocktail, Gil said, "We invited ten or twelve writers to participate because we had a pretty good idea that they might be a good fit for our company. We don't have enough capital to pay for a team of writers and artists, so we need someone who can do both. And a good sense of humor is a must."

"In other words, they have to be as warped as the rest of us," said Jeremiah.

Stephanie shook her head. "We're not all warped."

"Oh, please. One more bubble martini, and they'll be hearing your donkey laugh from the pickleball court," teased Gil.

"Worth it," Stephanie said before tilting her glass so that the bursting bubbles slid into her mouth.

Jeremiah mimicked the motion. "Hmm. Passion fruit?"

"And lychee," said Jane.

Their server whisked away the empty glasses and returned a minute later with a fresh round of Poetry in Motion martinis.

Jane popped her smoke bubble but left her glass on the table. Her guests, however, reached for theirs with gusto.

While they sipped, Jane told them what it was like to grow up at Storyton Hall. And by the time she circled back to the writing competition, Gil and Stephanie had shining eyes and flushed faces. Jeremiah seemed to be enjoying himself as much as his colleagues, and Jane decided it was safe to ask more pointed questions.

"How did you end up recruiting Professor Ashley?"

Gil pointed at Jeremiah. "He did a feature story on Dodge Ashley and was really impressed by him. He's an award-winning poet and an incredible teacher. He also gets what we're trying to do with Current Mood because he's been trying to do the same thing for contemporary poetry. His stuff is down-to-earth and hits you right here." He thumped his chest. Jeremiah gave an enthusiastic nod. "When Gil and I were looking for a poet to help us run this competition, we knew Ashley was our guy. I was a fan from the moment I read his poem about a guy riding the subway. Right, Gil?"

"Right. The poem was less than twenty lines about a man heading home from work, but it speaks to anyone who keeps giving their all to a job that gives nothing back. The emptiness of living to pay the bills. The end dares the reader to live for something more. It's a powerful poem."

Jane said that she'd like to read it.

"The writers don't know it yet, but they're all getting a copy of Professor Ashley's first poetry book. Their conference fee covers the cost of their stay and the book. We have a copy for you too," Stephanie told her.

After thanking her, Jane said, "I remember reading about Professor Ashley's summer program. It's in North Carolina, right? Someone told me it's the most prestigious creative writing workshop in the country."

"It is!" exclaimed Stephanie. "And Professor Ashley made my job super easy. He reached out to his best and brightest students, and they signed up for this competition."

"Sounds like a class reunion," said Jane.

Jeremiah's left shoulder rose and fell in a lazy shrug. "The workshop's been going on for ten years, and very few of the poets here now attended at the same time. A few of them know each other, but anyone from Brightleaf—that's the name of the summer program—entered this competition in hopes of winning. There are probably thirty writers who came here seeking to hone their craft, but the rest want to win the contract. I expect the tension will increase every day."

It already has, Jane thought.

"There's plenty of tension already," Stephanie admitted. "After today's sessions, I heard whispers about which poets were the obvious leaders. All three went to Brightleaf. I just hope the conference is a positive experience for all the writers, even if they don't win."

Jeremiah put a hand on her arm. "We all want that. For the sake of our company's reputation and because we understand how scary it is to chase an impractical dream."

Gil plucked a bursting bubble from the bottom of his empty glass and said, "To borrow from Ray Bradbury, 'Do what you love and love what you do. Imagination should be the center of your life.' It's definitely the center of Mateo's life. That man's a maestro of mixology."

Jane was too busy mulling over the exchange between Stephanie and Jeremiah to respond. She remembered the video footage of Jeremiah retrieving Gretchen's pen. The look on Stephanie's face—had it been jealousy? As she tried to find a way to mention the incident, she realized that she'd missed a conversation between Gil and Stephanie. But as it turned out, they were just arguing over who had the biggest bags under their eyes.

Stephanie took a compact out of her purse and examined her reflection. "Okay, Gil, you win. Which means you need to take better care of yourself. Book a massage while we're here. Read poems in the spa's relaxation area. Invest in some self-care."

"Or get outside and take another hike," Jane suggested. "Did you see anything interesting yesterday? My great-uncle spotted a great blue heron."

Jane searched their faces for any sign of surprise or guilt, but their expressions were guileless and affable.

Maybe the drinks worked too *well,* she thought.

Gil leaned forward and spoke in a stage whisper.

"I'm not going back out there. Bugs love to bite me, the sun loves to burn me, and grass is overrated. Sorry, Walt Whitman, but it's either itchy, sharp, or wet. Or it has bugs in it, which takes me back to my first point."

When Gil's friends started to laugh, Jane couldn't help but join in.

"I love the great outdoors," said Jeremiah. "Rock climbing and mountain biking are my jam. I'm trying to talk Stephanie into a white-water rafting excursion. She's my only hope because Gil will never go."

"My face might not be as pretty as Steph's, but that doesn't mean I want to smash it into a bunch of rocks."

Stephanie picked up her glass, saw that it was empty, and darted a look at her smart watch.

"We should get going." Gil directed a smile at Jane.

She rose to her feet and returned the smile. "Enjoy your dinner. I'll see you later for the scavenger hunt."

Jeremiah shook her hand and thanked her for the drinks. The rest of the party followed suit.

Stephanie wobbled a little as she walked away. Mateo's cocktail had rendered her cheerfully tipsy, but not drunk.

"I wouldn't mind feeling like that," Jane muttered under her breath.

Before she headed out to meet her sons, Deputy Emory, and a few Cover Girls, Jane stopped by the bar to tell Mateo that his Poetry in Motion cocktail had earned a permanent place on the menu.

"We have a plan," Hem announced as Jane reached for a plate.

Everyone else had already served themselves from the dishes lined up on the break room's counter, and it took all of Jane's willpower to choose grilled prawns, heirloom tomato salad, and asparagus instead of mozzarella fritters and flatbread topped with bacon, fig, and caramelized onions.

The wedding's in two weeks, niggled the voice in her head when her hand starting moving toward the fritters of its own accord.

"Mom? Are you listening?"

Jane turned away from the food. "Yes. You have a plan."

Hem waited until his mother sat down between Deputy Emory and Eloise before continuing. "Fitz and I are going to play cribbage without a board."

Fitz tapped the pencil behind his ear. "We'll write our scores on a piece of paper. That way, if we overhear anything, we can write it down."

Mrs. Pratt tapped her temple. "Good thinking."

Hem, who'd already cleared his plate, reached for the fritter tongs. "Will all the scavenger hunt groups come to the Jane Austen Alcove?"

"Yes, but not at the same time," Jane said. "All the clues are hidden in the library and reading rooms, but each group has a unique set of clues. The Austen Alcove is the perfect place for you two. It also has that lovely bookcase with the glass doors—"

"That always get stuck," interrupted Hem.

Phoebe flashed him a conspiratorial grin. "Good. That'll delay the groups a little longer."

Jane turned to Deputy Emory. "Deputy Em—sorry—Amelia, I told my son and my friends to watch for dirty looks and to listen for gossip. What else should we look for?"

"Signs of hostility, anger, or jealousy. Pay close attention to arguments or behavior that seems out of place.

I'm going to leave now so I can eat with the writers, but if you need to get my attention, find me and say the code word loud enough for me to hear it." She turned to Fitz and Hem. "Okay, gentlemen. You wanted to choose the code word, so what's it going to be?"

Hem said, "Brouhaha," just as Fitz said, "Malarkey."

Eloise laughed. "They're fun, but we need something more subtle."

"We could pretend to be looking for Muffet Cat," suggested Phoebe.

After everyone agreed to "Muffet Cat" as the code word, Deputy Emory wished them luck and left the break room.

"Jane, are you sure the boys will be safe?" Mrs. Pratt asked as she topped off her glass of iced tea.

The twins stiffened.

Mrs. Pratt flicked her napkin at them. The motion dislodged her purse from where it hung on the back of her chair, and it fell to the floor. "Don't be offended. I know you've been taking karate or whatever it is since you were knee-high and that you're smarter than most boys twice your age, but one of the guests might be dangerous. I can't help but worry."

Hem retrieved Mrs. Pratt's purse and presented it to her with a flourish. "Milady."

"Such a charmer," Mrs. Pratt said, giving Hem's shoulder an affectionate nudge.

Eloise asked Jane to share some of the scavenger hunt clues.

"The most important clue will lead the searchers to a book of poems by Thomas Hood. The ominous card I found in the lobby after the wine tasting quoted Hood's poetry, and we want to see if anyone reacts to the clue. The poets aren't allowed to use their phones to find answers. If they get stuck, they're supposed to ask Sinclair, Butterworth, or myself for help. All the clues lead to a particular book." Jane put down her fork and tried to remember one of the clues. "Okay, here's an example: *These shipwreck survivors built a house in a tree.*"

Phoebe cried, "Swiss Family Robinson!"

"Wow! You answered that in, like, two seconds," said Eloise. "Meanwhile, I'm sitting here, picturing the cover of *Magic Tree House.*"

"Tell us another one," Phoebe pleaded.

Jane glanced at the clock. She would've liked a few minutes to tell the Fins about her conversation with the Current Mood folks, but she had to be ready and waiting for the start of the scavenger hunt.

"One more before I go. Ready? *A zebra, a tiger, and an orangutan in a lifeboat.*"

"*The Life of Pi!*" the three Cover Girls shouted in unison.

Eloise looked at the twins and said, "That was one of our book club picks. I bet you two know the answers to lots of clues."

Fitz shrugged. "We'd rather spy than play games, anyway."

"We certainly don't look like spies, which makes us perfect for the job," exclaimed Mrs. Pratt.

Jane reminded everyone about seeking out Deputy Emory if necessary and, after carrying her dirty dishes to the dishwashing station, hurried through the staff corridor to the Madame Bovary Dining Room.

Butterworth was waiting for her outside the dining room. Taking her by the arm, he steered her around the corner. "Deputy Phelps conducted a thorough search of the secret passage. Here's what he found." He pulled a folded piece of paper from the inside pocket of his coat and handed it to Jane.

She studied the printout in silence, her forehead wrinkling in confusion. The image showed a piece of paper covered in cursive writing.

"I'm not familiar with this poem."

"Not many people are, but Mr. Sinclair claims that it was written by Walt Whitman. It was meant to be included in the first printing of *Leaves of Grass*. For whatever reason, Mr. Whitman changed his mind, and the poem wasn't included. The original copy was given to your great-grandfather for safekeeping."

Jane frowned. "Then how did it end up in some dusty passageway behind our walls?"

Butterworth's expression was grave. "All I know is that Mr. Sinclair is waiting for you *upstairs*. The guests are still enjoying their dessert, so you're free to join him. If you don't return in time to review the rules, I'll see to it."

Jane knew what Butterworth meant by upstairs, so she headed to her great-aunt and -uncle's apartments without delay. Once inside, she found Sinclair pacing the living room. Muffet Cat was there too. He sat on a gold satin cushion as if it were a feline throne, casting his reproachful stare on the head librarian.

After a quick word with Sinclair, Jane walked through the living room and master bedroom and came to a stop at the back of Aunt Octavia's closet. She pulled aside a shoe rack to reveal a return air filter grille. Using the small screwdriver hidden inside Aunt Octavia's rain boot, Jane removed the grille.

The grille didn't conceal an air duct but a lever and a keyhole. Jane took out the key she kept on her person at all times and fitted it into the keyhole. She turned the key while simultaneously pushing down on the lever.

Behind the wall, gears and pulleys groaned. The mechanism would cause the china cabinet in the living room to shift, and a narrow opening would appear.

Sinclair stood next to the china cabinet, a battery-powered lantern in his hand.

They didn't speak as they ascended the narrow staircase leading to a locked steel door. Using another key stashed behind a bit of loose mortar, Jane unlocked the dead bolt and stepped inside the secret library.

Despite the number of materials that had been donated, returned to the families of the original owners, or sold, the secret library was still replete with literary treasures. These included a Gutenberg Bible, sequels to famous novels, and undiscovered works by some of the world's most celebrated writers. There were dozens upon dozens of drawers filled with documents, books, maps, and scrolls.

While it had been easy to donate a Shakespeare play with an alternate ending to the Folger Library, it was more difficult to know what to do with the materials entrusted to past Guardians to forever keep out of sight. These works had disturbing and dangerous ideas, such as the mass sterilization of all females without a genius IQ, a treatise on the supremacy of the Aryan race, and detailed instructions on how to keep minorities and immigrants from gaining equality in a young nation called the United States of America.

This was not the time to dwell on specifics of the collection, no matter how astounding or astonishing, so Jane turned on the light and said, "Do you know which drawer we need to open?"

Ignoring the antique card catalog cabinet to the right of the door, Sinclair said, "I do."

He opened the top drawer of the cabinet and retrieved two pairs of white gloves. He then made a beeline for the fireproof drawers on the far wall.

"Whitman is here." He tugged at the drawer pull, and it slid open with a whisper.

For a moment, they both stared at the collection of papers with reverence. Here were the writings of one of America's greatest poets. And in his own hand, no less.

The documents lay flat, enveloped in archival sleeves, and as Sinclair gingerly transferred each document from the drawer to a velvet-lined box, he said, "When the first version of *Leaves of Grass* was published in 1855, it consisted of twelve poems. Multiple editions followed—all of which included edits and corrections made by Whitman. Anyone in possession of the 1855 version owns a piece of history worth a small fortune. A poem written in Whitman's own hand is an even greater fortune."

"I read an article saying that Whitman is one of our most controversial poets. His poems were considered scandalous by many of his contemporaries. Despite that—or because of it—his popularity grew and grew."

Sinclair paused to scan another document before gently setting it aside. "Four years ago, a book from the first printing fetched over three hundred thousand at auction. Everyone believes the original manuscript was destroyed in a fire. It wasn't. Whitman gave it to the Guardian of Storyton Hall."

Jane drew in a sharp breath. "That must be worth a million. Or more."

"Indeed. Ah, here's a discarded draft from the printer's copy page. Look at the notes over the crossed-out lines. Now, imagine a whole collection of those papers handed off from Whitman to the printer."

He picked up a letter, and suddenly, they were staring at the bottom of the drawer.

"No, no, no," Jane whispered. "How could it be gone?"

Only she could access the secret library, and only a select number of people were aware of its location. Jane trusted all of them with her life.

The idea that someone had stolen from the secret library made her stomach turn.

She pressed her hand against the wall of drawers and took deep breaths until the queasiness abated. There was no relief for her dread, however. As she stared at the dozens upon dozens of drawers, the feeling intensified.

"What else is missing?" she croaked.

Sinclair didn't reply. He just took her hand, offering comfort through touch.

No warmth permeated the silky fabric of his glove, but Jane held on tight all the same.

Chapter 7

Jane was still reeling from her brief visit to the secret library when she entered the dining room. She gripped the hostess podium for support and waited for Butterworth to ring the gong.

The moment he struck the metal with a soft mallet, the low, rich note reverberated through the room. He hit the gong a second time, and all chatter ceased.

The hum of the gong echoed in Jane's dazed brain, and she stood as if in a trance.

"Miss Jane?"

When Butterworth's whisper didn't snap Jane out of her stupor, he pinched her arm. She gave a little jump and picked up the handheld microphone.

Forcing a smile, she began to speak.

"Good evening, ladies and gentlemen. I hope you've dined well and are ready to exercise your minds. Hopefully, you had double dessert because you'll burn plenty of calories racing around Storyton Hall in search of clues."

Jane moved forward until she stood behind the table closest to the door and said, "Some of you may have guessed that your dining companions are also your scavenger hunt teammates."

She paused. This was the moment to bring up Gretchen's name—to use the verbiage she and Sheriff Evans had come up with a few hours ago. However, she was drawing a complete blank.

Gretchen West is dead. She was tied to a canoe. Which one of you did that to her?

Of course, that wasn't what she was supposed to say, but all she could think about was the drawer in the secret library. The drawer and the stolen poems.

Suddenly the words came back to her, and Jane's panic subsided. She made a sweeping gesture, encompassing the whole room, and said, "Before I go on, I'd like to share a concern regarding one of your fellow writers. Gretchen West signed up to participate in both the morning and afternoon writing sessions but didn't attend either. She isn't here tonight, and we've been unable to reach her by phone. We're asking for your help in locating her. This wouldn't be the first time a guest strayed off a hiking trail and ended up lost in the woods, so if you've seen Gretchen in the last forty-eight hours, please let me know right away."

Her announcement didn't provoke any dramatic responses. People exchanged whispers or looks of concern, but that was all. No one averted their eyes or rearranged their features into a blank expression. There were too many guests for Jane and Butterworth to study at once, and even with Deputy Emory in the crowd, the person responsible for Gretchen's death might lack a visible tell.

Jane plastered her gracious-hostess smile back on and pointed at the table in front of her. "There are small bags taped to the underside of your chairs. Inside each bag is a bandana. This is your team color. Please wear the bandana so that everyone can see it. Use it as a headband or scarf, for example."

There was a great deal of tittering as the guests retrieved the bags and discovered their team colors.

A man at the table near Jane held his orange bandana up to his face. In a singsong voice, he said, "'My eyes are grayish blueish green, but I'm told they look orange in the night.'"

"That's Shel Silverstein!" cried the young woman to his left.

"Our team should be the Tyger, Tygers," the man suggested.

Jane gave him a thumbs-up. "You should also take this time to invent a name for your team. The staff will be coming around with paper bags and markers. You have five minutes to come up with a team name. When you've got it, please write the name in big, bold letters on both sides of your bag. As you find clues, you'll drop them in the bag."

Jane turned off the microphone and put it on the host stand. Signaling for a server, she ordered a coffee brandy.

"Quickly, man," Butterworth chided when the server paused to watch the guests.

He put a hand on Jane's shoulder and studied her face for a long moment. "Your trip upstairs has upset you."

"Yes," Jane admitted in a small voice. "Once, we had twelve poems. All handwritten by Whitman. Every page included notations and edits. It's the literary equivalent of the Hope Diamond. Or was. Deputy Phelps found one of the poems in the passageway. The rest are . . . missing." A buzzing noise sounded in her ears.

Butterworth leaned down. "Focus on my voice. *You* are in control of your body. *You* are in control of your mind. Don't let the circumstances take control. You are Jane Steward, Guardian of Storyton Hall."

The buzzing receded, and Jane gave Butterworth a grateful look. "Sinclair stayed behind to see if they've been misplaced by accident, but it's unlikely. We've spent the past two years redistributing our works of British literature. Other than a few titles, we haven't dealt with works by American writers at all. I didn't donate the Whitman poems by mistake or anything."

Butterworth's expression turned dark. "Has there been a theft?"

"Without my key? Without Aunt Octavia and Uncle Aloysius's knowledge? It doesn't seem possible!" Jane lowered her voice. "Getting agitated won't help matters, but it's very hard not to. I can count the number of people who've seen the inside of that library on two hands. I love—and trust—each and every one of them."

"Unless evidence points to the contrary, you should continue to love and trust these individuals."

At this, Jane's tension eased a little. "You're right. Jumping to conclusions is never the answer. I'm going to give my full attention to my guests and our immediate goals of observation and eavesdropping."

"Excellent. Here's your coffee." Butterworth took the coffee cup from the server and pressed it into Jane's hands. "Have a few swallows before you address the guests. As an Englishman, I find nothing restores one's senses more effectively than a generous dose of brandy."

Jane took a sip and puckered her lips. "Oh yeah, that's generous."

This time when Jane picked up the microphone and turned to the guests, her smile was genuine.

"Let's go around the room and hear the team names. I'm going to start with the green team. What's your official scavenger hunt name?"

A woman jumped up and shouted, "The Clever Kiplings."

"After Rudyard Kipling, I assume?"

"The one and only!"

Jane moved to the next table. This team's members waved their bandanas in the air and cheered when a man yelled, "We're the Boozy Brownings!"

The blue team became the Blue Bells, the purple team chose the Violet Verses, the red team picked Rhymes with Dead, and so on.

The guests were clearly excited to start the hunt, so Jane quickly reviewed the rules and then asked if there were any questions.

"Are we allowed to take our wine with us?" someone shouted.

Judging by the mild slurring of his words, the man didn't need any more wine.

"It's best to keep the wine away from the books," Jane replied amiably. "Any other questions?"

A woman said, "What happens if someone uses a phone?"

"That will lead to automatic disqualification. If your team needs a hint, feel free to ask the room monitor. For example, if you're stuck on a clue and you're in the Henry James Library, Mr. Sinclair, our head librarian, is there to help. I'll wander between the library and the lobby, so feel free to ask me, or Mr. Butterworth, for assistance. If there are no more questions, we'll head to the lobby, distribute the first clue, and start the clock. And don't forget to let me know if you have any information to share about Gretchen West."

A voice from the other end of the room called out, "What does the winning team get?"

Jane mimed a head smack. "The prize! Of course! Since I have no idea, I'm going to ask Jeremiah of Current Mood Cards to tell you what's in store for the winning team."

Heads swiveled as Jeremiah strode to the front of the room. Jane offered him the mic, but he waved it off with a grin.

"I have one of those voices," he told her before facing the crowd. Then he reached into his jacket pocket and drew out a box. "Good evening! I'll keep this short because you're obviously raring to go. Each member of the winning team will receive a Montblanc gold-coated LeGrand ballpoint pen. Because great writing deserves a great pen."

His announcement elicited *oohs* and *aahs* from the crowd as well as a flurry of animated whispers. A subtle change came over the writers. Whereas a moment ago they'd been energized and excited, competition had now given their eagerness a sharp edge.

It's just a pen, Jane thought as she drank more coffee.

But a Montblanc pen didn't have the same significance to her as it did to these writers, many of whom had charged their room and conference fee to a credit card they couldn't afford to pay off.

"If this is how they respond to the idea of winning a fancy pen, imagine how they feel about the greeting card contract," she whispered to Butterworth.

"They remind me of a pack of bloodhounds picking up the scent of a rabbit. There's no telling how they'll behave once they're let loose to hunt their quarry."

Jane said, "There's nothing like a competitive game to bring out a person's true nature. It's why I never play Monopoly. It turns the nicest people into jerks."

The guests moved to the lobby, where Sinclair, Phoebe, Mrs. Pratt, and Eloise waited to hand out clues. As Sinclair distributed clues to Jane and Butterworth, the set of his jaw made it clear that he hadn't located the missing Whitman poems.

"We'll find them," Jane said, hoping she sounded more convincing than she felt.

After introducing the helpers to the writers, Jane asked a representative from each scavenger hunt team to come forward. Once they'd lined up facing a helper, Jane counted down from ten. When she reached zero, she handed her clue to the representative of the pink team.

The woman who received it cried, "Please make this be an easy one!"

A few teams were already racing toward the library or the reading rooms while the rest stared at their first clue and tried to puzzle out the answer.

A debate between two members of the yellow team became so heated that Butterworth had to ask them to lower their voices.

"If we don't get those pens, it won't be my fault," said a young woman wearing a floral dress and combat boots. She crossed her arms over her chest and pouted like a two-year-old.

A woman ten years her senior curled her lip. "If we don't get the pens, it'll be because *you* wasted our time."

Before the argument could resume, the rest of the team members took a vote and decided to look for their next clue in the Daphne du Maurier Drawing Room.

Jane walked over to Butterworth. "Talk about starting off on the wrong foot. What was their clue?"

" 'Rose of Sharon is pregnant at the beginning of this novel about the Dust Bowl.' "

"I assume one of the women guessed *The Grapes of Wrath*. What other book was suggested?"

Butterworth said, "Karen Hesse's *Out of the Dust*."

"There's no 'Rose of Sharon' in that novel."

"The younger of the two women believes there is." Butterworth touched his ear. "I shall now fade into the walls and eavesdrop."

"Butterworth, you have many, many skills, but fading into the walls isn't one of them."

The butler's mouth twitched in the approximation of a smile, and he glided away.

Jane lingered in the lobby for a while, and when no one asked for her help, she quelled the temptation to check on Fitz and Hem and went to the library.

Sinclair was behind his desk, presumably giving the red team a hint, while the purple team flipped through an atlas of constellations. The book was a beauty. It was also huge. When opened, it took up half a library table.

"That's not it. Keep going," a middle-aged man told the woman turning the pages.

"You'd better take over," she said, stepping aside. "My arms are too short. I'm like a T. rex in a rowboat."

Her teammates chuckled.

"What would it be like for a T. rex to row across Storyton Lake?" asked a man in a Hawaiian shirt and pink board shorts. In his hand, he carried a metal water bottle covered with stickers.

A tall woman with cat's-eye glasses rolled her eyes. "Okay, Connor. What would it be like?"

Connor placed the bottle on the table and performed a little drumroll with his fingers. "It would be quite an oar deal!"

"Can you lay off the Dad jokes until we've found the next clue? And I don't think you should be drinking kombucha near the books."

"It's my magic elixir! Okay, fine, but *you* should skip to the Greek section. None of the constellations are named after Egyptians."

His teammate did as he suggested, and the clue was there, nestled in the gutter between a page of text and a full-color plate of Orion the Hunter.

"Nice one, Connor," said the woman with the glasses.

While the group huddled closer to read the next clue, Jane studied him.

Connor had shiny, shoulder-length blond hair and elfin features. He was a cross between Legolas from *The Lord of the Rings* and a surfer.

Someone else on the purple team was assessing Connor. Deputy Emory shot Jane a quick glance as if to say, *"I heard the canoe reference too."*

When Connor's team hurried out of the library to search for their next clue, Jane had just enough time to return the celestial atlas to its shelf before the white team stormed in.

As the hunt progressed, the teams quickly learned to rely on the strengths of their individual members. There was minimal bickering, and nothing ever escalated beyond a dirty look or snide remark.

More than anything, the guests were having fun.

An hour later, many of the teams were on their last clue, so Jane headed to the lobby to join the Current Mood trio to await the winning team.

Jeremiah, Gil, and Stephanie had made themselves comfortable in the seating area near the massive fireplace. Professor Ashley was there too, and as Jane approached, he got to his feet and offered her his chair.

Jane had seen Dodge Ashley around the resort, but she'd yet to speak with him. From a distance, he hadn't made much of an impression on her. He was a man of average height and build with brown hair, glasses, and a pleasant smile. Up close, she noticed that his eyes were a captivating shade of gray, and his face had the ruddiness of an outdoorsman. His smile was electric.

"How are you enjoying your stay so far?"

The professor swept a hand around the room. His fingers were long and elegant. "So much that I won't want to leave come Wednesday. You've created a real literary haven here."

Pleased, Jane said, "Thank you. I hope the environment is inspiring the writers."

"From what I've read so far, it definitely is."

When Jane asked about his summer program, the professor told her that it was always the highlight of his year. As he shared details of what he called his "writer's boot camp," he spoke with such passion and energy that Jane forgot about the Current Mood trio. Like all the best teachers, Professor Ashley had a certain magnetism.

If I'm hanging on his every word after five minutes, then his students must adore him.

The professor glanced at Jane over the rim of his wineglass. "Do you write, Ms. Steward?"

"Not a lick. But I read everything."

"That's the first step toward becoming a good writer. Aspiring poets must experience the power of the written word in many forms. Every summer, I start off the class by playing music. Hip-hop, country, gospel, opera—poetry is everywhere. That's the most important lesson I have to teach."

"I wish you could tell that to my sons. They think poetry is for old people."

Professor Ashley threw back his head and laughed. "The boys in the card room—are they yours?"

"It depends. Were they behaving?"

"Like one of William Blake's angels," he said with a chuckle. "Would they mind if I interrupted their game to perform my *Dead Poets Society* act on them?"

"Does it involve standing on a table?"

"Since I've been eating like a horse since I got here, I'd better not. A sturdy chair should do the trick. I'd like to recite Rupert Brooke's 'The Soldier.' After that, I'll challenge them to a haiku duel. With your permission, of course."

Adore isn't a strong enough word. His students must worship him, Jane thought. Aloud, she said, "I'd be delighted."

The teal team jogged into the lobby, heading straight for the Current Mood trio.

Stephanie jumped up, her face shining. "Are you done?"

"No!" cried a young woman with large dark brown eyes and skin the color of chai tea. "Can we ask Professor Ashley for help?"

When Stephanie looked to Jeremiah and Gil for guidance, they nodded in assent.

The professor put a hand on his chest and bowed his head. "I'm at your service, Farah."

"Last year, when I was at Brightleaf, we read a poem about death. I know a pre-Raphaelite poet wrote it, but I can't remember if it was a Rossetti. And if it was, which one? Christina or Gabriel?"

"Here's your hint: The poem was written from the deceased's point of view."

"Christina!" Farah shouted. "Thank you, Professor. You're the best!"

Farah's team dashed off.

"How many of the competitors have you taught?" Jane asked the professor.

"Twenty, including Gretchen West. I don't know if anyone's talked to you about her yet, but I saw her twice on Friday. During the morning session on using comedy, and again that afternoon for the session on marking milestones. I also saw her in the tea room. She stopped by my table to say hello. When I taught Ms. West two years ago, she was painfully shy. It seems that hasn't changed. But she was clearly excited about the competition. She might be insecure around other people, but she's a confident and competent writer."

Jane had to tread carefully. As much as she wanted to glean more information about Gretchen, she needed to keep her tone conversational.

She looked around the lobby as if expecting another team to run by and said, "Is anyone else from Gretchen's class here now?"

Professor Ashley wrinkled his brow. "From that summer? Yes. Mavis Trudeau and Connor Jensen. Mavis is a grandmother. Connor is a tall kid with blond hair. When he's not catching waves, he's writing."

"A surfer poet?" Jane nodded in approval. "If you had to guess, which of your former students are favored to win the competition?"

The professor mulled this over for a moment before answering. "Connor is one of three shining stars in this contest. The other two are Gretchen West, and the young lady who just asked me for a hint. Her name's Farah Khan."

"You must get to know your students on a deep level after reading their work. I mean, all writing is personal, but poetry is . . ."

"A diary in verse. It's very intimate." He sipped his wine and gazed off into the middle-distance. "In my classes, my students have to reveal their souls. The best poets are willing to bare the good, the bad, and the ugly—to show me their scars and secrets. They also need to be strong enough to go back to the drawing board if their work fails to cause a reaction."

"Isn't that something all successful writers need to do?"

Professor Ashley shook his head. "There are places to hide in fiction. Only in poetry, and in memoirs too, is the writer laid open. It's like standing naked on the fifty-yard line in a packed stadium."

Jane pulled a face. "I'm not that brave. But it sounds like Gretchen, Connor, and Farah are."

"Brave *and* honest. Through their poetry, I learned that cancer took Gretchen's mother from her when she was a teenager and that her father is serving a twenty-year prison sentence for vehicular manslaughter. Connor is a water baby. He surfs, kayaks, swims—you name it. If there's water involved, that's where Connor wants to be, even though he watched his sister drown when he was in high school. She fell through the ice, and he couldn't pull her out in time."

At Jane's sharp intake of breath, the professor gave her a somber nod. "And Farah? She grew up in extreme poverty, is a sexual assault survivor, and immigrated to the States with her father. Her mother and sister weren't able to immigrate, and eventually they stopped trying." Turning to Jane, he gave her a small smile. "It sounds grim, I know, but the three of them transformed their worst memories into powerful poems. They're flowers growing out of cracks in the concrete. Tough and beautiful."

"Is writing humor a challenge for them?"

Professor Ashley shrugged. "Connor is known for his corny jokes. He can make anyone laugh. Farah and Gretchen are better with sarcasm. Snarky humor, that sort of thing. It's a close race between those three."

"Speaking of close races, look! Two teams are running our way from opposite directions."

"And people think all writers are introverts. They should see this!" He laughed. "I'm going to make some room for the winners and work my magic on your sons. It was lovely chatting with you. I hope we can do this again."

Professor Ashley thanked the Current Mood folks for the wine and walked away.

Thirty seconds later, the yellow team came to a stop in front of the group of chairs, beating the blue team by a nose. There was a great deal of panting and grinning as a man presented their final clue.

Gil gave it a quick scan before asking for the rest of the clues.

"We'll check these over while you guys go back to the dining room for some well-deserved drinks." Seeing the crushed looks on the faces of the blue team, he added, "We'll take your clues too. The yellow team got here first, but that doesn't mean all of their clues will be correct."

Accepting this crumb of hope with good grace, the members of the blue team followed their competitors down the hall.

Jane's phone buzzed in her pocket. She took it out and read the text message. She then showed the message to Gil.

"Her teammates are *not* going to be happy."

Stephanie scooted to the edge of her seat. "What happened?"

"Riley Gruber used her phone to find an answer. She was seen by someone on another team who'd prefer to remain anonymous."

Stephanie groaned. "I told you those pens would take the fun out of this."

Gil frowned at her. "They *all* had fun. And isn't it better that we know what Riley's like before we offer her a job? Or anyone else who'll cheat to get ahead?"

Jeremiah said, "Gil's right. We want to trust our new hire. We're such a small company that we should feel good about the people on our team. And I wouldn't feel good about Riley."

"I get that, but is it wrong to punish her whole team

if they didn't know what she was doing?" Stephanie countered.

After a brief conference, they decided to speak to Riley in private before making a decision.

"This will give people time to come forward with info on Gretchen," Stephanie added. "I hope she's okay."

Her colleagues murmured in agreement.

Jeremiah volunteered to meet with Riley alone. "We shouldn't gang up on her. Even if she did cheat. I'll meet you guys in the dining room. This shouldn't take long."

As it turned out, Riley's team was fully aware that she'd cheated. Riley went to her room, and Jeremiah reconvened with Jane and his colleagues at the hostess podium.

"The yellow team is DQ'ed. We don't need to call them out in front of everybody. We'll just announce that the blue team won and end the night on a positive note." He looked at Jane. "Did anyone come forward with information about Gretchen?"

"A few people saw her on Thursday. One person heard a server in the Rudyard Kipling Café address her by name, a handful of people remember her from Friday morning's poetry session, and Professor Ashley saw her at afternoon tea the same day."

"What about Friday night?" asked Stephanie.

The worry in her eyes seemed genuine, and though Jane hated to deceive her, she said, "Not yet, but I'm sure to hear from more people on their way out."

In truth, she was waiting for one person in particular to approach her. She'd watched him when the winning team was given their prize pens. She'd watched him as they left the dining room to celebrate in the Ian Fleming Lounge. She'd watched as guests trailed out to join the victors or to call it a night.

Finally, she'd watched him leave.

Connor Jensen had spent an entire summer with Gretchen West, but he walked away as if he had no idea who she was. He walked away as if he didn't care that a former classmate and fellow writer had gone missing.

Then he got in the elevator.

As the doors closed, Jane muttered, "You can't hide from me. This is *my* house."

Chapter 8

"I think I heard something important," said Mrs. Pratt, puffing out her chest. She waited until all eyes were on her before adding, "I don't know what it *means*, but I think it was important."

Deputy Emory, Fitz, Hem, Eloise, Phoebe, and all four Fins had gathered in the William Faulkner Conference Room to share what they'd seen and heard that evening.

Jane had barely taken up her position in front of the wall-mounted whiteboard when Mrs. Pratt made her announcement.

"You're going to want to uncap that marker," she said.

Jane picked up the black marker and raised it in the air. "Ready when you are."

For once, Mrs. Pratt opted for brevity. "I overheard a conversation between two guests—Connor and Farah. Connor would look right at home on a California beach.

Farah has striking, dark brown eyes, and her hair is pulled into two, I don't know, topknots?"

When Mrs. Pratt fisted her hands and put them on top of her head, Phoebe said, "They're called 'space buns.' "

"I like that. Anyway, Connor and Farah weren't on the same team, so I was surprised when she pulled him into the reading room. They didn't see me, so I ducked down behind a sofa and tried not to move. Farah sounded angry. She said, 'Everyone's looking for Gretchen! I know you know something!' "

Deputy Emory interrupted to ask the approximate time of this exchange. Mrs. Pratt said that it was half past nine, give or take a few minutes.

"Farah was obviously upset, and Connor responded by snapping at her. He told her to chill out. Then he said, 'Gretchen's somewhere, crying a lake of tears, because she can't win this thing. She has no sense of humor, and she's never been in love. This isn't Brightleaf, Farah. Greeting cards are for real people.' "

Jane turned and wrote the word BRIGHTLEAF on the whiteboard. Directly under that, she added three names: GRETCHEN, CONNOR, and FARAH.

Circling Connor's name, she said, "He mentioned a canoe in the library and the lake in the reading room."

"Was that the end of their conversation?" Deputy Emory asked Mrs. Pratt.

"Farah said something I couldn't hear, but on their way out, Connor told Farah that she was his biggest threat."

Deputy Emory's pen flew across her notepad. "Was his tone hostile?"

"No. It was matter-of-fact."

Jane said, "Thank you, Eugenia. Anyone else?"

Fitz raised his hand. "Hem and I heard people talking about which poet was in the lead."

"Some of them said Connor. Some said Farah. But most of them think Gretchen will win," Hem said.

"People talked about how funny Connor is and how Farah's poems make them cry. Someone said Farah can't be funny, even when she tries."

"One lady said Gretchen's poems are so good that she can tell which ones are hers even if her name isn't on them," Hem put in.

Eloise and Phoebe had heard similar comments.

Sinclair was the only Fin with something to add.

"A few guests are clearly envious of the front-runners," he said. "Though their remarks were spiteful, I'm pleased to say they weren't well-received by their teammates. Most people believe they have something to gain from this experience and wish it to remain as friendly as possible. A handful of writers are here solely to improve their craft and aren't invested in the competition. Everyone spoke highly of Professor Ashley. They admire his work as a poet and his skills as a teacher."

Jane glanced at Deputy Emory. "You were closer to the guests than any of us. Did your teammates offer any insight?"

Emory made a seesaw motion with her hand. "They had plenty of theories about Gretchen's absence. Rumor has it that she was agoraphobic. Others thought she was trying to increase her mystique for the benefit of the judges. The rest had no clue. The names you wrote on the board were considered the favorites by my team too."

"If there's nothing else, we'll call it a night. It's getting late, and I know Sheriff Evans is waiting on our findings. Thank you all for your help."

Though the twins wanted to stay, Jane sent them home with a gentle reminder to walk the dogs.

Deputy Emory stepped out of the room to call Sheriff Evans. While she was gone, Butterworth picked up the phone in the conference room and dialed the extension in the kitchens. He ordered several pots of coffee and a tray of sandwiches, then sat back down to await Jane's orders.

"Sinclair, please take a deep dive into the background of the guests on the whiteboard. Especially Connor and Farah. I'm especially interested in any financial info you could glean. I assume the sheriff will want to interview them both. I just don't know when."

She glanced from the whiteboard to Sterling. "You've had to sift through enough footage for one day. Landon? Would you follow Connor Jensen's movements from check-in until now and make notes on the times we weren't able to track him. Butterworth, would you do the same with Farah Khan?"

Butterworth inclined his head.

"I know everyone here shares my anxiety over the missing Whitman poems and the implications of their disappearance. I'll speak with Aunt Octavia first thing in the morning to see if any staff members entered their apartments in the past week. Outside of Mrs. Templeton, of course. It's too late to do that now. As for me, I'm going to ask the Current Mood folks for poetry samples from all the writers on our list."

They all filed out of the conference room. Deputy Emory was still on the phone, so Jane lingered a bit until she was done.

"The sheriff wanted me to tell you that we'll reconvene early tomorrow morning. He'd like to conduct interviews before he tells the guests about Ms. West. According to the event schedule, the poetry panel starts at nine. He'd like to meet you in your office at seven."

I don't think I'll make it to church tomorrow, Jane thought.

Deputy Emory checked her watch. "I'm going to hang out in the lounge for a bit. Order a mock gin and tonic and keep my ears open."

"I'm heading there too," Jane said.

But when she saw that none of the Current Mood people were there, she backtracked to the Henry James Library.

The library was closed for the evening, so Jane used her master key to enter. As soon as the door shut behind her, Edwin sent her a text.

Busy night. Big birthday party and several anniversaries. Magnus has a summer cold, so I told him to knock off early. I hope your hunt was a success. You'll probably be asleep when I get home, but I'll still whisper I love you, I love you, I love you in your ear.

Edwin's words wrapped around her like a blanket fresh from the dryer.

Her reply said, **The hunt is ongoing. Will be up early to meet sheriff, but you can wake me up when you get home.**

Sinclair's office door was ajar, and he was standing in front of a board of guest printouts. When Jane stepped into the office, he opened his arms to her.

She moved into his embrace. How often had she felt the tweed of his suit coat against her cheek? How often had his familiar scents of aftershave and peppermint soothed her? As a child, he'd been the one to doctor her scrapes and dry her tears. He'd consoled her when she got a bad grade or when someone hurt her feelings. And when she'd returned to Storyton Hall as a pregnant widow, he'd held her just like this while she'd cried and cried.

His gentle, fatherly support fortified her as it always had. When she pulled away, she gave him a grateful smile and pointed at the printouts. "Any luck?"

"Not yet. Both Mr. Jensen and Ms. Khan have active social lives and steady employment. They're well-educated and have been published in prestigious poetry journals. Not as many as Gretchen West, but still impressive. There isn't much more we can do tonight. I can't call their employers or landlords until Monday. Our best option is get our hands on their work. Even if their poetry isn't autobiographical, it will give us a glimpse into their true selves."

"In that case, we should turn in. We can start fresh tomorrow," Jane said.

Together, they walked into the library. Sinclair stopped near one of the chairs facing the fireplace and waved at the walls of books. "I'm going to sit and think awhile. Don't worry, I'm in good company."

When Jane's alarm went off the next morning, she hit the snooze button, rolled over, and reached for Edwin.

Not here, her mind told her body.

Her body sighed in disappointment.

The house was quiet. Unusually quiet. The arrival of Merry and Pippin meant an ever-present cacophony of yips, whines, barks, grunts, snorts, sneezes, and growls. Because they were puppies, they needed lots of sleep, but their slumber was never silent.

Jane had never had a pet and was both wary of and fascinated by the poodle pups. After reading books on dog ownership and listening to advice from other pet parents, she grew more confident with their new family members. In a matter of weeks, Merry and Pippin had licked and snuggled their way into her heart. She couldn't imagine life without them.

As if thinking of the puppies had summoned them, she heard the click of paws on hardwood and a sudden weight on her bed.

"Oof!" she cried as she was assaulted by puppy kisses and the smack of wagging tails. Jane's hand met with damp hair, wet noses, and more licks. The puppies smelled of fresh grass and soil.

"Now that you're up . . ." came a voice from the doorway.

Jane pushed her hair out of her eyes and saw Edwin leaning against the door frame. He wore an apron printed with the text: MAY THE FORKS BE WITH YOU.

"Their fur's damp. Is it raining?"

"It was coming down in buckets, but it's easing up now. And don't worry, I made them wipe their paws before I sent them up to be your puppy alarm clock."

Jane scratched Pippin behind the ears. "The boys are responsible for these fuzzballs. You have enough to do without taking over their potty training."

"I only did one chore." From behind his back, he produced a coffee mug.

"Oh, you marvelous man."

Edwin crossed the room and put the mug on Jane's nightstand. He leaned over, kissed her on the forehead, and said, "My oven timer's about to go off. Otherwise, I wouldn't have let the dogs get you up. I would've found a better way."

"Better than puppies and coffee?" Jane scoffed.

"Ingrate," said Edwin, throwing a pillow at her on his way out of the room. He whistled softly and the puppies raced after him.

After a few sips of coffee, Jane threw on a robe and went downstairs. The kitchen smelled like apples and cinnamon. Edwin was at the sink, washing a mixing bowl.

"Are we having pie for breakfast?" Jane asked as she slid her arms around Edwin's waist.

He turned around and bent his head to kiss her. Then he said, "Crêpes with baked apples for the boys. Crêpes with spinach and eggs for you. I just need to sauté the spinach. While I'm doing that, tell me everything that happened last night."

Jane plunked down on a stool and started talking. Edwin didn't interrupt until she mentioned the missing Whitman poems.

"Who better to trace a thief than a thief? Will you let me look into this?"

Not so long ago, Jane would have refused him outright. After all, Edwin lived a double life. When he was in Storyton, he was a restauranter. But when he traveled abroad, posing as a travel writer, he was really fulfilling missions for a secret sect. These missions often required that he steal books from one owner to return them to another, and Jane had never come to terms with this side of him.

Still, she knew she could trust Edwin Alcott. He would never do anything to harm her, her family, or Storyton Hall. He'd proven time and time again how much he loved her and the twins. He'd been young and head-strong when he'd sworn an oath to his Order, but his goals had changed. All he wanted now was to be the man Jane and the boys needed.

"You can help by going to see Aunt Octavia and Uncle Aloysius. Tell them that someone may have gained access to the secret library and find out who's been in their apartments. If I can leave that to you, I can focus all my energy on finding Gretchen West's killer."

"Our investigations may lead us to the same person," Edwin said, placing Jane's breakfast on the counter.

She looked down at the golden-brown crêpe, which was filled with scrambled eggs, goat cheese, and sautéed spinach. Though she knew every bite would be delicious, she didn't pick up her fork.

"Hey." Edwin sat down next to her.

"Sorry. I just need a minute."

He smiled. "That crêpe is still steaming. It's not going anywhere, and neither am I. We're in this together, Jane."

"And we can handle whatever comes our way."

Jane wrapped her arms around Edwin and hugged him fiercely. She was just releasing him when the puppies shot out of their crates and ran over to the back door.

"What do you guys hear?" she asked the puppies. "A squirrel?"

They whined, their tails furiously whipping from side to side.

Jane peered out the window but saw nothing unusual about the patio and garden. Then she moaned. "Damn. I forgot to put my bike away. I'm going to wheel it to the garage in case it starts raining again. It'll give my crêpe time to cool off."

Grabbing a dish towel, she opened the door and followed the puppies outside. They bounded over to the lawn, their black noses quivering as they detected interesting scents.

"If only those noses could track a killer," she said ruefully.

She dried the seat of her bike and was running the towel over the handlebars when she suddenly froze.

"Edwin!" she called.

He was beside her in a flash.

"Is that—?" he trailed off, staring into the basket attached to her handlebars.

"One of Whitman's poems? If so, it's been out here all night. In the rain."

Sheriff Evans looked with naked desire at the plated crêpe Edwin held out to him.

"Baked apple, you say? I know I shouldn't, but I'm only human."

"And while this isn't lobby coffee, you might like it even more," Jane said, placing a mug on the kitchen table.

The sheriff gestured at the back door with his fork. "From the look on Mr. Sinclair's face, that poem is authentic and worth a ton of money. Is it ruined?"

Jane winced. "I don't know. The ink has run in places. Sinclair doesn't dare touch the paper when it's still wet. If he isn't insanely careful, we'll end up with shreds only good for a hamster cage instead of an original poem by one of America's most famous poets."

"How long was your bike parked on the patio?"

"Two days. No, wait. Make that three. I've been so busy . . ."

After a swallow of coffee, the sheriff said, "First there was a poem in a secret passage inside the manor house. Now, there's a poem in your bike basket, parked behind your home. Ms. Steward, this person is no stranger to Storyton Hall. They know where you live. They know how to move behind the walls without being seen by your guests, staff, or great-aunt and -uncle. I have to assume they're also aware of the security cameras and know how to avoid them."

"Edwin is going to ask Aunt Octavia and Uncle Aloysius which staff members have been in their apartments for the past week or so." With a troubled frown, she looked at Edwin and said, "I guess you should ask about all of their visitors—even friends."

The sheriff finished the last bite of his crêpe. "I decided to curtail individual interviews until after I address the guests as a group. It's been forty-eight hours since Ms. West was found dead, and there's no sense in withholding the truth any longer. However, I will not share details. I don't want to give the person who tied up her up the attention they seek. As far as the guests are concerned, Ms. West was found in a canoe, dead from unknown causes."

Jane glanced at her watch. "In twenty minutes, the guests will be in Shakespeare's Theater. I'll bet the Current Mood folks are there too. I need to speak with them anyway because I'd like copies of all the poems the contestants have submitted up until now."

Edwin offered the sheriff a travel mug. "Fuel for the road?"

"When I show up at someone's house unannounced, I rarely receive a warm welcome. This has been a pleasant change. Thank you both. Ms. Steward?" He waved in the direction of the front door. "Let's go break the bad news and hope that it elicits a reaction."

Together, Jane and Sheriff Evans crossed the Great Lawn and entered Storyton Hall from the terrace. In the lobby, they found Deputy Phelps conferring with Butterworth. The Current Mood execs were helping themselves to coffee from one of the silver urns.

Jane caught Stephanie before she had a chance to sit down.

In response to Jane's query, Stephanie said, "I can forward all of the submissions to your email."

Gil, who'd overheard the exchange, was reluctant to fulfill Jane's request. "Considering what's at stake, I don't think we should share their work until we have a winner. We need to keep our cards close to our chest, if you'll forgive the lame metaphor."

Jane said, "I'm not asking out of idle curiosity. I'm asking because I'm the manager of this resort and one of those poems might tell us what happened to Gretchen West."

Stephanie put a hand over her heart. "Did you find her? I've been so worried!"

"Yes."

Though Stephanie and Gil looked genuinely relieved, Jane knew that certain people were adept at hiding their true feelings. But even their body language showed a release of tension. Their shoulders dropped, and they audibly exhaled.

Suddenly an impish spark ignited in Gil's eyes. "I propose a trade. I'll run up to my room and send you all the poems if you'll give me the lovely Phoebe's number."

"Please give it to him," Stephanie pleaded. "He's

been talking about her since the wine party. He had so much gelato yesterday afternoon that he could barely eat dinner. And I'm pretty sure he'd sell our company if it meant he could buy one of those naked women. Creepy!"

Gil's fair skin flushed tomato-red. "They're not creepy. They're art! Phoebe used scrap metal to make them. She even stamped words into their books. I think they're fantastic!"

"I was calling *you* creepy, not the sculptures," retorted Stephanie. She then told Jane she'd go to her room and send the email because she wanted to brush her teeth.

Jane knew Phoebe would love to hear from Gil, but Jane couldn't give him her number. Right now, everyone under her roof was a suspect.

"I'll text Phoebe first. If she gives me the green light, you can have her number."

Gil's face glowed. "Perfect. Thanks!"

Excusing herself, Jane entered Shakespeare's Theater. Lachlan and Sterling were already inside. They would seat the guests and study them as Sheriff Evans shared his grim tidings. How Jane wished they hadn't seen him deliver terrible news multiple times before, but they had. Jane had made similar announcements herself too. She'd had to look out at the sea of curious or anxious faces and witness their transformation.

Today was no different. Eyes widened. Mouths opened into ovals. There were gasps and soft cries. Hands gripped armrests, handbags, or another person's hand. Whispering always followed the initial blow. Neighbor turned to neighbor as an entire roomful of people was instantly united by the shocking revelation.

Only it wasn't a shock to at least one person in the theater. And if that person wasn't here, they were going about their business as a staff member of Storyton Hall.

Where are you? Jane thought, scanning the faces of her guests.

There were no answers. The sheriff, however, had to field plenty of questions.

He provided the pertinent information before repeating Jane's appeal of the previous night.

"Please speak with me, Deputy Phelps, or Ms. Steward if you have any information that might help us understand how Ms. West ended up in a canoe before daybreak. Time is of the essence. Even if you think something you overheard or saw is irrelevant, it might be the very thing we need to know. Robert Frost, who knew how to string words together better than I ever could, said, 'Courage is the human virtue that counts most.' If you know something, I ask that you think of Gretchen West and be courageous."

Jane followed the sheriff by doing what she could to reassure her guests. She told them that their safety was paramount to her and her staff and that they would be assisting the sheriff and his team in the investigation.

She then surrendered the podium to Professor Ashley, who invited the poets to express everything they were feeling by engaging in a stream-of-consciousness writing session. As pens and paper were distributed, Deputy Phelps signaled to Connor Jensen.

Heads swiveled when the lanky lawman and the towheaded poet exited the room together, but Professor Ashley quickly reclaimed their attention.

Jane turned to give him a grateful wave before trailing after Connor and the deputy. She knew they were headed to the William Faulkner Conference Room, and though Sheriff Evans hadn't invited her to sit in on his interview, that wouldn't stop her from listening in.

A narrow space ran between the two conference rooms, and if a person was very, very quiet, they could crouch in that space and overhear what was being said on the other side of the wall.

The space was accessed through a broom cupboard. If Jane pushed past the mops and brooms and pulled a lever at the back of the cupboard, an opening would appear. Unlike the Narnian wardrobe, this aperture led to a dark and dusty place. There was no tea with Mr. Tumnus, and she would have to be absolutely silent to avoid detection.

As there was no one in the hallway, Jane sent a text to the Fins telling them where she was going and that she was going radio silent until further notice.

Slipping into the cupboard, she fumbled about for the lever. It was cleverly hidden, but her fingers remembered its exact location. Seconds later, the back panel opened outward and she stepped into the blackness beyond.

She inched forward a bit before pausing to listen. The rumble of a low voice probably belonged to Sheriff Evans, but since Jane couldn't hear distinct words, she had to get closer.

The light from the conference room streamed through the air vent and cast a diamond pattern on the floor directly in front of Jane. She moved with infinite care and stopped just shy of the vent. She then crouched down, wincing as her knees let out soft cracks.

Wheels squeaked as someone shifted in a chair on the other side of the wall, and she heard Connor give the sheriff permission to record the interview.

Sheriff Evans then stated the time, date, and the names of the people in the room. This included Connor, Deputy Phelps, and himself.

In the heartbeat of silence that followed, Jane thought she heard a sound coming from the blackness a few feet away.

She stiffened.

It can't be, she told herself. *No one's here. It's just you.*

But then she heard it again.

Though it was little more than a disturbance of air, she knew she wasn't alone.

For about a body's length away, shrouded in darkness, someone else was breathing.

Chapter 9

Jane's heart pounded so loudly that she was sure everyone in the conference room could hear it. She tried to stay calm, to breathe slowly through her nose, but it felt like there wasn't enough air to be had. Her body flared with warmth, and her skin turned clammy.

It has to be Sinclair.

She seized hold of this idea like it was a ring buoy in a choppy sea.

Sinclair wasn't in Shakespeare's Theater, but he would've known about the sheriff's interviews. The Fins are always updating one another by text.

It had been nearly an hour since Jane had looked at her phone. She'd probably missed lots of messages.

Sinclair did what he could about the water-soaked Whitman poem and then came in here ahead of the sheriff. That's the only logical explanation.

As she pictured the beloved face of Storyton Hall's head librarian, Jane's panic abated. The more she visualized Sinclair's silver spectacles, tailored suits, and whimsical bow ties, the more foolish she felt for nearly coming undone.

She and Sinclair had developed ways of communicating with each other in the darkness. A light touch on the arm meant "I'm here." Two quick taps were a warning. A firm squeeze of the hand meant "Time to go."

Sinclair could move with catlike stealth, but since Jane had never been particularly light-footed, she waited until someone made noise in the conference room before crab-walking past the vent.

It was a risky thing to do because anyone staring directly at the vent would notice the movement, but she had to confirm that Sinclair was the person sharing the dark space with her.

As she stretched out her hand to touch him, she heard him breathe again.

Her hand froze in midair.

Sinclair never made a sound when he was back here.

But it was too late to stop now. Either the person in the dark was Sinclair, or it wasn't. Jane had no choice but to find out if it was friend or foe.

After all, someone had discovered the secret passage behind the walls. The person who'd tied Gretchen's body to the canoe had used that passageway to avoid detection. This person might know all of Storyton Hall's secrets—from its hidden passageways to the library in the attic turret.

Jane lowered her hand until it landed on an arm, and alarm bells instantly sounded in her head. Her fingers didn't encounter the fabric of a suit coat or dress shirt. They rested on bare skin.

The person jerked their arm away and breathed like

a horse pushing air out of its nose. Jane reared backward. Her palm slapped against the floor as she lost her
balance, and without caring about what anyone in the
conference room might hear, she spun around and
scurried back to the cupboard.

As she slipped through the opening, she heard Connor shouting.

The noise provided cover for her swift exit, and when
she burst out of the cupboard, the hallway was empty.
But she was too frightened to feel relief. Her hands
shook as she reached for her phone and sent a message
to the Fins: **Need help. Someone hiding between conference rooms.**

Before she could be seen by a guest, she ducked into
the ladies' room to wash her hands and brush the dust
off her clothes. She expected to hear back from one of
the Fins right away, and when she didn't, her fear grew
exponentially.

Glancing at herself in the mirror, she saw a woman
with wild eyes and stained clothes. She did her best to
pull herself together before hurrying back to the main
lobby.

In the lobby, she heard the din of many voices and
saw the guests streaming past the elevator banks toward
the back of the manor house.

"What's going on?" Jane asked the bellhop on duty.

"I don't know. They're following a man with glasses."

Jane approached a middle-aged woman with a kind
face and said, "Is your morning session over?"

The woman shook her head. "Someone told Professor Ashley that they couldn't write after hearing about
Gretchen. Lots of us felt the same way, so he said that
we all needed to get outside. We're going to sit on the

lawn and listen while he reads us some of his work. After that, he wants us to go off on our own, find a peaceful place, and see what words come to us. I'll probably go back inside. My brain can't function in this humidity."

The woman walked off. Jane waited until all the guests had vacated Shakespeare's Theater and entered the room. There wasn't a Fin in sight.

Where are they?

Even if two of them had accompanied the guests outside, one of the others should have responded to her text by now.

When Jane returned to the lobby, she was surprised to see a group of people mingling near the entrance of the conference room wing. In the middle of the group, she spied a nimbus of blond hair.

The sheriff had obviously released Connor, and the young man was now being questioned by his peers. Closed in by a semicircle of writers, Connor couldn't move unless they moved. And yet he didn't seem to mind the attention. He gesticulated as he talked and shook his head often. Though Jane couldn't hear his exact words, his tone of righteous indignation was perfectly clear.

Farther down the hall stood another group of people. Aunt Octavia and Uncle Aloysius were speaking with Mrs. Templeton. Jane's great-uncle had his back to her, but she noticed that he wasn't wearing his fishing hat again.

I really need to talk to Aunt Octavia about taking him to the doctor, she thought.

She'd barely added this to her mental list of concerns when Deputy Phelps rounded the corner with Farah Khan at his side.

The writers milling around Connor stopped talking. The silence was instantaneous, like someone had flicked a switch from on to off.

Farah looked terrified. She walked with her arms crossed over her chest. Her dark eyes were glassy, and she gnawed at her lower lip.

Jane knew that fear wasn't necessarily a mark of guilt. Most people were intimidated by the idea of a police interview. Even innocent people were scared. The justice system was flawed. Inadvertent errors could cost a person their freedom.

Sheriff Evans hadn't used the word "murder," but that didn't stop people from leaping to conclusions. Gretchen's death had winnowed the unofficial leaders down from three to two. If the other poets hadn't known Farah's name before, they did now. Jane couldn't blame them for being anxious or for seeking answers. She doubted she could go outside and listen to poetry after the sheriff's announcement.

Farah progressed down the hall until Connor stepped right in front of her.

"Why are you talking to Farah?" Connor shouted at Deputy Phelps. "Are you targeting Brightleaf writers? How come you won't answer our questions, but you expect us to answer yours?"

Phelps squared his shoulders and asked Connor to move. He refused to budge.

Jane rushed to intervene before the situation could escalate. She put a hand on Connor's arm and said, "I know this isn't easy, Mr. Jensen, but the sheriff and his team are trying to learn everything they can about Ms. West. To do that, they'll need to talk to anyone who knew her or had something in common with her. No one's being targeted. Why don't we get something to eat? I bet you could use a coffee or a smoothie. How does that sound?"

Connor nodded. "Yeah. I think I need some electrolytes. Not a smoothie, though. I make my own kombucha. I'll get one from my room." His gaze slid sideways and came to rest on Farah's face. "Don't worry. Everything's cool. You're going to be fine."

Was that some kind of code? Jane wondered.

Farah didn't reply as Phelps pushed past Connor.

Connor turned to the other writers. "I'll meet you guys outside. We all came here to write, so let's write!"

As Jane watched him walk away, her phone vibrated in her pocket. Now that the poets were heading out to the terrace, she decided to touch base with the Fins from the privacy of her office.

Dropping into her chair, she read through her text messages. Sterling and Butterworth were on their way to the cupboard to check out the space between conference rooms. Lachlan was observing the *en plein air* poetry session with Professor Ashley, and Sinclair was closeted in his office with Edwin.

Sinclair's message said: **Mr. Alcott and I are looking into the other matter. Forgive my delayed response to your SOS message. I was on the phone and didn't read it until after Mr. Sterling and Mr. Butterworth confirmed that they were on their way to investigate.**

Jane guessed that he and Edwin were reviewing Storyton Hall employee files. Sinclair must have put Jane's bike in a secure location and then met up with Edwin. By that time, Edwin had probably acquired a list of those employees who'd entered her great-aunt and -uncle's apartments within the past week or so. Discovering how the secret library had been infiltrated was of paramount importance, and Jane prayed that Sinclair and Edwin would soon have an answer.

The texts weren't the only notifications on her phone. She'd received an email from Gil as well. The email attachment was labeled POEMS.

Too agitated to stay in her office, she crossed the hall into the surveillance room and shut the door behind her. She stood in front of the screens without really seeing them. To clear her head, she decided to call home and check on the twins.

Fitz answered with a barely intelligible "Hey."

"Hi. What are the two of you up to?"

"We're trying to sink an Athenian ship, but Fitz keeps steering us into the rocks."

Jane heard a bleat of protest in the background.

"Well, when you're done defeating the Athenians, would you give your Spartan warriors a break and go fishing with Uncle Aloysius? I think he'd like the company."

"Use arrows!" Fitz cried. Then, "Sorry, Mom. An Athenian tried to board our ship, but he looks like a porcupine now. We'll be done with this mission when we take their captain hostage. Is Uncle Aloysius at the lake?"

"Not yet. Before you go out, make sure you all have plenty of water."

After urgently murmuring something to Hem, Fitz said, "Got it."

Confident that he and Hem would do as she asked, Jane hung up. The boys loved being outdoors as much as they loved playing Assassin's Creed, and as long as they were out on the lake with Uncle Aloysius, she wouldn't worry about them.

Jane's gaze moved from screen to screen. All the guests were outside, so there was very little activity. The housekeeping staff bustled about, while two members of the kitchen staff broke down the coffee service in the lobby. Before they had a chance to finish, Gil approached the table. When he held out his empty coffee cup, the staff member smiled and gestured at the urn. Gil said something that made both staff members laugh, then he saluted them and carried his cup to a nearby sofa. Pulling a wad of papers from his messenger bag, he settled back and began to read.

I should be reading poems too.

The thought vanished the moment the camera outside the conference room picked up Sterling and Butterworth. Their faces were grim. Jane sat down and waited for them to join her.

Butterworth entered the room carrying a damp rag. He set to wiping dust from his livery jacket while Sterling picked a cobweb out of his hair.

"No one's there. Not anymore," he said.

Butterworth tossed the rag aside with a grimace. "They left marks in the dust. The footprints are large, which means the person is probably of above-average height."

Jane frowned. "But where did they go? Is there another way out?"

Sterling wiped the cobweb on a tissue and tossed the sticky mess in the trash. "It's unlikely, but I'm going to put on coveralls and go back in."

"There were no footprints beyond where this person was sitting," Butterworth said. "Unless they apparated through the opposite wall into the empty conference room, they had to exit through the cupboard or climb through a hidden aperture in the ceiling."

Jane shook her head. "It's too high. Unless you're Spider-Man, you'd need a ladder."

Sterling went off to change, and Jane asked Butterworth to help her review the file of poetry Gil had emailed her.

The downturn of Butterworth's mouth indicated his displeasure, but he followed Jane into her office and patiently waited while she printed a stack of papers. She divided the stack in half, grabbed a pen from the mug on her desk, and said, "I'm going to read on the terrace. I could use some fresh air."

Butterworth's eyes were already moving over the poem on the top of his stack. "I'd prefer to read them with a large supply of whiskey at the ready, but as that isn't a viable option, I'll be at the bellhop stand."

Jane smiled at him. "You might enjoy them more than you think. After all, the work of one of these poets will soon be printed on greeting cards across the nation."

Tapping the top sheet of his stack, Butterworth murmured, "Not this one."

Jane found a terrace table in the shade and sat down to read.

The first poem on her stack was called "The Memory of Dough" and was about a mother teaching her son how to bake bread. It was sweet and sad. It felt like every word had been carefully chosen to evoke the sights, scents, and emotions of the kitchen from the poet's childhood home.

The author's name did not appear at the end of the poem. Instead, there was a number code. Jane assumed that every poet had been assigned a unique number.

That way, the judging was more likely to remain unbiased.

But who has the key?

Though she needed to know which poems had been written by Gretchen, Connor, and Farah, she decided not to contact Gil just yet. She still wanted to go through as many poems as possible, setting aside those replete with anger, bitterness, or jealousy. She didn't expect to come across any references to Tennyson or the Lady of Shalott, but if any of the writers mentioned a woman in a boat, a broken mirror, Arthurian legend, or the idea of embracing one's destiny—even if it led to death—then Jane would need to know the writer's identity.

After reading for almost an hour, she decided to get a glass of iced tea from the kitchens.

As she passed through the smaller of the two kitchens, where the prep cooks were washing and chopping vegetables, she thought of the images in the poem she'd read earlier. The kitchens were large rooms with high ceilings, gleaming steel countertops, and commercial appliances, but they operated inside of a home. They were still the heart of the house, regardless of their size.

In the bigger kitchen, pots of sauce simmered, rolls baked in the oven, and sous chefs scaled fish and butterflied meat.

Mrs. Hubbard was inspecting a tray of green and red macarons when Jane appeared.

"Didn't Jessie do a lovely job?" she asked.

"They're beautiful. The colors remind me of red and green apples."

Mrs. Hubbard put an arm around Jessie. "See that? You were born to be a pastry chef, my dear."

Beaming with pride, Jessie offered Jane a red macaron. "Apple with a white-chocolate filling."

Jane bit into the cookie, and a rush of flavors filled her mouth. The macaron was tart and sugary with a smooth and creamy interior.

"Wow. What a flavor combo. What are these for?"

"This afternoon is the Robert Frost Apple Picking Tea Party," said Jessie.

Mrs. Hubbard chuckled. "Try saying *that* three times fast. I want you to see the other treat Jessie and I have whipped up. Hmm, maybe after I get you something to drink. You look thirsty."

She left Jane and Jessie chatting and returned a few minutes later with a pitcher of iced tea and a tall glass containing several mint leaves.

"Green tea with mint leaves—very refreshing." Mrs. Hubbard filled the glass and handed it to Jane. "Now, the savory items on today's tea menu are turkey, Gouda, and apple tea sandwiches; an apple-shaped cheese ball surrounded by raw veggies; and a salad of apples, feta, and walnut served in a hulled apple. Our sweet treats are Jessie's marvelous macarons, apple upside-down cake, apple cider cutout cookies, and this yummy confection."

Jane cast an admiring gaze at the layered cake positioned squarely in the middle of a wooden stand at Mrs. Hubbard's station.

"This is my apple spice cake. The layers are filled with cinnamon cream cheese frosting, and the whole thing is topped with a tasty crumble. It's a cake posing as apple crisp topped with ice cream. You know I'm a sugar fiend at heart, but this naked cake will be a sweet, cinnamon overload. A little piece will go a long way, which is always good when you're feeding a crowd. Want a taste?"

It took all of Jane's willpower to politely decline. "I'm going to hold off until this afternoon. The boys went fishing with Uncle Aloysius, but I know they'll be back in time for tea." A thought struck her. "Aunt Octavia will be good and cross because she didn't make it to church this morning. Having to pass on cake and cookies will make her even crankier, the poor thing."

Mrs. Hubbard was holding a piping bag with both hands, so she jerked her head toward the walk-in fridge. "Not to worry, my sweet. I made two diabetic-friendly treats just for her. An apple yogurt parfait and an air-fried apple fritter. I have apple cider for the boys and an apple tea for the grown-ups."

"You think of everything." Jane gave Mrs. Hubbard a one-armed hug. She then refilled her glass and carried the stack of poems to her office.

She'd just put them down on her desk when Sterling appeared in her doorway. His blue coveralls were nearly gray with dust.

"I looked at every crack, seam, and nail hole in that space. There's no other way out other than the cupboard. Whoever went in must have exited shortly after you did and either joined the group of people in the hallway, hid in the bathroom, or busted into the William Faulkner without knowing the sheriff was there. I'll check the footage again—see if anyone has dust on their face or in their hair."

By lunchtime, Jane had read through all the poems in her stack. She walked to the lobby to see if Butterworth had finished his allotment.

He handed over the papers. "Fortunately, they improved after that first one. I found four meriting a closer look. You'll have to get the code from the Current Mood collective. The two gentlemen passed by a few minutes ago, bound for the Rudyard Kipling."

Jane brushed at a smudge of dust on Butterworth's lapel. "There. Now you're as dapper as always."

Butterworth pulled a face and then signaled a bell-boy. "Man the door, Pete. I need to change into a fresh suit."

Turning on his heel, Butterworth marched down the hall.

A crowd of writers was lined up at the café host stand, and as Jane approached, she couldn't help noticing the darkened, damp fabric on the seats of their shorts, pants, and skirts.

"Once we get a table, we can take turns running up to our rooms," one woman said to another.

Her companion nodded vigorously. "Oh, please. I can't sit through lunch in these jeans. I don't know what that man was thinking having us park our derrieres on that wet grass. It rained all night, and I'm soaked through."

The first woman pursed her lips. "Maybe we were supposed to be uncomfortable—you know, to help us express our feelings about Gretchen."

"Well, it didn't work because I couldn't concentrate on her. I kept thinking about how I should have brought another pair of pants. *That* got me thinking about how my ex used to overpack and how we always fought before every trip. I ended up being more annoyed than sad."

Jane didn't catch the rest of their conversation because she saw a break in the line and slipped through, directing a smile and an "excuse me" to the guest behind her.

Jeremiah and Gil sat at a table in the back of the café. Gil spotted Jane and gave her a friendly wave.

"Would you like to join us?" he asked when she came over.

"Thank you, but I just wanted to ask how I could identify the authors of the poems you shared with me."

Gil shook his head. "Stephanie's the only one who knows the key. Jeremiah and I wanted to judge purely on merit, and we figured the best way to do that would be to use numbers instead of names. The numbers change for each category too."

Jeremiah had been watching Jane closely. Now he cocked his head and said, "Why do you want to know who wrote what?"

Jane should have been prepared for this question, but she wasn't. She'd set aside all subtlety and tact in her determination to aid the sheriff in finding out how Gretchen West had ended up in that boat.

"I'm sorry. I should have explained myself first." Jane sat down in the empty chair. "The sheriff asked me to get to know the guests better. I thought the quickest way to do that would be to read their poetry. Poetry is personal. Not all of it is autobiographical, of course, but every writer leaves a bit of themselves in everything they create. Poems, novels, plays, songs—pieces of the writer's soul exist in those words."

Gil seemed satisfied by her answer. Jeremiah did not.

Something shifted in his gaze. It was no longer inquisitive, but as sharp as a knife's edge. Anger was there too, sitting just below the surface, out of sight. Jane could feel its presence.

Jeremiah leaned over the table, his eyes boring into Jane's. "Is that why you asked us for drinks? So you could get to know us?"

"Yes."

Gil reared back as if he'd been struck. "You knew that Gretchen was dead, but you kept that from us."

Jane nodded. "I found her the same morning I ran into the three of you out walking."

Looking pained, Gil said, "I guess I understand why you did what you did. You don't know us and we were right there, near the lake. Still, I wish you could have been straight with us."

"We were near the lake because we were on a walking trail," Jeremiah cried. "We weren't plotting the demise of one of our contestants! Why would we? And why wouldn't you tell us the truth so we could help? The future of our company is at stake!"

Jeremiah's anger had broken through, igniting sparks in his eyes and adding gravel to his voice. Gil put a hand on his friend's arm, but Jeremiah shook it off. "So, now what, Ms. Steward? Are we suspects? The three of us?"

Locking eyes with him, Jane answered, "Yes, you are."

Chapter 10

A ccording to Gil, Stephanie had rented a bike earlier that morning, intent on riding to Storyton village. Though they expected her back soon, Gil said
he'd send a message asking her to send Jane the name-
and-number key right away.

As her current line of inquiry was stymied, Jane
walked to the Henry James Library to see how Sinclair
and Edwin were progressing, but the door was locked.

Jane knocked three times and was gratified to hear
Sinclair call, "Coming!"

He opened the door for Jane, then closed and locked
it again.

"Why the extra precautions? Have you found something?" she asked.

"Not yet. The apartments have been cleaned by Mrs.
Templeton, with help from Martha, for the past year.
Every Wednesday at nine like clockwork. Mrs. Templeton records the areas requiring special attention in her
weekly planner. For example, on the second Wednes-

day in July, she and Martha polished all the wood furniture. On the last Wednesday, they washed the windows."

He led Jane over to a table strewn with papers and file folders and laid his hand down on a monthly planner with a floral cover.

"Mrs. Templeton has been with us for twenty years. And Martha? Five or six?"

"Seven."

Jane pointed at the planner. "Since they're above reproach, who else are you looking at?"

"First I had to be sure they were above reproach. It's been some time since I reviewed the personal and financial status of the staff members who clean and deliver food to your great-aunt and -uncle. As you know, Carlos and Nadia are in charge of delivering meals to their apartments. If they're not available, Mrs. Hubbard takes them up. After reviewing their files and speaking to each staff member, I can safely say that the culprit lies elsewhere."

At that moment, Edwin stepped out of Sinclair's office, carrying a stack of file folders. Seeing Jane, he smiled and said, "What do you think of our situation room? Looks a bit like an accountant's office during tax season, doesn't it?"

"It does. Are those work orders?"

He nodded. "For the past six months. Aunt Octavia remembers calling maintenance over a leaking faucet and hiring a local electrician to replace the ceiling fixture in their kitchen. She also hired a painter to paint her library and your uncle's study. Everyone checks out except for the electrician. I haven't been able to track down the person she used yet."

"What about Uncle Aloysius? Does he remember any projects or repairs?"

Edwin jerked his head at Sinclair. "He won't let me out, not even for lunch, so I haven't spoken with Aloysius."

"He's probably fishing now, anyway," Jane said.

When Jane turned to Sinclair, his eyes were filled with worry.

"He did mention a project—a sink installation for the half bath—but that was two years ago."

Jane's gaze moved to the shelves as if the answers to every question were hidden within the pages of the books, but the colorful leather and clothbound spines couldn't chase all the shadows away. Not this time, anyway.

"He's been more and more confused lately," she told Sinclair. "Tomorrow, I'm going to call Doc Lydgate's office and make an appointment for him. I'm sure Aunt Octavia is scared of what might be happening. I am too, but we can't help if we don't know what's wrong."

"I agree." Sinclair pulled out a chair for Jane. Once she was seated, he said, "Sterling discovered an anomaly. He found video footage of Deputy Emory. She stopped by last week, and your great-aunt met her in the lobby and led her to the elevator. Ms. Emory was in plainclothes. She stayed for a little over an hour and was noticeably happier upon leaving."

Jane wondered why Aunt Octavia hadn't mentioned the deputy's visit. She shared this thought aloud and was surprised to hear Edwin say, "She wouldn't go into details. She said it was a private chat *just between us chickens.*"

"I'll get her to elucidate. She's usually at her most congenial after she's had her tea."

Sinclair asked if any of the poems had caught Jane's notice. She explained how each poem had been assigned a number code and that she was waiting for Stephanie to send her the key.

"The mystery of the person in the passageway is at a dead end—unless Sterling spots someone on camera with cobwebs in their hair."

Edwin cocked his head. "Cobwebs?"

Jane moved closer to him. "I'm sorry I didn't tell you before, but I was in the passage between the two conference rooms earlier because I wanted to listen in on Connor's interview. I didn't stay long because I heard someone else breathing a few feet from me."

Edwin's jaw dropped.

"I thought it was Sinclair, so I reached out to touch his arm. But I ended up touching bare skin. It felt like tissue paper." Seeing the look on Edwin's face, Jane was quick to add, "Don't worry, I hightailed it out of there. I'm not brave enough to confront a boogeyman in the dark."

"They didn't speak? Or try to touch you?" Edwin asked.

"No. Butterworth and Sterling scoured the space and are positive they entered through the cupboard. All we know is the boogeyman has big feet."

Edwin's body went rigid. "I don't like this. It takes a special skill set to discover the secret architecture of a building this size. Even though the original blueprints were supposedly destroyed, I have to wonder if a copy still exists. Think about it. The missing Whitman poems. Someone moving behind the walls. How could a stranger discover these things? What if Gretchen West died because she saw this person in action? Maybe her death has nothing to do with the poetry competition."

Gooseflesh erupted on Jane's arms. "I never considered that."

"Where are Fitz and Hem?" asked Edwin.

"Fishing with Uncle Aloysius." She passed her hands over her face. "We need to take inventory of the secret library, but we don't have the time. We need days, not hours. We're stretched too thin."

"Let's focus on what we can do. We can learn why Deputy Emory visited your great-aunt. We can find out if the sheriff's interviews have produced a lead. We can examine the poetry and make a list of the guests requiring further study."

Sinclair's logical approach restored Jane's equilibrium. She flashed him a grateful smile and pulled out her phone to send instructions to Sterling, Butterworth, and Lachlan.

Her finger was poised over the screen when her phone began to buzz. Someone was calling her from her house.

"Hello?"

"Mom!" Hem shouted. "Come quick! Uncle Aloysius is sick!"

Jane was already moving as she replied with a shrill "I'm coming!"

Edwin beat her to the door and threw it open wide. Together, he and Jane ran down the hall, over the terrace, through the gardens, and across the Great Lawn.

When she burst into her house and saw the terrified faces of her sons, Jane feared the worst.

"Where is he?" she panted.

Fitz pointed to the living room, and Jane rushed in to find Uncle Aloysius in a fetal position on the sofa. His face was the color of aged parchment.

Jane dropped to her knees and put a hand to his cheek. "Uncle Aloysius? It's Jane. I'm here. Everything's going to be okay."

"Can you get a glass of water?" Edwin said to Hem as he phoned for help.

Jane heard him tell the person on the other line to send Doc Lydgate to their address without delay. While he tersely answered questions, Jane looked over her great-uncle, searching for an apparent injury. His shoes and pants were peppered with dried mud, but she saw no cuts in the fabric or bloodstains.

Returning her attention to his face, she saw that his lips were moving and bent closer to his mouth to hear the faint words.

His breath tickled the damp hair on her temple, but his whispering was more like a whimper. It was the frightened sound of a cowering dog or an injured animal.

Hem held out the glass of water, and Edwin moved forward to ease Uncle Aloysius onto his back. Jane propped his head on a pillow and coaxed a little water into his mouth.

"Try to drink," she said gently.

He managed a sip, and Jane coaxed him into taking a second.

"There you go. That's good. Edwin, run a washcloth under cold water and wring it out. Fitz? Hem? What happened?"

The boys stood shoulder to shoulder, their sun-kissed faces flushed and fearful.

Fitz spoke first. "We were going to go fishing, but we couldn't find Uncle Aloysius anywhere. Aunt Octavia said he was probably on his way to the lake, so we went down there."

"His boat was still at the dock. His pole and tackle-box were there too," Hem said.

Fitz leaned closer to his brother. "Mr. Lachlan was hanging out with the guests on the lawn, so we couldn't ask if we could borrow a Gator, but we took one anyway."

"We were worried about Uncle Aloysius," Hem added, mirroring Fitz's movement.

A powerful wave of tenderness rolled over Jane. Tears threatened, but she blinked them away. "You did the right thing. Where did you find him?"

"In the orchard. He seemed . . ."

"Lost."

A lump formed in Jane's throat as she accepted the damp washcloth Edwin handed her. She placed the cloth on Uncle Aloysius's forehead and got him to drink a few more sips of water.

"It's me. Jane." She spoke to him as if he were a spooked horse or a child with night terrors. "You're in my house. You're safe. Are you in pain? If you can't talk, can you nod or shake your head?"

Uncle Aloysius closed his eyes.

When Jane told him she was going to check him over for injuries, he didn't respond. She rolled up his pants to look at his ankles and saw no sign of swelling. She then gently squeezed his arms and legs. He had a few minor scratches on the backs of his hands and an angry red slash on the side of his neck. Otherwise, he appeared unhurt.

Did he have a stroke? Is that why he's weak and confused?

She turned back to her sons. "Can you meet the doc in the driveway so you can tell him what happened?"

Dual whines drifted in from the kitchen. The current of anxiety flowing through the house had reached

Merry and Pippin, and the young dogs needed reassurance.

"I'll let them out in the garden," Edwin said.

Jane heard the dogs yip and shift excitedly in their crates. Moments later, their nails clicked on the kitchen floor as Edwin herded them outside. "Come on, lads," he cooed. "Are you the best dogs? Yes, you are. You're the best dogs in the whole world."

Five minutes later, the twins returned with Doc Charles in tow.

Jane was only partially relieved to see him. He was too new and unfamiliar. His father knew everything there was to know about Uncle Aloysius's health. His was the calming, comfortable presence she'd been expecting.

If Doc Charles noticed her disappointment, he didn't let it show. He put his bag down and laid a hand on his patient's shoulder.

"Mr. Steward. I'm Doc Charles. Can you hear me?"

Uncle Aloysius moaned and slitted his eyes. Then his lids dropped like stage curtains, and he murmured what sounded like, "My. Hat. He . . ."

Doc Charles held his patient's right hand. "We're going to take care of you, sir. Can you squeeze my hand?"

Jane saw her great-uncle's fingers press into the back of the doctor's hand and had an irrational desire to squeeze him too. Doc Charles wasn't his father, but he clearly knew what he was doing.

After getting Uncle Aloysius to do the same thing with his left hand, Doc Charles took his blood pressure. He didn't do anything without first carefully explaining his actions to Uncle Aloysius, and even though the patient didn't respond, Jane appreciated the respect and care the younger Doc Lydgate was demonstrating.

"Your blood pressure is elevated, and you're dehydrated. I'm going to listen to your heart now."

Doc Charles also took his patient's temperature and shone a penlight into his eyes. Uncle Aloysius objected to this, which he demonstrated by shaking his head and murmuring, "Get the girl. The *girl*."

His voice was faint and slightly slurred. Doc Charles lowered his penlight and put a hand on Uncle Aloysius's shoulder. "We're all done. You can rest now. You did very well."

He pulled out his phone and sent a quick message. Then he met Jane's fretful gaze.

"An ambulance is on the way. Your uncle may have suffered a minor stroke. His weakness and confusion might also be the result of heatstroke. His pulse and temperature are higher than I'd like to see. Right now, he needs fluids and a more thorough evaluation."

"I'll call Aunt Octavia," Jane said.

Edwin put a hand on her shoulder. "I'll go see her. And after I tell her, I'll drive her to the hospital. You should stay with Uncle Aloysius."

Jane put her arms around Edwin and said, "I love you" in a quavering voice.

"I love you too," he whispered into her hair. After briefly tightening his embrace, he let her go and rushed out of the house.

The twins returned to the driveway to wait for the EMTs. When they arrived, Doc Charles gave them a quick summary of the situation before stepping aside to grant them access to Uncle Aloysius.

The EMTs spoke to Uncle Aloysius, but he didn't respond. However, the second they lifted him and transferred him to the gurney, words wafted from his mouth.

Thin as moth wings, they fluttered into the air and vanished.

Though the EMTs tried to calm him, he grew more and more agitated. When they strapped him on the gurney, his face crumpled in anguish.

"The girl!" He strained against the strap traversing his chest and thrashed his limbs. "Help . . . the girl!"

As an EMT slipped an oxygen mask over his face, Jane rushed to her great-uncle's side. "It's okay!" she cried. "I'll help the girl."

"Is someone injured?" an EMT asked Jane.

Without taking her eyes off Uncle Aloysius, she said, "I think he's talking about the guest who died two days ago. Everyone's distressed about what happened."

The words were no sooner out of Jane's mouth than Uncle Aloysius began jerking his head from side to side. He managed to dislodge the oxygen mask and gasp, "The girl. In water. *Help.*"

As the EMTs wheeled the gurney through the house, one of them said, "Don't worry, sir. You'll feel much better once you've had some fluids."

Tears slid down Jane's cheeks as she gathered her sons to her. After a quick hug, she told them the dogs were in the back garden and that she'd call the house as soon as she had news.

She was at the door when Hem said, "What if he's right, Mom? What if a girl needs help?"

Jane turned around. "We'd better make sure no else is in danger. Take a Gator and check any place that has water. The lake, the pool, the spa—all of them."

"We'll handle it," Fitz said.

For a brief moment, Jane saw the men her boys would become. Her strong, handsome, confident sons. She said, "I love you," and turned to follow the EMTs.

Uncle Aloysius didn't make a peep on the way to the hospital. Jane held his hand and reminded him of the time he'd taken Fitz and Hem fishing and Fitz had thrown his sandwich in the lake to attract a tuna fish. She didn't expect her uncle to respond, but his stillness was more unnerving than his distress, so she kept talking to him.

"It's been a while since you were over the mountain," she said in a high, bright voice.

"Over the mountain" was a term the locals used for the larger towns and cities beyond their isolated little valley. These places had strip malls, car dealerships, fast-food chains, and office buildings with enormous parking lots. They had lots of traffic lights and coffee shops, and the people living and working there moved at a much faster pace than those living in the tiny village of Storyton.

"Do you remember our last trip?" Jane went on. "We visited that specialty pet store and bought cookies for the puppies. The cookies looked like something Mrs. Hubbard would make. All of those different shapes. All perfectly frosted. You thought the fire hydrant and mailman cookies were hilarious. After we spent way too much money in that store, we had lunch at the Japanese restaurant. Remember how the chef built a volcano out of onion rings and set the whole thing on fire? Aunt Octavia screamed."

It took forty-five minutes to reach the hospital, and Jane talked the entire time. When the EMTs finally stopped and the rear doors of the ambulance were flung open, Jane suddenly felt seasick. The rocking motion of the ambulance coupled with her anxiety had her stomach in twists, and she had to lean against the ambulance as Uncle Aloysius was wheeled into the hospital.

A woman in scrubs with an ID badge swinging from a lanyard around her neck said, "You okay, hon?"

Jane nodded, but the woman wasn't convinced. She forced Jane to sit on the bench outside the emergency room doors and take deep breaths. After a minute or two, Jane felt well enough to ask where Uncle Aloysius had been taken.

"I'll show you."

Inside, she saw Edwin and Aunt Octavia standing in front of the desk in the emergency room waiting area. Aunt Octavia had a handkerchief pressed to her face, and Edwin was speaking softly to her.

Seeing Jane, Aunt Octavia began to cry.

"He's going to be okay," Jane said, wrapping her arms around her great-aunt.

"This is my fault!" Aunt Octavia wailed. "He hasn't been right all summer. And I didn't want to admit that he was forgetting things. I couldn't stand the thought that he might forget us—that he might forget *me!*"

While Jane did what she could to comfort her aunt, Edwin went off in search of strong coffee to give them something to do while they waited.

He'd barely returned with a drink carrier when the doors leading to the patient area opened and a nurse with a clipboard called out, "The family of Aloysius Steward?"

They followed her through the triage room until they reached a curtained area with a bed. Uncle Aloysius lay in the bed with his eyes closed. There was an IV pole on the right side of the bed, and a pulse oximeter covered the index finger of his left hand. He no longer wore an oxygen mask.

The nurse addressed Aunt Octavia. "Your husband is receiving fluids to treat his dehydration. He got very agitated when we tried to insert the catheter, so he's been given a mild sedative. His pulse is a little high, and we're keeping an eye on his oxygen levels. Do you know how long he was out in the heat?"

Aunt Octavia could only focus on her husband. She leaned over, stroked his hair, and whispered to him.

Jane replied to the nurse's question. "He was outside for a few hours. But that's not unusual. He goes fishing for long stretches of time and never had an issue with the heat before."

"He's sitting in a boat then, though," Edwin added. "He usually goes out early in the morning, and he always wears a hat. Today, he was walking around without a hat or water to drink."

"Any particular reason?" asked the nurse.

Jane stared at her uncle. "I wish I knew. The last time I saw him, he was inside. It was around eleven when I asked my sons to see if he'd like to go fishing with them. It was humid, but the rain had taken the edge off the heat, so I figured they'd be fine on the water for an hour. My sons couldn't find him for a while, and when they did, he seemed confused."

The nurse took a few notes. "Doctor Martinez is the attending overseeing Mr. Steward's care. He'd like to run some tests when Mr. Steward's feeling better. We'll move him to a room in a bit. Depending on how things develop, he may end up spending the night with us."

Aunt Octavia turned to face the nurse. "We haven't spent a single night apart for the past sixty years. If he's staying, so am I."

The nurse smiled at her. "I'm sure we can work something out. For now, we need to let Mr. Steward rest and wait for the fluids to do their job. One family member can stay with him."

Everyone looked at the single chair near the bed. There was no question who'd take it.

Aunt Octavia dropped her handbag on the chair and said, "Edwin, you're such a dear for driving me here. Jane, I may need you to get a few things from home and have a driver deliver them here. Not Sterling, of course. You need him back at the manor house."

"But—"

"Don't argue, my sweet. You have important things to do, which means you can't waste the day pacing around in the waiting room. Your uncle is going to be fine. He's in the best of hands. And you don't need to worry about me either. I just need a book and a sweater—these places are always so cold—and I'll be all set."

Jane was torn. She knew she should return to Storyton Hall. She hadn't touched base with the sheriff for hours, and Stephanie should have emailed by now, which meant Jane could match the poets to their poems.

And yet Uncle Aloysius was here. Aunt Octavia was here. How could Jane leave them?

Aunt Octavia took Jane's hand. "Do you think a few mountains can separate us? A few miles of road? Do you think I won't feel loved and supported because you need to go home and make things right there? Darling girl. That isn't how love works. I carry your love in my handbag of a heart, and I can take it out any time I need it. Go home now. We'll be fine."

Relenting, Jane gave her a hug and kissed her uncle's cheek, which was as dry as onion skin, but no longer waxy or pale.

With a final wave to Aunt Octavia, Jane and Edwin left.

They were halfway to Storyton when Jane realized that she hadn't called her sons and immediately dialed her home number. The phone rang and rang.

"No answer," she told Edwin.

"They were going to drive around the grounds, right? They're probably still doing that."

But Jane felt that twisting sensation in her stomach again, and she knew something was wrong. "Drive faster," she whispered.

They were ten minutes from Storyton when Jane's phone rang. She recognized the number. It was the phone in the archery hut.

"Mom!" Hem panted. "Uncle Aloysius was right! There *is* someone in water. You know that big hole they dug at the folly? It's full of water, and someone's floating in there."

"Oh God."

Edwin heard the fear in her voice and hit the gas. The car shot forward, racing toward another disaster.

Chapter 11

Fitz and Hem met Jane and Edwin in front of Storyton Mews. They both spoke at once, but Jane couldn't hear anything over Merry and Pippin's frenzied barking.

The dogs tugged on their leads, desperate to reach the aviary cages. Inside the cages, a motley collection of hawks, falcons, and owls flapped their wings and screeched with agitation.

Edwin took charge of the dogs. He commanded them to heel and led them to the Gator. The barking ceased.

"Now," Jane spoke into the blessed quiet, "say that again. One at a time."

"Mr. Butterworth wants you to meet him by the construction fence at the folly," said Hem.

Fitz said, "Is Uncle Aloysius okay?"

Jane wanted to put an arm around each of her sons and pull them close. She wanted to hold them and stroke their hair like she used to when they were small. Now she'd have to make do with words.

"He's stable. He's getting fluids and will stay in the hospital overnight. He'll get good rest there, and Aunt Octavia is with him. Because of you two, Uncle Aloysius is going to be okay. You found him and got him to our house. I'm so proud of you." She smiled tenderly at her sons. "Take Merry and Pippin home now. You all need a rest. But give me a hug first."

The boys smelled of cut grass and sweat. Their shirts clung to their torsos, and their sun-warmed hands pressed against Jane's back as they each gave her a quick, but fierce hug.

As Edwin passed the dog leads to Fitz and Hem, he said, "Well done, gentlemen."

The boys were glowing as they turned toward home.

Jane slid into the Gator's driver's seat and waited for Edwin to climb in. When he sat down, she leaned over, cupped his bristled cheek in her palm, and kissed him. She tried to infuse the kiss with all the love and gratitude she could.

After they broke apart, she faced forward and metamorphosized. She no longer looked like a mother or a lover. She looked like the Guardian of Storyton Hall. Her eyes were as hard as flint as she pushed the Gator to its top speed.

She brought the vehicle to an abrupt halt within inches of the orange safety fence and hopped out. Butterworth stood inside the fence, his face set in an inscrutable mask.

But Jane, who'd known him her whole life, saw beyond the mask. Two tiny lines had sprouted between his

brows, and his fingers curled inward like talons. Butterworth was upset.

"This way," he said, beckoning Jane and Edwin past a
mound of debris to the area earmarked for the new
folly. The foundation hole had been dug two weeks ago,
and the footings had gone in on Monday. Since then,
there'd been two heavy rains.

Starting on Monday night, the remnants of a tropical
storm had soaked the valley for a solid twenty-four
hours. Because the folly was at the bottom of a hill,
water had sluiced into the foundation hole the whole
time. Last night's downpour had filled the hole with
more water.

It was in this muddy pool that a body floated.

The woman was facedown. Her bent arms bobbed
like goalposts on either side of her head, and her wet
hair fanned out in the water. She wore a white floral
shirt and turquoise shorts. The heels of her bare feet
looked like two turtle heads poking through the water.

A drowned woman was bad enough, but the scatter-
ing of wildflowers in the water was even worse.

"Ophelia?" Jane asked, staring at the great blue lo-
belia, cowbane, and butterfly weed. There were oxeye
daisies and golden asters too, suspended half-in and
half-out of the water. The flowers reminded Jane of
foundered ships.

Butterworth said, "That was my thought as well. All
of these flowers grow in the meadow between the orchard and the woods."

Edwin got down in a catcher's stance. "They haven't
started to wither, which means they can't have been
here very long."

Jane glanced around the site. "Did you see shoe
prints?"

"None." Butterworth pointed at the edge of the hole to the left of the dead woman. "The killer probably stood there, in that patch of gravel, and lowered the body into the water. If they'd gone into the hole to drown him, they'd have left tracks in the mud."

The pronoun startled Jane.

Him?

She scanned the body more carefully. Between the lean limbs and long hair, she'd erroneously assumed this was a woman. Now she noticed the abundance of hair on his arms and legs. She also saw the collection of bracelets made of braided hemp on his right wrist and a smart watch with an orange band on the opposite wrist.

Edwin skirted around the edge of the hole and peered down at the body. "His hair is dyed. The roots are just starting to grow out, but his natural hair is a few shades darker. He has an athletic build and the kind of tan you get from spending lots of time outside."

"Connor," Jane said. "He surfs, swims, kayaks—you name it. His hair is platinum blond."

"Shall I call the sheriff?"

Jane nodded at Butterworth before taking out her own phone. She punched in a number and waited for Lachlan to answer. "We have a Rip van Winkle at the folly. We can't say for sure, but we think it's Connor Jensen."

Lachlan made a strangled noise.

"When the professor was reading to the poets on the Great Lawn, did Connor leave the group? Did anyone else?"

"There were a few latecomers, but once the professor got started, no one left. He read three poems and then talked about how to channel disbelief or horror into words. At that point, he encouraged the poets to find a comfortable place to just sit with their feelings until they were ready to write. He wanted them to hear the words in their head before committing any to paper."

Jane grunted in frustration. "Which means people were wandering all over the grounds."

"Yes. I decided to follow Farah at a safe distance. She went to the Anne of Green Gables Gazebo, lay down on the bench seat, and cried. Eventually, she sat up and threw her notebook and pen onto the grass. After she went inside, I read all the poems in her notebook. Some are pretty dark. She's angry at a certain man. She doesn't name him, but she wishes him dead in several poems."

Jane went very still. "Including drowning?"

"Drowning, stabbing, poisoning, suffocating. Pushing him off a bridge. In one line, she impales the guy with a spear."

For a moment, Jane was whisked back in time to a Halloween night when the twins were in third or fourth grade. After an evening of trick-or-treating with their friends, the boys spent the night with Aunt Octavia and Uncle Aloysius. They'd watched *Hocus Pocus,* and Uncle Aloysius had read them Edward Gorey's *The Gashly-crumb Tinies.*

The book used verse to tell the story of how twenty-six children had met with their deaths. Because of the various methods in which the children died, coupled with Gorey's morbid drawings, some found the book nightmarish. Others found it amusing. Naturally, the twins had loved it. A year later, Uncle Aloysius had given them their own copy.

'I *is for Ida who drowned in a lake.* J *is for James who took lye by mistake.*'

"Are you there?" asked Lachlan.

"Yeah. Sorry. When did you last see Connor Jensen?"

After a pause, Lachlan said, "Walking to the conference room to meet the sheriff."

Jane thought of the stranger in the secret space between the walls. She'd never stopped to consider why someone would be there. Had they wanted to listen to the interview too? "After the interview, I saw him in the conference room wing. He and Deputy Phelps exchanged words, and then Connor went to his room to get something to drink. I need to know where he went next. Do you remember seeing him outside?"

"I remember seeing him on the lawn, but I don't know where he went after the group separated."

"We need to track his movements. Maybe Farah ran into Connor on her way back inside. With him gone, she's now favored to win the contest."

After a brief moment of silence, Lachlan said, "I don't think she could overpower him."

"He's floating facedown in a hole filled with muddy water. We don't know how he ended up like that, and our best chance of finding out what happened is to learn whom he interacted with in the past two hours."

Lachlan was already walking to the surveillance room. He promised to locate Farah and track Connor's movements as soon as possible. Jane hung up and looked a question at Butterworth.

"The sheriff's on his way," the butler said.

Edwin touched Jane's shoulder. "Unless you need me to stay, I'll go check on the boys and see if Sinclair could use my help. Should I ask Mrs. Templeton to pack a bag for Aunt Octavia?"

"Yes, please." Jane lowered her eyes in shame. "For a second, I forgot they were at the hospital."

"They'll be having tea on the terrace soon enough," Edwin whispered.

Not long after Edwin ascended the hill and disappeared from view, another Gator approached. Sterling was in the driver's seat. His passengers were Sheriff Evans and Deputy Phelps.

Sterling stopped the vehicle outside the construction fence and called to Jane, "I'm going back to the garages to direct the coroner's van!"

Jane and Butterworth remained near the fence to give Phelps and the sheriff the space and quiet they needed to assess the crime scene. As much as Jane wished Connor's death could be accidental, it was extremely unlikely that he'd drowned in a very deep puddle.

"I wish we'd found him in the river," she whispered to Butterworth. "He loved being in the water. He should have been where it was clean and clear. This brown, muddy mire feels undignified. Especially if he's supposed to represent Ophelia."

Keeping his eyes on the sheriff, Butterworth said, "Either someone wanted to disgrace or humiliate this young man, or this was simply a convenient and isolated spot where the killer could meet their victim."

As if he'd heard Butterworth's observation, the sheriff put his hands on his hips and turned in a circle. When he finished taking in the surrounding landscape, he said, "How long does it take to get here from the house? Fifteen minutes? Twenty?"

"Twenty. Unless you're moving at a brisk pace."

Sheriff Evans pointed at the ground. "And these shoe prints? Are they yours?"

Jane glanced at her mud-crusted ballet flats. "Mine,

Edwin's, and Butterworth's. And maybe the twins' too. They found the body."

The vexed tone of the sheriff's previous question vanished. "That's unfortunate. Are they alright?"

"I don't think the enormity of what they saw has hit them yet. Between this and seeing Uncle Aloysius taken away in an ambulance, they've had a helluva day. We'll talk it through later on. No matter what else is going on, I'll make time to do that."

Jane knew she shouldn't direct her anger at the sheriff, but she wanted to lash out at someone. Two people had been killed on her property. Two guests who'd come to her resort hoping to change their lives for the better were now dead. Uncle Aloysius was in the hospital, and she knew that his issues were more serious than dehydration or heatstroke.

Sheriff Evans interrupted her pity party by saying, "With all the guests moving around outside, it won't be easy to know who was here with Mr. Jensen. Hopefully, Deputy Emory saw something useful. Were there any anomalies this morning? Other than the professor moving his session outdoors?"

Jane repeated what Lachlan had told her about Farah Khan.

"Where is that notebook now?"

"Lachlan probably left it on my desk. I should also have an email from Stephanie explaining who wrote which poems."

The sheriff said something else, but Jane didn't hear him. "Sorry. I just realized that Stephanie went for a bike ride to the village this morning. I don't know when she got back, but I'll find out. There isn't much to do in the village on a Sunday morning. Almost everything's closed except the Pickled Pig and The Old Curiosity Shop. And Phoebe will open the Canvas Creamery if one of the high school kids is available to work. I'll call and ask if Stephanie came in for a coffee."

"Please do. Ah, here comes the doc."

Jane turned to see Doc Lydgate picking his way over the uneven ground. Sterling followed in his wake, carrying the doc's bag.

"You're going to make sure I go out with a bang, aren't you, Miss Jane? Can't you tell the villains to book their stay elsewhere?"

"I wish I could." Jane smiled at the man who'd taken care of her entire family for most of their lives.

The doc's gentle gaze moved from Jane's face to the body in the water.

"Ready when you are, Sheriff."

The sheriff signaled to Phelps. They each grabbed hold of a foot and pulled Connor toward the edge of the hole. Together, they eased him out of the water and rolled him onto his back. He lay on the ground like a beached seal, his milky eyes gazing skyward.

Sheriff Evans gave Phelps a few minutes to photograph the body. Then he looked over at Jane, Butterworth, Doc Lydgate, and Sterling and said, "We could say something before we continue."

They all knew what he meant.

If Sinclair were here, he could recite a poem or a passage from memory. It would be short but poignant—a respectful farewell. And even though Connor was a stranger to them all, Sinclair would find the right words for his send-off.

Jane didn't share Sinclair's gift. Her mind was too

full of questions and fears to recall a single line of poetry, let alone an entire verse.

Butterworth came to the rescue.

He moved closer to Connor's body, clasped his hands in front of his waist, and closed his eyes.

"Toni Morrison once said, 'All water has a perfect memory and is forever trying to get back to where it was.'" He let the words linger in silence for a moment before continuing. "You loved the water, Connor, and in the end, you were surrounded by it. We hope that your last perfect memory was being held in its arms as it took you back to where you began."

Tears danced on Jane's lashes as she listened to Butterworth. She never took him for granted, but times like this made her acutely aware of how lucky she was. She was surrounded by several amazing father figures—all of whom possessed great strength and tenderness.

They'll see you through this.

Doc Lydgate approached Connor's body, and Sterling followed with the doc's bag. He helped the doctor get down on his knees, which snapped like twigs as he bent his legs.

"Old age isn't always dignified," he announced to the group at large. "But it's better than the alternative. Who knows what this young man would've experienced had he'd lived as long as I have?"

Doc Lydgate peered into his patient's ears, eyes, and mouth. He picked up his hand and studied the fingernails. After unbuttoning his shirt, which was white with a pattern of orange and green palm leaves, he gently probed the dead man's abdomen.

"Based on how he was found, we might assume the

cause of death is drowning. However, there's bruising to the front of the neck, which makes me wonder what happened before the young man fell, or was dropped into, the water."

The sheriff leaned over to examine the bruises. "Asphyxiation?"

The doc glanced up at him. "It's possible. There's no bruising to the back of the neck, so if something cut off his air supply, the pressure was applied here." He made a wide circle around Connor's Adam's apple. "That's not all. We also have pinpricks in the pupils and swelling to the tongue and throat. And the abdomen feels distended."

Jane remembered what the ME had said about Gretchen's death. "The ME believes Gretchen West ingested some kind of drug. A sedative. Do you think that's what happened here too?"

"Until the lab results come back, that's just a theory," clarified the sheriff. "The ME put a rush on them, so we should have them back by the end of the day."

"I imagine the postmortem will hold the answers to this young man's death as well. I'll ask Charles to head over to the coroner's office and offer his assistance."

Once again, the doc held Sterling's arm. The head chauffeur slowly raised the older man to his feet and picked up his medical bag.

Turning to Jane, Doc Lydgate said, "I heard about your uncle. The hospital folks will call Charles with an update, and he'll reach out to you soon afterward. I know that you're one tough cookie, but there's a limit to the amount of stress a person can handle at once. Over the next twenty-four hours, I want you to find time to sit quietly, drink plenty of water, eat high-energy foods, get a good night's rest, and ask for help when you need it."

Jane latched on to the warmth in the doc's voice and the kindness in his eyes. "If I do all that, do I get a lollipop?"

"I'll put one aside. If I remember correctly, you like green the best."

"I sure do. Does Uncle Aloysius take a lollipop after he sees you?"

Doc Lydgate cupped Jane's chin and smiled. "Every time. He closes his eyes, holds out his hand, and says, 'Surprise me.'"

After Sterling helped the doc into the Gator and drove off, the sheriff told Jane there was no need for her to wait for the coroner's van.

"I know you want to have a second look at the poetry."

This was true. Jane also wanted to call Phoebe and check the bike rental log at the recreation desk. The log would tell her when Stephanie had left Storyton Hall that morning and when she'd returned.

Jane glanced at Connor's face in farewell before shifting her gaze to Sheriff Evans. "I can't help wondering if Connor let something slip during his interview—something that got him killed. Or if his killer wanted to be sure Connor was out of the running to win the contract."

"As a whole, the writers agree that Gretchen West, Farah Khan, and Connor Jensen were each favored to win. But why? Because they'd attended Brightleaf? Because they've had more poetry published? Or because their work is clearly superior to everyone else's? I put this question to Ms. Khan and Mr. Jensen. Ms. Khan told me that her poems are known for being honest and empathetic. Mr. Jensen said that optimism sets his poems apart. These two have been in competition for years. There's no love lost between them, but they're always polite to each other."

"In public, that is."

The sheriff nodded. "True. During our interviews, they both were very open about wanting to win. They both believed they had a good shot. They claimed to have known Ms. West by her work only, though Ms. Khan had heard rumors about animosity between Ms. West and Mr. Connor. They spent a summer together at Brightleaf and were always vying for Professor Ashley's approval. We've contacted several other students from that year's program, and they agree that the mutual dislike between the two writers was obvious to all."

With little else to learn from the sheriff's interviews, Jane left Butterworth with Connor and returned to the manor house. At the recreation desk, she asked the staff member for the bike rental log.

Stephanie's was the most recent entry. She'd checked out a bike at ten and returned it a little after one. Unless she'd spend hours drinking coffee in the Canvas Creamery or perusing the shelves of the Pickled Pig, it had taken Stephanie a very long time to ride to the village and back.

Jane replaced the log and headed to her office. She shut the door, guzzled some water from the bottle she kept on her desk, and dialed Phoebe's number.

"I was *just* thinking about you," Phoebe trilled. "I'm planning my fall coffee menu and just added a cinnamon latte to the list."

"My favorite fall drink. What time did you open today?"

Over the whir of a blender in the background, Phoebe said, "Nine thirty. I didn't want to, but I had no choice. With all the people coming from over the mountain to see Pig Newton, I figured there'd be a riot if they didn't get their caffeine fix."

Jane had no idea what her friend was talking about but could only focus on one line of questions at a time. "Who else is open?"

"Roger opened The Old Curiosity Shop at eleven, and Geppetto's opened at noon," Phoebe said, referring to the toy store.

Maybe Stephanie could've spent a few hours in the village.

"Did you serve Stephanie Harbaugh this morning? You'd remember her from the wine tasting and last night's dinner. She's the PR person for Current Mood. The pretty blonde?"

Phoebe hadn't seen Stephanie, but she put Jane on hold to ask her high school helper. Seconds later, she was back. "Katie said that a woman named Stephanie ordered a café au lait with oat milk. She was very friendly and put a five-dollar bill in the tip jar. This was around ten thirty. Why do you want to know?"

"This is for your ears only, but we've had another suspicious death."

"*No,*" gasped Phoebe. "Oh Jane. I'm so sorry. How can I help?"

Jane wished there was something her friend could do. And then she realized that Phoebe could help her track Stephanie's movements. "Could you find out which businesses she visited? She rented a bike for several hours, and I want a picture of how she spent her time. It makes no sense for her to be involved in either of the deaths, but the sheriff asked me to consider all anomalies."

"I can totally do that. I'll just say that we're looking for her credit card. I'll text you as soon as I've talked to the other merchants." Lowering her voice, Phoebe said, "Gil called. He asked me to be his dinner date tonight. I was thrilled because I really like him. But Jane . . . is he a suspect?"

"Until the sheriff rules him out, everyone is. I'm really sorry."

Phoebe sighed. "It's hard to be single these days. Dating can be downright dangerous."

Jane placed her phone on its charging pad and touched the space key to wake up her computer. She clicked on her email inbox, opened the file attached to Stephanie's message, and hit the print button.

Next, she spread out the poems she'd set aside and began matching names to the numbers on each poem.

Jane was unsurprised to discover that most of the poems in her folder had been composed by Gretchen, Connor, and Farah. Most, but not all. There was one poem that started off with a person floating in water until memories of violence slowly weighed them down until they couldn't keep their head above water. In the end, they drowned. The poem, called "The Buoyancy of Forgetting," had been written by Amelia Emerson.

"Deputy Emory? Did she submit this yesterday?"

Jane cross-referenced the date of the submission. She couldn't believe what she saw, so she checked it again. Deputy Emory had submitted the poem months ago, when she'd registered for the conference. According to Stephanie's records, she'd submitted a poem for every category since the competition started on Thursday.

This is news to me, thought Jane.

She couldn't understand why Deputy Emory would have kept this information from her. What did she have to hide?

Four people had poems containing powerful emotion and violent imagery. Two of the four were now dead. How many secrets were the remaining two keeping?

Jane's hand trembled as she picked up her phone to call Sheriff Evans.

Chapter 12

When Jane's call to the sheriff went straight to voice mail, she left a message asking him to get back to her as soon as possible. Her next call was to the department's non-emergency number.

"How may I direct your call?" said the desk sergeant.

"This is Jane Steward up at Storyton Hall. Is Deputy Emory available?"

Paper rustled in the background. "Ma'am, Deputy Emory is at your place. Would you like me to radio her?"

"That's okay. I'm bound to bump into her sooner or later. What about Deputy Phelps?"

"He's with the coroner. The sheriff dispatched two more officers to Storyton Hall twenty minutes ago. Can they assist you?"

As much as she welcomed their presence, Jane couldn't ask those officers about Deputy Emory's behavior, so she thanked the desk sergeant and ended the call.

Rocking back and forth in her chair, she stared at her phone screen and wondered what to do next. Nothing came to her. She felt like a cracked egg—empty of any substance. A headache was flowering behind her eyes, so she let her lids fall shut.

She tried to relax, but when her headache became more pronounced, she opened her eyes and rifled through the top drawer of her desk for a bottle of Tylenol. As she popped two capsules into her mouth, her Hopes and Dreams board caught her eye.

It was so colorful that it was hard to miss. Pink, yellow, orange, and green stickie notes in neon hues covered the board. Jane had written a goal on each one. When her gaze landed on "Rebuild the Folly," a wave of sadness rolled over her.

"I'm so sorry, Connor."

Saying his name aloud conjured an image of the Connor she'd seen at last night's scavenger hunt. He'd been so animated. His liveliness and sense of humor made him the center of attention. With his shining hair, easy smile, and relaxed manner, he probably stood out in any crowd.

His life wasn't all sunshine and rainbows, or he wouldn't have become a writer. He'd been brave enough to tap in to the memory of his sister's death and use words to express his pain, regret, and deepest longings.

Did Connor's poetry hint at those longings? Did they contain his secrets? What would his guest room tell her about him?

"Only one way to find out," she mumbled.

She'd just sent a text to the Fins, asking if anyone could meet her in Room 213, when there was a knock on her door.

"Come in."

Sue Ross, the reservations manager, stepped into Jane's office.

"I just got off the phone with the governor's communications director. Apparently, the governor forgot that it's his wedding anniversary tomorrow, and he's asking to book a last-minute stay with us. His wife is crazy about Pig Newton, and Tobias Hogg agreed to let her take a photo with Virginia's most famous pig. Move over, Wilbur and E. B. White. Pig Newton and Tobias Hogg are trending. They have over a million social media followers!"

Jane gestured at the chair facing her desk. "You'd better sit down."

"Okay, but I have to call the governor's office back in five minutes."

Passing a hand over her face, Jane said, "He can't stay with us, Sue. There've been two suspicious deaths on our property in the past seventy-two hours. Storyton Hall isn't safe for our current guests, let alone the governor and the first lady."

Sue wasn't the slightest bit ruffled by what she'd just heard. Ever the professional, she simply nodded her head and said, "Understood. I'll see if the governor is willing to postpone his visit until this weekend."

"Offer him a private cottage. Tell him it's even more romantic than a suite."

"The same one we rented to the writer who gave the twins their poodles? What was her name?" Sue snapped her fingers. "Ms. Limoges!"

The thought of Olivia Limoges and her faithful canine companion, Captain Haviland, nearly brought a smile to Jane's face. Her facial muscles refused to move, but there was more warmth in her voice when she said, "The one and only. Thank you, Sue."

Lachlan had a falconry lesson in an hour, which gave him plenty of time to help Jane search Connor's room.

"We need to hurry," he told her as she used her master key to unlock the door.

"Because of your lesson?" Jane asked once they were both safely inside.

Lachlan shook his head and held out a pair of disposable gloves. "No. Butterworth is supposed to get the key to this room and hand it over to the officers waiting in the lobby."

Jane felt a stab of panic. "Is one of them Deputy Emory?"

"She's still pretending to be a guest. These officers arrived fifteen minutes ago."

"I'll take the writing desk. You check the bathroom," Jane said, already moving toward the desk. She let her eyes roam its surface as she stuffed her hands into her gloves.

If she expected to find notebooks of poetry as she had in Gretchen's room, Jane was to be disappointed. Connor had a laptop, but it was password-protected, as was the phone plugged into a charger on his nightstand.

"This is interesting."

Jane glanced over to where Lachlan stood in the bathroom doorway, an orange pill bottle in his hand. He gave it a shake and said, "Tramadol. It's for back pain. It's a controlled substance that should never be combined with alcohol."

"Maybe that's what killed Gretchen. A bunch of

those pills combined with her anxiety meds?" Jane shrugged. "Anything else in there?"

"No. I'll check the closet next."

While Lachlan hastily searched the pockets of Connor's shirts and pants, Jane opened the mini fridge. Inside, she found three glass bottles. She took out a bottle, unscrewed the top, and sniffed. It smelled a bit like vinegar and a bit like a wet sponge.

How does anyone drink this stuff?

Jane replaced the bottle and turned her attention to the nightstands. Both were empty, so she headed over to the bureau. The top drawer held socks, boxer briefs, and a wallet. She was reaching for the wallet when Lachlan grabbed her arm.

"We have to go." He shut the drawer and ushered Jane out the door. "Gloves!" he whispered as they jogged to the stairwell.

Behind them, they heard Butterworth's deep baritone. "This is Mr. Jensen's room. I'll be right outside should you require any assistance."

On the way back to the ground floor, Jane told Lachlan how Deputy Emory had registered for the poetry conference months ago.

Lachlan frowned. "Did she deceive the sheriff? Or does he already know?"

"He hasn't returned my call yet, so I have no idea. Everyone knows that Amelia Emory is artistic. She paints, draws, writes, gardens, and bakes treats for her coworkers. Sheriff Evans raves about her pastries, though he's always quick to assure me that Mrs. Hubbard is still Top Chef in his book." Jane sighed. "Think of how many times she's wandered through this house. How many investigations has she worked? What if she's been studying Storyton Hall from the beginning? What if she didn't transfer to our little village to escape the violent big city, but to gain access to my family home?"

After taking a moment to mull this over, Lachlan said, "It's possible, but I've spoken with her about PTSD and some of the coping mechanisms I've learned. If she wasn't sincere when she asked for my help dealing with trauma from her time as a city cop, then I should consider a new career."

Jane wagged her finger at him. "You can't do that. I can't imagine a life where Eloise and I don't live in the same town."

"I'd better get to the Mews. Ms. Khan is part of my group lesson, which is a good thing because the birds will sense if she's nervous or scared."

As Lachlan walked away, Jane took a seat on one of the steps. "We must be pretty desperate if we're hoping some injured raptors can identify our murderer."

Her phone buzzed, and she read the text from Phoebe.

Not only had Phoebe spoken to all the merchants open for business that morning, but she'd created a rough timeline of Stephanie's movements. She'd visited the Canvas Creamery, the Pickled Pig Market, and Storyton Pharmacy. According to Anna, she'd come in around eleven and spent fifteen minutes looking at greeting cards before buying a pack of gum and a roll of tape. She then hopped back on her bike and rode off toward Storyton Hall.

Jane organized her thoughts by voicing them. "She's in great shape, which means she could have been back on our grounds by eleven thirty. If she took the service road, no one would've seen her return. But how to get Connor to meet her at the folly? Or incapacitate him once they were alone together? She's a beautiful woman. Did she seduce him? Drug him? But why would she want to kill one of the contestants in the first place? She wouldn't seek negative publicity when she's in charge of PR. Or would she? Maybe she's not as loyal to Current Mood Cards as she pretends to be."

The sheriff would need a warrant to access Stephanie's phone, and he couldn't even interview her until he finished meeting with the medical examiner.

A line from *War and Peace,* which had taken Jane the better part of July to read, popped into her head.

"The strongest of all warriors are these two—Time and Patience."

Jane was running out of both. The winner of the poetry contest would be announced at the end of tonight's Poetry of the Plate banquet. All the guests were scheduled to depart by noon tomorrow. But with two unsolved murders, things couldn't unfold as they should.

Sitting alone in the cool stairwell, Jane felt despondent. She'd been in this position before and had always rallied.

You can't wait on the sheriff. You need to act.

Jane's inner voice rarely steered her wrong. In this quiet place, the simple thought rang with truth. She nodded to herself and sent a text to the Fins.

Meeting in the surveillance room. Fifteen minutes.

She closed her message app and dialed her aunt's number.

"Oh, Jane! The doctor was just here. He asked me all these questions about your uncle's memory. If he's been forgetting the time or date. If he seemed confused about things that didn't used to confuse him. If he's been losing or misplacing things. When he asked if he could follow a recipe, I laughed. Aloysius? Cooking! The very idea. Do you know what else? He wanted to know if my husband had good hygiene and was showering, shaving, and brushing his teeth regularly. I know he's been getting more forgetful lately, but the man hasn't become a lesser life-form over the past few months!"

"Have they ruled out heat exhaustion as the cause?"

Aunt Octavia sucked her teeth. "They're still saying they don't know exactly what's going on with him, but the good news is that he's awake."

Jane's heart leaped. "That's such a relief! Does he know what happened?"

"At first, he was terribly groggy. When that wore off, he got very agitated. I think it was a shock for him to look around and see that he wasn't at home. They wanted to restrain him so he wouldn't hurt himself, but I wouldn't hear of it! All I had to do was sing a few lines of 'Fascination,' and he settled right down. Your uncle's always loved Dinah Shore."

"I should be there with you."

Aunt Octavia heard the hitch in Jane's voice and tut-tutted. "None of that, sweetheart. Women always feel like they should be wearing ten hats at once. We have one head, darling, which means we can only wear one hat at a time. I'm right where I need to be. As are you. Now, tell me what's happening with the investigation."

Refusing to compound Aunt Octavia's worries, Jane said, "We're narrowing suspects down."

"That a girl. Your uncle is asking for water. I'll talk to you later."

She was gone before Jane could tell her to send her love to Uncle Aloysius, so Jane made her way to the surveillance room. She was writing on the whiteboard at the far end of the room when Sinclair walked in. Jane was pleased to see a file folder in his hand.

"Information," she said. "Good."

Sterling was the next to arrive, with Butterworth on his heels. By the time Lachlan appeared, Jane had finished writing on the whiteboard.

As soon as the Fins were seated, she tapped the board with her marker. "We need to figure out what we've been missing. I've started with the suspects. Farah, Stephanie, Amelia Emory, and a question mark in case the first three are wrong. Next, we have motive and means. We don't have a minute to lose, so let's get started."

Sinclair opened his folder. "I gathered as much financial information as I could. Ms. West, Mr. Jensen, Ms. Khan, and Ms. Emory have their fair share of debt. These include car payments, student loans, and mortgages or rent. However, none of them are living beyond their means. Stephanie Harbaugh's situation is different. She comes from money. She has no debt and earns an above-average salary."

Butterworth grunted. "She seems the least likely to have committed these murders. She doesn't need money, making her less susceptible to bribery, and I can't see her killing two poets to gain publicity for her employers."

"I agree. Her motive would have to be personal," said Lachlan.

Jane gestured at Sinclair's folder. "Let's move on to the personal stuff, then. Romantic partners, hobbies, causes, etcetera."

"As previously mentioned, Gretchen West was fairly reclusive. She went to work, wrote poetry, and played video games online. Between the gaming and anxiety support groups, most of her social interactions occurred online."

"Her prowess as a poet was seen as a threat by one of her competitors. It's the most logical reason for her death," said Butterworth.

Lachlan was gazing into the middle distance. Jane could practically hear his gears turning, so she stayed quiet. Eventually, he turned to her and said, "I don't think her killer posed her in that boat out of mockery or spite. She was dignified. She was a lovely, tragic heroine, just like in the poem. It's as if her killer regretted taking her life and tried to make up for it by turning her into the Lady of Shalott."

Butterworth's right brow twitched. "What of Mr. Jensen? He was dumped in a muddy puddle."

"It might have been the closest water source at the time," said Lachlan.

Jane pictured the foundation hole. "We can't forget the flowers, either. Even if the killer wasn't trying to evoke Ophelia, I think the flowers were meant as some kind of tribute to Connor."

"One of the poets might be responsible for the killings, but there's another person to consider," Sinclair said. "Someone who respected both of our victims and who knew them better than anyone here. A teacher, mentor, and friend."

"Professor Ashley?" Jane's voice betrayed her skepticism.

Sinclair shuffled through his papers. "The professor has authored four poetry books. Though he's an award-winning poet, his writing career is hardly lucrative. Thus, the teaching job. Between the two vocations, he's financially solvent. The professor is divorced and has no children. His ex-wife lives on the other side of the country. His father is deceased. He'd previously shared a house with his mother, but she moved into an assisted living facility specializing in Alzheimer's and dementia care last year."

A weighted silence descended upon the company. Jane knew that everyone in the room was thinking of Uncle Aloysius. Like her, they were deeply concerned about her great-uncle's health. It was also comforting to know she wasn't alone in her fears. Nor did she have to hide them from these four men, as she trusted them with every fiber of her being.

"He'll be back, catching catfish and running his model trains, before you know it."

Jane smiled gratefully at Lachlan. She couldn't have chosen a better life partner for Eloise if she'd tried.

Eloise is getting married in two weeks. I need to solve these murders and restore peace to Storyton Hall long before she walks down the aisle. I can't let anything put a damper on her wedding day.

After adding Professor Ashley's name to the white-board, she said, "I see no obvious motive for the professor to kill his former pupils. If a former student won the competition, it would only enhance his reputation. Both Gretchen and Connor attended his summer workshop. What would make him turn violent? Jealousy?"

Butterworth tented his hands on the table. "Jealousy is rarely powerful enough to lead to premeditated murder. I don't know about Mr. Jensen, but Ms. West's death was planned. How long has it been since the professor published a collection of poetry?"

Sinclair consulted his notes. "Three years. *A Trick of Memory* wasn't as well received as his previous work, *Songs of the Working Man*. I read a few from the recent collection and thought they were quite good. On the surface, they're about a son losing his mother. On a deeper level, they're about loneliness."

"That's probably why his students can relate to him. And vice versa. They're all willing and able to put their hardship into words. Most of us aren't brave enough to do that, let alone publish those words for the whole world to judge," Jane said.

Butterworth cleared his throat. "How could these poets, the professor included, discover any of Storyton Hall's secrets on their first visit?"

Pressing her hand to her forehead, Jane moaned. "I forgot to ask Aunt Octavia why Amelia Emory came to see her. We need to know what they discussed during that meeting and if my aunt was in the room the whole time. Amelia is the only suspect on the board with plenty of time and opportunity to study Storyton Hall."

Jane put her phone on the table, set it to speaker mode, and called Aunt Octavia.

"Yes, dear?" her aunt answered.

After hurriedly explaining her reason for calling, Jane let her know that the Fins were listening in on the call.

"If you must know, I ran into Amelia at the post office a few weeks ago. She was holding a letter and looked so happy that I knew she'd received good news. When I pointed out that she was glowing, she showed me the letter. It was from a university—I can't remember which one—informing her that they meant to publish two of her poems in their next journal. I had no idea she wrote poetry and congratulated her on her success."

They heard raised voices in the background, followed by the sound of an alarm. Aunt Octavia said she needed to move away from the din.

"Take your time," Jane said.

When it was quiet again, Aunt Octavia kept talking as

if there'd been no interruption. "On our way out of the post office, I praised Amelia for cultivating so many talents. To my amazement, she responded to my compliment by bursting into tears."

"Why?"

"That's what I wanted to know, but it wasn't the right time or place, so I invited her for tea. We had such a nice chat." Aunt Octavia sighed. "I know you have to turn over every stone, but Amelia doesn't have the stomach to commit such atrocities. Remember that she started her law enforcement career in a big city but left because she was so shaken by the violent acts she witnessed. She hoped Storyton would be a refuge from such horrors. Alas, we have more than our fair share of troubles, and Amelia has been considering a career change."

"She wants to quit?" Jane asked.

Aunt Octavia said, "Yes—to pursue a career in the arts. However, she also wants to remain in Storyton. Her idea was to open a painting studio. One of those places where adults drink wine and have painting parties. She'd hold after-school and summer painting classes for children and evening classes for adults. I think it would be a wonderful addition to our village."

"Does she have the capital to start such a business?"

"I don't know, my dear. Right now, this is just a seed of an idea. But Amelia's inner voice is telling her to chase this dream, and you know I place a great deal of stock in listening to one's inner voice."

Jane made a noise of agreement. "During her visit, did you ever leave the room? Or did she? I'm wondering if she had an opportunity to search for the door to the secret library."

"I'm afraid I left to tend to Muffet Cat. He was in your uncle's study, gagging and coughing up a storm. By the time I rushed to his aid, he'd deposited the hair-ball—and a glob of regurgitated cat food—on the Turkish carpet. I had to clean up the worst of the mess and pour some club soda on the stain before it set. I was absent for nearly ten minutes. Your uncle wasn't at home."

While the Fins exchanged meaningful glances, Jane said, "Thank you, Aunt Octavia."

"She's a gentle spirit, my girl. In light of recent events, you must look closely at her. I understand that. But please don't accuse her without irrefutable proof. I don't think she'd recover if her own community turned on her."

The Fins nodded, but Jane was distracted by the image on her screen indicating that she had an incoming call. After thanking her aunt again, Jane told her she needed to go. She then pressed the END CALL button. Before she could tell Sheriff McCabe that he was on speaker, his voice boomed out of her phone.

"I hope you're free to talk, Ms. Steward. I have news, and I'm sorry to say that none of it is good."

Chapter 13

"Let's start with the lab results," the sheriff continued. "Doc Charles was correct in thinking Ms. West's death was related to drugs or a toxic substance. She'd ingested ten times the recommended dose of antianxiety meds, along with a powerful dose of pain meds. According to the ME, the chemical signature matches the Tramadol found in Connor's room. Her stomach contents included yeast, bacteria, fermented tea, blueberry juice, and sugar—the ingredients match those of Mr. Jensen's homemade kombucha."

Though Jane had heard of kombucha, she'd never tried it and wasn't entirely sure what it was. When she admitted this to the sheriff, he let out a snort of disgust.

"I wouldn't touch the stuff with a ten-foot pole, no matter how good it's supposed to be for my gut. The *fermented* bits floating around in there are basically a colony of helpful bacteria and yeast. That glob of microorganisms is called the SCOBY. The SCOBY converts sugar into acetic acid and ethanol. It has a sour taste, which some describe as vinegary—ideal for camouflaging the taste of medication."

Jane thought of the glass water bottle Connor always seemed to be carrying. "Does all kombucha have to be chilled?"

"Apparently. The mini fridge in Mr. Jensen's room contained several bottles of the stuff, all homemade. We also found a cooler in his closet, which means he probably brought the kombucha from his home in Virginia Beach."

Sterling and Butterworth exchanged grimaces.

"This leaves us with three possibilities," Jane said, her eyes on the board. "Connor killed Gretchen and then committed suicide, Connor killed Gretchen and was later killed by someone else, or that someone else killed both Connor and Gretchen."

"We think it's the latter. The real culprit may have tried to frame Mr. Jensen for Ms. West's murder. We found a gray hoodie and a pair of dark-blue sweatpants balled up inside one of the plastic laundry bags found in every guest closet. The bag was stuffed in the back of a dresser drawer in Mr. Jensen's room. The long, dark hair found on the hoodie's sleeve belongs to Gretchen West."

Jane didn't remember seeing the laundry bag. She and Lachlan had been pressed for time while searching Connor's room, but she chided herself for not examining the dresser's contents more carefully.

Sheriff Evans continued. "Our working theory is still riddled with holes. If one person killed both poets, why did they bother to frame Connor?"

Tapping his folder, Sinclair said, "Connor could have been an accomplice. If helping the killer meant that he'd win in the competition, he might have been tempted.

Maybe he changed his mind. Or the killer decided to silence him. If they were able to lure Connor to the folly, then there was a measure of trust between them."

"I know I started off this call with doom and gloom, but we did get one break, and it's a big one. The ME was able to confirm Doc Lydgate's preliminary diagnosis: Connor Jensen was poisoned."

Jane frowned down at her phone. "With another cocktail of kombucha and medication?"

"No. Connor had an immediate and acute allergic reaction to whatever he ingested. His whole mouth was inflamed, which means whatever he swallowed caused his throat to swell. His gums, tongue, and lips were enlarged too. The ME thinks the poison came from one of the flowers we bagged from the water where Connor was found."

"Those flowers are from our meadow!" cried Jane.

"Poison water hemlock is white with clusters of tiny petals. It looks like Queen Anne's lace but is extremely toxic. This is the first case of water hemlock poisoning the ME has seen in our area, but the number of nationwide cases is increasing. At one point, the plant was found growing in roadside ditches, on creek banks, and in waste areas. Now it's popping up in fields and backyard gardens. All it needs is clay soil and a bit of moisture. The root is the most toxic part, but people have gotten sick from merely touching the plant."

The habitat Sheriff Evans described fit not only the meadow bordering the orchard, but also the patches of long grass near the lake and the hiking trails and ditches along the service road and archery fields. The soil piled next to the foundation hole was mostly clay, which meant the killer might have found the plant in multiple locations.

"Do we need to locate this plant?" she asked.

"I was going to assign that job to Deputy Emory, but it would be better if you could spare someone from your staff instead. I'm going to need all the help I can get interviewing the guests."

Jane met Lachlan's eyes, and he jumped up from his seat and out the door in a flash. "If anyone can find that plant, Mr. Lachlan can," she told Sheriff Evans. "There's something I need to tell you about Deputy Emory before you involve her in the interviews."

"Oh?"

Knowing she had to tread carefully, Jane said, "Amelia registered for this event months ago. When she volunteered to mingle with the guests as a fellow writer, she wasn't putting on a show. I'm not sure why she wasn't more transparent about her interest in poetry or the fact that she was already registered under a false name."

The sheriff was silent for so long that Jane wondered if the call had been dropped. Finally, a sigh rolled through the speaker.

"I had no idea that she planned on participating. I know she's a gifted painter—she gave me a wonderful watercolor last Christmas—but I didn't realize she wrote poetry as well. Maybe she wanted to keep her private and public lives separate. Lots of people in law enforcement do that. We're fiercely protective of our families and hobbies—of the person we are out of uniform."

When the three Fins nodded, Jane wondered if those who'd served in the military felt the same way.

"I just thought you should know and, well, you might want to take a look at one of her poems. I'm sending it to you now." Jane opened a new window on her phone, found the saved document, and forwarded it to Sheriff Evans. "I'd like to sit in on Farah Khan's interview. I've read her work and learned a few things about her from Professor Ashley, so I might be able to help."

In truth, Jane doubted she could help anyone at this point, but she wanted to be there should Farah have any pertinent information to share. A killer was still moving freely around Storyton Hall, and Jane was desperate to apprehend them before tonight's Poetry of the Plate banquet.

Not only did she believe the killer should be held accountable for their crimes, but Jane didn't want a villain to walk away with the Current Mood contract.

Will the greeting card company end up with the best person for the job? Or is that person already dead?

"Of course," the sheriff answered. "Please have Butterworth escort Ms. Khan to the conference room. I'm getting in the car now."

Butterworth was heading to the door before the sheriff could finish his sentence.

"Should I ask Stephanie Harbaugh to wait in the other conference room? We can't account for her movements from the time she left the village at eleven thirty to the time she met her coworkers two hours later."

"Yes. I also have a warrant permitting my team to search the guest rooms. I don't plan on being subtle today, Ms. Steward. Quite the opposite."

"I understand."

Jane disconnected and looked at the wall of screens behind Sterling. Other than two guests walking through the lobby, the only people moving about were Storyton Hall employees. Scanning the library and reading rooms, Jane saw that every seat was occupied.

"They're so intent on their work," she murmured.

Sterling held up a piece a paper. "According to today's schedule, this is their last chance to dazzle the judges. They have until five o'clock to hand in seven unique greeting cards. The categories are I Love You, I'm Sorry, Congratulations, Happy Birthday, Hang in There, Thank You, and Smile. They can use photography or drawings brought from home. Photos taken with their smartphones over the last few days or simple sketches are also accepted."

Sinclair got to his feet. "The library is without its librarian. Unless you have a different task for me, I'd like to make myself available to the guests."

Jane walked over to him and straightened his bow tie. "As you should. Even now, at the eleventh hour, we should do what we can to give them the experience they were promised."

"Not only that, but someone needs to keep an eye on them," added Sterling in an ominous tone. "All those people. All that quiet. And all that time to think? Sounds dangerous to me."

Sterling's words followed Jane as she hustled to the kitchens. She knew the sheriff would arrive at any moment, but she wanted to put a few cookies and tea sandwiches on a plate. The sheriff and his team had been working nonstop all weekend and could use a little pick-me-up.

Jane was delighted to see her sons perched on stools at one of the prep stations, chattering away with Mrs. Hubbard. The head cook was kneading dough, her deft hands folding and flattening, folding and flattening.

"Uh-oh, here comes your mother!" she said in a stage whisper.

The twins swiveled in their stools. Their eyes glinted, and their cheeks were stuffed.

"I'm glad your official taste testers are on duty," Jane said as she put an arm around each boy.

Fitz and Hem accepted her one-armed hug with good grace. Since their mouths were full, they grinned at her before spinning around to face the counter again.

Mrs. Hubbard beamed at the twins. "I just love feeding my two favorite men. And what about you, Mother of Dragons? Would you like a cookie or a scone?"

"The sheriff is on his way, so I thought I'd grab some food for him and his team."

Covering the dough with a white tea towel, Mrs. Hubbard dusted off her hands and beckoned for Jane to follow her. She walked straight through the kitchens and down the hall to the cookbook nook.

"I didn't want to say anything in front of the boys, but I've sent a hamper to your aunt and uncle. No one is going to eat hospital food on my watch! One of my staff is driving it over the mountain. I packed enough for tonight's dinner as well as tomorrow's breakfast. If the need arises, I'll send more food in the morning."

This unexpected kindness made Jane misty-eyed.

"Oh, sweet girl!" Mrs. Hubbard opened her arms.

Jane stepped into the embrace and was immediately comforted by Mrs. Hubbard's warmth. She smelled like buttered bread and was as soft and pillowy as fresh dough.

"Thank you," Jane said. "For the hamper, for feeding Fitz and Hem, and for always being a port in the storm."

Mrs. Hubbard dabbed her eyes with the corner of her apron. "No more of that. I have prep cooks, sous cooks, and pastry chefs to cow into submission, and I can't do that when my lips are trembling. Speaking of chefs, Jessie saw the coroner's van drive past the garages. What happened?"

Telling Mrs. Hubbard about Connor was the same as broadcasting the news over a loudspeaker. Still, there was no reason to keep his death from the staff. She'd be doing a disservice to pretend that this was like any other Sunday.

Lowering her voice out of respect for Connor, Jane said, "We had another Rip van Winkle. Another poet. It seems that Uncle Aloysius found his body at the construction site. My uncle had been wandering the grounds for a long time—hours, maybe—so we're not sure exactly when the young man passed away."

Mrs. Hubbard put her hand to her mouth. "You mean, your uncle found the body, and then the boys found *him*?"

"Yes."

"What a terrible, terrible day." She shook her head in sorrow. "Is that why the sheriff's on his way?"

Jane said, "I'm afraid so. I'd appreciate it if you'd let the staff know that they have no need to fear. And if anyone sees any unusual or suspicious behavior, they should report it to me or to a department head right away. Can you get the word out?"

Mrs. Hubbard grunted. "Do you even have to ask? Let's get you those cookies and sandwiches. You and Sheriff Evans have work to do."

Jane ate one sandwich and a cookie as she proceeded through the staff corridor and out into the lobby. Her timing couldn't have been better, for just as she passed the main door, a bellboy opened it for Sheriff Evans.

His gaze locked on the tray in her hands. "Is that for us?"

"Yes. Would you like to eat and walk?"

"Don't mind if I do," he said, helping himself to a sandwich. "Deputy Emory is waiting at the end of the hall. I've asked Phelps to search Ms. Khan's room. Another pair of officers will take Ms. Harbaugh's room. If anyone asks, the warrant is in my pocket."

Is he going to let Amelia slide? Or did he talk to her on his way over?

They reached the William Faulkner Conference Room to find the door closed. There was no sign of Deputy Emory.

Jane's mouth went dry, but the sheriff was unperturbed. He knocked on the door, and when it was cracked by Deputy Emory, he asked her to step out into the hall.

"Emory, I hate to put you on the spot, but I have no choice. Why didn't you tell me that you'd already registered for this event and submitted work as an official contestant?" His brows drew together as he glared at his deputy. "Damn it, Emory. What are you playing at?"

Deputy Emory turned scarlet. "I'm sorry, sir. I didn't mean to deceive you or let you down in any way. You've been so good to me. It's just that, more and more, I've been feeling like . . ."

"You want to get off this ride?"

"Yes." The word was soft with gratitude. "I haven't made any plans yet because I wanted to be sure. Entering the competition was like dipping my toe in the water."

Sheriff Evans reached into his shirt pocket and withdrew a folded piece of paper. Holding it out to his officer, he asked, "I'd like you to explain this."

Seeing her poem, all the color drained from Deputy Emory's face. She'd gone from cherry red to coconut white in an instant.

"The boat. The references to drowning." The sheriff shook the paper. "Well?"

"I wrote that months ago. I can show you the file on my computer. The date's right there." For the first time, Amelia Emory looked at Jane. "It was back when the cooking show filmed here. When that grill exploded—I couldn't stop thinking about how many innocent people might have been hurt because someone tampered with that grill. And then the Berry Festival got ruined too. It's like everything I look forward to is ruined by violence. Over and over."

Jane felt like she should be apologizing. How many times had strangers come to Storyton carrying suitcases in their hands and malicious intentions in their hearts? How many times had Storyton Hall hosted a conference that had ended in tragedy? How many times had one of her guests had a negative effect on the village?

"I understand how you feel," she told the younger woman.

"Because you care about the people around you. Just like I do. I feel like I've let the people of this town down so many times." Her gaze shifted back to the sheriff. "I'm letting them down now because I can't figure out who's doing these things."

The sheriff gave her arm a paternal pat. "All we can give of ourselves is our best. That's what we'll do today and tomorrow and until this case is closed. After that, the only person you have to please is yourself." Again, he gestured at the poem. "This doesn't come as a surprise to me. I know you love Storyton, and I know you're close with your colleagues, but it's okay to walk away from this job. No one will think less of you. Right now, however, I need you to be fully invested in this case."

Deputy Emory sagged in relief. "Thank you, sir. And I'm totally committed. I'll do whatever it takes to see that justice is done."

The sheriff had his hand on the door handle when Jane said, "You'll also have to withdraw from the competition. You've been investigating the other poets, as well as the Current Mood folks. It's not a good look."

Abashed, Deputy Emory murmured, "You're right. I'll withdraw as soon as we're done here."

Having made his point, the sheriff opened the door and held it for Jane. She entered the room and deposited the plate of food on the mahogany sideboard.

The sheriff sat down at the head of the table, and Deputy Emory remained standing next to the sideboard. Jane took a seat in the middle of the table, which gave her a clear view of all parties.

Farah Khan's dark eyes were round with fear. Her arms were crossed over her chest, and her hands were burrowed in her armpits. Her chin quivered, and as Jane watched, she drew in her shoulders, as if trying to make herself as small as possible. She looked like a rabbit cornered by a fox, and Jane felt sorry for her.

"Would you like a glass of water?"

Farah darted a glance at Jane and shook her head.

Sheriff Evans informed Farah that he'd be recording the interview.

"I'd like to begin with the morning session with Professor Ashley. You went outside with the other poets. Is that correct?"

Farah nodded.

"Please speak your answers out loud, Ms. Khan."

Her eyes glued to the table, Farah said, "Yes."

"I understand that at one point, the professor told everyone to find a place on the grounds where they could sit by themselves and contemplate. Where did you go?"

"The gazebo."

Keeping his tone conversational, the sheriff asked, "How did your work go?"

At this question, something shifted in Farah. Anger smoldered in her eyes, and all traces of timidity vanished. "I'd just heard about Gretchen's death. I was too shocked to write. We were supposed to channel our feelings into words, but I couldn't even process it. I mean, one of us was dead! And there was an investigation going on!" With a little shake of her head, she added, "I don't even know what I did with my notebook. I think I left it outside, but I was too upset to go back for it."

Sheriff Evans pulled it out of his bag. "This one?"

Farah was horrified to see the book in his hands, and Jane couldn't blame her. Poetry was personal. That notebook was stuffed with her feelings—some of which Farah never intended to share.

"I have to ask about two of your poems. 'The Enemy Within' and 'I'd Kill You If I Could.' Are those poems about a particular person?"

"Yes."

"Have you seen that person recently?"

Farah's anger had lost its edge, but she remained guarded. "The person is my uncle, and I haven't seen him since I immigrated from Malaysia with my dad."

"Did you know Gretchen West personally?"

Though Farah was momentarily confused by the abrupt change of subject, she answered without hesitation. "I know of her. Except for Professor Ashley, she's been published more than anyone at Brightleaf. I saw her picture in a bunch of journals, and I remember looking her up on social media, but that was just me being curious. In all the time we've been here, I've said hi to her twice. Another time, I told her that I liked her poem."

"Did you consider her your biggest competition?"

"Her and Connor, yeah."

The sheriff made a contemplative noise. "You and Connor were at Brightleaf together, correct?"

"Yes. He's really talented. He's one of the few here who can write poems that make people laugh out loud." She gestured at her notebook. "I'm not good at that."

"Are you and Connor friendly?"

"Not really. He rubs me the wrong way. He always wants everyone to like him. And he pretends like nothing bothers him—like he's got it all figured out. But I've read the poems he wrote about his sister. I know that she died when they were kids and that he blames himself because he couldn't save her. He can write about all these other sides of himself, but in person, he hides behind the laid-back surfer-boy act. It gets old after a while."

Sheriff Evans cocked his head. "Doesn't everyone have something to hide?"

Farah let out a sigh that was too world-weary for a woman in her late twenties. "Of course. Everyone has secrets. But people who hide their true selves behind

charming smiles and silly jokes aren't trustworthy. I
learned that the hard way when I was still a girl. My
poems are angry because I *am* angry. I can't forget that
I was abused. I can't forget that my mother chose not to
believe me. I've been through too much to joke
around, and I don't like fake people."

"I'm sorry to bring up painful subjects, Ms. Khan. I
truly am. I wouldn't ask about your poems without a
valid reason, but Ms. West's death is suspicious. People
say that you and Connor were her biggest competitors.
That's why I've asked to speak to you. It's also why I
need to know where you went after tossing your notebook on the grass and leaving the gazebo."

"I walked to the lake. I couldn't stop thinking about
Gretchen, and I wanted to see where it happened. I
know that her death improved my chances of winning,
but I didn't do anything to her. I swear! I could never
hurt a woman. Not after what I've been through. And
Gretchen was a survivor, like me. I've read enough of
her poems to know that."

Tears beaded Farah's lower lashes, but Sheriff Evans
was unmoved. "You mentioned 'poisoned water' in several poems. Why?"

"Oh God, was Gretchen poisoned?"

"Just answer my question, Ms. Khan."

Farah pointed at the water pitcher on the sideboard.
"You can't understand this, because you didn't grow up
in a little village in Malaysia, but our rivers were conta-
minated. Contaminants leached into our wells. Our
water supplies were literally poisoned. That's why I
write about water so much. In America, everyone has
access to fresh water. It's such a gift. I still remember

how amazed I was when I saw an American bathroom for the first time. I thought everyone was rich because so much clean, clear water flowed out of the faucet. It just kept coming and coming."

"Thank you for the explanation. I can see that I misinterpreted your meaning. I did find it interesting that you and Mr. Jensen frequently mention water in your work."

Farah frowned. "Connor has a complicated relationship with water. It killed his sister, and I think he's spent his life trying to master it—trying to make it his playground. Now I have a question of my own. Why do you keep asking me about Connor? I thought I was here to talk about Gretchen, and I told you that I didn't do anything to her. I need to get back to writing. Every minute I spend in here takes away from the time I need to polish my work. So, can I go now?"

Hearing the desperation in her voice, Jane wondered if it stemmed from guilt and fear or from a genuine desire to present her best work to the judges.

"We're almost done," said the sheriff, consulting his notes. "I'd like to clarify something. You said you went down to the lake because Ms. West was on your mind. Did anyone see you there?"

"Not by the lake, no. But on my way back to the hotel, I saw Stephanie from Current Mood. She was riding a bike. She waved, and I waved back."

"What time was that?"

Farah thought for a moment. "I don't know exactly. Around twelve thirty."

"Was she heading to the manor house?"

"I guess. I didn't see her inside, but I wasn't really paying attention. I didn't feel like hanging out with other people, so I went up to my room and ate some nuts and fruit for lunch."

"When did you last see Connor Jensen?"

Farah frowned. "He was out on the lawn with Professor Ashley and the rest of us. I have no clue where he went after that. Why? Do you think he had something to do with Gretchen's death?"

"Do you?"

Farah put her hands up as if warding off a blow. "I don't know! I keep telling you—I didn't know Gretchen or Connor. I've read their work, but we're not friends. I've had a few interactions with Connor in the past few days, but that's it. I don't know his favorite color or if he has a pet. He's a good writer with bad breath from the stuff he's always drinking. And I think his jokes are dumb. That's all I know. Can you just talk to Connor yourself and let me get back to work?"

"I wish I could, but Connor Jensen is dead."

The silence following this statement was absolute. Farah stared at the sheriff with openmouthed horror.

"Did you see Connor when you left the gazebo?"

Farah seemed to have vacated her body. She'd gone completely still and stared at the table through hollow eyes. The sheriff had to repeat his question. Farah's reply was barely audible.

"No."

The word had no substance. It was more like the ghost of a word. A breath of air tinged with sound.

"Did you kill Connor Jensen?"

"No."

"Did you kill Gretchen West?"

"No." And then, "No, no, no!"

Farah began to sob. Deputy Emory stepped forward and handed her a wad of tissues.

"Alright, Ms. Khan. That'll be all for now. You can—" He was interrupted by sharp knock on the door.

When Deputy Emory opened it, Jane saw Butterworth's face on the other side. He leaned down and spoke into the deputy's ear. After a quick nod, she hurried over to the sheriff and whispered, "Professor Ashley's in the hall. He wants to confess."

Chapter 14

Sheriff Evans told Farah Khan that she was free to leave, but she didn't seem to hear him. When Deputy Emory placed a hand on her shoulder, she flinched.

The deputy said, "Ms. Khan. You can get back to your writing. You still have time."

But Farah was looking at the closed door. Her face was ashen, and she gripped the arms of her chair as if she might break into a million pieces should she let go.

It's too much, Jane thought. *She just learned about Connor's death, and now the man she admired as a poet and a teacher is on the other side of that door, waiting to confess.*

Jane got out of her chair and stood in front of Farah, blocking her view of the door.

"You came here to win a competition, right? You're shaken. The wind's been knocked out of you. Most people wouldn't be able to see this through, but you're not most people. You're a fighter. You've worked hard for this chance, and the finish line is so close. Can you cross it? *I* believe you can."

Farah's gaze snapped back into focus. She stared at
Jane for a long moment before dipping her chin in the
semblance of a nod. Jane opened the door and beckoned Butterworth inside.

"Would you escort Ms. Khan and see that she gets a
strong coffee or tea?"

"Perhaps a mug of *teh tarik?*" Butterworth asked Farah.

Farah brightened. "You have that?"

"Not only will I make it for you myself, but I'll sneak
a piece of banana cake from the kitchens too." Butterworth offered Farah his arm.

After a brief hesitation, she took it and was led out
into the hall.

Deputy Emory also left the room. She returned seconds later with Professor Ashley in tow.

Sheriff Evans beckoned to the seat Farah had just vacated and cautioned the professor that he would be
recording their conversation.

Jane found it interesting that he called it a "conversation" instead of an "interview."

Maybe he doesn't want to spook the professor.

Professor Ashley didn't look frightened. If anything,
he looked resigned.

He accepted a glass of water from Deputy Emory and
drank it down in greedy swallows.

"Guilt makes the mouth go dry," he said.

The sheriff laced his hands and adopted a relaxed
posture. "I'm here to listen to whatever you'd like to say.
Where would you like to start?"

"This story, like so many stories, begins with my mom."

If this opening surprised the sheriff, he didn't show
it. He simply waited for the professor to continue.

"Poets aren't exactly one-percenters," the professor

said with a self-effacing grin. "The royalties for my books are a tiny drop of what someone like George R. R. Martin or Nora Roberts makes. I never wrote poetry expecting to become rich. I don't think anyone does. Unless you can charge high fees for being a guest speaker, most poets must teach to earn a comfortable living. That's what I've been doing. Writing, teaching, and living comfortably. At least, that's how it was."

Gazing into the middle distance, the professor seemed to be caught up in a memory, so the sheriff brought him back by saying, "Until something changed."

"Two things, actually. First, my wife left me. She said she was tired of playing second fiddle to my muse. Our divorce was friendlier than most, but still expensive. Splitting our assets meant dipping into my savings to buy her out of her half of the house and so on. At the same time, my mother, who lived several states away, had a bad fall. When I got to the hospital, she seemed confused."

Jane pictured Uncle Aloysius lying on her sofa. She saw his waxen face and wild eyes. Her throat tightened, and she willed the professor to hurry up.

"I thought she was just rattled from the fall. Until I saw the state of her house." He shook his head. "It was bad. Not just messy, but dirty. She barely had any food. Her parakeet was dead in its cage. God knows when it was last fed."

A soft squeak came from Deputy Emory, and she covered her mouth in embarrassment.

Professor Ashley smiled at her with his eyes. "You're right. It *was* sad. The whole mess was sad. My mother had always kept a shipshape house. She was smart, independent, and charismatic. This new version of her was fretful and meek. She would slip between the past and the present a dozen times a day. She couldn't live alone anymore, so she came to live with me."

"How did you manage your work?" the sheriff asked, not without sympathy.

"I hired someone to be with her when I was teaching. I stopped traveling. Then I stopped doing guest lectures and readings altogether. This allowed me to be with my mother in the evenings, but losing that income hurt. I wasn't writing, either. The publish-or-perish maxim is legit. To stay relevant, I had to come up with fresh work. But the well was empty." He let out a humorless laugh. "Actually, the well was full of fear and anxiety. In short, I was too drained to be creative."

He looked at Jane and must have seen something in her eyes, because his next words had nothing to do with him. "You've been there, haven't you? Was it one of your parents?"

For a fleeting moment, Jane forgot about the investigation, the murders, and the writing competition. Sheriff Evans and Deputy Emory faded away. It was just her and this man, united by circumstances beyond their control.

"My great-uncle. He's at the hospital right now after wandering the grounds for hours. I think this was our wake-up call. Like your mother's fall. You didn't know what was happening to your mom, but my uncle lives here. The signs have been right in front of me—I just didn't want to see them." She put a hand to her mouth to cover her trembling lips.

"I'm so sorry."

Jane felt the weight of the sheriff's gaze and knew she had to redirect the conversation.

"You might have seen my uncle before he got lost. He left the manor house around the time you finished reading to the poets on the Great Lawn."

Professor Ashley said, "I'm afraid not. As soon as the writers separated to find a place to work, I went looking for Jeremiah and Gil. I had to tell them what I've come to tell you."

"Which is?" prompted the sheriff.

The professor filled his lungs with air and slowly let it out through his nose. "This competition was rigged from the start. I accepted a bribe to push a particular poet to the top of the heap. There was no guarantee that my influence would seal the deal, but I was supposed to do everything in my power to see that this writer won the contract."

"Which writer?"

"Connor Jensen."

The sheriff sat up in his chair. "Who offered you the bribe?"

"I don't know. Someone contacted me by email explaining what they wanted me to do. At first, I deleted the emails. I did this twice. The third email was different. The message came from a money-sending service, indicating that I'd received a payment. I can't remember the name of the site, but I can show you the email. I Googled the company, saw that it was legit, and accepted the money. It was for five grand. That would cover a few of my mom's assisted-living payments. She's in a special memory care center because she needs 'round-the-clock supervision. It's expensive."

"Did the payment come with instructions?"

Professor Ashley held up his phone. "The email's here if you'd like to read it. I turned my passcode off.

Feel free to look at anything—emails, texts, photos—I don't care. I don't want to carry this secret around anymore."

Deputy Emory took the phone from the professor and passed it to the sheriff.

"For the sake of the recording, I'm going to read the email out loud."

The sheriff pulled his reading glasses out of his shirt pocket. Once they were perched on the tip of his nose, he recited the date and time the email was received, as well as the sender's and recipient's account names. Then he glanced from the phone screen to the professor and said, "The email is addressed to 'The Artful Dodge.' Why?"

"I assume the sender was making a play on my name by combining Dodge and the Artful Dodger from *Oliver Twist*. The Artful Dodger was a skilled pickpocket and the leader of a gang of child criminals. I think it was meant as an insult—like I had to decide if I was willing to be insulted, manipulated, and bribed." He splayed his hands. "Obviously, I was willing."

The sheriff proceeded to read the whole message:

"'For the Artful Dodge. You were a lousy husband and son, but you're finally doing right by your mom. Seasons isn't cheap. How long can you swing it? How long can you ride the success of your aging publications? If you don't come up with new work, no one will pay you to lecture.'"

Those aren't questions; they're arrows, Jane thought. *Whoever sent this knew exactly how to wound this man.*

"'This is a proposition. Not the kind you get from your love-struck students. This a business transaction. Later this summer, you'll be running the competition at Storyton Hall. You will convince the judges to award the Current Mood contract to a particular person. If you succeed, you'll receive twenty-five thousand dollars. The five thousand dollars attached to this message is your first installment. The balance will be paid when the right person wins the contract. If you accept the offer, claim the down payment. The poet's name will follow.' "

After announcing that he'd read the message in its entirety, Sheriff Evans said, "You had no idea who sent this? The author seemed to know you quite well."

Professor Ashley shrugged. "It wouldn't be hard to learn any of those details. I discussed my mother's health and my writing struggles in front of colleagues, students, and strangers attending my readings. I've never been afraid to express my vulnerability."

"Why would someone say that you were a lousy husband?"

Jane saw a subtle hardening of the professor's jaw. "My wife filed for divorce. If I'd been a better husband, I'd still be married. I've been pretty open about the mistakes I made. My career always came first—my writing, my students, my fans. I *was* a lousy husband."

The sheriff made a noncommittal noise. "Okay, so you accepted the money. Then what?"

"A few days after my summer session at Brightleaf ended and I was prepping to come here, I got another email with the name. It came from one of those sites specializing in emails that disappear after twenty-four hours. If you close the window on the screen, you can see it for yourself."

The sheriff tapped the screen and frowned.

"I got it," volunteered Deputy Emory. She leaned over the phone, tapped twice, and returned the device to her boss.

As he read the time, date, and account information aloud, Jane wanted to scream, "Just tell us the name!"

And then he did.

"Connor Jensen."

The professor massaged his temples. "I would've pushed him through, anyway, based on merit. Connor is an excellent poet. His only area of weakness is writing about grief. His sympathy cards will need work, but he'll get there. After his younger sister died, Connor's parents refused to talk about it. Connor bottled the memory until it came out in his writing. He needs more practice accepting and expressing sympathy, but he's getting there."

"How were you supposed to influence the judges?"

"By talking him up to Jeremiah and Gil. It was easy to do. From day one, the competition was a toss-up between Gretchen and Connor." A look of pain flashed in his eyes. "Until she was killed."

The sheriff studied the man at the other end of the table. He stared at him so long that the professor began to fidget. He worried his fingernails and shot a nervous glance at Jane.

When the air held enough friction to produce an electrical charge, the sheriff said, "Did you kill Gretchen West?"

Unlike Farah, Dodge Ashley didn't rear back or shrink inward. He looked directly into the sheriff's eyes and said, "No, I didn't. I'm guilty of accepting a bribe. I'm guilty of trading my integrity for money. Between my mom's Medicaid and the payout I'll get if Connor wins, I can cover the cost of assisted living for a whole year. With my money troubles on hold for a bit, I can get back to writing. I could stop being so anxious."

"The money gives you a motive."

For the first time, Professor Ashley looked scared. "I know. With Gretchen gone, Connor will probably win. That looks very bad for me. But I could never silence another writer's voice. I've taught for nearly two decades, and I care about my students. Gretchen's loss *hurts*."

Jane didn't approve of the professor's actions, but she didn't think he was a murderer. He was a good person who'd made a bad decision. She wondered what she'd have done in his position. If Uncle Aloysius required special assistance—costly assistance—would she accept a bribe to pay for his care? What if her income fell short of was what needed to ensure his safety and comfort?

"Why did you choose to come forward now?" the sheriff asked.

"I kept telling myself that I can't bring Gretchen back. I also can't help my mom from jail. I have a motive. I took that five grand. I planned on earning another twenty. But when I was outside with the poets, I looked around and knew my mom would be ashamed of me. I'm ashamed of me."

As if the weight of his remorse was too great to bear, the professor put his head in his hands.

Deputy Emory turned to the sheriff and raised her brows. At his nod, she refilled the professor's water glass and said, "How well did you know Connor Jensen?"

The professor gave her a puzzled look. "As well as I know any of the poets I've taught at Brightleaf. I only teach one group of twenty-five or thirty writers, and they're with me for eight weeks. During the day, we work. At night, we have family-style meals. I interact with my students the whole time, so I get to know them pretty well. For example, I know that Connor loves the water and that he's very popular with the ladies. I know that he makes his own kombucha and that his little sister fell through the ice and drowned. Connor is outgoing and extremely confident. He charms everyone he meets but doesn't have close friends—just acquaintances and admirers. He keeps people at a distance. He manages a sporting goods store in Virginia Beach. The job and the city are a good fit for him."

Deputy Emory poured herself some water and sat down next to the professor. After taking a drink, her expression turned pensive.

"The person who emailed you is no stranger. They know you, they know literature, and they know Connor Jensen. Whom did Connor hang out with during his time at Brightleaf?"

Emotions warred on Professor Ashley's face. After a brief hesitation, he said, "He got along with everyone. The women flirted with him whenever they had the chance, and I know that he had a physical relationship with at least two people. He made it clear that he wasn't interested in anything serious, and there were no hard feelings. Only one person disliked him, but she was too friendly and polite to let it show."

"Farah Khan?"

The professor nodded. "In every group, there are always people who don't get along. As long as everyone's respectful, we can work together. Connor's a good guy. Farah's a good woman. They don't have to like each other to be successful writers."

"Makes sense." Deputy Emory had another sip of water. "This morning, after the poets went off to work on their own, you said that you wanted to come clean to Jeremiah and Gil. Did you?"

"Yes. They were finishing their lunch in the café and invited me to sit down. That's when I told them."

"How did they react?"

The professor's despondency lifted. "They were incredibly gracious and were willing to forgive me as long as I made things right. I feel horrible for adding to their stress. They're still reeling from Gretchen's death, and now they know someone wants to determine the outcome of the competition."

Deputy Emory nodded her head in understanding. "I crossed a line too. Months ago, I entered the competition under a false name. I should've told my colleagues about that as soon as we started looking into Ms. West's death, but I didn't. I deceived the other poets too. I never told them my real name or what I did for a living. I don't know who I am anymore."

"What's your pen name?"

Averting her gaze, the deputy said, "Amelia Emerson."

The professor smiled. "Deputy, you're a talented writer and artist. If you have a dream to chase, do it now, when you're young. The older you get, the harder it is to take risks."

Isn't that the truth? Jane thought.

The sheriff told Professor Ashley that a deputy would drive him to the station, where he'd be asked to provide a formal statement. When the professor left, his footfalls were noticeably lighter than they'd been when he'd first entered the room.

Jane said, "What now?"

"Let's see what Phelps found in Ms. Khan's room."

Phelps entered the conference room with two evidence bags in hand. One bag held a glass bottle. The second held a thin sheaf of papers.

The sheriff pointed at the bottle. "More kombucha?"

"Whatever it is, it smells rank." His eye fell on the platter of sandwiches and cookies, and the grimace vanished. "Are those for us?"

"Help yourself," Jane said, moving the platter to the table.

The sheriff put two cookies on a napkin. "You'd better eat something too, Emory. With the way the day is going, we should grab food while we can."

Phelps slid the evidence bag with the papers across the table to the sheriff. "These are jokes written by Connor Jensen."

The sheriff slipped a disposable glove on his right hand, removed the papers from the bag, and spread them out on the table. Jane and Emory angled their chairs so they could read them too.

The first page was titled, CARD IDEAS: DAD JOKES, and under that, Connor had listed twenty examples.

WHAT DO YOU CALL A LAWN MOWER WITH HICCUPS? A GRASSHOPPER!

WHAT DO YOU CALL A PLANE WITHOUT WINGS? A BUS!

WHAT DO YOU CALL A BOXING BEETLE? A PUNCH BUG!

Jane groaned. "These are horrible, but dad jokes are supposed to make you roll your eyes, right?"

"I love dad jokes," the sheriff said. "I have a whole arsenal, but I save them for my family. I like to torture them at the dinner table."

"No wonder your kids only visit on major holidays," teased Phelps.

There was no reason to read every dad joke, so Jane

moved on to the next sheet of paper. The page header was: SNARKY POSTCARDS FOR STRANGERS (PROPOSAL).

"This sounds like a good way to start a fight," Emory remarked. "I'm not sure if anyone would buy these."

As she wanted to form her own opinions, Jane read the first few examples.

DID YOU KNOW?
Your car goes in the space BETWEEN the white lines.

DID YOU KNOW?
You shouldn't pick the express line if you can't see the bottom of your cart.

DID YOU KNOW?
When the flight attendants tell passengers to turn off their devices, they're talking to YOU.

DID YOU KNOW?
Tailgating the car in front of you will cause them to SLOW DOWN. Kind of defeats the purpose, doesn't it?

If she wasn't pressed for time, Jane would've read them all. "Honestly, I think these would sell. It's trendy to judge strangers these days. I could see these postcards tucked under wiper blades across America."

Sheriff Evans examined the cartoonish drawings accompanying each postcard. "We could hand these out with our parking tickets."

Jane said, "Why was Connor's work in Farah's room?"

"We'll have to ask her. Phelps, that drink needs to be analyzed as quickly as possible."

"Can Sterling have a sample?" Jane asked as Phelps

gathered the evidence bags together. "I know his findings wouldn't be official, but he can tell us if the bottle contains ingredients that don't belong."

"Have him meet Phelps in the garages, and please ask Mr. Butterworth to fetch Ms. Khan again."

Jane sent the text, and Phelps left.

"What about Ms. Harbaugh?" asked Deputy Emory.

"I'll let you handle that interview. Get an account of her movements from the time she woke up this morning until now." He held up a cautionary finger. "Don't go easy on her. We're still hunting a killer."

The sheriff stood and rubbed his lower back. As he massaged the aching muscles, he said, "Hearing the professor talk about his mom was hard for you. I could see that. But you don't know that your uncle will share the same fate. Wait and hope, Ms. Steward. Wait and hope."

A buzz from Jane's phone saved her from having to respond. She glanced at the screen and said, "It's Butterworth. A staff member saw Farah at the recreation desk. Let me call over there and ask what she was doing."

Jane dialed the number. When Eloise answered, Jane thought she'd misdialed.

"When did Lachlan recruit you?"

Eloise's musical laugh bubbled through the speaker. "I'm just covering the desk until he finishes looking for a certain plant. It's been an easy job so far. For the past hour, all I've done is read and rent out one bike."

Blood rushed into Jane's ears. "To which guest?"

"What was her name? I saw her at the wine tasting and again at the scavenger hunt. She's really pretty. Such gorgeous hair and eyes. Let me check the ledger.

Here we are. It was Farah Khan, and she said she was heading into the village."

"When was this?"

Eloise said, "Exactly thirty-two minutes ago."

Plenty of time to get to town. But for what reason?

"Did she have anything with her? A purse or—"

"She had a backpack. It looked full too."

Jane thanked Eloise and turned to the sheriff.

"I heard," he said. "When she left this room, I assumed she'd go back to her poems. But I think she planned her escape instead. Would you like a ride into town, Ms. Steward? I promise to exceed the speed limit."

"Good. We have a murderer to catch."

Chapter 15

J ane's phone was pressed to her ear as she burst through the door to the loading dock. She was listening with such intensity that she didn't hear Gil Callahan creep up behind her.

"Phoebe, I don't know what you're talking about. What mob?"

"I told you earlier! They came from over the mountain to see Pig Newton." Phoebe panted. "We haven't had this many people in the village since the Berry Festival, and *that* crowd was nice. This one isn't. They surrounded the market and are demanding to see Pig Newton!' It's scary."

And half of the sheriff's department is at Storyton Hall, Jane thought.

Jane's earring was digging into her neck, so she put the phone on speaker. "Why today?"

Phoebe shouted over the gurgling of the espresso machine. "Apparently, there was a social media post inviting influencers with fifty thousand or more followers to pose with our famous pig. The post just went up yesterday, but a bunch of influencers showed up today. Celebrities too. And they *all* brought entourages. I've never had a security detail come into my shop to buy a cappuccino for a pop star or a skinny iced latte for a style guru. It's surreal! A rumor's going around that Reese Witherspoon is coming. I really hope it's true. I love her book club picks."

For the moment, Jane forgot her reason for calling. All she could think about was that sweet little pig. Could he handle all that noise? And what about Tobias? He was a quiet, gentle soul. He'd shy away from that kind of attention.

"I'm out at the loading dock, waiting for the sheriff to drive me into town. I bet he's not out here yet because someone called to tell him about the crowd."

"They're angry because Pig Newton isn't here," explained Phoebe. "A few people got to see him this morning, but Tobias didn't think the fuss was good for either of them, so he took Pig Newton home."

Relieved, Jane said, "Thank goodness. I just hope the mob doesn't find out where he lives. For the right amount of money, his brothers would give up his address."

"Ugh, they need to stop being so jealous! When I think how they mocked him for writing that book in the first place—or how much they protested having Pig Newton at the market—I'm tempted to serve them day-old coffee."

"Speaking of coffee, has Farah Khan been in your shop in the last half hour or so? She left Storyton Hall after being interviewed by the sheriff, and we need to find her. At this moment, she's our prime suspect."

Jane gave Phoebe a brief physical description of Farah.

"I remember her from the scavenger hunt, but I haven't seen her. It won't be easy to find her with all these people milling about, so I'll start looking. Catching a killer is way more important than making lattes."

Behind Jane, a man cried, "Phoebe don't! It's too dangerous!"

Jane whirled around to face Gil. "How long have you been standing there?"

"Long enough." Gil's face was flushed. "Please! Tell Phoebe to wait. If Farah killed Gretchen and is desperate to get out of town, there's no telling what she'll do. I'll come with you, but tell Phoebe to stay where she is. I couldn't take it if anything happened to her!"

A happy sigh drifted out of the phone speaker. "Aw, isn't he sweet?"

Jane glared at Gil. "Fine. You can come. Phoebe? I'm going to text you a photo of Farah. Share it with as many merchants as you can. We can't let her get away."

At that moment, Sheriff Evans appeared on the loading dock. Jane told him that Gil wanted to help, and the three of them jumped into the sheriff's SUV.

As they took off for town, Jane turned to Gil and said, "Where's the rest of your crew?"

"Jeremiah's reviewing the final submissions, and Stephanie's talking to Deputy Emory."

"Don't you need to review submissions too?"

Gil shook his head. "Like Phoebe said, catching a killer is more important."

"Do you mean that, or are you just trying to impress Phoebe?"

"I want to protect her *and* find Gretchen's killer. This person has probably sunk our business. No one's going to buy greeting cards from a company associated with a murder."

Gil sounded bereft, and for good reason. Could Current Mood get off the ground after such a disastrous start? Jane wasn't sure. She also noticed how Gil referred only to Gretchen's death, which meant either he hadn't heard about Connor, or he was feigning ignorance.

"It might take time, but don't give up hope." When Gil didn't reply, she asked, "How's Jeremiah holding up?"

"Not great. We're both upset about Gretchen, and we're worried about Stephanie and our company. We don't have a Plan B, Ms. Steward. We put all of our eggs in this basket. Not only will we be broke, but I'll lose my shot at impressing the woman of my dreams."

"Phoebe's the woman of your dreams?"

Gil laughed softly. "I know it sounds crazy, but she hit me like a lightning bolt. She's smart, funny, sexy, sweet, and fun. Ever since the wine tasting, I've been trying to figure out how to make her fall in love with me before I leave. But will she want someone with no future?"

"The best way to help your company is to cooperate with the investigation, and here you are, trying to help. But what about the rest of your team? Is there a chance they could be involved?"

"Jeremiah is my brother from another mother. I'm not kidding. I'd trust him with my life. He's all about integrity. Ethics matter more to him than money. And Stephanie hates violence. She won't watch horror movies, she faints at the sight of blood, and she cries during sappy commercials. She gets mad if someone kills a spider. She's a softie. Putting those things aside, why would any of us want to sabotage our dream? By hurting the poets, we'd be hurting ourselves."

Jane wasn't ready to concede the point. "So you know Stephanie as well as you know Jeremiah?"

"Does that even matter? If Current Mood goes under, Stephanie loses her job. She's our only salaried employee, and she's already going to have to perform a PR miracle if she wants her job to exist after this competition is finally over."

They entered the village, and Jane was stunned by what she saw. Not only was every parking spot taken, but so were the loading zones, alley entrances, and private driveways.

"Whoa," Gil said, his head swiveling from left to right.

As they got closer to the Pickled Pig, the parking violations became more flagrant. Vehicles sat on sidewalks, were parked on lawns, and were packed into the school's bus lot.

The sheriff skirted around a knot of people and turned into the department parking lot. He'd barely stopped before he was out of the SUV. "I'm going to check in with my officers," he told Jane. "Call me if you spot her."

"We will."

Jane led Gil to the Canvas Creamery. Instead of walking through the front garden, she turned down the lane and approached the building from the back. She knocked twice, and Phoebe stepped outside.

"Oh!" she exclaimed as her gaze landed on Gil.

Bowing gallantly, he said, "I'm not quite a knight in shining armor, so I hope you'll settle for a squire in a T-shirt."

Phoebe grinned. "I like your shirt. Green's my favorite color."

"Any sign of Farah?" Jane asked.

"Not yet. One of the guys from Spokes said a bike was left outside their door, but they have no idea when it was dropped off. Eugenia and Violet are at the antique shop. They want to help."

"Okay. You and Gil can search from here to Storyton Outfitters. I'll pick up Eugenia and Violet and work the other side of the street."

Jane didn't need to knock on the door to The Old Curiosity Shop because Violet and Mrs. Pratt rushed out to greet her the moment she walked through the front gate.

"I never thought I'd be involved in a manhunt," said Mrs. Pratt. She was glowing with excitement.

"Is it a 'manhunt' if you're looking for a woman?" asked Violet.

Ignoring their comments, Jane told her volunteers to check every garden and peer inside every parked car. She'd cover the alleys and the back lane.

"Don't forget the trash cans. She could be hiding in a recycling bin, waiting until it gets dark," Mrs. Pratt said as she hurried away.

The idea hadn't occurred to Jane, and though she felt a little foolish, she followed Mrs. Pratt's suggestion.

There were no people hanging around in the lane behind the shops. In fact, it was eerily quiet.

Jane had just passed the rear entrance of the Daily Bread when she heard footsteps in the alley behind her. Someone was running.

She stiffened, waiting for the runner to appear in the lane. The footfalls were heavy. Too heavy to be Farah's. Was it a villager or an angry visitor from over the mountain?

Some deep-seated instinct warned Jane to prepare for flight, so she pulled her key ring from her pocket.

Separating one key from the rest, she edged closer to Edwin's door and stared down the lane.

The man who rounded the corner moved like a retired linebacker. Tobias Hogg had played football in high school, but that was a long time ago. Since then, age had softened his body and stiffened his joints.

The big man barreled toward Jane, his arms pumping as he ran, His face and neck were pomegranate-red, and his shirt was soaked with sweat.

"Help!" he wheezed. "They're after me!"

Jane fitted the key into the lock and gestured for him to hurry.

By the time he reached her, Tobias was too winded to talk. He pressed his palm to the brick wall and sucked in great gulps of air.

Jane heard more footsteps in the alley. More people were coming, and they were all running.

She unlocked the door, pulled Tobias inside the building, and slammed the door behind him. She clicked the dead bolt into place and put a reassuring hand on Tobias's arm.

"You're safe now. Come sit down. I'll get you some water."

Jane hit the light switch inside the commercial kitchen, illuminating the stainless-steel counters. She filled a glass with cold water and gave it to Tobias. She then ran a dish towel under the tap and handed it to him.

As he wiped his face with the towel, he said, "Do you have a phone? I need to call Barbara."

Jane passed him her phone. "Who's chasing you?"

"A bunch of people from over the mountain. They came here to see Pig Newton, but he's home, with Barbara." He held up a finger, signaling that he needed to pause their conversation. "Barb? Yeah, I'm okay. I was rescued by Jane Steward. She's letting me hide in Edwin's café." He paused to listen and then started shaking his head. "They *will* come to the house! My brothers are sharing our address for a *fee*. You and Pig Newton need to get out of there!"

Barbara's panicked voice burst through the speaker. "Where can I go? I can't take Pig Newton to your mother's place. She'll just tell your brothers!"

Jane knew where Tobias and Barbara lived. Their house was at the end of a narrow road on the hillside, and one could sit on their front porch and look down on the village. It was a peaceful and private place, with only one way in or out. If Barbara left right now, she'd probably run right into her pursuers.

"I have an idea," Jane told Tobias as she hurried over to the cordless phone on the desk. "Tell Barbara to hold on for a second."

She punched in a number and was relieved to hear, "Hilltop Stables. Sam speaking."

"Sam. Thank God. We need a hero on horseback. Pig Newton's in danger."

As quickly as she could, Jane explained the situation. Sam was Edwin's oldest friend. He was a good man with a natural affinity for animals. He had a stable full of horses, most of whom were gentle creatures, because his income came from riding lessons and trail rides. But Sam's personal horse was a fleet-footed gelding named Samson. If Sam saddled his horse right away, he could race through the woods and beat the crowd to Tobias's house.

"I'm on my way. Tell Barbara to leave a key under the mat and then drive away like she's trying to escape. People will follow her car, but Pig Newton won't be in it. He'll be with me. I'll keep him safe until things calm down."

Jane relayed the plan to Tobias, who passed it on to Barbara. As he returned Jane's phone, he seized her hands and cried, "I can't thank you enough. Barbara's going to meet me at Storyton Outfitters. Do you think it's safe to go outside?"

"I'd give it a few minutes if I were you." Jane pulled up Farah's photo and showed it to Tobias. "This is a long shot, considering how many faces you've seen today, but does she look familiar? She's one of my guests. I came to town to find her."

Tobias was still on edge. The fear he felt for his partner and his pig wouldn't abate until he knew they were both safe. But he was in Jane's debt, so he carefully studied the photograph.

"I think I saw her. The store was so packed—none of our regulars could get in—and I was trying to clear a path for Mrs. Chambers. I was worried someone would knock her over, and the last thing she needs is another broken hip. I got her and her groceries into her car, but she couldn't back out because a big SUV was blocking her way." He pointed at Jane's phone. "The driver had his window down, and that woman was talking to him. It looked like she was offering him money. And she was crying."

"Then what happened?"

"I shouted at the guy to move his car. He told the woman to get lost and drove off. She ran to another idling car and showed the driver her money again. That's all I saw. As soon as Mrs. Chambers was able to back out, I went inside to call for help."

Jane tapped her phone. "Can you show me the post that caused this chaos?"

Tobias opened a browser window, typed a few words, and angled the screen to give Jane a better view. "This is the original Twitter post. It was shared to every social media site. The people with the right number of followers came to see Pig Newton. The rest came to mingle with the celebrities. Personally, I can't tell the difference."

"The original post came from PigNewtonNation. The account has been active since June and has thousands of followers. They share your Instagram posts, book news, and photos of Storyton. They're basically a fan page. And you have no idea who this is?"

"Nope."

Jane returned to the most recent post and studied the photo. "Did you take this?"

"That's the craziest thing about this whole thing. I *didn't* take that photo. It's definitely Pig Newton. He has a spot on his nose that looks like a side view of the man in the moon. Another pig might have similar spots, but not the exact same. And since the background is blurry, I can't tell where this was taken."

The timing of this post is suspect. Was someone trying to create a diversion? Did they orchestrate an event to bring in a big crowd and put a strain on local law enforcement?

As Jane stared at the image of Tobias's adorable miniature spotted pig, a thought struck her. She sent a text to the Fins and then drummed her fingers on the counter as she waited for a reply.

Three dots appeared within seconds, but it took much longer for a link and a short list of instructions to appear on her screen.

"I'll try to find out exactly where this photo was taken. If it was taken in Storyton, then someone you know well posted it or sent it to the person behind PigNewtonNation."

Tobias stared at her in amazement. "How can you do that?"

"Sterling told me that the EXIF data—whatever that is—would reveal GPS coordinates. Oh, look. Here they are." Jane copied the coordinates and pasted them into the search bar of Google Maps.

"That's my house!" Tobias yelled. Pressing his hands to his cheeks, he murmured, "My brothers. They did this. That thing on the ground is a blanket. A few weeks ago, Barbara and I had Mama and my brothers over for supper. Companies keep sending me free stuff that I don't need and didn't ask for, but my brothers love freebies, so I invited them over to have their pick. I thought they'd stop being so jealous if they could share in my success."

Jane could see that Tobias was hurting, but she didn't have time to console him. She needed to search for Farah before she caught a ride out of town.

"So, one of your brothers took the photo. Did they create the account?"

Tobias let out a derisive snort. "No way. They can barely use the registers at work. My brothers didn't start that Twitter account, but I bet they know who did."

Jane's phone vibrated, and she glanced at the screen. "Sam has Pig Newton, and Barbara's on her way to get you."

Tobias was about to hug Jane when he caught sight of his sweaty shirt. Instead, he clasped his hands together and said, "Thank you so much."

"Now, I need your help. Today's social media fiasco might be connected to my missing guest. I think she's trying to buy a ride out of town. She's desperate, Tobias, and she might be a murderer. That's why I need you to confront your brothers. I know you don't want to go back to the store, but you have to get them to cough up a name."

Though clearly aggrieved, Tobias promised to do as she asked.

Jane grabbed a chef's coat from the hook by the door and told Tobias to put it on. She then handed him a black bandana.

"Tie that around your head and keep your eyes lowered as you walk. Hopefully, no one will look at you too closely and we'll get to the market in one piece. If Farah hasn't found a ride yet, she'll be hanging around a parking area. We need to move quickly."

The crowd surrounding the Pickled Pig was noticeably smaller than it had been before. There was no sign of Farah, so Jane followed Tobias to the delivery door at the back of the store.

In the office, Tobias picked up the phone, pressed a button, and said, "Duncan Hogg, please report to the manager's office. Duncan Hogg, Code Brown."

"What does that mean?" Jane asked.

"It means that we need to call the sheriff's department. Duncan has his faults, but he respects officers of the law. It's the only way I could think of to get him back here."

Tobias knew his brother well. It wasn't long before Duncan Hogg was darkening the doorway.

He was about to berate Tobias when he noticed Jane and attempted to rearrange his features into a smile.

Because he couldn't quite force his lips to curve upward, his expression was caught between a snarl and a sneer.

"Ms. Steward! What a surprise. I, uh, I didn't expect to find you here."

"I asked Tobias to call you because I'm assisting Sheriff Evans with his investigation. It's a murder investigation, Mr. Hogg, and *you* might hold the key to the killer's identity. We're running out of time and really need a hero. I'm hoping that hero is you."

Jane was laying it on thick, but Duncan puffed up with self-importance and said, "Some people consider me to be a leader of this community, so I see it as my duty to help wherever I can."

Tobias opened his mouth, undoubtedly preparing to rip into his brother, but Jane clamped her hand around his arm and gave him a hard stare. "Show Duncan how the investigation ties to this influx of unexpected visitors."

"She's talking about this." Tobias showed Duncan the photo of Pig Newton. "The authorities can trace where the photo was taken. Someone took this in my house on a Sunday in June. You, Rufus, and Mama were there that day. No one's in trouble for taking the picture, but Ms. Steward and Sheriff Evans need to know who paid you for it."

"How did you—?"

Jane didn't give him a chance to finish. Smiling benevolently, she went on. "Mr. Hogg, there's nothing wrong with sharing a photo of that precious pig. Nothing at all. The sheriff isn't interested in the folks who came to see Pig Newton. He only cares about the identity of the person who asked you for that photo. There's no time to waste. The killer could be out there at this very moment"—she pointed toward the front of the store—"trying to escape!"

Looking a little green, Duncan crossed the room to the wall safe and opened it. His hand shook as he retrieved two scraps of paper and offered it to Jane. "They offered us money for a picture. Rufus didn't believe that someone could send money through the computer, but I thought we should take a chance. And it worked! I kept copies of the emails. I kept it in case they tried to back out."

A quick scan of the email left Jane feeling deflated. The sender's name was a random assortment of letters and numbers and was probably sent using an email server that deleted its messages after twenty-four hours. The messages could probably be retrieved, but going through the correct legal channels to gain access would take days or weeks. They didn't have that kind of time. They had hours.

"Unfortunately, this doesn't tell us anything." Jane's voice was leaden. "Was this the only communication you received?"

Duncan nodded.

Jane used her phone to snap a photo of the email and sent it to the Fins. She then thanked both Hogg brothers and hurried back outside to search for Farah.

She was heading for the post office parking lot when she heard her phone ping. Sterling had sent her a text that made her stop in her tracks.

Looked up the IP address of the PigNewtonNation's social media accounts. The geolocation is in Chicago. The accounts were created from a computer at the offices of Current Mood Cards.

Before Jane could unpack the meaning of Sterling's message, she saw movement across the parking lot. Farah Khan was climbing into the bed of a pickup truck.

Shoving her phone into her pocket, Jane started to run.

Chapter 16

By the time Jane reached the pickup and peered into the bed, Farah was completely hidden under a large canvas tarp. The cab was empty, which meant Farah was planning to hitch a ride out of town without the owner's knowledge.

After firing off a text to Phoebe, Jane sent one to the Fins.

I found Farah. Waiting for reinforcements before I confront her. Gil came with me. He wanted to help.

Sterling replied, **Be sure to bring him back to Storyton Hall. The Current Mood folks have been asked to stay in the Safari Room until the sheriff tells them otherwise. Gil should join them when he gets back.**

Jane typed, **What about Stephanie?**

Deputy Emory didn't get much out of her, but she thinks she's hiding something. Sit tight. I'm on my way.

There was no movement from under the tarp, but Jane kept glancing from the tarp to the street and back again.

Finally, she saw Phoebe, Gil, and Mrs. Pratt heading her way. Mrs. Pratt returned her wave and then stepped into the middle of the street. Horns blared, but she raised her hand like a traffic cop and pointed at the pedestrian crosswalk. A silver Porsche kept inching forward and the driver rolled down his window to vent his indignation. Unfazed, Mrs. Pratt beckoned for Phoebe and Gil to cross. Once they were in the clear, she wagged her finger at the driver. He responded by flipping her the bird.

As soon as she was within shouting distance of Jane, Mrs. Pratt bellowed, "Such a bother over one little pig! Don't people have better things to do? Books to read? Cookies to eat? For heaven's sake, I've never seen such a circus."

Gil and Phoebe, who were walking so close together that their shoulders touched, exchanged grins.

Jane wanted to pull Phoebe aside and whisper, "Don't fall for him," but since Phoebe and Gil were practically joined at the hip, she pointed at the pickup truck behind her instead.

"What do we do now that we've found her?" Mrs. Pratt asked *sotto voce*.

"First of all, we have to be calm. We're going to talk to her until Sterling gets here. She can't run with all four of us surrounding the truck bed, but I'd rather not cause a scene—especially since all of these people are looking for something to post on social media. They're upset because they've been denied their moment with Pig Newton. If they see the four of us ganging up on a woman, the truth will be twisted into knots for the sake of a juicy story."

"She's right," said Gil. "All is takes is one video clip, taken out of context, to ruin reputations."

Phoebe was gazing at Gil like he'd hung the moon while Mrs. Pratt focused her attention on the pickup truck.

"The three of us should spread out around the truck bed," Jane said, gesturing between herself, Phoebe, and Mrs. Pratt. "Gil? Would you keep an eye out for bystanders and warn me if someone heads our way?"

"You got it," said Gil.

He really acts like one of the good guys. What if he ends up being a nightmare instead of Phoebe's dream man? She'll be devastated.

The thought had barely crossed Jane's mind when Mrs. Pratt reached into the truck bed and rustled the tarp. In a singsong voice, she said, "Come out, come out, we know where you are. You didn't fly in on a tornado or fall from a star. You're a guest from Storyton Hall, so come out, come out, or the sheriff we'll call."

Phoebe clapped softly. "Maybe *you* should've entered the greeting card contest."

Mrs. Pratt was too busy preening to see Farah's head appear on the opposite side of the truck bed. However, Jane saw the terror etched on the younger woman's face.

"It's okay," she said, holding her hands out in a pacifying gesture. "I just want to talk to you."

Farah clung to the tarp as if it were a very large security blanket. She whispered something, but Jane didn't catch it.

"Sorry, but I didn't hear that."

After darting a quick glance at Phoebe and Mrs. Pratt, Farah turned to Jane and whimpered, "Please. Please let me go."

"You know I can't. Two people are dead, Ms. Khan."

"And I'll be next if you don't let me go!"

Her words gave Jane pause. "What makes you say that?"

Farah stared at her in disbelief. "Either Gretchen or Connor would've won the competition. Now that they're gone, everyone thinks I'll win. Do you know what that means? It means *I'm* going to be next. I came here to compete, but I'm not willing to die for the chance!"

"Running away makes you look guilty, Ms. Khan. Do you know what else makes you look guilty? Those jokes you had in your room. The ones Connor wrote?"

Again, Farah looked at Jane like she had two heads. "Why? He read them out loud during our session on writing humor. He made extra copies, so I took one. I was trying to figure out if his words were funny or if it was just his delivery. I stink at writing humor, but it's not like I was going to plagiarize Connor."

"What about the kombucha?"

Farah's face clouded in confusion. "What about it?"

"Why did you have a bottle of Connor's homemade kombucha in your room?"

"I didn't. That stuff's disgusting. I'd never—wait! Someone must have put it there. But why? Are they trying to frame me? Was there something in that bottle besides kombucha?"

Jane's expression turned hard. "You tell me."

Tears sprang into Farah's eyes. "I can't! I don't know what happened to Gretchen or Connor! I just want to go home. I'll never write another poem if I can just make it out of here alive. Why won't you let me leave?"

Jane edged closer to Farah. "No one's allowed to leave without the sheriff's permission, so you're going back to Storyton Hall. But I *will* see to it that you're guarded at all times. No one will lay a finger on you."

When Farah glanced to her right and saw Sterling standing next to Mrs. Pratt, she began to sob.

Mrs. Pratt bustled around the truck and put her arm around Farah's shoulders. "Hush now. Running away won't fix anything. The best way to deal with fear is to face it. And you don't have to do it alone. We want to help." She dug around in her purse and came up with a wad of tissues. "Dry your eyes, my dear. That's it. Now, let's get you out of this truck."

Sterling helped Farah climb down, but as soon as her feet touched the ground, she released his hand and reached for Mrs. Pratt. "Would you come with me?"

Mrs. Pratt looked to Jane for guidance. At Jane's nod, she said, "Of course."

Sterling opened the car door for Farah and Mrs. Pratt. After they were settled in the back seat, he looked at Gil and gestured at the passenger seat. "Mr. Callahan?"

Gil took Phoebe's hand and said, "I don't want to leave, but I also don't want you to come back with me. I don't want anything to happen to you."

"Well—" Phoebe began, but before she could continue, a pair of bearded giants wearing black T-shirts, cargo pants, and combat boots were suddenly looming over her.

"Hey, lady! What are you doing around our truck?" barked the first man. He folded his massive arms over his tree-trunk chest and glowered at their entire party.

Stepping in front of Phoebe, Gil said, "We saw a woman climb under your tarp. We thought she might be hurt, so we came over to check on her. We helped her get out, and she's in that car now. No harm done."

"We'll see about that," growled the second giant,

lumbering over to the truck bed. He pulled back the tarp and examined the contents concealed beneath it. Jane had no idea what the assortment of black cubes and metal poles were, but it seemed highly unlikely that Farah had damaged them.

"Anything missing?" demanded the first giant.

"No, but if there's even the tiniest scratch to the paint—"

Gil splayed his hands. "The woman didn't touch anything. She hid because she's upset, which is why we need to get her back to her hotel. Have a nice day."

The first giant barred his path, and Jane steeled herself for a fight. She could never overpower the second giant, but Sterling could. Before anyone had a chance to move, however, Phoebe intervened.

"You guys look super thirsty. See that shop down the street there? The Canvas Creamery? I own it. If you'll follow me, I'll treat you to an iced coffee. Or a gelato. Today's flavors are strawberry cheesecake, coconut, lemon-lime, dark chocolate chip, and hazelnut."

The second giant said, "I like coconut."

"Go," Phoebe mouthed to Jane before smiling at the giants. "This way, gentlemen."

Gil was about to follow after Phoebe, but Jane seized his arm and muttered, "She defused those walking bombs so that we could get out of here, so let's go."

"I can't leave her alone with the Testosterone Twins!"

Jane propelled him toward the car. "She's handled worse."

Inside the car, Gil let out a defeated sigh. "I had the chance to impress her, and I flubbed it."

"Because you didn't take a swing at that giant?" Jane scoffed. "You were calm and reasonable. Rational people settle things using their words, not their fists."

"Not exactly hero material," mumbled Gil.

He looked so forlorn that Jane almost laughed. "You've been watching too many action movies. Phoebe would rather hang out with Tom Hanks than Dwayne Johnson."

"Don't sell The Rock short. He's a wrestler, actor, hip-hop artist, and the father of three girls. The guy's a Renaissance man."

"He still can't top Tom Hanks," said Mrs. Pratt. "The Rock couldn't pull off Mr. Rogers, and the whole world loves Mr. Rogers."

Gil conceded the point.

Everyone fell quiet as Sterling drove down Main Street. The traffic congestion had eased a bit, and they passed through the iron gates leading to Storyton Hall in under fifteen minutes.

Butterworth and Deputy Emory were waiting for them on the front steps. Butterworth escorted Gil to the Isak Dinesen Safari Room, and Jane asked Deputy Emory to take Farah and Mrs. Pratt to the cookbook nook. Farah would be safe there, and Mrs. Pratt would see to it that she had something to eat and drink.

Jane waited for Butterworth to return to the lobby.

"What did I miss?"

"For starters, a love poem was found inside Mr. Jensen's wallet. It's an exact copy of the love poem found in Ms. West's phone case. Same font, same paper, same words."

After briefly mulling this over, Jane said, "Did Connor write it for Gretchen? Or vice versa?"

"Mr. Sinclair doesn't think it was penned by either of them. He believes the style is too different. An online search for the poem yielded no results, but it's important. Both of our victims had a copy. Both of our victims handled the poem until the paper turned butter-soft. That means they read it again and again."

Jane bunched her lips to the side. "I wonder if Farah has a copy."

"We should ask."

Lowering her voice, Jane said, "Has Jeremiah picked a winner yet?"

"He has. Right now, he and Mr. Callahan are selecting a runner-up, just in case their first choice ends up behind bars."

Jane glanced at her watch. The Poetry of the Plate banquet would be starting in ninety minutes, and as much as she'd hoped for a different outcome, it looked like the final event of the competition would occur with a killer still at large.

"I wish I could see inside Farah's head," she told Butterworth. "I'd love to know if she was running away because she didn't want to be caught by a murderer or because she didn't want to be caught by Sheriff Evans. Either way, she was ready to forfeit the Current Mood contract."

Butterworth tilted his head. "We've been operating on the assumption that money is at the heart of this mystery. But what if it's something else entirely? Vengeance? Unrequited love? Poetic justice?"

"The Lady of Shalott. Ophelia. Brightleaf. The love poem. Those center around emotions, not money. Poetry is emotion put into words. What emotion has the killer conveyed to us?"

A spark ignited in Butterworth's eyes. "Both victims were memorialized. Their deaths were turned into a tableau. Tragic, beautiful, haunting. What if it was more than respect? What if the killer truly cared for Ms. West and Mr. Jensen?"

"Someone cared enough to give them a love poem."

Butterworth stroked his chin. "If either victim had a romantic relationship with the killer, it was a well-kept secret."

"If the sheriff doesn't make an arrest after speaking with Farah and Stephanie, then we'll have no choice but to use words as a weapon."

"At the banquet?"

Jane nodded. "I think we'll kick off the evening with a poetry reading."

After hearing that Sheriff Evans had questioned Gil, Jeremiah, and Stephanie to no avail, Jane went home to dress for the banquet. She had twenty minutes to get ready before the Cover Girls showed up for a pre-banquet cocktail, and a small part of her wished she could cancel their plans. But the thought of venting to her friends over a glass of wine trumped her desire for some alone time.

Edwin entered the bedroom while Jane was twisting her right arm behind her back in a fruitless attempt to zip up her dress.

"Isn't this why you keep me around?" he teased, pushing her hand away. He finished zipping the dress and bent to kiss the nape of her neck.

Jane turned around and rested her head on Edwin's shoulder. She closed her eyes and breathed him in. She didn't want to move. When his hands began massaging the tight muscles of her back, she put her arms around his waist and sighed.

"Tough day, huh?" he murmured into her hair.

"Just a bit."

His fingers worked the knots just below her shoulder

blades. "You always hold tension here. You should get a proper massage once this is all over."

Jane sighed. "*If* it's ever over. We're not even close to catching the killer. The sheriff won't let the guests leave tomorrow without definitive proof of their innocence. That means watching hours upon hours of camera footage to trace everyone's movements. What am I supposed to do with the incoming guests? Call them tonight and ask them to rebook? I don't think an apology and a full refund is going to cut it, and when they learn that a murder investigation is the reason we canceled, I doubt we'll see them in the future. Why wouldn't they look for a nice, peaceful place to stay?"

Edwin lifted Jane's chin with a finger, forcing her to meet his eyes. "Hey. It might feel like the midnight hour, but we're not there yet. We still have tonight and tomorrow morning to expose the killer. I know you're tired. I also know that you won't give up. So tell me what I can do to help."

"Make me forget about all of this for a few seconds." She put her hands on either side of his face and pulled him in for a kiss.

Edwin pressed her to him, his fingers sinking into her hair as he traced a line of kisses from her jawline to her ear.

"I love you," he whispered. He gently nipped her neck. "But if we don't leave now, I won't be able to stop." He slid his fingers under the collar of her dress, eased the fabric aside, and kissed the swell of her collarbone. "If we don't leave this room, I'm going to unzip this dress and take you to bed."

Jane let out a groan of frustration and stepped out of

his embrace. "When this is all over, we're going to stand here, just like we are now, and you *will* unzip this dress."

The chime of the doorbell floated up the stairs. Jane kissed Edwin one more time before she hurried downstairs to greet her friends.

Unsurprisingly, Eloise was the first to arrive. She always seemed to know when Jane needed an extra dose of support.

"You look beautiful." Eloise gave Jane a quick hug.

"I look tired. *You* look beautiful. That dress is pure poetry. Is it one of Mabel's?"

Eloise spun around, causing the long, dusky-rose skirt to flare out and the gold tulle embroidery to catch the light. "Yep. She made it for my honeymoon. What about yours?"

Jane's maxi dress was white with a pink floral pattern. It had a tight bodice and a long, loose skirt. "No. I bought this online years ago. Come on into the kitchen. I need at least two servings of liquid courage if I'm going to make it through the night."

In the kitchen, Eloise watched Jane open a bottle of cabernet and a bottle of prosecco. "Landon told me about the water hemlock. That's really scary. I never knew we had such dangerous plants growing here."

"Me either." Jane was about to fill two wineglasses, but she lowered the bottle and looked at her friend. "Wait. Did he find some?"

"I think so. He and Sterling were examining it, which means you should hear from him any minute now." Eloise took the bottle from Jane and waved for her to sit down. "Landon said the village was packed with people today. What was going on?"

Jane told her about the Twitter post and how Sam had to rescue Pig Newton.

Eloise was completely riveted. When Jane finished with her story, Eloise raised her glass and said, "To Sam. Tamer of stallions and hero to miniature pigs."

Smiling, Jane said, "To Sam."

"Well, no wonder the sheriff was giving the Current Mood squad the third degree. If the post came from their office building, then Stephanie must have done it. She's in PR, after all, and I doubt she rode to the village this morning on a whim. I bet she went there to make sure her post had the intended result."

This hadn't occurred to Jane, but it made perfect sense. "Do the other Cover Girls know about the poison hemlock?"

"No. Landon only told me because I was going to hit one of the trails this afternoon, and when he asked me to stay close to home, I knew something was up. I know about Connor too. I'm really sorry, Jane." Eloise's eyes filled with sympathy. "You're probably running on empty by now."

The doorbell rang, and Betty called out, "We're here!"

"In the kitchen," Jane shouted back.

Eloise jerked her head toward the front door. "You're not alone. We'll do whatever you ask. Just give us an assignment."

Her words reminded Jane of what Mrs. Pratt had said to Farah. She'd told her that she wasn't alone.

"Assignment? Did we have homework?" asked Mabel. She wore a pale pink dress patterned with fuchsia roses.

Mrs. Pratt bustled in behind Mabel. Her dress featured tropical flowers on a field of navy. "No, dear. They're probably talking about the investigation."

Violet's floral dress was a soft lilac, and she'd woven

sprigs of lavender into her braided hair. She handed Jane a bouquet of daisies. "These are for you. I can put them in water if you want to tell us what's going on."

Jane thanked Violet and told her friends to help themselves to wine. The sunflowers on Betty's skirts rippled as she moved forward to fill the wineglasses. Phoebe, who wore a sage-green dress with splashes of poppy-orange, passed a glass to Anna.

"Most of us have one kind of flowers on our dresses, but you have the whole garden," Phoebe said to Anna.

"What can I say? I'm an overachiever."

Mabel swept her arm in an arc. "We look like extras from *The Nutcracker*."

"You look lovely," Jane said as she led her friends into the living room.

By the time she'd summarized all that had happened since they'd last been together as a group, everyone's glasses were empty.

After retrieving another bottle from the kitchen, Betty said, "Stephanie definitely sounds shady."

"She needs to confess," cried Anna. "The competition will be over after the winner's announced at the banquet. We can't let her get away with murder!"

"If the sheriff can't get her to do that, how can we?" asked Violet.

Jane told her friends that even if Stephanie was responsible for the social media post, she wasn't necessarily the murderer. The Cover Girls were too keyed up to listen to reason and continued to plot Stephanie's demise.

Mrs. Pratt cleared her throat. When she was certain she had everyone's attention, she said, "We could write an anonymous poem." Holding her hands over her heart, she intoned,

"I know what you did.
"You poisoned those kids.
"We can make a deal.
"My lips will stay sealed.
"Meet me in the gazebo at eight
"With all your cash—don't be late!"

The other Cover Girls stared at Mrs. Pratt. She blushed and reached for her wineglass, muttering something about the pressure of impromptu performances under her breath.

"That was impressive, Eugenia. I couldn't come up with anything like that on the spot," Jane said.

Mabel gave Mrs. Pratt a playful nudge. "Okay, Emily Dickinson, so what happens after she shows up at the gazebo?"

"Yeah, who'll meet her?" Phoebe looked at Jane. "You?"

Eloise shook her head. "Someone more imposing. No offense, Jane. What about Butterworth? With a few deputies hiding in the bushes?"

"It's worth a try," Violet said. "But I don't think we should focus all our energy on Stephanie. That media post could have been created by Jeremiah or Gil."

Jane and Phoebe exchanged glances, which didn't go unnoticed by Mrs. Pratt. She studied Phoebe's face for a moment before her eyes widened, and she covered her mouth with her hand.

Anna said, "What am I missing?"

"Phoebe doesn't want Gil to be involved because she's sweet on him," declared Mrs. Pratt.

"She's right." Phoebe sounded dejected. "I don't want him to be mixed up in anything bad because I like him. I really, really like him."

Violet squeezed Phoebe's hand and told her that Gil was probably innocent. Jane knew this might not be the case but understood that Violet was trying to reassure Phoebe. She was about to agree with her friend when someone knocked on the front door.

"I'll get it!" Eloise sprang up and hurried out of the room. Seconds later, she returned with Lachlan in tow.

After taking one look at his face, Jane said, "You found the hemlock." When he didn't answer right away, she gestured at the Cover Girls. "It's okay. They know everything and want to help."

Lachlan nodded. "I found the plants and a partial shoeprint too. I took images and sent them to the sheriff. He wants us to examine the guest's closets during the banquet. If we find the shoe, we find the killer."

"Sounds like a twisted Cinderella story," said Mabel.

Mrs. Pratt got to her feet and put her hands on her hips. "It'll take a small army to search all of those rooms."

Eloise looped her arm through Mrs. Pratt's and smiled. "Jane doesn't need an army. She has a book club."

Chapter 17

The terrace had been transformed for the Poetry of Food Feast, and a few guests were already wandering around admiring the assortment of wines on offer or reading the names of each dish as written on the chalkboard placards lining the buffet table.

Weeks ago, when Jane and Mrs. Hubbard had begun planning the feast, she'd envisioned a Bohemian-style setting with whimsically elegant food. The Storyton Hall staff had gone above and beyond to turn her vision into reality. The ground was covered with mismatched rugs, a network of string lights and lanterns illuminated the terrace, and dozens of plants and small trees in multicolored pots divided the five buffet stations.

Each station represented a poem about food. Moving from left to right, diners began their food journey with an enormous cheese and cracker board in homage of Katherine Mansfield's "Countrywomen." The next table featured ingredients from Ben Jonson's "Inviting a Friend to Supper," like a salad of olives and tomatoes with a lemon-caper dressing, Japanese egg custard, and wine-infused mutton with wild mushrooms.

"I won't have a problem finding things to eat here," one guest said to another. "Sometimes events like this have limited vegetarian choices, but I'm going to eat like a king tonight."

The two guests were standing by the Shel Silverstein station. The dishes, which were based off his poem, "Italian Food," included fettucine with pesto and peas and sweet potato ravioli in a basil brown-butter sauce. Silverstein shared a table with Elizabeth Bishop. In her poem, "A Miracle for Breakfast," she wrote about a "crumb of bread." The reference had inspired Mrs. Hubbard to produce herbed garlic rolls, crab and avocado crostini, pimento and bacon bruschetta, and baked vegetables with Parmesan breading.

A smaller station was dedicated to D.H. Lawrence's "Figs." Though the poem's title was short and sweet, the dishes created to highlight the fruit were full of depth and dimension. Jane remembered asking Mrs. Hubbard if it was necessary to serve roast chicken with figs and rosemary in addition to honey-glazed salmon with caramelized onions and figs.

" 'Necessary'? When has that word ever been associated with a feast? To celebrate food, we must present a dazzling variety of dishes," had been Mrs. Hubbard's rejoinder.

Despite her belief that they didn't need quite so many savory items, Jane had bowed to the head cook's expertise. She knew better than to argue with Mrs. Hubbard over the desserts, which meant the final buffet station was so laden with decadent delights that Jane half-expected the table to collapse.

Several guests were reading the placards aloud. Others were trying to decide which treats to sample.

"Everything sounds so good!" a woman said.

"Maybe we should eat in reverse order." Her companion waved her arm around the terrace. "If I don't have room for cheese, I'll live, but my life won't be complete if I don't try the pineapple tiramisu or that chocolate pavlova with Nutella and strawberries."

The woman pointed at the printout of the first stanza of Christina Rossetti's "Goblin Market" and said, "I've never read the whole poem, but she's got to win the prize for most fruit mentioned in a single verse."

Leaving the guests to drool over the rest of the desserts, Jane wondered if Mrs. Hubbard had set aside servings of salted caramel grilled peaches, blackberry mousse, apricot and almond Linzer torte, cherry and dark chocolate brownie bites, orange cream cupcakes, or melon in coconut sauce for the twins.

Luckily, they were having dinner with Edwin in the kitchens. He'd make sure they ate their veggies and protein before he let them loose on the desserts, and after their meal was finished, Edwin would keep Fitz and Hem close.

"I don't want to leave them home alone, but I also want to be available if you need me, so we'll hang out in the surveillance room. The boys are eager to prove their usefulness, and I want to keep an eye on the guests."

He'd shared these plans with Jane as she and the Cover Girls walked through Milton's Gardens. Jane's friends headed straight for the manor house to receive further instructions from Butterworth, but she'd paused under the garden arch to speak with Edwin.

As they'd stood in the jasmine-scented air, Edwin had brought her hand to his lips and whispered, "'In your light, I learn how to love. In your beauty, how to make poems.'"

"That sounds like Rumi."

Edwin had smiled and said, "No other poet but Rumi could understand how I feel about you."

Now, as Jane entered the manor house, she touched the back of her hand where Edwin's lips had brushed her skin. With that simple gesture, he'd reminded her that she was loved and cherished. He'd renewed her strength and shored up her resolve.

How I love that man.

The thought barely had time to form before someone came up behind her and grabbed her arm.

Jane spun around to face Jeremiah.

He immediately released her arm. "Sorry, I didn't mean to creep up on you. I just wanted to ask you if anyone's been arrested without drawing too much attention." He retreated a step so that he was no longer invading Jane's personal space and gestured down the hall toward the door leading to the terrace. "It doesn't feel right—to eat this beautiful food and drink fine wine. To talk about our company and pick a winner. I don't think I can do it."

From the outside, Jeremiah looked completely put together. His sand-colored suit was perfectly pressed, and his Converse sneakers added an element of playfulness to his outfit. But his handsome face was drawn with worry, and his brown eyes held no spark.

"No, there hasn't been an arrest yet."

Jane recognized the look of defeat on Jeremiah's face. How often had she felt exactly what he was feeling right now?

"I could really use a drink," she said. "Would you join me?"

After a quick glance at his watch, Jeremiah accepted her offer.

They sat at the bar in the Ian Fleming Lounge, and Jane ordered two spitfires.

"Never had one of those. What's in it?" asked Jeremiah.

The bartender showed him a bottle of cognac. "A shot of this along with white wine, egg white, lemon juice, and simple syrup. Shaken and served cold. The name sounds like it should have a fiery taste, but it's the citrus kick that makes a spitfire special. It'll wake you up, from head to toe."

Jeremiah said, "I wish it would take me back to this morning and let me wake up to a totally different day, but I know it won't. I'll take one if you can make it without the booze."

"Two mocktails, please," said Jane.

They watched the bartender add the ingredients to a cocktail shaker. He gave it a shake, added ice, and repeated the process. He then poured the chilled liquid into martini glasses. He dropped a twist of lemon peel into each glass and placed them on napkins. To give Jane some privacy, he came out from behind the bar and began to wipe off tables at the opposite end of the room.

There was no one else in the lounge. The low lighting, soft music, and quiet were like the calm before a storm.

"Here's to a better tomorrow," Jane said.

She sipped her drink. It had a wonderful taste, but she doubted it would help loosen Jeremiah up. He was wound way too tight.

"Jeremiah, I'm not going to mince words. Stephanie's behavior is suspicious, and no one is satisfied by the answers she's given. You know her better than we do, so be honest. Do you think she's hiding something?"

Anger flared in Jeremiah's eyes. "She's no stone-cold killer, that's for damn sure."

"That's not what I asked."

He grunted in annoyance. "Just because she can't account for every minute of her day, doesn't mean that she's lying. If she'd known we were going to be in this mess, she'd have paid more attention."

Softening her voice, Jane said, "You're frustrated. I get it. You're loyal to Gil and Stephanie. I get that too. I care about my staff. And I care about my guests. I'm furious and deeply sad that two of my guests lost their lives. I'm also desperate to keep the rest of them—and my coworkers—safe. That's why I can't give Stephanie a break. Let's be real for a second. She wasn't wandering the grounds for ninety minutes after a long bike ride. And unless you or Gil put up the Pig Newton post, then you don't know Stephanie as well as you think."

Jeremiah was deflated. "Maybe not, but she's been an incredible asset. I've never met anyone with such creative marketing ideas or enthusiasm. If there was an espresso-drinking, Einstein-kind-of-thinking, Boss Babe Barbie, that'd be Stephanie. That woman is always smiling. She's always positive. And man, does she like pink."

"Are you two involved outside of work?"

"No, it's not like that. I live with my high school sweetheart, and I don't want anybody else. I admire Stephanie as a person, that's all. She gets the job done."

As Jane considered what to say next, Jeremiah polished off the rest of his drink. He put the glass down and stared at it. Jane turned her head and caught the bartender's eye.

"Maybe she posted that thing about the pig. Maybe she wanted to get a bunch of celebrities to come to Storyton while we were here. Maybe she wanted to cash in on the publicity. That would be her kind of out-of-the-box thinking. But murder? No way, no how. Why would she sabotage this competition? We can't launch our first wave of cards without an amazing writer. And if Current Mood fails, Stephanie's out of a job."

"I had the same thought," Jane admitted. "But if you're right about her motives for putting up that social media post, then why deny it? She hasn't broken any laws."

Jeremiah glowered at Jane. "She's probably scared! Two people are dead, but everyone can go back to their lives if there's an arrest, right? Maybe she's worried that if she tells the truth about the post, she'll end up behind bars with no hope of getting out."

"Sheriff Evans wouldn't put her jail out of convenience or to make the department look better. He's not like that at all."

"I'm a Black man in a small, southern town in the middle of nowhere, so forgive me for not sharing your faith in local law enforcement."

Holding his gaze, Jane nodded in understanding. She let the silence sit between them for a bit before saying, "Is Stephanie closer to you or to Gil?"

"As in, who could get her to talk?" Jeremiah shrugged. "Probably Gil. He's got that golden retriever vibe about him—he's always the most approachable person in any room."

"Do you trust him?"

Jeremiah bristled. "With my life. And before you ask,

he already tried talking to her. We both did. Stephanie just cried and said she knew nothing about the post or the murders. She's done talking to us, and she's not even coming to the feast. After all of this, she'll probably quit."

The bartender asked if they'd like another round, but Jane didn't reply.

She's not coming to the feast.

"Not for me, thanks." Jeremiah smiled politely as he slid off his stool.

Jane got up too. "I won't rest until we have all the answers. I give you my word."

Considering all that Jeremiah stood to lose, words were insufficient. But Jane had nothing else to offer.

As she watched him leave the lounge, Jane steeled herself to follow. The feast was about to start, which meant the Fins, the Cover Girls, and officers from the sheriff's department would be free to enter the guest rooms to examine the soles of their shoes.

But not all of the rooms will be empty. Stephanie isn't coming to the feast!

Jane hurried through the lobby and into Shakespeare's Theater.

Inside, Sheriff Evans was addressing his officers and volunteers. Behind him, the image of a partial shoe print filled the oversized screen.

"Based on the tread, we're looking for a boot or a sneaker. Note the pattern here." He pointed at the photo. "These wavelike ridges are meant to provide traction. If we're lucky, we'll find mud in the groves between the waves. If you think you've found the shoes, call me immediately. Don't touch anything else in the room, and be sure to wear gloves at all times."

Betty's hand shot up. "What should we do if a guest comes in while we're searching?"

"Good question. Ask them to wait while you call an officer. There'll be at least one on every floor." He glanced around. "By now, you should all have a copy of this print on your phone. If you haven't received a text, see Deputy Phelps right away. As soon as Mr. Alcott gives me the all clear, we'll move out."

Edwin's giving the all clear? Jane was momentarily confused, but then she remembered that Edwin and the twins were manning the surveillance room.

Sheriff Evans switched off the mic and met Jane in the middle of the aisle.

"I heard back from the ME. Ms. West and Mr. Jensen were both poisoned. They ingested a fatal quantity of poison water hemlock, which had been macerated and mixed into Mr. Jensen's homemade kombucha."

"If that's true, is suicide still on the table? What if Connor took his own life after killing Gretchen? Connor could've paid Professor Ashley to help solidify his win."

The sheriff was clearly running on fumes. His uniform was rumpled, the skin around his eyes was puffy and discolored, and his five o'clock shadow had spread over the bottom half of his face. "If we accept that possibility, we also have to accept that Mr. Jensen scattered flowers in what would become his grave, swallowed a substance that would lead to a painful death, and opted to die in a mud puddle. From what everyone tells me, this young man had a lust for life. I don't think he'd have chosen such a sad exit."

"And this print didn't come from his shoes?"

"No. We found hiking boots in Mr. Jensen's closet,

but the pattern on the sole is different. He had three pairs of shoes in total: the boots, loafers, and the sneakers he had on when he died. All three pairs are the same size. All are smaller than the shoe in our photo."

Jane thought about the everyday items she'd seen in Connor's room. A toothbrush, socks, a soft hoodie, a book, shoes—they were all significant because they were the last things Connor had touched. These were the relics of a life. To anyone who cared about Connor, a line of his handwriting on the hotel notepad or the T-shirt he'd worn to bed were now precious memorabilia.

"Have you spoken to his family?"

"I have." The sheriff's voice was weighted with sadness. "Mr. Jensen's parents were vacationing in Australia when they got the news. They'll be here as soon as they can, and I want to have answers by then because closure is the only comfort I can offer. They've lost both of their children. There's no solace in the world for these people. There's only the truth."

Jane gave his arm a squeeze. "No one sleeps until this is resolved. Not us. Not the guests. Not the staff. No one."

"Agreed."

The sheriff glanced down at his phone and then turned to face his officers, the Fins, and the Cover Girls.

"It's time," he said. In the dead silence, his words struck like thunder.

As people began filing out of the theater in teams of two, Jane noticed that one of her Fins was missing. She waited for Sterling and Lachlan to walk by before approaching Butterworth.

"Where's Sinclair?"

"He left for the hospital an hour ago. With so many unknown factors surrounding these deaths, he deemed it prudent to guard the other members of your family."

Jane's cheeks went hot with shame. It had been over an hour since she'd thought about Aunt Octavia and Uncle Aloysius.

Butterworth gestured toward the exit. "After you."

"I'm bound for Stephanie's room," she said as they headed for the exit. "She's abstaining from the feast, and since I haven't had the chance to question her on my own, I'm going to have a go at her. I'll also examine her hiking boots. I know she owns a pair because I've seen her wearing them."

A steely glint appeared in Butterworth's eyes. "Shall I accompany you?"

"It's probably best if you wait in the hall. I'm going to play the sympathetic host. If that fails, we'll have to be more aggressive, even if it means a negative Yelp review."

Butterworth made a small sound that was almost a laugh.

The DO NOT DISTURB sign hung from Stephanie's door handle. She didn't respond to Jane's knock.

"Ms. Harbaugh, it's Jane Steward," Jane spoke in a loud, clear voice. "I need you to open this door. If you don't, I'll assume you need help and will use my master key to open the door."

This did the trick. Stephanie called out, "I'm fine! I just want to be alone."

Irritated, Jane knocked again. "Ms. Harbaugh, I'm worried about you. Please let me see that you're okay."

Stephanie finally relented. As soon as she opened

the door, Jane slipped into the room. Stephanie shut the door, slid the chain lock into place, and took a seat at the end of her bed.

Jane quickly scanned the room. It was pin-neat because Stephanie was clearly ready to check out, whether she had permission to do so or not. Her suitcase, which sat on the luggage rack, was full but not yet zipped. As for Stephanie, she was dressed in black yoga pants and a plain gray sweatshirt.

A hoodie! Jane thought, her heart jumping a beat.

"I'm sorry that I haven't stopped by before now," Jane said in a honeyed voice. "You've had an awful day, haven't you?"

Stephanie visibly relaxed. "You have *no* idea. My whole world's been turned upside down! The people I trusted—who supposedly cared about me—aren't who I thought they were."

"It might feel that way, but it might not be true. Everyone is incredibly upset. These deaths, well, they're hitting everyone really hard. Sometimes people act out of character when they're scared."

Stephanie pulled her long ponytail over one shoulder and began to twist it around and around. "Do I look like a murderer? Do I act like one? I'm all about connecting people, not killing them. Ugh!" She flapped her hands next to her face. "I can't talk about this anymore!"

I wonder if this was how she played it with the sheriff.

Jane sat in the desk chair. "Tell me how I can help. Can I order something for you? A little comfort food or a big drink?"

Stephanie shook her head. "I can't eat. My stomach is in knots."

"Listen, maybe you'd feel better if you knew that the

Pig Newton post brought a ton of business to the village. A bunch of my friends own shops, and they were beyond thrilled. Sundays are usually slow, but not today. The post gave Tobias's book such a huge boost in pre-orders that his publisher is already planning a second printing!"

"Well, I'm glad something good happened today." Her eyes went to her suitcase. "But Current Mood is finished. Everything's ruined. Even if the company survives this nightmare, I can't work there anymore."

Very gently, Jane said, "Because you didn't tell them about the post."

Realizing this was meant as a statement, not a question, Stephanie opened her mouth to protest but changed her mind.

Jane pressed her advantage. "You were just doing what you said—trying to connect people—right?"

"Yes."

It was a single word, but like so many words, it had a powerful impact.

"Talk me through it so I can understand what you were thinking. When did you first get the idea to do a post about Pig Newton?"

Stephanie's glance skittered to her suitcase. "Back in June. I was researching Storyton. I'm always looking at things through a PR lens. Our company is new, which means I have to make it a known brand fast. And when I found out Pig Newton was here, well, that was a gift from the social media gods!"

"I bet."

"So, I reached out to Tobias's brothers, got them to send me that photo, and arranged the invitation-only event with them."

Jane acted surprised. "The Hogg brothers don't usually interact with people outside the village. You must have given them quite the incentive."

"I paid them the same amount I'd pay an influencer. Not big-time influencer money. More like a micro-influencer fee."

Having no idea what the difference was, Jane said, "Did you send them a company check?"

"I wanted to take the money out of petty cash, so I was going to use Venmo or Apple Pay, but they've never heard of those apps. Can you believe it? I had to use an online money service."

"Was this the same money service you used to pay Professor Ashley?"

In a flash, Stephanie was on her feet. She shed her sensitive, mistreated woman act like a snake wriggling out of its skin.

"I don't know what you're talking about, but if you think you can come in here, pretending to be kind—only to turn on me like everyone else, you're wrong! I'm *done!*"

Stephanie started zipping her suitcase, but Jane rushed over and slammed her hand down on the lid. "You're not going anywhere," she said, grabbing the suitcase and dumping its contents on the bed. An avalanche of clothes fell out, followed by a pair of silver heels and pink flipflops. The heaviest shoes, the hiking boots, remained on the bottom of the suitcase.

"What the hell?" Stephanie shrieked, lunging for the suitcase.

Jane thrust out her arm to stop her.

"Get back," she commanded. "Every room in this hotel is being searched. Officers from the sheriff's department and Storyton Hall staff members are right outside that door, so back off!"

The tension between the two women was palpable. The air molecules bouncing around them had the charging voltage of an electric fence. One touch and someone would be burned.

Stephanie held Jane's gaze for what felt like an eon but was probably no more than ten seconds. Then she turned and bolted for the door.

Jane didn't pursue her. She folded her arms over her chest and watched as Stephanie swiped the chain lock off its track and yanked the door open. Before she could dash out, a bear of a man stepped in front of her.

"Ms. Harbaugh. I suggest you remain in your room."

"*No!* I need to go! You can't make me stay, so *move!*"

Keeping his arms at his sides, Butterworth advanced. Stephanie could either catapult into his chest or backpedal. She chose the latter.

Butterworth shut the door and looked a question at Jane.

"Hiking boots," said Jane, picking up one of the boots. She turned it over and examined the pattern on the sole. Her face fell, and she whispered, "The pattern doesn't match."

Chapter 18

Deputies Phelps and Emory escorted Stephanie to a sheriff's department cruiser. Despite her ardent protestations, they were taking her to the station for further questioning.

"Why are you doing this?" she'd shrieked at Jane. "Because I posted about that stupid pig? I did you and everyone in this village a favor!"

Jane's reply was frosty. "It's less about the post and more to do with the money-sending site you used. The Hogg brothers weren't the only ones to receive a payment from that site. Another person was offered money to throw the competition. Add the suspicious deaths of two contestants to that mix, and you have some explaining to do."

Stephanie's mouth fell open and her breath hitched. She looked and sounded like a panting dog. "What? I didn't do that! I only sent money to the brothers!"

Deputy Emory opened the back door and took hold

of Stephanie's arm. "Save it for the station, Ms. Harbaugh."

For a moment, Jane thought Stephanie might try to bolt again, but after glancing at Butterworth, she practically vaulted into the back seat.

Butterworth watched the car drive off. When it disappeared around a bend lined by ancient magnolia trees, he let out a satisfied grunt.

"You think she's guilty," said Jane.

"What do you learn from her body language?"

Over the years, Butterworth had taught Jane how to interpret body language and facial expressions. Though she never expected to achieve his level of mastery, he kept pushing her to hone her skills.

"She alternated between fear, anger, and guilt. One moment, her hands were restless. The next, she wrapped her arms across her torso like she was trying to hold herself together. She looks people directly in the eyes when she's lying. It's when she turned away that I saw how scared she was. The rapid breathing and pacing underscored that. Her anger was genuine too."

"Was it directed at you?"

Jane recalled the fury in Stephanie's hooded brow and the tense cords in her neck. "No. She feels betrayed. By her colleagues, maybe? She's still holding back, and that's generating acute anxiety. She's on a cliff's edge. When she got in the car just now, it was like she knew she was going to fall."

Butterworth gazed up at the clock tower. It glowed like a moon from its spire high above the main doors, its giant hands shifting as another minute ticked by. He laced his fingers together as he mulled over Jane's assessment.

"If Ms. Harbaugh is responsible for these crimes, her motive remains elusive."

Jane had also glanced at the clock and, having decided it was time to head to the banquet, started walking toward the manor house. "She'd be putting her job and lifestyle at risk to control the outcome of this competition. The only thing that would make a smart, successful, optimistic woman cross a line would be love. Either she did it to prove her love to someone, or she did it because someone broke her heart."

Butterworth nodded. "If so, we'll have to work quickly to identify that someone."

"We need to find those boots too. Would you update the Fins? I'm going to grab my friends and go to the feast."

Jane convened the Cover Girls in the lobby and told them about confronting Stephanie Harbaugh.

"Does that mean we can eat?" asked Mrs. Pratt. "I did a year's worth of snooping in thirty minutes, so I've worked up a serious appetite."

Jane smiled and led her friends out to the terrace.

By the time the women made their selections and sat down at their reserved table, the banquet was in full swing. Mrs. Hubbard's sumptuous fare coupled with free cocktails had erased all traces of gloom, and the atmosphere, if not merry, was upbeat. Jane heard laughter and lively snippets of conversation over the smooth jazz music being piped through the terrace speakers. The happy noise made it seem like the trials of the past few days were finally coming to an end.

A server with a cocktail tray appeared behind Jane's shoulder. "Ladies, could I interest you in this evening's signature cocktail? It's called the Last Word."

"That sounds rather ominous," said Eloise.

Though Jane knew Eloise was joking, she wished she'd changed the cocktail before the feast. In light of the current circumstances, the name was in poor taste.

Violet pointed at the tray. "What's in it?"

"Dry gin, green chartreuse, maraschino liqueur, and fresh lime juice. Shaken and poured into a chilled coupe glass."

Mabel used her fist to mime banging a gavel. "Sold."

"Based on the size of those glasses, we're going to need at least two," added Phoebe.

Anna looked at Betty. "You're the alcohol expert. What's a coupe glass?"

Betty chuckled. "Honey, I serve beer from a tap. That hardly makes me an expert. But I actually know the answer because of a trivia night we had at the pub. The coupe glass, or champagne saucer, was rumored to have been molded in the shape of Marie Antoinette's left breast."

"What was wrong with her right breast?" asked Jane.

Everyone laughed and raised their glasses in a toast.

"To our left breasts!" exclaimed Phoebe, which caused another ripple of laughter.

Jane took a sip of the pale yellow cocktail and was pleasantly surprised by its sweet, citrusy sharpness. "Whoa."

"Yeah, whoa," agreed Eloise. "Talk about your palate cleanser."

Anna licked her lips. "I like a drink with a bite. Do you have a signature wedding cocktail, Eloise?"

"We're having a strawberry champagne punch because I wanted to use Storyton Hall's old-fashioned punch glasses. Mrs. Hubbard found a huge box of them in the attic. They're crystal with etched stars around the rim."

"I *cannot* picture your future husband holding a punch glass," said Violet.

"A Viking drinking horn would be more like it," added Mrs. Pratt.

Eloise smiled. "Maybe he can order a set for the groomsmen."

"Who else, besides me, would pay money to see Butterworth drinking champagne out of a horn?" asked Mabel.

The women chortled with glee.

Betty waved at their server. "Sir, may we have another round?"

Jane didn't protest when a fresh cocktail was placed in front of her. She couldn't remember the last time her mind and body had felt this relaxed. The food, drinks, and company had done much to revive her flagging spirits, but she knew she could lower her guard only so much. There were still questions needing answers, and no one could predict if more secrets would bubble to the surface after the contest winner was announced.

She surveyed the other diners. The guests seemed determined to enjoy the lovely summer evening, and their last night at Storyton Hall, before returning to their everyday lives. Jane was eager to get back to her routines as well. She was more than ready to watch the boys play with Merry and Pippin, visit with Aunt Octavia and Uncle Aloysius, and sip wine with Edwin on the back patio.

Turning her attention to her friends again, Jane saw that Phoebe had gotten to her feet. "I don't know about the rest of you, but I have a teeny, tiny bit of room left for dessert."

"I have an extra stomach reserved for treats," said Mabel.

Violet grinned. "You're a goat?"

"If you mean the Greatest Of All Time, then yes."

Eloise leaned against Jane. "I can't go up there. There are too many temptations. Would you go bring me *one* thing? Just one. Please?"

"What are you in the mood for?"

"Whatever you pick will be perfect. You know what I like."

This brief remark gave Jane a jolt of happiness. At the dessert table, she selected a salted caramel grilled peach and a slice of the chocolate pavlova with Nutella and strawberries. Moving behind the table, she used a clean knife to split each dessert in half. Her head was bent in concentration when she heard Phoebe's voice.

"I want to. Believe me, I do. It's just that, well, you're leaving tomorrow."

"Even if I'm allowed to leave, I won't. I want to spend a day with you. Just you and me. I'll be your barista. Or your gelato scooper. I'll mop the floor and take out the trash. Anything, as long as I'm with you."

Gil and Phoebe were standing in front of the orange dream cupcakes. They both held a cupcake in their hands and were too busy staring at each other to lower the treats to their plates.

"I like you, Gil. I did from the first, but—"

"That's all I need to hear. The timing is awful, I know. This weekend has been horrible in so many ways. I could end up without a job or a dollar to my name after all is said and done, but if you like me, I can bounce back. For you, I can be my best possible self."

Phoebe couldn't control the smile pulling at the corners of her mouth. "You're crazy! You don't even know me."

"Not true," Gil protested. "You're smart, funny, artistic, and insanely sexy. You love your friends and your community, and they love you right back. You light up every space you enter. You're a birthday candle, and summer fireworks, and a Christmas tree star. I've wanted to kiss you from the moment I saw you. I want to kiss you so much it hurts."

"Oh," was all Phoebe could manage.

Jane couldn't blame her for being speechless. Gil certainly had a way with words.

"So, will you come with me? As soon as this is over?"

Phoebe nodded.

Beaming, Gil took the cupcake from her hand and put it on her plate. He then captured her free hand in his own and kissed the dab of frosting on the tip of her finger.

Jane straightened just as Mrs. Pratt declared, "That boy is smitten! And you, Phoebe. In that dress, with your fiery hair cascading down your back, you look like a heroine from a Barbara Jewell novel. What would the title of your novel be? *Seduced by the CEO*?"

"Stop it, Eugenia," chided Betty. "Let her revel in this feeling for a hot second. It doesn't come along every day. Here. Why don't you get a cupcake for Roger?"

Anna sniggered as she passed a cupcake to Mrs. Pratt. "The name of *your* book would be *How to Seduce a Shopkeeper*."

In a flurry of animated whispering, the women returned to their table. Eloise was delighted by the desserts Jane had chosen, and the two friends ate in companionable silence while the other Cover Girls asked Phoebe question after question about Gil.

Finally, it was time for Jane to step up to the mic. She wished she'd heard from Sheriff Evans before the big announcement, but she hadn't missed any calls or texts.

She put on a brave face and excused herself. As she walked to the corner of the terrace, she peered up at the place where the security camera was mounted above the door frame and blew it a kiss. The three men she loved most would be watching. They'd know the kiss was meant for them, just as Jane knew they were ready to leap into action the moment her safety, or that of the guests, was threatened.

The Fins were also watching from their locations around the terrace. Lachlan had the path to the gardens covered while Sterling guarded the path leading to the kitchens and loading dock. Butterworth was closest to Jane, but she doubted anyone could see him. He stood behind a pillar, cloaked in shadow, and held himself so still that he seemed invisible.

Jane tested the portable microphone by tapping on it. Usually, several muffled thumps were required to gain the crowd's attention. But tonight, they went quiet in an instant. The silence descended so quickly and with such weight that Jane felt like they were in the eye of a hurricane.

"Ladies and gentlemen, good evening. I hope you enjoyed your Poetry of the Plate Feast."

She paused to allow for a round of applause.

"I know that your time here didn't turn out as planned. For that, I am very, very sorry. I want to thank you for bearing with us as we pursued the truth. I'm not

at. I'd rather focus on how lovely it was to have
nner with my closest friends."

. Pratt beamed at Eloise. "The next time we get
ssied up, it'll be for your big day, my dear."

ise put an arm around Jane's shoulders. "Please
all the murderers packing before then, okay?"

After the Cover Girls left, Jane walked to her favorite
nch in Milton's Gardens. She gazed skyward, finding
ace in the steadiness of the stars, and breathed in the
rfumed air. Then she called Sinclair.

He answered right away and told her that Uncle
loysius was resting peacefully. He also confessed that it
had been exceedingly difficult to convince Aunt Octavia that she needed a good night's sleep, but she'd finally relented. She'd rented a two-room suite, which
meant Sinclair could guard her from the relative comfort of the sitting room.

"I'm so grateful that you're with them. I wish I could
be there too," Jane said when he'd finished briefing
her.

She heard the crunch of footsteps on the gravel path
and turned to see Professor Ashley heading her way.
When he was within speaking distance, he gave her a little wave and said, "I didn't mean to disturb you. I'm sure
you need a moment of peace and quiet after today."

Jane told Sinclair she'd call him right back and lowered her phone.

After apologizing for intruding, the professor said,
"Before I go, I wanted you to know that I left copies of
my books at the front desk. It was a few hours ago, but I
overheard a conversation about your great-uncle, and I
was going to suggest that you read out loud to him. It

at liberty to provide updates about the investigation,
but I want to assure you that a resolution is in sight."

A wave of muttering swept over the terrace.

"Tomorrow morning, you'll receive a notification
asking you to gather in Shakespeare's Theater. Sheriff
Evans will share his findings, and you'll have a chance
to ask questions. If there's anything I can do to ease
your mind before then, feel free to find me at the con-
clusion of tonight's event. And now, I'd like to turn
things over to Jeremiah Okoro and Gil Callahan."

Jeremiah and Gil slowly made their way to the front
of the terrace. Their movements were wooden, and
their expressions were fixed, though Jeremiah smiled
politely as he took the mic from Jane.

"Thank you for your hospitality, Ms. Steward," he said
before turning to address the writers. As he scanned the
faces of the participants, Jane did the same. She saw a
wide range of emotions. Hope, excitement, and curiosity mingled with resignation and glumness. Once again,
Jane wished her guests had known a happier time at
Storyton Hall.

"When Gil and I came up with the idea for this competition, we thought it would be an amazing way to recruit new talent. We were both journalists before we
quit our jobs and decided to launch a greeting card
company. Neither of us read much poetry before we
started Current Mood, but we've fallen in love with it,
haven't we?"

Jeremiah looked to Gil for confirmation. Gil smiled
and said, "Absolutely."

"We both want you to know how impressed we've
been by the work you've submitted," Jeremiah continued. "Every single person is this group is talented. Even

if you don't win the contract, we hope you'll rise above the hardships you experienced this weekend and any challenges you'll face in the future. We want you to remember that you came here because you're a writer. No one but you can take that title away. We hope you made friends, honed your craft, and will continue writing."

He paused to let the words of encouragement sink in. Dozens of people nodded. Two women used their napkins to dab the corners of their eyes.

Jeremiah passed the mic to Gil, who cleared his throat and said, "Do you know the difference between successful and unsuccessful writers? The successful ones never quit. If this is your dream, don't ever let it go. Fight for it. Believe in yourself and believe in your words. Jeremiah and I believe in all of you. And now, on behalf of Current Mood Card Company, I'm pleased to offer a contract to Ms. Farah Khan."

Jeremiah led the applause, and the crowd quickly joined in. Everyone glanced around to see how their fellow poet would respond to her good fortune.

Farah didn't jump out of her seat and shriek with joy. She didn't race over to Jeremiah and Gil and throw her arms around them. She didn't put her hand over her heart, cry, or fan herself. She didn't do anything. She sat there, frozen with fear, until someone at her table touched her hand.

The man's touch startled Farah, and she snatched her hand away as if she'd been burned. She then looked at Jeremiah and Gil and shook her head.

Jeremiah's congratulatory smile slipped.

Gil turned to Jane. "What should we do?"

Pointing at the mic, she whispered, "You can talk to Farah later. In private. For now just thank everyone again and wish them a good night."

This did the trick. As soon as [...] turned to their seats, a swell of [...] through the crowd. Some of the old[...] side the manor house while others [...] table for the second time. No one see[...] upset by Farah's win. A few people stop[...] to congratulate her, but most of the w[...] bemused glance before going about thei[...]

Butterworth suddenly appeared behi[...] bent over, murmured something close to [...] offered her his arm. She took it, leaning [...] him as he led her inside.

"She looks miserable," said Eloise.

Betty shrugged. "It has to be a bittersweet [...] mean, she won, but two of her competitors are [...]

"Gretchen West and Connor Jensen may hav[...] favored, but Farah still believed she stood a c[...] Eventually, I think she'll be able to celebrate he[...] and her new job. Right now, she's too scared to e[...] anything," Jane said.

Phoebe stared at Farah's empty chair. "I don't blan[...] her."

"Me either. I'd be looking over my shoulder for a long time," said Anna.

More and more guests trickled inside. Jane studied as many faces as she could but saw no signs of anger or malice. She saw only fatigue.

I'd love to go home and flop on my bed.

As if hearing her thoughts, Violet said, "So what now?"

Jane let out a sigh. "I have to wait for Sheriff Evans to contact me, which could happen two minutes or two hours from now. If Stephanie confesses, the guests can leave tomorrow. If she doesn't—I don't even want to think doesn't have to be my poetry, of course, but my mother responded very well to being read to, so I just thought I'd mention it."

When he made to leave, Jane got to her feet. "That's very kind, thank you. I hope you'll visit again in the future. Writers tend to be very productive when they stay with us. After all the mentoring you've done, especially over the past few days, it would be my pleasure to offer you a complimentary weekend."

He smiled. "That would certainly give me something to look forward to."

"And I look forward to you seeing us at our best," she said.

"This is a bit awkward, but some of the writers have asked if they're allowed to check out tomorrow. What should I tell them?"

Jane wished she had a definitive answer to that question. "I haven't received word from the sheriff's department yet. As soon as I do, we'll contact all the guests either by text, email, or a note under the door."

"Considering the circumstances, I feel like I shouldn't leave you here alone. Could I walk you somewhere?"

Is he being a gentleman, or is he flirting? Jane wondered.

"I appreciate the offer, but I'm going to sit here a little longer. Good night, Professor."

"Good night, Ms. Steward."

As he walked away, it occurred to Jane that, like her, the professor had probably come to the garden to decompress. In retrospect, she should have given up her spot and headed home. She considered going after him but decided against it. Instead, she called Sinclair back.

"Don't hang up again, no matter who wants to talk to you," Sinclair's voice was sharp. "I brought Professor Ashley's collection of poems with me and have been reading since your aunt retired. Certain lines and phrases have been leaping off the page because they seem familiar. Do you know why? Because I've read them before: in the love poem found in both Ms. West's and Mr. Connor's rooms."

"What?"

She heard the rustle of papers. "That love poem is cobbled together using lines from Dodge Ashley's poems. Either someone knew his work extremely well or—"

"He wrote it," interrupted Jane. "Maybe there was more to the bribe than he originally told us."

"Quite."

Thoughts tripped over themselves in Jane's head.

The professor walked our trails.

The boots we were looking for weren't found in his room.

He took a bribe.

Connor didn't win because he was killed.

What if the person who bribed the professor was also bribing someone else?

He knew the top contestants better than anyone.

He knew Connor made his own kombucha.

Did he know about Gretchen's anxiety meds?

Eventually, one thought won out over the rest. "Professor Ashley said he didn't recognize the love poem. He must've been lying."

"He's been the common dominator all along, which means he's very, very dangerous. Do not confront him alone."

Jane promised to be careful, then hung up. She sent a quick text to the other Fins, asking them to find Professor Ashley and alert Sheriff Evans. Then she headed for the manor house.

As she emerged from the gardens, she heard the gentle hiss of water. The irrigation system was on, and droplets beaded the grass bordering the flagstone path. An irrigation head appeared to be leaking because a thin stream of water covered the surface of one of the stones. On the next stone, Jane saw the ghost of a shoeprint. She drew up short.

The professor is wearing *the boots. He's the killer.*

Jane paused to snap a photo of the boot print when she felt a breath of movement from behind and a sudden pressure against her throat. An arm pulled her backward until her torso slammed against a muscular chest. She started clawing at the steel-like forearm cutting off her air supply, but a sharp point against the small of her back forced her to stop.

"Keep struggling and I'll sever your spinal column." The hoarse whisper belonged to Dodge Ashley. "Nod if you understand."

The grip around her throat was so tight that Jane couldn't breathe, let alone nod. She made a strangled sound but lowered her hands.

"Good girl."

The pressure against Jane's neck eased just enough for oxygen to enter her airway.

"We're going to take a few more steps back now. If you try anything, these will be the last steps you take. I think you know that I'm deadly serious."

Jane knew. She weighed the risks of an elbow to his ribs or jerking her head so that the back of her skull slammed into his face, but the knife was too much of an impediment. This was no butter knife. The tip of the sharp blade had already sliced through the material of her dress and pierced her skin. She felt a warm trickle of blood sink into the waistband of her panties.

"Why didn't you just go home?" he growled as he pulled her toward the shrubbery.

Jane stared at the lights glowing behind the curtained windows of the manor house and willed Edwin to see her. She knew the camera didn't pan this far, but he was her only hope.

No, he isn't. The Fins will come.

She believed this with her whole heart. But she wasn't sure if they'd come in time.

Once they were safely in the shadows, the professor said, "That wasn't too hard, was it? Keep listening to me and you'll live. I don't want to hurt you. I just need a little more time. Tomorrow this will all be over."

Behind her, Jane felt him shifting. The pressure on the knife point eased. Seconds later, it was back.

Jane cursed herself for not reacting the moment she sensed her assailant was distracted. She'd missed her chance, and it might have been her only one.

The professor held a bottle in front of her face and said, "You're going to drink this. It won't kill you. It'll make you sick, and I'm sorry about that, but you'll live. I'm showing you mercy because you're a mother, and everything I've done is for my mother. You won't thank me, but one day your sons will. If you don't swallow this—if you spit it out or spill it—you get the knife. Now, open your mouth."

He's lying. If I drink, I won't survive.

Without warning, the knife bit into her skin. The pain was a surprise, but that sensation was instantly replaced by anger. The pain woke the fighter inside of her. Instead of opening her mouth to scream, Jane turned her head to the left and sank her teeth into the professor's arm.

He bellowed in surprise and pain, and she abruptly twisted her body away from his. She knew she might be cut or stabbed trying to escape, but if she didn't take the risk, she'd surely die.

Suddenly she felt a searing pain along her side. It was so intense that she stumbled but didn't fall. While she fought to stay on her feet, a rock crashed into the professor's face. It was immediately followed by a second rock, which smacked against his temple.

Jane's attacker crumpled, and she heard voices crying, "Mom! *Mom!*"

Her vision blurred. The lights from the windows merged with the light of the stars, and all she could see was white. And after that, only blackness.

Chapter 19

When Jane came to, the first thing she saw was Edwin's face.

He smoothed her hair and smiled. "Hello, love. You're in a spa treatment room, making a big mess of the white sheets and towels. Doc Charles is on the way to stitch you up."

"How bad is it?" Jane whispered. Her mouth was dry, and her head felt foggy.

Edwin pinched his thumb and index finger together. "It's just a scratch. A little nick. You won't even notice it when we're dancing at Eloise's wedding. Would you like some water?"

He held a glass up to her mouth, but when she tried to sit up, he put a hand on her shoulder to stop her. "Just tilt your head. If it spills, it spills. I can get more."

Water made it into her mouth, but it also dribbled down her chin to dampen the tender skin of her neck. She explored the area with tentative fingers.

Watching her, Edwin's expression darkened. "What

I'd give for five minutes alone with that bastard. What kind of man sneaks up on an unarmed woman from behind?"

Jane replayed what she'd seen before passing out. "The rocks. Was it the twins?"

Edwin lit up with pride. "It was. They saw Ashley approach the house by the terrace. When he backed away instead of entering, they thought he might be up to something. Where was I when this was happening? In the kitchens, making hot chocolate. In August."

"Let me guess. Fitz and Hem thought they'd feel more like professional security guards if they had coffee."

"You nailed it." Edwin laughed. "I figured hot chocolate in coffee mugs would do the trick. Next thing I know, the surveillance room is empty. I'm standing there with two cups in my hands, staring at the screens, when I see the boys dashing across the terrace, slingshots in hand."

Jane pressed her palm to his cheek. "And you ran out after them."

"Not fast enough. Those sons of yours already had their man down." Edwin shook his head in wonder. "They never hesitated, Jane. They saw that you were in grave danger, loaded their weapons, and took aim. As scared as they must have been to see you like that, they were still able to wait for the right moment. They fired their missiles and saved their mother."

Smiling tenderly at the man she loved, Jane said, "Those sons of ours, you mean."

Edwin lowered his eyes. When he raised them again, they were glassy with unshed tears. "When I saw them on the monitor, I was petrified. The thought they might get hurt—because I couldn't move fast enough. And when I got to them and saw they were okay, I wanted to hug the life out of them. Then I saw you, and I was terrified all over again."

Jane gestured for him to come closer. When he did, she wiped away his tears and kissed him. They stayed there, their foreheads pressed together, until Jane couldn't hold her head up any longer. Every movement, no matter how small, made the cut in her side pulse with pain, but she didn't care. She was alive. Thanks to her sons, she was here with Edwin. And once she was stitched up, she could hug and kiss Fitz and Hem too. She could visit Uncle Aloysius in the hospital, watch her best friend walk down the aisle, and join the Cover Girls in a champagne toast.

Overcome by gratitude for the future she'd been granted, Jane couldn't speak for a long moment. Finally, she said, "That beach vacation we've been talking about sounds pretty good right now. I think we should tell Olivia Limoges that we'll be coming to Oyster Bay next month. October at the latest."

Someone knocked on the door.

Edwin moved to open it. "This should be the doc. The boys are out in the hall with Butterworth. He'll tell you where things stand with the investigation when you're ready."

"Where's Ashley?" Jane couldn't call him "Professor" after he'd threatened to poison her. He was no longer worthy of her respect.

Edwin grinned. "We trussed him up like a Christmas goose and dumped him in Deputy Emory's car. He'll be in a comfy, cozy cage by now. I hope he likes prison orange because he's going to be wearing it for a long time."

Once Doc Charles had been admitted, Edwin slipped into the hall to tell Fitz and Hem that they could see their mother in a few minutes.

"Thanks for coming out again. We're not exactly easing you into things, are we?" Jane told the doctor.

"I prefer jumping in with both feet. Let's see what we're dealing with." He peeled back the bandage Edwin had applied. "Someone did a fine job cleaning you up. I'm going to sterilize the area, give you a localized anesthetic, and suture this laceration. Part of the wound is deep, so I'll be using absorbable stitches here." Jane felt a light touch to the left of her spine. "For the rest, I'll use nonabsorbable stitches because they're stronger, and unless you plan on spending the next week in bed, this area will be affected by movement. Any questions before I get started?"

Jane returned the doctor's steady gaze. "Be honest. Do I look like Pac-Man?"

Doc Charles pretended to give this serious thought before replying, "More like Ms. Pac-Man. You'll have to take it easy for two weeks. No running marathons, steeplechase racing, or pickleball tournaments, okay?"

Jane laughed. "Okay."

"Ready?"

"I'd like to ask Butterworth to come in first. He'll distract me."

By the time Jane's wound was sterilized, stitched, and bandaged, she'd learned that Dodge Ashley had been formally charged for the murders of Gretchen West and Connor Jensen, as well as attempted murder. There'd been enough poison hemlock in the bottle he wanted Jane to drink from to fell a horse.

"Sheriff Evans believes Ms. Harbaugh is the professor's accomplice. He doesn't have enough proof to substantiate his theory but is hopeful that Professor Ashley's arrest will inspire a confession."

Doc Charles interrupted to give Jane instructions on washing her wound and changing her bandages.

"Don't let her overdo it," he told Edwin on the way out.

Edwin had the good sense to say, "Jane's her own woman, but I'll do what I can."

Fitz and Hem waited for the doctor to exit the room before rushing in.

"My brave boys!" Jane cried. She opened her arms and gingerly hugged them both. "Thank you for saving me. And promise never to do that again, okay?"

"It's cool, Mom," said Fitz. "We knew we wouldn't get hurt."

"Because Edwin had our backs," Hem said.

Edwin ruffled his hair. "Always."

Hem's gaze strayed to Jane's bandaged middle. "How many stitches did you get?"

"Forty."

"Whoa," the twins said in unison.

Jane nodded. "It would have been worse if you two hadn't come along. And I take back everything I said about those slingshots. A murderer will face justice now, and that's no small thing." She examined her sons' faces. "Are you sure you're both okay?"

"Totally," said Fitz.

Hem glanced at his brother. "We just wish we'd gotten there before—before he cut you."

Jane rubbed his arm. "I'll heal. And if it leaves a scar, I'll think of you two every time I see it. It'll always remind me of my heroes."

"Well, you know what they say—sleep is the great healer," said Edwin. "Let's get you home."

The skin around Jane's wound was still numb, which made it easier for her to change into her pajamas. Edwin brought her a cup of chamomile tea and placed it on her nightstand.

It was too hot to drink, so Jane decided to call the sheriff. She knew she wouldn't rest until they'd talked.

"Ms. Steward, how are you?"

"I'm fine. And you?"

Sheriff Evans chuckled. "I'm feeling like I should deputize your boys."

"Better not. The power might go to their heads."

Issuing a wry snort, the sheriff said, "If only my power could influence Stephanie Harbaugh. She's sticking to her story like a gnat on flypaper. Actually, all I'm getting now is the silent treatment."

"And Ashley?"

"Oh, he's spinning a fine tale. In his land of make-believe, Connor gave Gretchen the poisoned kombucha and then drank it himself out of guilt. He claims *you* attacked *him* and has plans to sue you."

The idea was so asinine that Jane burst out laughing. Her abdomen shook, which made her newly stitched side hurt. "Oof," she wheezed. "Don't make me laugh, Sheriff."

"I have to admit, I wanted to roll my eyes while listening to the man, but after so many years on the job, I just gave him my best blank stare and moved on to my next question. So here's what we have. Ashley's boots match the prints in the mud. Connor was killed around noon today and the professor has no alibi for the time following his outdoor session with the writers and the time he was picked up by the camera on your terrace. I asked Mr. Sterling to send me the footage, and Ashley was wearing his boots when he reentered the hotel."

Jane remembered how the professor had led the writers outside and inspired them with his words. He'd sounded so sincere. Listening to him, one would never have believed that he'd murdered a former student and fellow poet. Or that he was planning to kill another student within the next hour or two.

"What about the bribe? Did he make that up?"

"He couldn't show me a bank deposit for the five grand he supposedly received. There's no trace of that money. The money site is legit. It's because of that site that I won't release Ms. Harbaugh. She used the same one to pay the Hogg brothers. That can't be coincidence. She and Ashley are in this together. I just don't know how all the pieces fit together yet."

His voice was thick with fatigue. And while Jane was grateful to be propped up in bed, sipping a cup of tea, she also felt sorry for the sheriff. When had he last slept? Or eaten? She couldn't run around searching for clues, but she could still use her brain to help him reach the end of this nightmarish investigation.

"Gretchen and Connor had the same love poem. From the start, we thought it might be important because they both kept it close and clearly read it over and over. Tonight, Sinclair discovered that the entire poem is made up of lines from other Dodge Ashley poems. What if Ashley used that poem to seduce Gretchen? Connor too. Everyone assumed that Gretchen had no romantic attachments, but what if she did? And Connor wrote about loving someone in secret. What if that someone was Ashley?"

The sheriff grunted. "Even if it's true, we have no definitive proof of these relationships."

"Maybe not, but I think we can use that poem. Why would Stephanie Harbaugh behave this irrationally or take such unnecessary risks? She has a good job, a supportive family, and money in the bank. She's never broken the law before. If not for money, then—"

"She's in love with Ashley? I can test that theory by showing her the poem. Who knows? Maybe she got one too." The sheriff's voice was practically crackling with energy. "Would Juliet be happy if she found out Romeo was climbing two other balconies in Verona?"

Jane complimented the sheriff's literary reference.

"I'm going to let Deputy Emory take the lead on this," he said, clearly eager to get moving. "She'll be a sympathetic listener. I'm too tired and crabby to listen to that woman cry."

"If there's a breakthrough, no matter how small, please call me. I don't care if it's after midnight. I want to know if there's a chance this will all be over soon."

After promising to get in touch, the sheriff added, "And Ms. Steward, Charles Dickens would tell you to 'hope, hope to the last.'"

Jane put her phone and the empty teacup on her nightstand and switched off the lamp. For a while, questions cycled through her mind. She didn't understand why the professor had killed Gretchen and Connor. How would eliminating either of them from the competition earn him money?

Unless Farah was supposed to win all along.

It didn't seem possible for one person to seduce three women and a man at the same time. The very notion was ludicrous. But if the winner wasn't going to share their earnings with Dodge Ashley, what did he stand to gain?

Did he kill them out of envy? Because his words are running dry while theirs are flowing like a river?

Jane wondered if bitterness and defeat could drive a person to such extremes.

Desperate people do desperate things.

Her lids grew heavy, and she closed her eyes. Lucid thought faded, and for a little while a slideshow of faces played in her head: Dodge Ashley, Gretchen, Connor, Farah, Stephanie, Jeremiah, Gil.

The sound of laughter floated up from downstairs, and the faces of the strangers were instantly replaced by those of her beloved family. Just knowing that Fitz, Hem, and Edwin were close by allowed her to let go of her cares and surrender to sleep.

The first vestiges of dawn were appearing in the sky when a ringing phone woke Jane. As she twisted to grab her phone from its charger, the sharp pain in her side eradicated any residual drowsiness.

Next to her, Edwin groaned, rolled over, and mumbled, "Hmm?"

Jane told him to go back to sleep and whispered into the phone, "One second, Sheriff."

She tiptoed out of the room and made her way downstairs. When she reached the kitchen, she apologized for making the sheriff wait.

"I hesitated to call so early, but I made a promise."

"Did you get any rest last night?" she asked over a crescendo of excited whining from Merry and Pippin. The dogs were squirming in their crates, their little tails banging against the sides as they pawed at the doors barring them from freedom.

The sheriff said, "We made progress, which is more important than my beauty sleep. Your hunch about Ms. Harbaugh was spot-on. When Deputy Emory showed her the poem, she tried to pretend that she'd never seen it before, but she wasn't very convincing. After hearing that two other people received the same poem, she was ready to talk."

Jane opened the door to the patio before letting the dogs out of their crates. She scratched both dogs behind the ears in greeting before shooing them outside. Then she filled a glass with tap water and sat down at the kitchen table.

"She told us quite a story," continued the sheriff. "Days after she spoke to the professor about running the poetry competition, he started wooing her. No one uses that word anymore, but that's what he did. He sent her flowers, little notes, and drove from Madison to Chicago to surprise her with picnic lunches, walks in the park, and other romantic outings. He invited her to one of his readings. The last poem he read to the audience was the love poem. He looked at her the whole time he was reading. After that, she was a goner."

"Who could blame her? He seemed like the perfect gentleman."

The sheriff harumphed. "Ashley also invited Gretchen West to the reading, and he made sure she sat directly behind Ms. Harbaugh."

"So she'd think the love poem was meant for her. What a snake." Jane's voice was filled with loathing.

"We've asked Mr. Jensen's roommate to look through his things for any other notes or gifts from Professor

Ashley. The sheriff's department in Ms. West's area is working with her landlord to do the same. And thanks to Mr. Butterworth and Mr. Sterling, we have even more leverage over Ashley."

Jane assumed the Fins had stayed up late into the night, taking turns reviewing footage from the security cameras and standing guard outside Farah Khan's room. Though she was correct on both counts, she had no idea how their efforts had led to a piece of concrete evidence.

The sheriff went on to say, "Even the smartest criminal can make a mistake. Ashley made his after killing Mr. Jensen. He needed to dispose of the gloves he wore while adding the poison hemlock to Mr. Jensen's kombucha bottle. When one of your cameras caught our nutty professor entering the restroom lobby, Mr. Butterworth deemed a search of the trash can worthwhile. He was able to intercept the staff member who'd cleaned the bathroom this evening and luckily, the trash bag was still on his cart. Mr. Butterworth found the gloves, and Mr. Sterling bagged the trousers the professor wore earlier in the day. Both gloves and trousers have traces of the plant toxins."

Jane let out an audible breath of relief.

Sheriff Evans chuckled. "That's exactly how I felt."

"What did Ashley have to say in the face of this evidence?"

"We haven't told him yet. It'll take more than what we've got to make him confess. I know his type. He'll only cave when he sees no other way out. Right now, he's willing to lawyer up and go to trial. We don't want that. A confession means the rest of the guests can go home today."

Hearing a noise in the hall, Jane turned to see Edwin enter the kitchen. He put his finger to his lips and pointed to the coffeemaker. When Jane answered his questioning look with a nod, he began scooping grounds into the brew basket.

"Doesn't Stephanie have proof of what he had planned?" she asked the sheriff.

"He never told her about killing the contestants. All he said was that he wanted Ms. West to win because she'd been through hell and had nothing else going for her. He asked Stephanie to exert whatever influence she had over Jeremiah and Gil. But this was pillow talk. So it's her word against his."

Jane frowned. "He wanted Gretchen to win? Then why pick Conner to win in that bribery email he created?"

"Probably just smoke and mirrors. Provisions made by Ashley in the event he became a suspect."

"Why did he do any of this?" The all-too-familiar sense of frustration returned.

"I really don't know."

Edwin sat down across from Jane and held out his hand. As she took it, the coffeemaker started gurgling.

"Was he lying about his mother?"

"No," the sheriff said. "She's in a memory care facility. It's the best in the area and is quite expensive. The professor is facing a financial crisis."

Jane shook her head in disgust. "He can hardly help her from prison. He must've realized what would happen to her if things didn't turn out as planned."

"I asked him that very question, but Ashley didn't take the bait. He just sat there, looking smug."

Edwin jumped up from the table and grabbed a pencil and the pad they used for grocery lists off the counter. He wrote a single word on the pad and showed it to Jane. Her eyes went wide.

"If he got his hands on those original Whitman poems and squirreled them away somewhere, he'd have a reason to be smug. All he'd have to do is tap in to the antiquities black market, and his money troubles would be over."

The sheriff wasn't convinced. "If he knew about the secret passage or the location of the library, then why commit murder? Ashley would have been set for life if he'd just helped himself to a few literary treasures and run off before anyone noticed he was gone."

Jane couldn't refute this logic. She had a sinking feeling that her hope for a resolution had been premature. Without a clear motive or a confession, how could the sheriff build an airtight case against Dodge Ashley?

"Obviously, we've missed something," she said. "I'll assemble the troops, and we'll go back to the beginning. In all the best mystery novels, that's where the authors hide the clues."

Edwin offered to clean Jane's wound, but she wanted to stand in the shower and think. Every movement caused a twinge of discomfort, so she shampooed her hair with one hand, gingerly washed her stitched skin, and put on a dress with a long, loose skirt. Though the material brushed against her bandage every time her body shifted, it was better than wearing form-fitting clothes.

Downstairs, Edwin was making breakfast. He'd already added Greek yogurt and granola to a bowl and was busily slicing bananas and strawberries.

He waved at the door with his knife. "The dogs are napping on the patio. Go get some puppy love. I'll bring the food out in a minute."

As soon as Jane stepped onto the patio, Merry and Pippin dashed over to her and covered her hands with puppy kisses. She started to lean over to kiss their little black noses when a sharp pain reminded her to be careful.

She lowered herself into a chair and took in long, deep breaths of morning air. Feeling calmer and more centered than she had in days, she put her phone on the table and called Aunt Octavia.

"Hello, darling!"

Her aunt's voice was as bright and bold as the nasturtiums in Jane's garden.

"How are you?"

"Better. Having Sinclair here made a world of difference. I got some sleep, and when I woke up, I insisted he do the same. I'm with Aloysius now, and he's feeling much better. He's himself again."

Though Jane knew this might not be a permanent recovery, her relief was so profound that she closed her eyes and whispered, "Thank God."

"Believe me, I have," said Aunt Octavia. Then, "It's Jane, dear. She's beyond thrilled to hear of your improvement."

In the background, Uncle Aloysius murmured something about going fishing.

"You'll have to spare the fish for a few days, my darling. Just think of how slow and complacent they'll be by the time you get back out there. Jane? He wants to talk to you. Hold on."

There was a rustling noise, and then Uncle Aloysius said, "Hello, Jane."

The two words made Jane's heart swell. She'd never considered how precious her uncle's voice was until she feared she might never hear it again.

"Hi, Uncle Aloysius. I'm so glad you're feeling better. Everyone misses you. Even Muffet Cat."

"I doubt that very much! That mongrel fantasizes about using my grave as a litter box." He chuckled. "Your aunt doesn't like my jokes, but she brought me such a lovely breakfast of eggs and bacon that I feel like a new man. She told me how the boys found me. They probably saved my life." He paused to collect himself. "I'm sorry if I scared them. And you."

Even though he couldn't see her, Jane shook her head. "You have nothing to apologize for. You know Fitz and Hem. They'll milk their heroism to get double desserts as long as they can. All we care about is that you're okay."

"I wish I could remember why I was wandering around. Bits and pieces have come back, but not the important ones. I don't remember seeing the twins, but I do remember a man. His face won't come into focus, but he had my hat."

Though Uncle Aloysius wasn't agitated, Jane worried that he was heading in that direction. She was torn between asking him questions or telling him to focus on his rest and recovery.

Jane flashed to the image of her uncle lying on her sofa. She saw his waxen face and heard his reed-thin voice murmuring something about his hat.

"You were upset about your hat when they found you. Did someone take it?"

Uncle Aloysius didn't answer right away, but when he did, he sounded puzzled. "I was sitting in the boat. It was still tied to the dock. A man came over, and we started chatting about fish. He asked to see my hat. Then he ran off with it! At least, I think that's what happened. It's all rather muddled, I'm afraid."

In her bones, Jane knew that Professor Ashley had taken her uncle's hat. She just didn't know why.

Edwin appeared on the patio, carrying two bowls, napkins, and spoons. As he placed them on the table, Jane smiled and said, "Uncle Aloysius, I believe you just solved the case."

She and Edwin were in the car, heading for the village, when Butterworth called to confirm that Stephanie Harbaugh had purchased a roll of packing tape from Storyton Pharmacy. She'd dropped the plastic bag containing the tape and a pack of gum into her large purse before leaving the store.

Jane made a mental note to thank Anna for her help and then called Sheriff Evans.

"We'll be at the post office in five minutes," she said.

"I'll meet you there."

The post office had yet to open for the day, but Nandi, the postmistress, unlocked the door and waved Jane and Edwin inside. They entered to find Sheriff Evans pacing the lobby in front of the self-service kiosk.

Nandi shuffled through the many keys on her key ring. "Now that the party's all here, let's see what we've got."

She walked behind the counter and unlocked the door to the mailroom. Seconds later, she wheeled a canvas rollaway bin into the lobby. With gloved hands, she reached into the bin and withdrew a white mailing box.

"Priority-mail flat-rate box, size large, addressed to a one Professor Ashley of Madison, Wisconsin. Is this what you were looking for?"

Breathlessly, Jane watched the sheriff accept the box from Nandi. He set it down on a nearby counter and used his pocketknife to sever the packing tape. Removing a layer of newspaper revealed an object wrapped in a Storyton Pharmacy bag. The bag contained Uncle Aloysius's fishing hat.

Jane moved in for a closer look, and when the sheriff turned the hat over, she gasped.

Tucked inside a hat festooned with fishing flies and lures were several pieces of paper. The paper was covered in faded handwriting.

The hat contained a literary treasure. The bent pages were original poems by Walt Whitman.

Chapter 20

"**H**old up." Mabel raised her hand. "I need you to repeat that. Did you just say that your uncle had an *original* copy of *Leaves of Grass?*"

The Cover Girls gawked at Jane. All save Eloise. As the only member of the book club to have been introduced to the wonders of the secret library, she'd spent the last year helping Jane sell or donate dozens of its literary treasures.

Eloise said, "We can hear the whole story after we eat."

Jane smiled at her best friend, who, despite having a to-do list a mile long, had managed to organize tonight's potluck supper.

The moment Eloise heard about Jane's injury, she'd initiated the Cover Girl phone tree. Jane was resting after a long morning at the sheriff's department, followed by the departure of her current guests, when her best friend had shown up with a bouquet of flowers and a bottle of wine.

She'd knocked and let herself in while calling, "Don't get up! I'll come to you."

The rest of the Cover Girls had trickled in between five thirty and six. They all came bearing gifts. Before long, the bounty of food on Jane's kitchen island included curried chicken salad, spinach with strawberries, hummus and pita bread, German potato salad, honey barbecue meatballs, watermelon and feta skewers, BLT tartlets, fruit salad, blueberry pie bars, and salted caramel brownies.

There was enough food to feed the Cover Girls as well as Edwin and the twins. Jane appreciated her friends' kindness but was too emotionally and physically drained to play the part of gracious hostess.

Luckily, Eloise could read Jane like a book. After making her recline on a patio lounge chair, she fetched her a plate of food and a tall glass of water. She then told the rest of the women that they wouldn't be staying long because Jane needed to recover.

Eloise also knew that an hour spent in the company of friends would do wonders for Jane's taxed spirits. She was right, too. As Jane listened to the Cover Girls share anecdotes about their workdays, the combination of banter and good food on a balmy summer's evening was medicative.

After Eloise carried Jane's dinner plate into the house and returned with a blueberry bar, Jane was ready to talk to her friends about Professor Ashley.

Jane ate a bite of blueberry bar and sighed with contentment. "You gals are the best," she said to the group at large. "You knew just what I needed. I would've spent the rest of the day on the couch in a total funk, but you swept in with your special kind of sunshine and chased the clouds away. I couldn't have made it through the last few days without your help."

Mrs. Pratt saluted Jane with a brownie. "Lots of people are slowing down. I don't need to because you keep me young. Being your friend means expecting the unexpected. It's thrilling and dramatic, and there's never a dull moment. Of course, I'm going to have your back. You're the sun in the Storyton universe."

Violet chuckled. "It's true. Without you and Storyton Hall, we'd be just another sleepy small town."

"I doubt Jane enjoys all the drama," said Betty.

Jane gave her a fond look. "Definitely not, but this whole ordeal would've been a lot harder without all of you. Tomorrow's going to be rough because Connor's parents have asked to see where their son died. I need to do all I can to pretty up the construction site before I take them to it. I don't want them to see a hole with a few inches of muddy water. I don't want them to go away with that image burned into their minds. What do you think I should do?"

The Cover Girls made suggestions until Jane had an idea of how to proceed. She'd line the hole with a tarp, fill it with clean water, and place flowers and battery-powered candles around its perimeter.

With this burden lifted, she moved on to other subjects.

"On a more positive note, Uncle Aloysius is coming home tomorrow. By the time he's back in his apartments, Professor Ashley and his lawyer will be meeting with a prosecutor to iron out his plea bargain. Same goes for Stephanie Harbaugh. The charges against her aren't nearly as serious. She swears that she had no idea that the man she loved was a murderer. When she heard about Gretchen's death, she assumed it was accidental. By the time she heard about Connor, she sensed she'd made a grave mistake in doing the professor's bidding."

"Her biggest mistake was her taste in men," muttered Anna.

Phoebe turned to her. "Come on. Who hasn't fallen for Mr. Wrong? Love makes us believe what we want to believe and see what we want to see."

Mabel put an arm around Phoebe. "What about you, hon? It seems like you've fallen pretty hard. Is Gil Callahan a keeper?"

Looking aggrieved, Phoebe said, "I really hope so. I feel like I've known him my whole life. I really love being with him. I could talk to him for hours and hours."

"That's the most important thing, but other things matter too. What was kissing him like?" asked Mrs. Pratt, her eyes dancing with interest.

A dreamy smile lit up Phoebe's face. "It was like coming home."

Awed by the depth of these words, the women fell silent. Mabel gave Phoebe a squeeze, and Phoebe rested her head on Mabel's shoulder.

Anna was the first to break the silence. "So, Gil had nothing to do with the murders?"

"No!" Phoebe cried.

"Then there's no reason why you shouldn't be together. You like him. He likes you. Why not give him a chance? Not all men are Dodge Ashley. Mrs. Pratt has a Roger. Eloise has a Landon. Jane has an Edwin. Not a Dodge among them. So, why can't you have a Gil?"

Jane couldn't agree more. "I know he offered to delay his return by a day or two. Do you want him to stay?"

Phoebe blushed. "I do."

Mrs. Pratt clapped giddily. "That's what Eloise will be saying in ten days or so. You could be next, Phoebe."

Betty nudged Mrs. Pratt. "Stop it, Eugenia. Some people can live happily ever after without exchanging vows." Turning to Jane, she said, "As much as I love weddings, my mind is still stuck on murder. Why did the professor do it?"

"For money. His original plan was to seduce Gretchen West and convince her to share her Current Mood earnings with him. In exchange, he'd help her write the greetings and make her Mrs. Dodge Ashley. He knew she'd agree to his proposal because she'd been in love with him since the day they'd met at Brightleaf. He was right too. Evidence of their relationship was discovered in her apartment. However, Gretchen didn't know the professor was also wooing Connor."

Mabel grunted. "Guess he plays for both teams, eh?"

Jane went on as if Mabel hadn't spoken. "Ashley underestimated Gretchen. He told her they'd have to keep their relationship under wraps in public, but she began to suspect that he was involved with someone else. If he hadn't run into Uncle Aloysius the first morning of his stay, Gretchen and Connor might still be alive."

The Cover Girls exchanged confused glances.

"He's been forgetful lately," Jane said. "Well, more than lately. The whole summer, really. At first, it was little things. He had trouble finding papers in his office, or he'd mail envelopes without stamps. I guess that's why we didn't think much of it. Then he started mixing things up. Like dates or memories. He couldn't remember something Aunt Octavia had said the day before, but he was suddenly crystal-clear about which kids had attended his seventh birthday party."

Sensing what was to come, her friends didn't interrupt, and Jane went on to explain that both she and her aunt Octavia had refused to see Uncle Aloysius's memory issues as anything out of the ordinary.

"We all get more forgetful as we age, but he was putting himself in dangerous situations. Some of the childhood memories that resurfaced in his brain included the location of long-forgotten secret passageways and hidey holes. He got into a passageway on the second floor that ultimately led to an exit on the first floor. I went through it. You go in behind the stairs in the servants' hall and come out behind the grandfather clock in the lobby."

Betty exclaimed, "We've stood near that clock a hundred times! Why didn't we see it?"

"Because it's a rectangular panel under the stairs. It's in shadow, which makes it impossible to spot unless you know where to look. Still, Uncle Aloysius managed to crawl out of it and ran smack into the twins."

"I bet that made their day!" said Mrs. Pratt.

"It sure did. Uncle Aloysius wouldn't tell them where the entrance was unless they swore to keep his secret. They had no idea that he planned to hide his collection of rare books and papers back there and were way too excited about the passageway to notice what he held in his hand."

Unable to contain herself, Anna shouted, "The Whitman poems! Where did he get them in the first place?"

The lie rolled off Jane's tongue. "They belonged to his grandfather. Apparently, he and Whitman were close."

Her friends wanted to hear more details about this relationship. They also wanted to know what other treasures Uncle Aloysius had inherited, but Jane asked them to table those questions for another time as she had enough energy to get through this story, but not multiple stories.

"Despite what he told the twins, Uncle Aloysius decided to hide the poems in multiple places. He left one in the passageway and put one in my bike basket. On Thursday he was heading to the garages to hide another in a tool chest when he bumped into Gretchen and Professor Ashley in the gardens. When my uncle showed Ashley what he was carrying, Ashley knew his money troubles were over. He took the poem from my uncle and promised to put it in the tool chest."

Every Cover Girl was on the edge of her seat.

"These original copies of *Leaves of Grass* were written in Walt Whitman's own hand—to look at them is to feel like you're peering over the man's shoulder as he edited what would one day become an American masterpiece. Ashley could have taken that one poem and sold it for tens of thousands, but he wanted all of them."

"Was Gretchen onboard with stealing from an old man?" asked Mabel.

"No, which is why she was killed. Ashley asked her to meet him at the canoe hut late Friday afternoon before the wine tasting. He tried to convince her to go along with his new plan, but she couldn't hide her misgivings. Connor had left a bottle of kombucha in Shakespeare's Theater, and when the professor saw it, he knew he could kill Gretchen and frame Connor for the murder. All he had to do was mix poison water hemlock into the kombucha, get Gretchen to drink it, and plant the evidence in Connor's room."

Betty held up a finger. "Wait a minute. I thought Gretchen died Saturday morning."

Jane hesitated. She didn't want her friends to know the terrible suffering Gretchen had endured before she'd finally lost consciousness.

"He tied her up in the canoe hut and left her. When he came back around dawn on Saturday, she was dead. He cleaned up his mess and tied her to the canoe. It was too early to notice it out on the lake, and by the time I saw it, she'd been there for hours."

The Cover Girls bowed their heads in sorrow.

"He kept an eye out for my uncle and found another chance to talk to him on Friday, but he didn't get very far because all that Uncle Aloysius would say was that the rest of the poems were in a safe place."

Violet clasped her hands together. "Oh, let us guess! They were in a soup tureen in the cookbook nook?"

"Or inside a clock? Like in Nancy Drew?" said Phoebe.

"Both of those would've been better than the one he picked," said Jane. "He put them in his fishing hat. To him, this was a safe place because the hat is on his head most of the time. And when it's not, it's within sight. My uncle was sitting in his boat at the dock, organizing his fishing gear, when Ashley started questioning him about the missing pages. Uncle Aloysius kept touching his hat, and Ashley put two and two together. He snatched the hat and ran."

Betty frowned. "Too bad he didn't trip and break his ankle."

"Or his neck," added Phoebe.

Mabel shook her head. "He's about to spend lots of time facing his inner demons. That might be worse than a broken neck."

Jane admired Mabel's capacity for mercy. She hoped that one day, she would feel only pity for Dodge Ashley.

At this moment, her pity was reserved for Connor's parents and Ashley's mother.

"Anyway, Uncle Aloysius was so upset over Ashley stealing his hat that he got lost. Physically and mentally. In the meantime, Ashley tucked the other pages in the hat and gave it to Stephanie to mail to his home address. Because it was Sunday, the box was still at the post office this morning, and when Sheriff Evans showed it to Ashley, he folded and confessed all."

Eloise's face flushed with anger. "Lemme get this straight. He murdered Gretchen because she didn't want him to steal the Whitman poems, but why did he kill Connor?"

"Connor realized he'd left a bottle of kombucha in the room where the professor held the writing sessions. When he asked Ashley about it, the professor denied seeing it. But the seed of doubt was sown. And the more Connor thought about his deal with the professor, which was the same as Gretchen's, the more he wondered if he wanted to tie his life to a man he wasn't sure he could trust. He began asking himself if the professor had played him and Gretchen."

"If only he'd listened to those doubts," said Betty.

Jane pictured Connor on his guest room bed, staring up at the ceiling, as his mind and heart fought each other for dominance. "Connor decided to confront Ashley. Ashley knew he was being followed, so he led Connor to the folly. They sat down, and Ashley told Connor that he wanted to hold him before saying another word. As they embraced, he shoved poison hemlock into Connor's mouth. Then he wrapped his arm around Connor's neck and cut off his air supply. The water took care of the rest."

Mrs. Pratt sucked her teeth. "He was a respected poet and teacher. To think he turned into a thief, con man, and killer—all to pay for his mother's care. I doubt she'd approve."

"She'll never know what he did. I guess that's a small blessing," said Phoebe.

Anna picked up a spent marigold head and spun it around between her thumb and forefinger. "What was the point of posing Gretchen as the Lady of Shalott or dropping flowers around Connor?"

Jane said, "Ashley told the sheriff that he wanted to honor them as poets. He believed he was granting them posthumous fame—that the story of their deaths would spread, ensuring that tons of people would be introduced to their poetry. He said that he truly cared about them both."

Anna tossed the flower head into the mulch. "How could he be so deluded? Did he actually think he'd get away with two murders?"

He almost did, Jane thought.

Eloise held up an open wine bottle. "I don't know about you gals, but I need to wash the sour taste out of my mouth. Anyone else?"

Several hands went up. When Eloise looked a question at Jane, she shook her head. Her belly was full, the air was warm, and the surge of energy she'd felt thirty minutes ago was nearly depleted.

While some of her friends used their phones to determine how much the Whitman poems were worth, Betty and Mrs. Pratt asked Eloise about her September window display.

Eventually, Phoebe walked over to Jane's lounge chair. Jane moved her legs out of the way and signaled for Phoebe to sit.

"Are the poems okay?"

Jane smiled. "Considering they were folded, stuffed in the hat, and packed in a box, they're in pretty good shape. Sinclair knows how to fix the creases and folds. He'll put them in archival sleeves and find a safe place to store them."

"Imagine the money your uncle would make if he sold them. Your family would be set for life."

Gesturing at her house, Jane said, "I already have everything I want."

Phoebe nodded. "What I want is waiting for me in the Ian Fleming Lounge, but I can't meet him yet. I need to know that seeing us together won't remind you of this terrible time."

Taking her friend's hand in hers, Jane said, "If Gil makes you happy, then I'm happy to see him here. Now, get going. Your future might be sitting at the bar, trying not to check his watch for the millionth time."

Phoebe jumped up, waved good-bye to the rest of the Cover Girls, and left.

"Where's the fire?" Mabel called after her.

Mrs. Pratt put her hand over her heart and said, "In here."

The Cover Girls met the following week to discuss Rachel Hauck's *The Wedding Dress* and again the evening before Eloise's wedding. Knowing she'd prefer a casual dinner with her book club friends over a bachelorette party, her friends gathered at the Daily Bread to celebrate.

Each Cover Girl presented Eloise with a novel featuring a married couple. By the end of the meal, she'd unwrapped *Middlemarch*, *The Age of Innocence*, *Their Eyes*

Were Watching God, and *Olive Kitteridge.* In addition to these classic reads, she also received Anita Shreve's *The Pilot's Wife, To Have and To Hoax* by Martha Waters, and from Mrs. Pratt, *In Bed with a Highlander* by Maya Banks.

The night ended with hugs, well wishes, and a few tears.

There wasn't a dry eye in the church the next day when Landon Lachlan took his bride's hand and recited a quote from Richard Bach's *The Bridge Across Forever.*

" 'A soul mate is someone who has locks that fit our keys, and keys to fit our locks. When we feel safe enough to open our locks, our truest selves step out and we can be completely and honestly who we are; we can be loved for who we are . . .' "

As Lachlan paused to collect himself, Eloise gave him such a loving smile that it warmed the hearts of everyone in the building

"Eloise, you are my soul mate. You unlocked every part of me and let me be my true self. You love me for who I am, and I love you for who you are. You are the key to my future. You are the key to my happiness. I vow to be my best and truest self for you for the rest of our lives."

Jane dabbed her eyes with a handkerchief and looked at Edwin, who was channeling James Bond in a white dinner jacket and black pants, cummerbund, and bow tie. His eyes were moist as he returned her gaze. Smiling at her, he touched a finger to his chest. She repeated the gesture, and for a moment, they existed only for each other.

The spell was broken when Eloise leaned over to Jane and whispered, "Can I borrow that handkerchief?"

There was a ripple of quiet laughter from the Cover Girls. But when Mrs. Pratt covered her nose with a tissue and made a honking sound, more guests began to laugh.

This joyful levity prevailed during the wedding reception. Per the bride and groom's request, Mrs. Hubbard and the kitchen staff had created a casual buffet of finger foods. The champagne flowed, the strings of hanging lights twinkled, and the dance music pulsed.

A feeling of *joie de vivre* infected every guest, and the celebration lasted long into the night. Because her side was still healing, Jane didn't dance as much as she wanted to, but she sang and laughed with gusto. And with every song, toast, or embrace, she felt the dark shadows of the poetry competition recede.

Aunt Octavia and Uncle Aloysius were the first to retire for the evening. They'd had a grand time and had received a standing ovation after taking to the dance floor, where they waltzed, cheek to cheek, to Nat King Cole's "The Very Thought of You."

Jane also danced with her uncle. As he slowly moved her around the parquet dance floor, she sent up a silent prayer of thanks that he was here with her, waltzing under the stars.

Finally, it was time for the send-off. Eloise and Lachlan didn't change their outfits or drive away in a Rolls-Royce with tin cans bouncing behind them. Instead, they asked the guests to take a short walk with them to the lake.

Once everyone had gathered by the canoe dock, Jane addressed the crowd.

"A wedding marks the beginning of a marriage. Eloise and Landon are ready to embark on their journey as man and wife, and I'd like to ask you to join me in wishing them a long and fulfilling marriage by using one of these floating candles to represent a wish."

Jane held up a candle for all to see. "When we light these beautiful candles, Eloise and Landon will see dozens of lights shining in the water. These lights are a symbol of the community that will always be here to support them."

Turning to the bride and groom, she said, "I wish you a lifetime of laughter."

She then lit the candle, walked to the end of the dock, and lowered the candle into the water. Behind her, the Fins began distributing biodegradable candles while the Cover Girls spread out along the dock, lighters at the ready.

Unbeknownst to Jane, Edwin had tied a rowboat to the dock earlier that day. He now climbed aboard, untied the bow line, and called her name.

"What are you doing?" she asked with a smile in her voice.

"I've been asked to release a few of the candles from the middle of the lake. Care to join me?"

Abandoning her shoes, Jane gathered her skirts and took Edwin's outstretched hand.

After pushing away from the dock, Edwin dropped both oars into the water and began to row with strong, even pulls. Jane was too transfixed by the sight of the lights bobbing in the water to speak, and it wasn't long before the people standing by the lake edge receded.

Edwin stopped rowing and locked the oars. He began lighting candles and gently lowering them into the water. Jane gave each one a push, setting them on a course toward the candles released from the dock.

When they'd finished launching the candles, Jane and Edwin held hands. They sat in the little boat, bathed in star shine and surrounded by candlelight. In the distance, the dark woods were speckled with the glow of fireflies. The whole world had gone quiet. The air was full of magic.

Jane could have stayed just as she was until every candle flame went out, but eventually, she realized that the guests were leaving. When she turned to ask Edwin if they should head back, she saw an unlit candle in his lap.

"This one isn't for Eloise and Landon," he said. "It's for us. I've written the Order, Jane. I've asked to be released from my oath. I no longer want to be a Templar. I don't want to live a double-life. From now on, I want to dedicate myself to loving, protecting, and cherishing you and the boys. I want to be a husband to you and a father to Fitz and Hem. That's my one and only wish."

He lit the candle and cupped it in his hands. It was hard for Jane to see him clearly through her tears. His face was a radiant blur—a star Jane could wish upon.

She slipped her hands under his and whispered, "Will you marry me?"

Lights danced in Edwin's eyes, and his smile lit up Jane's entire universe. "I thought you'd never ask."

Together, they lowered their candle into the water and set it free.

Author's Note

If this book piqued your interest in poetry, here's a list of some of my favorite contemporary poets. I hope you'll enjoy their work as much as I do.

Maya Angelou
Robert Bly
Louise Glück
Galway Kinnell
Philip Levine
Frederick Morgan
Mary Oliver
Robert Pack
Gary Soto
Gerald Stern
Diane Wakoski

Looking for more Book Retreat mysteries from Ellery Adams? Don't miss this previous installment in the series . . .

MURDER IN THE COOKBOOK NOOK

Virginia is for lovers—and Storyton Hall is its best vacation spot for lovers of books. The big event this summer at Jane Steward's resort is A Bookish Cook-Off. It's a blend of the literary and the culinary—but someone's headed for the mortuary . . .

Six chefs are preparing to compete in an outdoor tent at Storyton Hall for prizes that will boost their careers—but is there someone who can't stand the heat? It looks that way when one of the contestants is found dead in a pantry packed with two centuries' worth of cookbooks, among other treasures and rarities.

Could there be a connection to other recent events in town, like the tampering with the costume of a local mascot? Jane isn't sure, but after someone serves a second course of murder, the kitchen must be closed and the killer must be found . . .

Available from Kensington Publishing Corp.
wherever books are sold

Chapter 1

Jane Steward, single mother to twin boys and manager of Storyton Hall, the renowned resort for bibliophiles, saw no cars on the narrow bridge she and her sons needed to cross as they headed home from the village.

Glancing over her shoulder, Jane adjusted her bike helmet and shouted, "The coast is clear! Catch me if you can!"

Her sons, Fitzgerald and Hemingway, responded with ear-piercing war cries that would have made Genghis Khan proud. They'd slowed down to polish off their ice cream cones, giving their mother a sizeable lead, and now pedaled like mad to catch her.

Jane was halfway across the bridge when the twins—known to all as Fitz and Hem—began singing "London Bridge Is Falling Down."

With the school year finishing three weeks ago, the boys were officially rising fifth graders and therefore, too old for nursery rhymes. It wasn't a lack of maturity, but a recent devotion to all things British that inspired the song about the famous London landmark.

The twins had become Anglophiles back in February when Jane's beau, Edwin Alcott, had given her a very thoughtful and generous valentine: a literary tour of London. Edwin had included the boys in the invitation, a gesture that elevated him even higher in Jane's esteem.

The trip had been scheduled for the beginning of June, and Fitz and Hem spent the months leading up to their departure researching British customs. And while Jane admired their enthusiasm, she could have done without their British accents or their obsession with certain British terms. They were particularly fond of "loo," "lift," "telly," "biscuits," "cuppa," and "crisps." By April, Jane was tired of her sons describing everything from food to books to television shows as dodgy, mental, or brilliant.

Hours after landing at Heathrow, the twins had talked Jane and Edwin into a tour of London Bridge. Jane had listened to the guide's disturbing tales of human sacrifice and the immurement of prisoners within the foundations without batting an eye. Unlike the other tourists, she knew that all old places had secrets, and it would take more than a whisper of skeletons to upset the heir of Storyton Hall.

Somewhere behind Jane, Hem now bellowed, "Take the keys and lock her up!"

"On death and darkness will she sup!" Fitz cried merrily.

Together, the boys finished the verse by shrieking, "My fair female bag of bones!"

Seeing as the current version of the classic nursery rhyme omitted much of the landmark's grim history, Fitz and Hem had decided to rewrite it. Over a dinner of roast beef and Yorkshire pudding the evening after the tour, they'd shared their new and improved "London Bridge Is Falling Down."

Edwin had applauded their efforts, calling their work clever and creative, but Jane had leaned over and whispered, "Don't encourage them. They're like the Vikings. Show the slightest weakness, and before you know it, they've taken all of your treasure."

"Then it's a good thing my treasure is right here," Edwin had said, squeezing Jane's hand.

But on this glorious summer afternoon, Jane felt like a warrior as she raced past Storyton Outfitters. She maintained a decent speed on the treacherous Broken Arm Bend and, feeling invincible, prepared to face the hill.

Crouching low over her handlebars, she pumped her legs even harder, trying to gain momentum before the road began its sharp rise. With the warm breeze caressing her flushed cheeks and her strawberry-blond ponytail streaming out behind her like a comet's tail, Jane felt unstoppable.

The feeling was short-lived.

She was still on the lower part of the hill when the twins caught her. Hem's front tire practically kissed Jane's rear tire, and Fitz was poised to overtake her as soon as the shoulder widened.

"Are you tired, Mom?"

"We can hear you panting."

Jane scowled. She *was* panting. It was a blisteringly hot day, the air was thick with humidity, and Jane was out of shape.

A guest had once told her that British food was awful, but Jane disagreed with this assessment. She'd eaten plenty of lovely food in England. After she and the twins had indulged in fish and chips, bangers and mash, Welsh rarebit, and ploughman's lunch, Edwin had taken charge of their restaurant picks.

In addition to running a restaurant in Storyton, Edwin was also a food writer. He'd travelled the world for years and knew exactly which dishes to order at which restaurants. Based on his recommendations, Jane dined like a queen in London. She ate amazing sushi, sumptuous savory pies, truffled egg toast, Peking duck, a flat-iron steak she chopped with her own cleaver, bao buns, and the best Indian cuisine she'd ever tasted. She also feasted on delectable desserts that included, but weren't limited to, puddings, pastries, gelato, pies, biscuits, teacakes, and scones.

Her delight in British cuisine was easily measured. Two days after returning stateside, she'd stepped on the scale and let out a squeak of dismay. The offending device was now under her bed—banished until further notice.

"I'm not panting," she protested as she tried to focus on pedaling and not on the pair of pants she could no longer zip. "I'm opening my lungs to get more oxygen in."

"You're panting like Lassie," said Fitz.

"Or Fang," Hem said in an English accent. "Hey, Fitz, do you think Mom could beat Hagrid up this hill?"

The twins laughed.

Jane wanted to sprint up the rest of the hill like a racehorse out of the starting gate, but her pace was more like a snail's than a thoroughbred's.

When she finally reached the top, she steered her bike into a patch of scraggly grass and waved for the boys to go ahead.

Instead of speeding off, they both stopped.

"Are you okay, Mom?" Fitz asked with genuine concern.

Jane waved again. "Just . . . catching . . . my . . . breath."

"You should be careful," Hem said with devilish glee. "Queen Anne wasn't much older than you when she died."

Fitz peered into the basket attached to Jane's handlebars. "Did you pack your smelling salts?"

Jane glowered at her sons. "I'm not . . . too tired . . . to think of extra chores for you two."

Suddenly, Hem's smile vanished, and he pointed at the woods. "Is that smoke?"

The sun's glare bounced off the road, so Jane shielded her eyes with her hand and followed her son's gaze.

He was right. A ribbon of smoke rose above the treetops.

"Mom? Is it coming from our woods?" Fitz asked.

"But we're under a fire restriction," Hem interjected before Jane could respond. "No campfires allowed. Mr. Lachlan told us to look for guests breaking the rules."

As Jane watched the smoke, a darker curl joined the pale gray coil. The fire was growing stronger.

"Should we ride over there?"

"Yes," said Jane. "If there's a wildfire, even a small one, use the phone in the archery hut to call 911. Got it?"

The twins said, "Got it," and sped off.

Knowing they'd reach the source of the smoke much quicker than she could, Jane stayed where she was and called Butterworth. A former member of Her Majesty's Secret Service, the butler of Storyton Hall was also an expert in marksmanship, reading body language, and remaining calm during a crisis. A bit of smoke wasn't a crisis, but when it came to the safety of Storyton Hall guests, Jane always erred on the side of caution.

"Good afternoon, Miss Jane." Butterworth's voice was as deep and constant as a mountain.

"The boys and I are on our way back from the village," Jane said. "We just crested the hill and saw smoke rising over the trees. I think it's coming from the archery fields. Has anyone heard from the film crew in the past hour?"

Butterworth replied, "Mr. Lachlan was scheduled to walk over after his falconry lesson, but I'll drive there posthaste and report back to you."

Jane thanked him, pocketed her phone, and followed after the twins.

She would have made better time if she didn't keep glancing skyward, but she couldn't help it. The smoke was no longer shaped like ribbons or curls. It had grown thicker, billowing over the treetops like dragon's breath.

Jane pedaled harder. The muscles in her legs ached. Her lungs burned. Sweat ran down her cheeks and dampened her shirt. The path was made of packed dirt, and her front tire flung dust onto her ankles and calves. The woods were quiet until the howl of sirens rent the air. Minutes later, two fire engines turned onto the service road leading to Storyton Hall's grounds, and Jane's imagination went wild.

The tent's on fire. The filming will be canceled before it can begin. I'll have to return the check to the production company. And it was such a nice check.

Apart from the money, Jane didn't want to disappoint the guests who'd booked rooms months in advance for the privilege of watching some of the greatest chefs in America in action.

Everything had been running smoothly until today. Last week, a construction crew had raised the tent and hooked up the appliances. After the set designer and her team had finished staging the interior, the director and film crew had flown in from LA. The six chefs had arrived at Storyton Hall last night, and the judges had checked in this morning. The international trendsetter, taste guru, social media influencer, foodie, and celebrity host of *Posh Palate with Mia Mallett*, would make her grand entrance this evening.

After several lengthy email exchanges with Mia's assistant, a young woman named Bentley, Jane came to understand that Mia Mallett's public image was meticulously curated and zealously guarded. Known as The Girl with the Midas Touch, Mia was a twenty-seven-year-old billionaire and social media darling. If she endorsed a product, her millions of fans would immediately buy it.

As the manager of a five-star resort, Jane had met her fair share of actors, politicians, writers, musicians, and media sensations, but none had made requests quite like Mia Mallett's. To guarantee her boss's privacy, Bentley had booked the entire third floor of the East Wing. Only Jane, select Storyton Hall staff members, and Mia's entourage were allowed to step foot on the floor while Ms. Mallett was in residence.

How will I fill those empty rooms if Mia checks out after a single night?

Jane pushed the thought aside. There was no sense in catastrophizing. All she could do was find out what was burning, and if the fire would affect tomorrow's filming.

"Don't be the tent," Jane chanted as she rode on.

Her phone was mounted to her handlebars. When it

rang, she pressed the speaker button and kept pedaling.

"The fire's in the archery field," Butterworth said. "Chief Aroneo has the situation well in hand, and the flames should be extinguished shortly. A gentleman from the temporary power supply company is talking to the chief. From what I understand, this is an electrical fire."

Butterworth sounded so calm that Jane's panic instantly subsided. "What kind of damage are we looking at?"

"The fire was restricted to the grass. It didn't have the chance to reach the tent, but the smoke and ash have severely discolored one side."

"Is the director there?"

Butterworth grunted in disapproval. "Mr. Scott is using his bullhorn to shout orders contradictory to those the chief is issuing. If I don't intervene, the firefighters may turn their hoses on him. If they do, I won't lift a finger to intervene."

"We knew this reality show would be a challenge, but I expected to only see flames when the chefs flambéed food," Jane said. "Please take charge until I get there."

After five more minutes of exertion, Jane emerged from the shady forest into a clearing filled with smoke, noise, and sunbaked spectators.

Jane leaned her bike against a pine tree and jogged over to where Butterworth stood. Though the butler was in his mid-fifties, he was tall and powerfully built. Most people found his physical presence and gargoyle stare intimidating, but Mr. Scott was clearly the exception.

Even though Butterworth's muscular chest was firmly pressed over the bell of Mr. Scott's bullhorn, the director didn't seem to realize that he was seconds away from having his legs swept out from under him.

"How am I supposed to tell people what to do?" he whined. "I'm in charge, man!"

Butterworth was as unmovable as a boulder "As I said, sir, Chief Aroneo is in charge. You will surrender your bullhorn until he and his firefighters have given the all-clear."

Jane pasted on her most winsome smile and approached the two men. "Thank you, Butterworth. I've got it from here." Turning to the director, she said, "I almost missed all the drama, and you haven't even started filming yet."

Butterworth retreated to a polite distance, bullhorn in hand, while Mr. Scott took in Jane's sweaty face and dirty clothes. "Ms. Steward? Whoa. I didn't recognize you in, well, looking like that." After raking his eyes over her once more, he pointed at the tent. "It's been a helluva day."

"How is it inside?"

The director chewed his lip. "Fine. But my opening shot is ruined. I wanted that *Little House on the Prairie* vibe. A picnic blanket here. A horse grazing there. A kid flying a kite. But I can't work with burned grass. I'm filming a cooking competition, not *Apocalypse Now*."

Since Jane had never seen the famous war film, she focused on the television show that would introduce Storyton Hall to hundreds of thousands of potential guests. "Maybe the burned grass could be a metaphor for cooking. Fire can transform food into something magical, right? When we were kids, putting a marshmallow on a stick and holding it over an open flame was one of the best things about summer. And adults love watching a chef prepare crêpes suzette. But too much fire, and that nice cut of Wagyu beef will taste like an old boot."

Scott touched his hair, which rose high over his forehead like a cresting wave. "That won't work for the opener, but I could use it when one of the chefs has a kitchen disaster."

Jane cupped his elbow and gently steered him toward the tent. "Does that happen often?"

"We hope so. With every episode." Scott grinned. "Drama makes for good television. If drama doesn't happen naturally, we create it. Things like this fire rarely happen on set. Too bad I wasn't filming. But I could always start another fire."

As they rounded the corner of the huge tent to face a patch of black and sizzling ground, Jane said, "Don't do that, Mr. Scott."

"I'm just kidding. And call me Ty. By the time this show wraps, we'll be good friends." He flashed her a bright Hollywood smile that Jane didn't find the least bit charming. Though she and the director were both in their late thirties, Ty looked younger than Jane. The skin on his face was smooth, his body was trim, and his hair—the color of a new penny—gleamed in the sun. The sleeves of his oxford shirt were rolled up to the elbow, exposing tan forearms and a gold Rolex. Designer sunglasses dangled from his breast pocket. He moved and spoke with the ease of a person who's never known true hardship.

We're not going to be friends, Jane thought. Aloud, she said, "Protocol requires that I stick with Mr. Scott. If I can help, let me know. I'm going to speak to Chief Aroneo."

Putting his hands on his hips, Scott frowned at the stained tent and the smoking field. "Wait! You *can* help.

Find me a company that can lay sod. *Today*. I want green grass for my opening shot. Cool?"

Jane bristled. She wasn't this man's lackey. "My first priority is to speak with the chief. After that, I need to clear my guests from the area. Don't you have an assistant to handle phone calls?"

Ty Scott waved in the direction of the manor house. "Everyone's busy. We start shooting tomorrow, remember? What about that grumpy butler? Can he help?"

Feeling wicked, Jane smiled and said, "You're free to ask him."

Leaving Tyler Scott to Butterworth's mercy, Jane looked for Chief Aroneo and spotted him talking to a man in coveralls. The man was red-faced with fury. He pointed from the burned grass to the tent and then jabbed himself in the chest. The chief held out his hands to show that he was listening before accompanying the man inside the tent.

Jane glanced around, expecting her sons to be among the spectators. When she didn't see two boys or two bikes, she assumed they'd gone home and slipped into the tent.

Though she'd been inside before, Jane was still amazed by how much work had gone into creating this set. Storyton Hall used upscale tents for outdoor weddings all the time, but they didn't have kitchen appliances, sinks with running water, granite countertops, or butcher block chopping stations. And that was just the cooking stations. The perimeter was lined with antique country furniture. Dry sinks, cupboards, pie safes, and hutches filled with stoneware, copper pans, milk glass vases, mason jars, and vintage kitchen scales. Other cabinets featured sets of jadeite, Lenox, Blue Willow, and Royal Albert dishes.

The ground had been leveled before the tent was erected so that a temporary floor could be installed. Between the floor, lighting, appliances, and décor, the tent was an interesting blend of an upscale restaurant kitchen and the kitchen in a country home.

Tomorrow, bucketloads of fresh flowers would augment that home kitchen feel.

"They'll be everywhere," the set designer had told Jane. "In vases. On top of cupboards. In baskets. It's how we'll get that outdoorsy summer vibe inside the tent."

"Are the flowers coming from the Potter's Shed?" Jane had asked. She wanted the local businesses to profit from the show along with Storyton Hall.

The set designer had consulted her clipboard. "Yes. Sunflowers, bachelor's buttons, coneflowers, and Queen Anne's Lace. But if Mia wanted Venus flytraps, she'd find a way to get them. Things tend to appear at the snap of her fingers."

"I wish she could snap her fingers and erase this fire," Jane muttered as she approached Chief Aroneo and the angry man in the coveralls.

The men were standing at one of the cooking stations, their backs to Jane. A large sheet of paper was spread across the counter and the man in the coveralls was tracing something with his finger.

"I've been doing this job for twenty years, Chief. I know how to avoid an overload. There's no way I plugged all that juice into one generator. None of my guys did either."

"How can you be so sure?" the chief asked. "Things seem pretty chaotic around here."

The man shrugged. "It's always this way around TV and movie people. Lots of yelling. Lots of freaking out over nothing. We ignore most of what they ask for because it goes against every safety protocol in the book. Scott wanted so many lights in this tent that the butter would have melted as soon as it came out of the fridge. I tell him what he wants to hear, but I stick to the contract." He tapped the paper. "The contract called for these lines. That's max capacity for the transformer."

"So who added an extra line?"

The man rolled up the paper. "Not me or my guys. Twenty years and not one fire, Chief. Maybe somebody wanted a fire, but it wasn't us."

"What's going on?"

Startled, the men spun around to face Jane.

"Please," she added. "I need to know if the fire was deliberate."

Jane saw the answer in the chief's face before he said a word. After glancing at the other man, he said, "I'll open an investigation, but considering all the people who've traipsed over this field lately, I don't expect to find much."

Someone called for the chief on his radio, and he excused himself and exited the tent. The man in the coveralls was staring intently at his cell phone when he suddenly went rigid.

"Just like I said," he mumbled. "It wasn't me or my guys."

Moving closer to the man, Jane introduced herself. "This is my resort, and I'm responsible for everyone here, so I'd like to know what caused that fire."

The man nodded. "I'm Jeff with Ashley Power Solutions. Our company provides temporary power for movies and TV shows. I'm in charge of this job. How much do you know about electrical systems?"

"Nothing."

Jeff showed her the image on his phone screen. "Pretend this box with all the wires and circuits is the brain of our system. These bigger cables have to plug in here. These skinny wires plug in here. And so on. All the wires have to be coated. Everything has to be clean and kept out of the weather. No water can get inside. Okay. See this red wire?" He tapped a red wire in a nest of black wires. "It shouldn't be there. Way too much juice went into the brain at this spot. That's where the fire started. See how black the board is around that wire? But there's more."

Though Jane didn't like where this was headed, she had to hear the man out. "Go on."

"Somebody helped create the overload by making sure the brain got wet. We haven't had a drop of rain since we've been here, but when the chief takes a closer look at this box, he'll see what I'm seeing. Wrong wire in the wrong place plus liquid. That's a recipe for an electrical fire."

"But aren't these boxes locked? To avoid tampering?"

Jeff looked aggrieved. "Once everything's up and running, yeah. But we were still tweaking things to make Mr. Scott happy. Anyone could have walked by, swapped a wire, and left a chunk of ice on top to melt into the box. I'm sorry to say this, but somebody has it out for this show."

After Jeff left the tent, Jane sent a text to Butterworth.

Fire wasn't an accident. Someone wants to sabotage filming. Since attempted arson failed, what's next?

Staring at her screen, Jane cursed her own stupidity. She knew better than to tempt the fates by wondering what else could go wrong.

Besides, she already knew the answer.

It was everything. Everything could go wrong. And that's when people got hurt.

Pushing her damp hair off her forehead, Jane glanced around the empty tent. "I'd like a summer without violence. A nice, easy summer filled with weddings, barbecues, and beach reads. Can I have one of those?"

The stain on the tent wall, which crawled from floor to ceiling like some multi-limbed shadow creature from a child's nightmare, felt like a sign that her wish had little chance of coming true.

Visit us online at
KensingtonBooks.com
to read more from your favorite authors,
see books by series, view reading
group guides, and more!

BOOK CLUB
BETWEEN THE CHAPTERS

Visit us online for sneak peeks, exclusive
giveaways, special discounts, author content,
and engaging discussions with your fellow readers.

Betweenthechapters.net

Sign up for our newsletters and be the first
to get exciting news and announcements about
your favorite authors!
Kensingtonbooks.com/newsletter